April 2003

Emma Lee-Pott... journalist on T... Evening Standar... writer and lives in a village near Oxford with her husband and children. She is the author of *Hard Copy*, also published by Piatkus Books.

Praise for *Hard Copy*:

'couldn't put [it] down'   *Best*

'A better read than Nicholas Coleridge's exposé of magazines'   *Independent*

'Entertaining . . . Lots of healthy cynicism'
Ms London

Also by Emma Lee-Potter
Hard Copy

To Marie-Claire

Moving On

Emma Lee-Potter

Lots of love

Emma

PIATKUS

For more information on other books
published by Piatkus, visit our website at
www.piatkus.co.uk

Copyright © 2000 by Emma Lee-Potter

First published in Great Britain in 2000 by
Judy Piatkus (Publishers) Ltd of
5 Windmill Street, London W1P 1HF
email: info@piatkus.co.uk

The moral right of the author has been asserted

A catalogue record for this book is available from the British Library

ISBN 0 7499 3193 0

Set in Palatino by
Palimpsest Book Production Limited, Polmont, Stirlingshire

Printed and bound in Great Britain by
Mackays of Chatham plc, Chatham, Kent

For Adam

With special thanks to eveyone at Piatkus, especially Judy Piatkus, Gillian Green and Sara Kinsella, to my agent, Jane Judd, to my friends Alex Lester, Ruth Thick, Colette Ward and Katie and Anthony Capstick for all their help and encouragement and to my fabulously supportive family. Thank you, too, to Lottie and Ned, for letting me write in peace . . . sometimes!

Prologue

Dodo Hollingberry wrestled with her conscience. A terrible sleeper, she'd only just fallen into a fitful slumber when a child's pitiful cry had immediately woken her again. She dozed for a few seconds longer in the hope that the wailing might stop. When it didn't, she wearily levered her middle-aged body out of her narrow single bed and headed up the steep wooden stairs.

By the time she'd reached the second floor, however, the sobs *had* begun to subside. As usual, the door had been left slightly ajar – the girls couldn't bear it shut tight – and there was a light glowing on the landing. Dodo peered short-sightedly into the cavernous room and nearly jumped back with fright. Apart from a battered-looking teddy lying on the pillow, one bed was completely empty. The old-fashioned blankets and rose-sprigged eiderdown were slung in a tangled heap on the floor, leaving just a crumpled sheet on the bed. Her heart beating wildly by now, Dodo glanced at the other divan, just two feet away from its twin, and sighed with relief. How could she have been so stupid? She should have known that Laura and Kate would be huddled up together, two small sad girls in need of consolation.

'It's all right, Katey-Kate,' soothed Laura's soft voice through the stillness. 'I'm here now. I'll never leave you. I promise.'

Dodo felt a lump form in her throat. Laura was only eight, and petrified of the dark. The little girl would have had to screw up all her courage to get out of her own bed and comfort her six-year-old sister. And she wouldn't have crossed the bedroom floor in the middle of the night for anyone else. Not in a million years.

Dodo cursed herself for not picking up on her nieces' mood earlier on. Admittedly it had been Sarah, their new Australian nanny, the latest in a long line, who had fed and bathed them. But Dodo had read them their bedtime stories as usual and tucked them up in bed for the night. Perhaps she was the least perceptive woman on earth but there had been no outward sign that anything was amiss.

The girls had been so brave over the past few months, thought Dodo, so valiant. It was almost impossible to believe that it was only a year since their mother had vanished into the wide blue yonder without a word of explanation to either of them.

'Do you think Mummy will come back soon, Laura?' whispered Kate's small voice through the darkness. 'I never thought she would be away *this* long.'

It was a few seconds before Laura answered.

'I . . . I don't know,' she said finally. 'I just don't know.'

'I wish she hadn't gone,' said Kate.

'Me too,' said Laura.

'Where do you think she is?' murmured Kate sleepily.

'I don't know. Every time I ask Daddy he goes all peculiar and cross, so I've stopped asking him now.'

'What do you remember about her best?' asked Kate.

'Her smell and her soft skin,' said Laura. 'And the way her eyes sparkle, even when she's a bit cross.'

'But she doesn't get cross very much, does she?'

'No. Hardly ever.'

'But Daddy gets cross with her sometimes, doesn't he?'

'Yes, and that makes Mummy cry . . .'

Laura's voice faltered and she fell silent again, clearly unable to be brave about it all any more.

A tear trickled down Dodo's cheek and she dashed it away angrily with the back of her hand. Damn Hubert. His daughters shouldn't have to cope with all this. No matter what their mother had done, they shouldn't have to cope without her. *No* child should, she thought fiercely.

It was November 1978. Almost a year to the day that Clare Hollingberry had stumbled down the front steps of her husband's elegant Chelsea townhouse for the very last time. Dodo would never forget the look on Clare's face as she'd lurched onto the pavement, her face white with grief, her usually immaculate short blonde hair all askew, her long, coltish legs almost buckling beneath her. The temperature had dropped dramatically over the few days before but she was only wearing a short navy pinafore with a stripy T-shirt underneath. No jacket or coat. She didn't have any luggage with her either, just a small leather purse slung over her shoulder and one of the girls' colourful paintings, wrenched hurriedly off the kitchen wall. Clare had glanced forlornly up to the top window one last time and disappeared from all their lives.

Dodo had seen it coming, of course. She'd seen that Hubert and Clare were set on a collision course. Hubert was absolutely impossible to live with, for a start. He always had been. Even as a small boy he'd refused point-blank to do anything he was told, whether it was washing his hands before meals or eating up his loathsome spinach or learning his twelve times table. Their own mother had pretty much given up trying the day he took the family Bentley for a spin down the King's Road at the age of fourteen. Dodo could still hear the poor woman plaintively shouting 'Hubert, Hubert . . .' from the corner of the street. And then the almighty crash as their father's pride and joy had smashed slap-bang into a lamppost.

After Clare's abrupt departure Dodo had moved into her brother's house, ostensibly to care for Laura and Kate, but, as things had turned out, to look after Hubert too. Dodo was three years older than her brother but he had been the boss for as far back as she could remember. He had always had the uncanny knack of getting everybody around him, Dodo included, to do exactly as he wanted. That was probably why he had been so successful in business, building up the modest family firm into the highly profitable regional newspaper group it was today. So Dodo had obediently let out her tiny mansion flat near Albert Bridge, put her most precious possessions into storage and decamped over the river to Chelsea.

It had been weeks before she'd got any sense out of Laura and Kate. Hubert had declined to discuss anything with any of them and the two little girls were so stunned by their mother's disappearance that for days they barely uttered a word. They were perfectly acquiescent, quietly doing precisely as their father and aunt instructed, but neither of them volunteered any information as to what was going on inside their heads. A year later, they still weren't exactly forthcoming, but at least they seemed reasonably settled. Now and again, when she was in a particularly sunny mood, Kate would even climb onto Dodo's knee for a cuddle. Laura, however, completely eschewed any physical contact, wriggling away whenever Dodo came near.

In private, Hubert claimed the girls had forgotten their mother but Dodo knew he was kidding himself. It was clear that they were both grieving for Clare. Dodo had often heard the murmur of childish voices late at night and realised that they confided in each other about Clare far more than Hubert imagined. But she'd certainly never found them like this before.

Now Dodo tiptoed across to Kate's bed, her old-fashioned nightgown swishing along the wooden floor. She switched the bedside light on and knelt quietly beside them.

Startled by their aunt's sudden appearance from nowhere, the two girls huddled even closer together. Kate's face was red and blotchy from crying but Laura looked curiously impassive. It was hard to tell what she was thinking. Laura never gave anything away if she could possibly help it.

Dodo touched Kate's cheek. It felt soft and downy, just like a baby's. She *was* only a baby really, thought Dodo, and her heart turned over with love.

'What's the matter, darling? I could hear you crying from downstairs.'

'I wasn't crying,' said Kate, sticking her bottom lip out in a gesture of defiance. Laura's arms tightened protectively around her shoulders.

'Darling, I heard you,' said Dodo, her voice gentle.

'What on earth's the matter? Do you want Daddy to come up and see you? I think he's home now.'

'Yes,' whispered Kate.

'No,' countered Laura quickly. 'You don't, do you?'

'No,' said Kate obediently. 'Not really.'

Dodo shrugged her shoulders. The pair of them were such a tightly-knit unit that it was difficult, almost impossible, to gauge what they were really thinking. Faced with Kate on her own, she was pretty sure she could have got to the bottom of all this. But Laura was a much tougher nut to crack. Dodo had no idea how to get through to her. She was a funny little thing really, painfully shy most of the time, but always fiercely loyal to her younger sister.

'Is it Mummy?' Dodo asked gently. She wasn't certain whether she should mention Clare or not.

Kate's face lit up.

'Yes,' she said. 'I miss her so much. Can you make her come back, Dodo?'

Dodo wrapped the little girl lovingly in her arms. If only things were that simple.

'Darling, I'm sorry. That's the one thing I can't do.'

'Why not?'

'Because . . . because . . . I don't know where she is.'

Kate's face instantly crumpled. Dodo could have kicked herself for admitting she had no idea what had become of Clare. She should have deflected the question. Or gone in search of Hubert. This was all his fault anyway. *He* should be the one dashing upstairs to comfort his daughters, not her. But Dodo was pretty sure that Hubert would be sleeping peacefully in his large Louis XIV bed downstairs, completely oblivious to the commotion going on above him. The only thing

6

that ever gave *him* sleepless nights was a tricky newspaper deal.

'Why did she go?' persisted Kate tearfully.

This time Dodo paused before answering. She had her own private suspicions but she could hardly discuss them with a six-year-old and an eight-year-old.

'I don't know exactly,' she said.

'I do,' said Laura suddenly.

Dodo glanced again at Laura's cool, imperturbable face. It was hard to tell whether she really knew anything or not.

'Why then?' asked Kate insistently.

'Because Daddy made her,' said Laura. 'I heard them shouting at each other just before she went. Daddy was yelling "Get out of this house and don't come back." And don't tell me he didn't, Dodo, because he did. I heard him.'

'Darling,' said Dodo, stroking Laura's fine blonde fringe from out of her eyes. 'I know it's hard to understand but grown-ups often say horrible things to each other when they're cross and upset. Daddy didn't mean it, I'm sure.'

Laura gazed at Dodo, the misery in her face quite clear.

'But he did mean it, didn't he?' she said. 'He did mean it, because Mummy hasn't come back, has she? And do you know what I think?'

The little girl paused dramatically before continuing.

'What d'you think, Laura?' pleaded Kate. 'Tell us. Please tell us. Please.'

'I don't think she ever *will* come back,' said Laura and promptly burst into floods of tears.

Chapter One

Sitting bolt upright in the corner of the busy morning train out of London, Kate pinched herself hard. A livid red mark instantly appeared on her forearm and she rubbed it absent-mindedly. She still couldn't quite believe that she'd actually done it at last. Actually told her father to stop interfering in her life for once and for all and fuck off.

It was a row that had been simmering for months. Probably even longer than that, come to think of it. But inevitably, when it had finally erupted, it had been sparked off by something completely trivial. Like a bowl of lentil soup.

Kate had been in the kitchen at home in Chelsea, cooking dinner and giggling with Laura about Dodo's fruitless attempts to persuade one of them to accompany her to a Wagner recital at the Royal Albert Hall. Dodo was only fifty-eight but she had grown increasingly eccentric over the years. Her mind was still as sharp as ever but it had become stuffed to overflowing with trivia. She fussed about everything, from the remote possibility that she might get her car clamped to the amount of council tax that she would have to pay in twelve months' time.

The bond between Kate and Laura was as strong as

ever but, for some reason, as the sisters had grown into adulthood, their interests had diverged sharply. Kate had matured into a bright, sparky twenty-two-year-old, filled with ambition and dreams of making a career as a newspaper reporter. She was small and blonde, with bright blue eyes that sparkled with mischief and a zany dress sense that sometimes worked and sometimes didn't. But as fast as Kate had blossomed, Laura seemed to have wilted. Perhaps the years of taking responsibility for Kate after their mother vanished had finally taken their toll, perhaps it was the constant sense of bereavement that, no matter how hard she tried, she could never quite shake off. Whatever it was, Laura seemed to live in a perpetual state of anxiety. When Kate suffered setbacks in her life, she put them down to experience and succeeded, on the whole, in laughing them off. Laura simply couldn't manage it. Her hair was white-blonde, much fairer than her sister's, and while Kate had a curvy, athletic figure, Laura was more delicate. Her sadness seemed to hang like a millstone around her neck, giving her, at the tender age of twenty-four, a troubled, careworn look.

At school Laura had excelled at art and design and both Dodo and Kate had tried their hardest to persuade her to go on to art college. But Laura had refused, protesting that her drawing wasn't nearly good enough and anyway, what would she do with an art degree? Instead she had gone straight to secretarial college before progressing to a dull PA job in the City. Kate, on the other hand, had recently graduated with a good English degree from the University of Manchester and, unbeknownst to her father, had written well over a hundred letters before landing her first job, sight unseen, on a weekly newspaper in Lancashire.

'Now if Dodo had got tickets for a Jarvis Cocker concert, I might have been tempted,' Kate had laughed as she stirred the lentil soup she was cooking.

Laura peered at the thick brown sludge in the saucepan and made a face. A pernickety eater, to put it mildly, she didn't share Kate's new-found enthusiasm for wholefood cooking at all.

'Ugh. That looks absolutely revolting,' she said. 'You could at least follow a recipe instead of making it up as you go along. Surely you're not going to eat it, are you?'

'Of course I am,' smiled Kate, licking the end of the wooden spoon. 'Mmmm, delicious. You can really taste the soy sauce. Here, try some.'

Kate ladled a spoonful of the soup into a spongeware bowl and picked it up to pass it to her sister. The bowl was boiling hot and she dropped it instantly with a yelp of pain. Tiny shards of smashed china flew across the room and the brown sludge she'd been cooking slid forlornly down the front of the immaculate cream Aga and onto the black and white tiled floor.

'Shit,' said Kate, before adding, 'oh well, I never really liked that bowl anyway.'

The girls burst out laughing together, but their merriment trailed away when they looked up and realised that a tall, thickset man with a ruddy complexion and a shock of white hair was watching them from the doorway. Hubert Hollingberry, his face racked with exhaustion, didn't seem to appreciate the joke at all. He needed peace and solitude when he got home, not two daughters behaving like hysterical teenagers. They were old enough to know better.

Over the past sixteen years Hubert's group of regional newspapers had expanded steadily and was now the

10

largest company of its type in the country. But HH, as he was known to almost everyone, Flatly refused to ease up. Where most bosses would have delegated the more tedious tasks to their minions, then sat back and enjoyed the advantages of life at the top, HH simply couldn't. He was fifty-five now, but, thanks to his horrendous hours and unhealthy lifestyle, looked a good ten years older.

'What the hell do you two think you're playing at?' growled HH.

'We're chucking soup around the kitchen for fun, of course,' said Kate lightly. 'What does it look like?'

HH's face flushed crimson. He wasn't in the mood for smart-arse cracks from his younger daughter.

'Well, clear it up then. *NOW*.'

Laura stood rooted to the spot with fear. Kate, however, wasn't in the least in awe of her father. She simply shrugged her shoulders and began searching under the sink for a dustpan and brush. When she sensed that he was still watching her like a hawk, she stopped what she was doing and stood up again.

'Look, Daddy, what's your problem?' she said, glaring at him. 'We all know you've had a hard day but there's no need to take it out on me and Laura. You're behaving like a bear with a sore head. For goodness sake, go and put your feet up in your study and I'll bring you a gin and tonic.'

HH glowered at his younger daughter. It was an appealing idea but he certainly wasn't going to be told what to do by a young slip of a girl.

'I'll have it here,' he snapped. 'There's something I want to have a serious talk with you both about.'

Laura shot a warning glance at Kate. As a rule HH *never* had serious talks with his daughters. Deep down

11

he adored them both and was intensely proud of them – though he found this hard to articulate – but he was usually far too busy to spend any time with them.

For one hopeful, fleeting moment it crossed Laura's mind that he might have come to his senses and decided to tell them the truth about their mother at last. Clare's name had barely been mentioned since the day she disappeared but Laura was convinced that HH's secrecy would have to come to an end eventually. They were both adults now; surely they had a right to know the truth.

Her hopes were soon dashed. As it turned out, HH only wanted to talk to them about their plans for the future.

'I know you're all sorted out, Laura,' he boomed, 'and about time too. I'm glad that you gave up all that art nonsense and settled down into a proper job. But now it's Kate's turn. Look, darling, I know you hate the thought of me pulling strings on your behalf, but I've been having a little chat with Gordon Osprey. I told him you're interested in the newspaper business and he's come up with something pretty good. He's looking for a new secretary and he said he would be more than happy to offer you the post. You'll have to polish up your typing and shorthand of course, but you'll really be in the thick of things. He wants you to start a week on Monday. It's exactly the chance you've been looking for, isn't it, darling?'

Kate rolled her eyes. She'd been waiting for the right moment to tell him her own news and now bloody Gordon Osprey, her father's creepy deputy, had gone and pre-empted her. She cleared her throat, unsure quite how or where to begin.

'That's terribly kind of him, Daddy—' she knew

from past experience that there was no point in going in with all guns blazing – 'but he needn't have bothered. You see, I've managed to sort myself out with something.'

HH's eyes bored into hers. His nostrils were starting to flare, like a bull that had spotted a red handkerchief fluttering in the distance.

'What do you mean you've sorted something out?' he asked. '*What* have you managed to sort out? Some poxy job on a listings magazine that'll pay you seven grand a year? Most girls your age would jump at a chance like this. Gordon is trying to do you a favour, Kate.'

'No, Daddy,' said Kate, steadily meeting his gaze. 'Gordon is trying to do *you* a favour. In fact, he wouldn't dare *not* to do you a favour, would he?'

Laura shifted uncomfortably from one foot to the other. She hated confrontation of any kind. Not that there was much of it in her life. She avoided it like the plague.

'I've just got a phone call to make,' she said, getting up from her seat. 'I'll leave you two to . . .'

'Sit down, Laura,' barked HH. 'You're not going anywhere. Stop skulking around like a frightened rabbit and sit down.'

Laura immediately did as she was told. Then HH turned to face Kate again.

'Right, Kate. I'll ask you a second time,' he said menacingly. '*What* exactly have you managed to sort out?'

Kate took a deep breath and plunged in. She could hear her heart pounding as she spoke.

'You know I've always wanted to be a reporter, Daddy?'

13

HH seemed to be ignoring the question so Kate hurriedly continued.

'Well, I have. So I've been writing letters to newspapers for months. I've written loads and loads and not got anywhere at all. I mean I haven't got anywhere until *now*.'

'And where have you got now?' asked HH.

'I've been offered a job on a newspaper in Lancashire. As a trainee reporter.'

She didn't let on that they'd offered her a job without even interviewing her – and at half the going rate too. She had a niggling fear that they probably hadn't been able to get anyone else. But then again, she was probably just as desperate as they were.

'One of ours, is it?' said HH. His newspaper group owned so many papers now that he frequently lost track of his smaller titles. 'It'll be pretty obvious why you got the job then, won't it?'

'It's not one of yours, no,' snapped Kate. 'It's the *Bowland Bugle*. And if you're assuming that I only got the job because I'm your daughter, then you're wrong. I used Mummy's surname. Not yours. So they know me as Kate Grant. Not Kate Hollingberry.'

Laura closed her eyes. She couldn't believe that Kate was talking to HH like this. Kate *knew* he couldn't stand even the merest mention of their mother's name. Dodo had warned them so often not to talk about Clare in front of him, and now here was Kate cheerily telling him that she'd decided to use Clare's name rather than his.

Kate stared defiantly at her father, almost willing him to fly into a rage. If he did that, she told herself, she'd walk out right here and now.

But HH hadn't got as far as he had in business by

14

losing his rag at inopportune moments. He was a man who relished a fight but he also knew his younger daughter. Of the two girls, she was easily the more like him. If he pushed her too far now, he wouldn't see her for dust. Perhaps it was time to try a more conciliatory approach, calm her down, make her see he was talking sense.

'Darling, I only discussed this with Gordon because I care. You know how much you used to enjoy working for us in your summer holidays and this would be the ideal way to learn more about the business. You'd be bored out of your skull up there. It's in the middle of bloody nowhere, for a start. And do you really know what junior reporters spend all their time doing?'

'What?' said Kate sulkily.

'They trail around to parish council meetings, flower shows, village fêtes. If they're very lucky, they might even get to go to a funeral once in a while. If they happen to get as much as a sniff of a real story they're edged aside by some cynical old hack who's full of resentment towards anyone under the age of twenty-five.'

'Really?' said Kate. It was perfectly clear what her father was up to. If he made the job sound boring enough, he reckoned she would knuckle down and agree to work for Grisly Gordon.

'Yes, really,' said HH, warming to his theme. 'So you can see you'd be much better off in the thick of things, can't you? And that's where you'd be with Gordon.'

'I suppose so,' said Kate.

'Good,' said HH, satisfied that she was coming round to his own way of thinking, as usual. 'Now, what was that you said about mixing your old dad a gin and tonic?'

It was after this episode that Kate had realised it was time she got her act together. She had to get out of London. And fast.

Now she looked at her watch and grimaced. She was itching to get to Lancashire but it was at least two hours before the train arrived at Preston and then a half-hour taxi ride after that to reach Bowland. To help pass the journey, she made her way down to the buffet car. The train was bumping all over the place by this time and twice Kate had to stop herself from falling sideways into passengers' laps. It was twenty minutes before she finally got to the front of the queue, paid for a carton of steaming hot coffee and turned to make her way back to her carriage. Just as she did so, the train shuddered abruptly to a halt. Kate tried frantically to keep her balance and, at the same time, to hold onto her coffee. For a moment she thought she had managed it and tentatively began walking. Then, almost as suddenly as the train had stopped, it lurched forward again. This time Kate collapsed heavily against a man in the buffet queue, sending her coffee flying in the process.

'Fucking hell,' yelled the man as the scalding hot liquid soaked through his once pristine white shirt. 'What the hell do you think you're doing?'

'Oh, I'm so sorry,' apologised Kate swiftly, scarlet with embarrassment. 'Are you all right? I really didn't mean to . . .'

'I'm sure you didn't fucking mean to,' retaliated the man. 'But you did, didn't you?'

This last remark was too much for an elderly woman in the queue. She stepped forward and wagged her finger in front of the man, protesting at his language.

'I can pick my own nose, thank you,' said the man nastily.

'Take no notice, love,' the woman instructed Kate. 'Some men just don't have any manners these days.'

At the old lady's intervention, however, the man suddenly seemed to pull himself together. 'Look, I'm sorry,' he said, grabbing hold of Kate's arm. 'I've had a lousy few days and now the office has sent me on a job I don't want to do. I shouldn't have taken it out on you. I'll buy you another coffee to keep the peace.'

Kate shook his arm off hers. Now he had calmed down a little, she took a proper look at him. Tall and broad-shouldered, he had dark curly hair and startlingly blue eyes. He was formally dressed, in a navy suit and a bright blue tie covered in sunflowers, and he looked as though he'd recently been on holiday somewhere hot. Only the coffee-stained shirt ruined the image, thought Kate. She grinned. It served him bloody well right too.

'You *are* joking, aren't you?' she responded sharply. 'I'm pretty choosy about who I take coffees off.'

The corners of the man's mouth twitched with irritation. He clearly wasn't used to getting the brush-off. Especially not from women.

He shrugged his shoulders, trying to look as if he wasn't bothered one way or the other. 'Suit yourself,' he said and turned away.

Kate was relieved to escape when the train finally drew into Preston station. The rest of the journey had passed uneventfully, thank goodness, and luckily she hadn't set eyes on the man in the sunflower tie again. But she was still fuming at the arrogant manner in which he'd treated her.

After toying with the idea of trying to find a room

17

to rent before she did anything else, she changed her mind and asked the taxi driver to take her straight to the *Bowland Bugle* office. She was desperate to get started before her nerve failed and, anyway, someone there might offer her a bed for the night.

Kate sat back to enjoy the ride. Once they'd crossed over the M6, the ugly outskirts of Preston gave way to the most breathtaking countryside she had ever seen. She'd once read that given the opportunity the Queen would have liked to retire to the Forest of Bowland – and now Kate could quite see why.

She was more used to the southern countryside, green and pretty and tame. This landscape was savage and raw and unforgiving. As the taxi turned off the main Preston to Skipton road and up into the hills, Kate caught her breath. Ahead of them lay a long lonely road heading up towards the moors, and, beyond that, to Bowland. There were no other cars on the road, just a couple of wild-eyed sheep who must have strayed out of their fields and over the cattle grid that was supposed to keep them confined to the moor. And suddenly, Kate wasn't at all sure why, she felt as if she'd arrived home.

Chapter Two

Laura hugged her knees to her chin and watched Robert getting dressed. He had his back to her now and was pulling his clothes on with almost indecent haste.

It was as if he couldn't get away fast enough. When he finally turned to look at her, she noticed that he'd done all his shirt buttons up wrongly. If she'd felt more sure of herself Laura would have pointed this out and they could have laughed about it; but she wasn't and they didn't.

'I've got to go. I'm sorry,' muttered Robert awkwardly as he flung a shabby old donkey jacket around his broad shoulders.

'I'm not,' thought Laura, only once again a sense of shyness stopped her from saying the words out loud.

For a couple of seconds, she clung to the forlorn hope that he might at least cross the room and say goodbye properly. But instead he lingered awkwardly by the doorway, clearly uncertain what to say or do, then blew her a kiss and dashed away. A shiver of pain ran through Laura as she heard the front door slam. She had the distinct feeling that she wouldn't be seeing him again in a hurry.

She turned and buried her face in the sheets. They

felt warm and threadbare and well-used. Laura was pretty sure that they wouldn't have been changed for weeks. Alexa was such a slut, come to think of it, that they probably hadn't been changed for far longer than that.

Half an hour later, she'd showered and dressed and remade Alexa's bed as neatly she could. She smoothed the creases over and over again, desperate to eradicate all evidence of the last few hours. Then, on the spur of the moment, she scribbled a note to Alexa and propped it up on the mantelpiece.

'Popped round to see you this afternoon but you must have been at the studio,' she wrote, before adding the now treacherous words, 'Robert let me in.'

When Laura had rung the doorbell of Alexa's scruffy flat in Clapham at lunchtime, Robert had been the last person she'd expected to see. She'd stood on the steps of the large Victorian house, waiting for Alexa's first-floor window to be pulled up as usual and the key to the front door to be chucked out onto the path. Only this time Robert's tousled blond head had appeared instead. He'd brushed aside her apologies for disturbing him and insisted that she come on up.

Laura had never been able to fathom Alexa and Robert's relationship. Robert was so calm and cool and self-contained, while Alexa . . . what words could you use to describe Alexa? She was the life and soul of every party, and, apart from her sister Kate, Laura's closest friend. Laura and Alexa had been at school together, a strict single-sex establishment in the wilds of Dorset. Out of the blue HH had suddenly decided that Laura and Kate were becoming far too dependent on each other, so at the ages of thirteen and eleven respectively he'd split them up and sent them to boarding schools at opposite ends of the country. 'They've got to learn to stand on their own two feet,' he'd told a weeping Dodo as Laura and Kate eavesdropped on the other side of the door. 'I know it seems harsh but it's got to be done. For their own sakes.'

When Laura had arrived at her new school, starting two years later than most of her class, she'd vowed to have nothing to do with the other girls. It just wasn't worth getting close to anyone because it always went wrong and they always left her. First Mummy. Now Kate. It was all too painful. She couldn't go through it again.

But somehow, and more than ten years later she still wasn't quite sure how it happened, Alexa Grainger had penetrated her defences. Like her, Alexa had been a new girl, but where Laura was quiet and reserved and desperate to keep herself to herself, Alexa was loud and boisterous and fizzing with energy. Despite their differences, she'd jollied Laura into being her friend and had remained devoted to her ever since. Even after they'd left the confines of school – unlike Laura, Alexa had gone straight to art school and started making lots of strange, bohemian friends – she'd loyally kept up the friendship. Laura, who couldn't help feeling a pang about giving up art, was grateful. Once Kate had left London and disappeared off to university, it was kind-hearted, gregarious, flame-haired Alexa who had kept her sane.

Then Robert had come along and ruined everything.

Kate stood and stared up at the battered sign above the fish-and-chip shop. 'First Floor. *Bowland Bugle*,' she repeated out loud. It wasn't the most glamorous location to launch her journalistic career, but everyone, she told herself, even her idol, John Pilger, had to start somewhere.

'This is it,' she told herself stemly. 'The start of your new life. The chance to prove yourself on your own terms. Go for it.'

She put her shoulders back, just like Dodo had always told her to, and pushed open the door. Instantly the smell of greasy fish and chips hit her smack in the face.

'How do I get to the *Bugle* office?' she asked the sullen-looking girl lurking behind the counter.

The girl, who wore a dirty white overall and an extremely unflattering pork-pie hat, jerked her head towards the staircase next to the fridge.

'Up there,' she said in a hard northern accent. 'But you won't find nobody there. They're always down the pub at dinnertime. Right load of piss artists if you ask me.'

Kate smiled at the girl. After her unpleasant encounter with the sunflower-tie man, she was determined to avoid getting off on the wrong foot with anyone else today.

'I'll go up and have a look anyway,' she said.

'You're wasting your time,' shrugged the girl and went back to shovelling chips.

Kate couldn't believe the sight that met her when she pushed open the heavy fire door at the top of the stairs. She'd visited loads of newsrooms up and down the country with her father and had felt pretty confident that she knew exactly what to expect at the *Bugle*. All the newsrooms she'd seen before had been huge, more the size of aircraft hangars than anything else, with fitted carpets, air conditioning, espresso machines and the most up-to-date technology. This place was like something out of the ark. It was tiny, for a start. Somehow six scruffy wooden desks had been crammed into the room, though God knew how anyone ever managed to squeeze between them and sit down. Each desk was crammed to overflowing with old-fashioned telephones, ancient-looking computers (she was amazed the *Bugle* had managed to progress into the technological age at all) and an assortment of mismatched – and mostly dirty – coffee cups.

As Kate stood there, trying to work out what to do next, the door was flung open and a flustered young man with a shaven head and battered leather jacket dashed in. He had three cameras slung round his neck and was panting heavily.

'Have I missed Thorndike?' he spluttered.

'Who?' asked Kate.

'Thorndike,' he repeated. 'Hey, who are you?'

'Kate Grant. The new reporter.'

'What new reporter? No one said anything about a new reporter. Where's Thorndike, anyway?'

This is a circular conversation, thought Kate, and couldn't help giggling.

'Look, you're going to have to help me out here,' she said. 'One, I haven't a clue who Thorndike is. And two, I haven't got a clue who you are either. Who are you, by the way?'

The young man banged his forehead with his fist.

'Bloody hell,' he said. 'Here I go again. My mum's always telling me to think before I open my big mouth.'

He thrust his hand towards hers.

'Danny Simpson – photographer extraordinaire. I

hope you don't mind me saying this when we've only just met, but you couldn't have picked a worse day to start.'

'Thanks a lot,' said Kate. 'What do you mean, anyway?'

Danny gaped at her.

'Don't you know what's happened up here?'

Kate racked her brains. She hadn't spotted anything about Bowland in the copy of *The Times* she'd been reading on the train on the way up. The paper had been full of boring stuff about the Labour Party conference.

'No. What?'

'Bloody hell, you're not exactly on the ball, are you,' said Danny. 'It's lucky you met me first. Thorndike would have hit the roof if he thought you hadn't been doing your homework.'

'What do you mean, doing my homework?' said Kate. 'No one told me I was starting at a new school. My dad told me nothing ever happens in Bowland anyway.'

'It doesn't usually,' said Danny grimly. 'But it has now.'

'So are you going to tell me, or what?'

'Bowland's a terrible place to be a hack,' said Danny. 'I've been here for two years and I seem to have spent most of my time doing pictures of sodding school fairs and golden weddings. It's quiet and sleepy and even though most Lancastrians I know have got the gift of the gab, for some reason they don't like talking about themselves round here.'

'So what's happened?' said Kate impatiently.

'So you've only gone and arrived on the one day that something actually *is* happening. A young girl called

24

Nicky Rawlinson has run away from home. She's only fourteen and she's disappeared off the face of the earth. Her mum and dad are worried sick . . .'

'Probably gone off to a rave with her boyfriend or something,' said Kate, a note of doubt creeping into her voice. 'I mean, I hate to pour scorn on what you're saying but you know what teenage girls are like.'

Danny gave her an odd look.

'Sure,' he said. 'I've got a sister of exactly the same age. And I'd go completely bloody apeshit if anything happened to her. Wouldn't you? If something happened to your sister, I mean?'

'How do you know if I've got a sister or not?' said Kate.

'Well, have you?'

'Yep.'

'And?'

'I'd go completely bloody apeshit.'

'Phew, I'm glad we've got that sorted out,' said Danny. He picked up a canvas bag off one of the desks and slung it over his shoulder. 'Anyway, are you coming?'

'Coming where?' asked Kate.

'To find bloody Thorndike, of course. Where did you think I meant?'

'Yep, of course I'm coming to find bloody Thorndike,' said Kate, scrambling after him. 'I'll leave my stuff here.'

'Bloody hell,' said Danny, suddenly noticing all Kate's cases strewn over the floor. 'You don't exactly travel light, do you?'

'This *is* me travelling light,' laughed Kate. 'I usually have at least double this. Now, you'd better explain who Thorndike actually is.'

25

She followed Danny out of the fish-and-chip shop and down a side street towards a grotty-looking pub. On the way he filled Kate in about Thorndike.

'He's the news editor,' said Danny. 'But he's the editor in all but name. The real editor's called Laurie Laing, but he's been here for donkey's years and he's completely past it.'

'It was Laurie Laing's name on the letter offering me the job,' said Kate.

'Really? That surprises me. Laurie Laing's not even up to getting up the office stairs these days, let alone drafting a letter. At least, not one that makes any sense.'

'Well if he's not important, tell me something about Thorndike. What's his first name anyway?'

'Bill,' replied Danny. 'But I don't even think his wife calls him that. He's Thorndike to everyone.'

'If he's the news editor,' said Kate thoughtfully, 'why do *you* need to find him? You're a photographer. Don't you report to the picture desk?'

'This isn't the *Manchester Evening News*, you know,' said Danny. 'There are only eight of us in total. Laurie Laing – and he hardly counts – Thorndike, two reporters, two subs, a sports guy and me.'

'*And* me,' said Kate indignantly.

'Mmmm, if you say so. Anyway, so Thorndike gives the orders on everything. Words, pictures, whatever. He's the man. So, if you want a piece of advice . . .'

'What is it?' said Kate urgently. They'd reached the door of the White Elephant by this time.

'Don't fall out with him. If you do, you're dead.'

It was strange, thought Kate, walking into a dark, smoky bar in the middle of the day. Outside, it had been bright and clear, a fine autumn afternoon. It was

26

hard to understand why anyone should want to while their daylight hours away in a dive like this. The White Elephant was almost as much of a dump as the *Bowland Bugle* office. There was no carpet on the floor for a start, just a sheet of shabby linoleum, and the few tables and chairs looked as if they'd fallen off the back of a skip. The television was blaring out the afternoon's racing but no one was watching it. In fact, the place was almost deserted, apart from a motley group of people congregated around a table at the far end of the bar.

'Come on Kate,' said Danny, putting his arm round her shoulders and propelling her forward. 'Come and meet Thorndike.'

As she crossed the room with Danny, Kate felt sick with nerves. She'd met loads of important people through her father, from the Prime Minister right through to Madonna, and thought nothing of it; but now her heart was beating so loudly that even Danny himself must be able to hear it.

'Thorndike,' announced Danny. 'This is Kate Grant. The new reporter.'

There were three men sitting in a huddle together and for a moment Kate couldn't fathom which one might be the dreaded Thorndike.

'Kate Grant, eh?' said the surliest of the trio, looking her up and down. 'Kate Grant you say? Mmmm? Come on, spit it out, girl.'

The man was small and wiry, with wispy brown hair that touched the back of his collar and the face of a weasel.

'Yes, Kate Grant,' said Kate firmly, wondering why he had twice questioned her name. On second thoughts, perhaps she was just getting paranoid about her father. 'And you must be Mr Thorndike.'

She offered her hand to him but he didn't take it. He laughed unconvincingly, showing a row of pointy teeth that made him look even more like a weasel.

'Oh forget the niceties, please, girl. Us gruff northerners don't bother with crap like that. Now, Kate Grant, what are you going to do for us?'

Kate shifted uncomfortably from one foot to the other. She wasn't sure what Thorndike meant, but it was pretty clear that she was going to have to watch her back when he was around. She couldn't comprehend why he was so instantly hostile towards her but one thing was for certain; there was no way this man was ever going to put himself out, either for her or for anyone else.

'Er, I'm not sure. What do you want me to do?'

At this the three men all burst into uproarious laughter. Danny's face went puce.

'Der, stupid me,' bellowed Thorndike, banging his fist against his forehead. 'I thought you said you were the new reporter. You're that strippergram girl Barney booked to gee up the lunchtime trade, aren't you? I don't think much of your clothes though. Or are you the schoolmistress type? All respectable on the outside and G-strings and suspenders underneath?'

Kate took a deep breath. She could see that if she didn't rescue the situation right now her career on the *Bowland Bugle* would be finished before it had even started, and she'd be on the 6.10 train back to London in double quick time.

'OK, boys, it was good while it lasted but the joke's over,' she breezed with all the confidence she could muster. 'I'm here to take the *Bugle* by the scruff of the neck and turn it into a newspaper. Not some pathetic freesheet that people chuck in the bin as soon as it plops through the letter-box.'

'Hear, hear,' said one of the older men. 'You tell 'im, lassie. Don't let this twisted old toerag here intimidate you. You start giving as good as you get and you'll get along just fine. I'm George Gibbs, by the way, chief sub.'

Then the man sitting next to George, a huge bruiser with shoulders the size of Mike Tyson's, jumped up and pumped Kate's hand so enthusiastically that she thought it was going to fall off.

'And if he gives you any more grief, you just tell me,' he boomed. 'I've knocked him senseless more than once and I'm quite happy to do it again. You just give the word and he's dead meat.'

Kate gulped. She wasn't totally sure whether he was joking or not.

'And you are . . . ?' Her voice was tentative.

'Steve Scarsdale. But my friends all call me Scar. Look at this.'

The bruiser proudly rolled up his shirt to show her a jagged scar running the full length of his left forearm.

'Good, eh? The joker who gave me this was soon laughing on the other side of his face, I can tell you. I really gave him what for.'

'Poof,' sneered Thorndike. 'Knocked me senseless? Gave him what for? I've never heard such a load of balls in my whole life. You wouldn't have the skin off a rice pudding.'

Scar's face fell. Thorndike always ruined his best stories. He looked like a small boy who'd just lost his prize conker.

'Are you on the *Bugle* too then?'

Kate couldn't help warming to Scar. He might have a nasty wound down his arm and he was definitely not superbrain, but at least he was a damn sight more welcoming than the creepy-looking Thorndike.

'Yep. Sports editor,' mumbled Scar under his breath. All of a sudden he looked a bit shifty.

'Balls,' said Thorndike again. 'So you cover the odd Rovers game; that doesn't exactly make you sports editor. Not in my book, any road. Just to put you in the picture, Kate Grant, our old mate Scar does most of our sports stuff but basically he's one of our run-of-the-mill reporters, just like you. In fact he can show you the ropes if you like. If you're going to be staying, that is.'

Kate met his gaze. Thorndike stared back at her unflinchingly for thirty seconds or so before, disconcerted, she was forced to look away.

'Of course I'm staying,' she said briskly. 'Laurie Laing offered me the job and I'm not going to let him down.'

'You've met old Laurie, then, have you?' enquired Thorndike.

'Er n-n-n-n-no,' stuttered Kate. 'Not exactly. But he did offer me the job. It was his name on the bottom of the letter.'

She fumbled in her pocket for Laurie Laing's letter, desperate to show Thorndike that she was genuine.

'Look. Here.'

Thorndike glanced at the letter in a desultory sort of fashion.

'Old Laurie wrote that himself, did he?' he asked.

'Yes,' said Kate proudly. 'At least some bosses can spot talent when they see it.'

Suddenly Thorndike snatched the letter from Kate's

hand and scrawled something across it in splodgy blue ink.

'Hey,' shrieked Kate. 'What do you think you're doing?'

'Just take a butcher's at the signatures, Kate Grant. That'll show us whether you've got anything up top or not.'

Kate studied the writing on the letter offering her the job. Laurie Laing's signature was tiny, black and spiky. Thorndike's version, just below, was tiny, blue and spiky. Identical. He'd clearly written the letter himself.

'Why did you . . . ?' she began.

'Shut up, Kate Grant,' hissed Thorndike. 'Just to teach you that things aren't always as they seem. If you're going to make any kind of reporter at all, and from what I've seen so far, I have my doubts, just remember not to jump to too many conclusions. Right? Now, we've got a big story on our patch and we go to press this evening. Rob Bennett – he's another of my so-called reporters – is covering the police end. Scar, I want you and Kate Grant to go and talk to the girl's parents.'

Kate glanced at Scar. So much for all his big, brave talk earlier on, she thought wryly. He looked bloody terrified out of his wits.

Laura clattered up the steps and pushed open the heavy black door of her father's house. Disgusted with herself for the way she'd betrayed Alexa, she felt as if she was going to be sick. The only person she could even contemplate telling was Kate. There was no way she could bring herself to confide in Dodo – Dodo was a dear but no, it was absolutely unthinkable – and

31

talking to Alexa was definitely out of the question. 'I'm afraid I've just spent the afternoon in bed with your lover,' muttered Laura, and, despite her misery, a ghost of a smile crossed her lips. No, she would tell Kate the whole sad story. She knew Kate would listen. Kate would listen carefully and sympathise and be wise and make everything all right.

For the last couple of months, since Kate had finished university, she'd been at home waiting for Laura at the end of each day, weird unstructured jazz pouring forth from her room till all hours or at least until HH got back and bellowed at her to turn it down, endless half-drunk cups of tea scattered around the house, and the smell of something absolutely unspeakable cooking downstairs in the kitchen.

Now the whole house was silent, and suddenly the truth hit Laura. In her haste to get home she'd completely forgotten that her sister had gone. Despite their father's dire warnings, this morning Kate had packed her bags and left to start her new life. Laura was all alone. Again.

Chapter Three

For all his bluster, Scar was virtually as inexperienced as Kate. The *Bowland Bugle* had a paltry circulation of twelve thousand a week, a figure that meant it barely broke even and was forced to operate on a shoestring. Apart from Thorndike, on whom the local verdict was 'he's so sharp he'll cut himself one day,' all the paper's employees were either has-beens with drink problems or naïve young trainees straight out of college. Scar himself had never even reached the giddy heights of college in the first place. He was Laurie Laing's nephew and had been foisted on the paper in a fit of magnanimity by his uncle. Now that Laurie Laing was almost permanently off sick, his illness inextricably linked with his forty-a-day smoking habit, Thorndike was forever threatening Scar with the sack.

'One more cock-up and you're out on your ear,' was the constant roar around the office and Scar would hang his head in shame and promise to do better next time. One of his early ignominies had been to ask the rest of the office what the foot pedal on his computer was for, only to be told by an incandescent Thorndike that it was the mouse and should be kept *on* his desk, not underneath it. And now, after being sent off to write a feature on traffic congestion in Bowland, only to face the humiliation of getting his own double-parked car towed away by the police, he was on a final warning.

'You know why Thorndike's sent the two of us round to Nicky Rawlinson's parents' house, don't you?' mumbled Scar to Kate as he raced through the back streets of Bowland in his bright green souped-up Ford Escort.

'Because we're his two star reporters, of course,' joked Kate. She felt so nervous that, despite the heavy-metal CD blaring out at top volume, she was certain Scar must be able to hear her teeth chattering.

Scar glanced sideways at Kate. He was astonished by her coolness. For someone who'd never worked on a newspaper before, or so she'd claimed earlier, she seemed remarkably composed.

'Is that what you really think?' said Scar.

'I was pulling your leg, you idiot,' smiled Kate good-naturedly. 'Come on, spill the beans, why *has* he sent us? Is it a question of giving us enough rope to hang ourselves?'

'You what?' gawped Scar.

Kate rolled her eyes. She couldn't believe Scar was such a dumbwit. A second later, however, she felt ashamed of herself. At least he'd made an effort to be friendly. Unlike some people she could think of.

'Come on. Why did Thorndike send us?' she asked again.

'He doesn't like you, that's obvious,' grunted Scar. 'And he sure as hell doesn't like me either. He knows that Nicky's family won't answer the door because he's had Pam Newbold down there all morning door-stepping the place. So he's sent us because he knows we won't get anywhere either and then he can go ballistic.'

Scar paused for a moment.

'And Thorndike likes going ballistic,' he added.

'Who's Pam Newbold when she's at home?' enquired Kate.

Scar gaped at her.

'You mean you haven't met her?'

'No,' said Kate patiently. 'You know perfectly well I haven't. I've only been in Bowland for about five hours.'

'She's the most senior reporter,' said Scar in hushed tones. 'You should see her in action. She's absolutely brilliant. She can get *anybody* to talk to her. She's . . .'

Kate was tempted to ask what Pam Newbold was doing on the *Bowland Bugle* if she was *that* brilliant. But Scar was clearly so smitten that she'd be unlikely to get an impartial answer anyway.

'What does she look like?'

Scar cleared his throat. How on earth could he do justice to Pam Newbold?

'She's the most . . . the most beautiful woman I've ever seen,' he said. 'She's got this rich auburn hair down to her shoulders, bright blue eyes and the sexiest legs.'

'Wow,' said Kate, totally underwhelmed. 'She sounds quite something.'

'Oh she is,' said Scar, then turned pale. 'But you won't tell any of the others what I said, will you? They'd only laugh at me. So would Pam, I should think.'

Kate couldn't help feeling sorry for the huge bulk of a man sitting next to her. She had the distinct impression that Scar didn't have much success with women. He might look like one of the Gladiators on the outside but on the inside he was painfully shy. He could barely string two words together, for goodness sake, let alone contemplate chatting anyone up.

'Of course not,' she said, and patted Scar's chunky arm reassuringly. 'You never know, if you're in luck, you might bump into Pam down at the house.'

'Don't think so,' mumbled Scar. 'I . . . I think she might be having a bit of a fling with one of the coppers from Bowland nick. That's the rumour going around. And she must have some inside contact down there because she's picked up some ace stories. That's why Thorndike likes her too. She brings in so many stories that he lets her do her own thing most of the time. A free spirit, that's what he calls her.'

'I bet he does,' thought Kate, making a mental note to avoid Pam Newbold like the plague.

'Here we are,' said Scar, spinning into a narrow terraced street called Moor View. He screeched to a halt outside number twenty-eight, a modest-looking two-up, two-down with a peeling front door and rotting window frames. It looked like something out of *Coronation Street*, thought Kate.

Scar and Kate sat silent in their seats for a couple of minutes, both of them reluctant to make the first move towards the door. Scar secretly thought Kate should ring the bell first. She was a woman, after all, and women were always better at times like this. Kate assumed that Scar would go; he was the one with the experience, wasn't he?

'Are you going to sit here all day, then?'

'You what?' said Scar.

'Are you going to ring the doorbell or do I have to?'

Scar still didn't move.

'Er, you do it, love,' said Scar, clinking the loose change in his pocket. 'It'll be good experience for you, won't it? And I'm sure there won't be anyone there anyway.'

In truth, Scar reckoned that there could well be someone inside the tiny terraced house, sandwiched between its two identical neighbours. A window upstairs was open a fraction and, although the jazzy floral curtains had been tightly closed when they arrived, he was certain that one of them had just twitched.

Kate groaned. Talk about being thrown in at the deep end.

'Has anyone told you before that you're as much use as a chocolate teapot?' she muttered, slamming Scar's passenger door as hard as she could.

'Hey, watch it,' growled Scar. 'I've only just had her resprayed . . .'

Kate took a couple of deep breaths to calm herself down, then walked slowly towards the door.

Scar watched her go, his heart beating wildly. Why was he always such a wimp? No wonder everyone in the office thought he was a joke. They'd all be laughing their heads off when they heard that he'd let the new trainee do his door-knock.

He pulled the rear-view mirror towards him and peered at his reflection. What an ugly mug, he thought, as he inspected his ruddy complexion and badly broken nose (courtesy of a pub fight a couple of years back). And now, just to set the seal on things, his hair was beginning to go too. It was perfectly obvious why Pam Newbold kept giving him the brush-off.

Suddenly Scar heard a door bang shut. He looked up, expecting Kate to slump grumpily back into the car. But Kate was nowhere to be seen. Puzzled, Scar glanced up and down the street several times. No, there was no one around. Scar buried his head in his hands. The girl had simply vanished into thin air.

'What do you mean, you've lost her?' growled Thorndike. 'She only set foot in the place a few hours ago, for God's sake. Even *you* can't have been so stupid as to lose her.'

Scar hung his head in shame. He would never live this one down.

'Where did you last see her?' demanded Thorndike.

Scar's brain clanked slowly into action.

'On the Rawlinsons' doorstep,' he muttered. 'I told her to stay in the car while I knocked them up. I knew she was a bit inexperienced like, so I thought it was better I did it on my own. She must have run off while my back was turned.'

Thorndike paced up and down the tiny newsroom. There was something distinctly fishy about all this.

'Why the fuck would she want to do a thing like that?' he said menacingly. He didn't believe a word of what Scar was burbling on about. To have one young girl go missing in Bowland was extraordinary. But for a second to disappear . . . No, it was bloody impossible. The kid had been so keen. There was no way she would have buggered off without telling anyone. Now, if it had been Scar walking out on a job it would have been completely in character. But Kate Grant? No. Definitely not.

'What happened when you knocked on the door?'

'What door?'

Thorndike jabbed his index finger at Scar.

'The Rawlinsons' door, you blithering idiot. Whose

door did you think I meant? Remember the story you and the Grant girl were supposed to be working on? Now try and get your pea brain in gear. What happened when you knocked on the Rawlinsons' front door?'

Scar's face went white.

Thorndike waited for a couple of seconds, then raised his voice by two hundred decibels.

'Tell me what happened,' he roared. 'Did you or didn't you knock on that door?'

Scar's shoulders slumped defeatedly.

'Didn't,' he mumbled.

'Did Kate Grant knock on the door?' demanded Thorndike.

'Don't know.'

Despite the fact that Thorndike was half Scar's size, he shoved him roughly onto a chair.

'You don't move an inch till I get back, Scar. I'll be dealing with you later. Either Kate Grant has got the biggest interview of all time or the Rawlinson boys have beaten her to a pulp. And if they have you know who will be held responsible, don't you?'

'Like another brew, love?'

Kate looked up from her notebook and nodded. After drinking three mugs of Bert Rawlinson's industrial-strength tea in quick succession she couldn't face even looking at another cup of tea. But then again she didn't want to appear ungrateful. Neither did she want to stop the Rawlinsons talking about their daughter and the reasons why they thought she might have run away.

She'd been sitting in the Rawlinsons' tiny shoebox of a kitchen for more than an hour now. She'd listened attentively as Violet Rawlinson tearfully recounted how she'd waved Nicky off to school the previous morning and hadn't clapped eyes on her since.

'I'm one of the dinner ladies at her school, you see, love, and when I got to work at dinnertime yesterday and found that Nicky'd never turned up for class, I just couldn't believe it.'

'Has Nicky played truant before, as far as you know?' asked Kate as gently as she could. She made a point of referring to Nicky in the present tense, not the past.

'Never,' bellowed Bert Rawlinson, slamming his hand down hard upon the yellow Formica table. 'Our Nicky's a good girl. Keeps her head down and gets on with her work. Her teacher says she'll probably get six GCSEs next year.'

'Would you like to see a picture of her?' said Violet. Without waiting for an answer she took a battered photograph album from the mantelpiece and began thumbing through it.

'There,' she said when she reached the page she was looking for. 'She's lovely, isn't she?'

Kate studied the picture. Nicky Rawlinson looked so young and fresh-faced staring out of the photograph in her school uniform, her long dark hair drawn back from her face in two fat bunches.

'You must be very proud of her,' murmured Kate.

At this, Violet Rawlinson buried her face in a large grey handkerchief once more and sobbed her heart out.

Kate shifted uncomfortably on her chair. Up until now her only journalistic experience had been the odd theatre review for one of Manchester's student papers. She didn't feel equipped for this at all.

'You're so young, love,' wept Violet Rawlinson.

'Too young to have lost anyone important to you. Too young to understand what it's like to lose a daughter.'

As she listened to Violet's sobs, a vision of an anguished young woman in a knee-length navy pinafore dress suddenly appeared in Kate's mind.

Oh, but I do understand what it's like, she thought fiercely. I understand completely.

Outside on the doorstep, the troops were starting to assemble. They looked more like an ill assortment of squaddies from *Dad's Army* than a group of working professionals. Alongside Thorndike stood Danny the photographer and Scar's pin-up, Pam Newbold. A tall, statuesque woman who claimed to be thirty-four but was in fact forty-one, Parn was livid to have been called away from her weekly session at the Beauty Spot – Bowland's one and only beauty salon gave her a free facial every week in return for the odd plug in the paper. Behind them were a couple of local radio reporters from Preston in grey anoraks and plastic loafers and a smooth-looking man in a navy suit who Thorndike assumed was either a detective or a reporter from one of the London papers.

'I'll give it another try,' said Pam Newbold, teetering forward in her brand-new snakeskin stilettos.

She banged the door hard with the palm of her hand. When that elicited no response, she gave it another whack.

Almost instantly the door was opened a crack and Bert Rawlinson's nose peeped out.

'What the bloody hell d'yer think yer doing? My wife's very upset inside here and you're making it all even worse than it already is.'

'Oh I'm so sorry, Mr Rawlinson,' said Pam Newbold smoothly. 'I didn't mean to alarm you. I just wasn't sure whether you'd heard the door or not.'

'I should think the whole street heard you making all that racket, missus,' said Bert Rawlinson. 'Now, sling your hook will you?'

Seeing that Pam Newbold was getting precisely nowhere, Thorndike stepped forward to try his luck.

'We're looking for a young reporter who's—'

Thorndike clearly didn't have the right approach either. Bert Rawlinson slammed the door in his face and slid the bolt across.

'I thought you called yourself queen of the door-knocks,' Thorndike hissed nastily at Pam once he'd retreated a few yards along the pavement.

'What about you, then?' said Pam, glaring at him. She wasn't going to take any nonsense from a no-mark like Thorndike. 'He hardly welcomed you in with open arms either, did he?'

'Now, now, you two,' said Danny, stepping between them like a referee at a boxing match. 'There's no point in the pair of you falling out, is there? We're here to find Kate. Remember?'

'Less of your lip, boy,' grunted Thorndike. He hated being shown up, especially in public.

Just then, the Rawlinsons' peeling door creaked open once again and Bert Rawlinson was seen to usher a female visitor out onto the front step. He gave her an awkward hug and promised to keep in touch.

'Thanks love,' he said gruffly and jerked his head towards the pavement. 'You're worth a million of that lot.'

The young woman – Pam took in her short blonde bob, large hoop earrings, jeans and flying jacket that looked at least two sizes too big, and wondered if this could possibly be the missing daughter – squeezed his arm and told him to keep his chin up.

It can't be the missing daughter, thought Pam. She doesn't sound very Lancashire, and she definitely looks older than fourteen.

The crowd all gawped at Bert's departing visitor. Thorndike and Danny were so shocked that it was a full ten seconds before either of them uttered a word.

'Blimey,' said Danny at last. 'It's Kate.'

Chapter Four

Kate sighed and buried her head in her hands. How the hell was she supposed to write the first and only news report she'd ever composed in her entire life with a crowd of people haranguing her over her shoulder?

'Look,' she said finally. 'I hate to be rude and I'm really grateful for all your suggestions but wouldn't it be better if I got on with it by myself?'

It was six pm and already turning dark outside. Kate had been working on her story for almost an hour now. In between trying to decipher the scrappy shorthand in her notebook and attempting to convey the agony the Rawlinsons were going through, she kept being interrupted by Thorndike and Pam Newbold bellowing bossy instructions about what to write.

'"We're so scared we'll never set eyes on her again,"' said Pam, reading the words off Kate's screen. 'You need that quote much higher up. Doesn't she, Thorndike?'

'Yep,' said Thorndike, drumming his nails on the desk, 'and we don't need all the crap about what her bedroom looks like.'

Kate rubbed her eyes wearily.

'But I thought that added a real poignancy to the story,' she said. 'It shows that she's just a normal fourteen-year-old girl who loves Robbie Williams and sleeps with loads of teddies on her bed.'

'It's balls,' said Thorndike. 'Look, spare me the sentimental details, will you? If that's the kind of garbage you're interested in churning out, then you'd better pack your bags and head off to *Woman's Weekly* now. You're not our resident agony aunt. Just give us the facts. That's all we're interested in here. Right?'

'Right,' said Kate grimly and began typing again.

'And get a bloody move on, will you,' he yelled. 'It won't be in the paper at all if you don't get it finished within the next ten minutes.'

Later, in the White Elephant, Thorndike took Kate to one side and demanded to know how the hell she'd managed to wangle her way into the Rawlinsons' house in the first place.

'I didn't wangle my way in,' said Kate, a note of indignation creeping into her voice. 'I just knocked on the door and told Bert Rawlinson how sorry I was about Nicky's disappearance. I asked him if he'd tell me a bit about her and he said that he would. He said that I was the first reporter who'd treated him with respect.'

Thorndike rolled his eyes at the ceiling.

'I know you're keen but you should have let Scar do it,' he hissed. Kate noticed that his thin lips barely moved as he spoke. 'You were completely out of your depth in there. Do what you're bloody told next time.'

'But Scar told me *I* had to go,' said Kate. Maybe someone more skilled might have asked more probing questions, but she didn't think she'd made that bad a job of it.

'Did he indeed?' said Thorndike and Kate could see

from the malevolent look on his face that Scar was almost certainly for the high jump.

'When will it be in the paper?' asked Kate, anxious to change the subject.

'Tomorrow,' grunted Thorndike. 'You made it by the skin of your teeth. If you hadn't filed when you did, the story wouldn't have made it at all. And it would have been old hat by next week's edition. Now let's just hope the Rawlinson girl doesn't turn up before we hit the streets tomorrow morning.'

Kate looked puzzled.

'But everyone wants her back as soon as possible,' she said. 'The Rawlinsons will be absolutely shattered if she isn't found by then.'

'*We* won't,' said Thorndike gruffly.

'What do you mean?'

'Bloody hell,' said Thorndike, raising his eyes to the White Elephant's cobwebby ceiling. 'Do I have to spell it out? If they find her in the middle of the night and the *Bugle* hits the streets first thing in the morning droning on about her still being missing, how will that make us look?'

'Stupid,' said Kate quietly.

'Yeah,' jeered Thorndike. He turned his curiously pale eyes full on her and Kate felt a shiver run down her spine. 'Yeah. Stupid.'

She was relieved when Thorndike lost interest in her and wandered off to the other side of the bar to bawl out the hapless Scar. She wished Danny would get a move on and finish his pint. He'd offered her a room in his house for a few days and she was desperate to get some sleep.

Suddenly, she felt a sharp tap on the shoulder from behind.

'I think we met earlier,' said a southern-sounding voice.

Kate whirled round to face a deeply tanned man of about thirty with dark hair and an immaculate navy suit. He was wearing a distinctive tie covered in – bloody hell, gulped Kate – sunflowers.

'Shit,' said Kate, instantly recognising the appalling man from the train. Overcome with confusion, she covered her face with her hand.

'You're every bit as charming as I thought earlier,' smiled the man. The expression in his eyes, however, was inscrutable.

'What do you think you're doing here?'

'It's a free world, isn't it?' said the man. 'Or have I wandered into some weird exclusive club?'

Kate ran her fingers through her ash blonde hair.

'It's weird all right,' she laughed, her eyes shining with amusement. 'I'm not so sure about the exclusive bit though. Who are you, anyway? Has my father hired you to tail me or something?'

The man looked puzzled.

'Oh, take no notice,' said Kate hurriedly. She could have kicked herself for mentioning HH. 'I'm just being tired and emotional. And you, by the way, haven't answered the question. What exactly *are* you doing here?'

The man laughed and Kate unexpectedly found herself warming to him. He no longer looked quite so arrogant and full of himself. He had a merry, animated face, and after the antics of Thorndike, Scar and Co. he at least seemed keen to be friends.

The kitchen table bore testimony to Laura's frantic midnight feast. A loaf of wholemeal bread lay mutilated on

47

the wooden chopping board, spilling crumbs everywhere. There were two ice-cream cartons, one chocolate, one coffee, both of them empty, a large can of baked beans with a spoon inside it – Laura had devoured them straight from the tin – a half-eaten pizza and the remains of a frozen strawberry cheesecake.

Now, in the attic bathroom, Laura, wearing a long white nightdress buttoned demurely to the top, was kneeling on the floor with her head hunched over the lavatory. She retched violently, the pain in her stomach so intense that she thought she might pass out. Revolted by what she'd just done and exhausted at the effort involved, she half-wished that she *would* pass out. That she would be overtaken by oblivion. At least then she might be certain of some peace in her miserable existence.

Half an hour later, when she could be sure that there was nothing else left in her stomach, she weakly rose to her feet and stumbled towards the stairs. She still felt as if she was going to faint but she must clear up the debris before morning. She would die if her father ever found out about all this.

Laura was disgusted with herself. How could she have done it? She had been doing so well until tonight. After Kate came back from university and the house seemed vibrant again, she'd cut these terrible binges, once an almost nightly feature of her life, right down. She'd really thought that she'd broken the dreadful cycle of bingeing and vomiting. But now that Kate had gone again, the truth began to dawn on Laura. She'd been kidding herself all along. She was just as pathetically weak as she'd always been.

*   *   *

'My name's Charley Stone,' said the sunflower man. He clasped Kate's hand firmly. 'I'm a reporter for the *Evening Clarion*. The office sent me up to this depressingly dire place to cover the Nicky Rawlinson story.'

'Gosh,' said Kate and then could have kicked herself for sounding so uncool. In fact her mind was racing, panicked by the thought that the *Evening Clarion* was one of HH's papers. But there was no way this man could have cottoned on to who her father was, she told herself quickly. She had to remember that she was Kate Grant now, an anonymous trainee whom no one was in the least bit interested in. If she told herself often enough she might even manage to convince herself.

'And are you going to introduce yourself?' asked Charley.

'Kate Grant. I work on the *Bowland Bugle*.' She wasn't going to tell him that it was her very first day.

'Pleased to meet you, Kate Grant,' said Charley.

'H-how are you getting on with the story?' asked Kate politely.

Charley Stone stared at her for a second, puzzled by the abrupt change in her manner. She'd looked so full of life when he'd first spotted her standing in this seedy-looking pub. She was the youngest there by far but it was obvious that she'd be the one going places. Her face lit up when she talked and even when she was speaking to the old duffer behind the bar, she'd seemed genuinely interested in what he was droning on about. Now, in an instant, the glow had faded and she appeared dull and mousy and rather unsure of herself.

'Not bad,' said Charley airily. 'I managed to file something for the last edition when I got here and I've got an absolute corker up my sleeve for tomorrow.'

Kate looked animated again.

'What's that?' she asked, curious to fathom how a real London reporter operated on a story like this.

'Promise you won't tell anyone?'

'I promise,' said Kate obediently.

'I've got Nicky Rawlinson's boyfriend to talk to me.'

A look of puzzlement crossed Kate's brow.

'But that's impossible,' she said finally. 'You can't have.'

Charley Stone laughed out loud.

'Oh no?'

'No,' said Kate firmly.

'Who says?'

'I say,' said Kate.

'And why's that?'

'Because Nicky Rawlinson doesn't have a boyfriend. Her parents told me so this afternoon.'

'Ah yes,' said Charley knowingly. 'You've had the privilege of an exclusive talk with them, haven't you?'

Kate looked confused again.

'How did you know that?' she asked.

'Because I was waiting outside with the pack when you came out,' he said. 'Now, how about passing on a few little snippets that they told you? You pat my back and I'll pat yours.'

'You'll have to buy the *Bugle* tomorrow,' said Kate obstinately. 'But tell me about this boyfriend you've found. Or are you making the whole thing up?'

'Bloody cheek,' said Charley. 'You'll just have to get hold of a copy of the *Evening Clarion* tomorrow, won't you?'

Kate pursed her lips with disapproval.

'You can't get it up here,' she said. 'And anyway, I

haven't the slightest intention of paying attention to a story that I know to be completely untrue.' She was well aware that she sounded pompous but she didn't want Charley Stone to assume she was a pushover.

'Is this your first job?' asked Charley, suddenly changing the subject.

When Kate nodded he smiled and said softly, 'Thought as much. Don't worry, Kate Grant. Give it a few months and you'll change your tune. You won't be quite so holier-than-thou when you've got a few stories under your belt.'

Charley plonked his empty pint glass down on the side of the bar and picked a smart black leather briefcase up off the floor.

'I'll be seeing you around then,' he said. 'And I'll send my dry-cleaning bill to you at the – what was the rag you said you worked for – the *Bowland Bugle*, shall I?'

51

Chapter Five

'Come on Laura,' yelled Alexa Grainger through the letter box after she'd tried HH's doorbell for the second time. 'We'll miss the band if you don't get a move on.'

When the door finally swung open to reveal Laura, wearing a red halter-neck minidress and far more make-up than usual, Alexa gasped with shock. She couldn't help it. She was stunned by Laura's appearance.

The two women hadn't seen each other for a while. Alexa had been immersed in her latest masterpiece, a huge splashy abstract that a couple of her unkinder friends privately thought looked more like a giant fried egg than a work of art. Underneath the chaotic exterior Alexa was kind-hearted and just as concerned about Laura as she'd always been. But for the last few weeks she'd neglected her in favour of her painting; now, however, she was determined to make amends.

Even so, the way Laura looked was a shock. It wasn't just the outfit she was wearing. Laura never wore sexy clothes as a rule, mused Alexa. What was she playing at tonight? But no, it was something else that set alarm bells ringing in Alexa's head. With her fine, shoulder-length blonde hair and slight build, Laura had always seemed waif-like and absurdly young for her age. At twenty-four, she was still occasionally challenged by pub landlords asking if she was eighteen or not. Tonight, however, she looked distinctly unwell. Even the heavy layers of make-up couldn't mask the puffiness in her face and her eyes looked hollow and unhappy.

'Laura darling,' cried Alexa, rushing to give her a hug. Once again, Laura's frailty struck her forcibly. Alexa had always been strong and robust; now she felt that if she hugged Laura just a little too hard she'd snap in two.

'It's lovely to see you,' said Laura. 'Why don't you come in for a minute?' Despite the warmth of her smile, she couldn't hide the vulnerability in her eyes.

Alexa followed Laura into the imposing hallway. A grandfather clock ticked reassuringly in the far corner and a full set of that day's newspapers was laid out on the large mahogany table in the middle of the hall. Alexa dragged her eyes away from the stunning picture of Mick Jagger's daughter on the front of the *Clarion* and stood back to take another look at Laura.

'Red really suits you, you know – you look absolutely delectable,' said Alexa. Her voice was gentle. 'But darling, are you feeling all right? Has something happened? Is it the old trouble?'

Bold and upfront as she was – her mother claimed that Alexa could always be relied upon to call a spade a shovel – she couldn't quite bring herself to mention by name the bulimia Laura had suffered since her late teens. Alexa had lost count of the number of times she'd heard Laura throwing up late at night Alexa knew for a fact that her periods had been completely erratic for a while, her poor, exhausted body unable to take the strains inflicted on it. She couldn't bear to think that the old problem had reared its ugly head all over again.

Laura shook her head obstinately. 'No, no, nothing like that.'

Alexa wasn't in the least convinced. She steeled herself to mention the unmentionable. It was obvious from years of trying that Laura couldn't bear to be questioned about her mother, but sometimes it simply couldn't be avoided.

'Your mother?' she said tentatively.

'No,' said Laura, more firmly than before. 'And how's your painting going? Is the masterpiece of the century finished yet?'

It was clear to Alexa in an instant that she was going to get nowhere with this line of questioning. Laura always reacted the same way when people got too close for comfort. She was a past master at taking the heat off herself by hurling another question straight back at her inquisitor.

Alexa grinned good-naturedly.

'About an hour ago. Look, I came straight from the studio. You can see the latest colours I've been using. Aren't they divine?'

Laura laughed as Alexa proudly showed her the stains of violet, cornflower and indigo paint she'd been slapping onto her canvas all afternoon. Both forearms were covered with splodges of it.

'You're hopeless,' laughed Laura. 'Why didn't you have a bath before you got ready?'

'I did,' said Alexa. 'But I decided to keep the paint on. Not only does it colour co-ordinate with my dress – clever, eh – but don't you think it makes me seem wildly exotic?'

'Mmmm,' giggled Laura, wondering how best to put it politely. 'Not exactly, no.'

Alexa groaned theatrically.

'Laura Hollingberry, you've got no romance in your soul.'

It was true, thought Laura. There was no romance there at all. She couldn't work out why it was that people like Kate and Alexa always looked on the bright side of everything, while she always saw the dark side. When they were children, Kate had been eternally confident that Clare would one day push open the door and walk back in as if she'd never left. But Laura had never managed to rid herself of the notion that it was probably her fault that Clare had gone in the first place. She felt rejected and unloved and was convinced deep down that she would never set eyes on her mother again. Perhaps if she'd been better, if she'd helped around the house more, if she'd been more attuned to Clare's distress . . . there were countless ifs, all of them totally and utterly unanswerable.

Alexa linked her arm through Laura's, the mass of silver bangles on her wrists jingling merrily as she did so.

'Come on, we'd better get down to the Seven Sisters,' she said. 'Robert will be really fed up if we don't turn up soon.'

Laura frowned.

'I didn't know Robert was coming with us,' she murmured. 'Anyway, I thought he didn't like jazz.'

'He doesn't,' laughed Alexa. 'I agree it's strange. Maybe he couldn't resist our scintillating company. But maybe it's Janey Bell, the gorgeous lead singer of the band who are on tonight. What do you think?'

Laura shrugged her shoulders wearily. She didn't

feel ready to face Robert again. Not just yet. In a way, he seemed to symbolise all that was wrong with her life. For that one split second in Alexa's flat, when he'd taken her face in his hands and dropped tiny butterfly kisses onto her eyelids, she'd thought that here was someone who might love her at last, someone who wouldn't reject her. But no. Like everyone else in her life, he'd only had a brief fling in mind. And, what was far, far worse, they'd both betrayed Alexa in the process.

HH lay in the bath and surveyed his huge bulk of a body. His rotund stomach, the result of a few too many business dinners, was now red and blotchy from the boiling hot water. He sighed heavily. Today ought to be one of the most triumphant moments of his life, the pinnacle of all that he had worked so hard to achieve. The only problem was that he had no one to share it with. Laura had gone out dancing with that crazy artist friend of hers, while, true to her word, Kate had disappeared into the back of beyond to join some downbeat paper up north. What a waste of her talents, he thought. She was bright and young and beautiful, she shouldn't be slumming it on a paper like the *Bowland Bugle*. It was time he took a proper look at that rag. There must be something he could do to help her on her way.

For all his wealth and success, HH was a disappointed man. He'd kept his nose to the grindstone for all these years, constantly telling himself that he was only doing it to make sure the girls' future was secure – though in truth he was addicted to the machinations of business. But when he'd finally paused for breath in his mid-fifties, keen, so he told his closer colleagues, to spend more time with his daughters, but in fact a little bit bored of the constant wheeler-dealing, it was too late. Kate and Laura had established their own lives. Whereas as little girls they'd craved his attention – HH felt a twinge of guilt when he recalled the number of times Kate had pleaded with him to teach her how to play chess, or Laura had tried to show him her ballet steps – now they weren't in the least bit interested in spending time with their father. Oh, they were quite fond of him, like a faded old slipper that had been around for a long time, but it was Dodo they went running to when they needed help, Dodo they really depended on.

So it was that HH had been all alone when he'd opened the thick cream envelope that had arrived by the afternoon post. The letter inside was printed on the best quality paper and embossed across the top was the magical address he had been longing to see for the last decade. Buckingham Palace. He'd scanned the contents of the letter frantically. When he realised that it was indeed confirming his innermost desire a smile of triumph crossed his face. He'd done it. He'd done it at last. All his achievements had been recognised. The depressing thing was that he had no one to tell.

Laura felt as if her heart was going to break. They had been at the Seven Sisters for more than an hour now and she'd spent most of that time sitting at a small table on her own, nursing one gin and tonic after another and trying not to catch anyone's eye. She hoped that she looked as if she was enjoying herself hugely but she suspected she probably wasn't fooling anyone. She could hardly bear to watch Alexa and Robert dancing together, Alexa's red curls flying as she swung her hips in time to the music, Robert laughing at her endless exuberance. At one stage Alexa had grabbed her arm and entreated her to join in with them, but Laura had shaken her head and smiled. She couldn't bear the thought of the two of them feeling sorry for her.

Awkward as ever, Robert had barely even acknowledged her. Alexa had thrown her arms around his neck and planted a huge kiss on his lips. Laura, however, had hung back, her eyes darting everywhere but reluctant even to meet his gaze. If Alexa had noticed her reticence, she didn't say anything, simply charged ahead to the bar to get the first round of drinks in.

Janey Bell was every bit as sensational as Alexa had predicted. The first half of her set had got virtually everyone in the pub apart from Laura up onto their feet, her music a clever mix of jazz and soul. Janey herself was an extraordinary sight. She must be almost six feet tall, marvelled Laura, with jet-black hair hanging right the way down her back and a voluptuous figure spilling out of a skintight vermilion leotard. The combination of watching Janey onstage and Alexa throwing herself around the dance floor, both of them larger than life in their own distinctive ways, made Laura feel even more mousy and insignificant than usual.

Gradually Janey Bell slowed the tempo right down, telling the punters in her deep, husky voice, 'If there's someone special you want to take home tonight, now's your chance . . .'

As the saxophonist began his sweet, plaintive solo, Laura, intoxicated by the potent mix of the music and the number of gins she'd drunk, rested her head on her arms and closed her eyes. She didn't want to watch

Alexa and Robert dancing to this. They'd be oblivious to the rest of the world, especially to her.

She was miles away when she heard the gentle murmur of a man's voice close to her head. She looked up lazily, and then, suddenly realising that it was Robert crouching down next to her with a look of almost unbearable fondness in his eyes, came to with a start.

'What . . . where . . . ?'

'Will you dance this one with me, Laura?' he said again, and like a sleepwalker Laura got up and blindly followed him on to the makeshift wooden dance floor.

Robert slipped his arms easily around her and without even thinking she rested her cheek against the rough cotton of his shirt. They stood like this for several minutes, swaying gently to Janey's velvety voice. Robert breathed in Laura's scent and a wave of regret swept through him. She was so delicate, so fragile. He knew he'd hurt her badly over the last few weeks but she was too emotionally complex for him to cope with right now. As his arms tightened around her again, he bent his head and kissed the top of her soft hair.

For the first time in weeks, Laura enjoyed the sensation of being held tight. HH and Dodo, probably as a result of their own rigid upbringing, weren't demonstrative people, and Laura had always yearned for cuddles and kisses that had never been forthcoming. She didn't have a clue what Robert was playing at, but for now she felt safe and secure. Just being in his arms brought a warm glow to her heart. Then she looked up and her eyes met Alexa's. She saw a myriad of emotions cross her friend's face – surprise, hurt, and utter bewilderment.

Chapter Six

'And the next planning application we shall consider has been submitted by Mr and Mrs David Porter, of Newton House, Church Lane, Bowland . . .' droned the balding chairman of the planning committee.

Kate tried to stifle a huge yawn but somehow couldn't quite manage it. Blushing with embarrassment, she took a seventh peppermint from the packet in her bag and unwrapped it under the table. The cellophane rustled noisily as she did so and several committee members shot disapproving glances at her.

Kate groaned inwardly. She'd been on the *Bugle* for almost seven weeks now and she had never been so bored in her entire life. After the drama of grabbing the front page with her exclusive interview with the Rawlinsons, the job had settled down into a monotonous routine. Nicky Rawlinson was still missing and no one, not even Danny, had commented on her scoop. The only sign that Kate had done a reasonable job had been the fact that virtually all the national newspapers had lifted the interview lock, stock and barrel and incorporated it into their own stories. The most galling thing of all had been the way that Thorndike had given Kate a joint byline with Pam Newbold on the story. When Kate had read the words

'*Nicky's mum and dad reveal their agony to* Bugle *reporters Pam Newbold and Kate Grant*', she'd scarcely been able to contain her anger. If she'd been six years old she would have stamped her foot and stormed off in a huff. As it was, she bit her lip and said nothing.

Thorndike definitely had it in for her, thought Kate, as she doodled in her notebook. Each day he seemed to take a perverse delight in sending her on the crappiest stories he could come up with. 'Sand stolen from toddlers' playground,' he'd say, looking up slyly from his paper-strewn desk next to the office's one and only window. 'Sounds like the perfect one for you, Kate. Right up your street. Give it all you've got, won't you?' Pam Newbold and Rob Bennett, the other two reporters, would snort with laughter and, one by one, all the others in the newsroom usually ended up joining in too.

Every Tuesday afternoon Thorndike despatched Kate to the offices of Bowland District Council, a horrendously ugly modern block in the centre of the town, to cover the weekly planning-committee meeting. It usually went on for at least three hours and although Kate meticulously churned out story after story of applications for barns to be turned into executive homes and pleas by farmers to convert their uncultivated fields to caravan parks, not a single one had yet made the paper.

The highlight of the week was Friday, when Kate was sent to college in Preston to study shorthand, law and local government with a handful of other trainees from local papers in the area. According to Danny, Thorndike had baulked at the cost of this, but a recent edict from the head office of Leadington Newspapers, the group that owned the *Bugle*, had insisted that all new trainees must be sent on bona-fide training courses. The men in suits professed themselves sick of forking out money for mistakes made by youngsters wet behind the ears, and said that it was high time trainees knew how to avoid getting their editors nicked for contempt of court.

Kate reckoned that if it hadn't been for Fridays, she would have gone completely stark raving bonkers. Lectures usually fizzled out at about four thirty pm and after that she and all the other students generally wound up in the pub to moan about the foibles of their news editors and compare horror stories.

They all agreed that Ben Maguire could usually trounce everyone else's tales of the ridiculous things they, as the most junior staff on their respective papers, were ordered to do. Ben was twenty-nine, a few years older than the rest of them and a former English teacher at an inner-city comprehensive.

'I had to do something to get away from all those adolescent pimples and snotty noses,' he'd breezily explained at the first pub session. 'Mind you, the snotty noses were almost certainly related to the vast quantities of coke the kids were snorting.' He had then proceeded to stun the other trainees with tales of drug-dealing in the playground and stand-up fights at the back of his classroom.

Kate giggled involuntarily as she recalled Ben's latest story, then tried to look serious again as the clerk glared at her for the third time that afternoon.

'You'll never believe what assignment those idiots sent me on this week,' Ben had announced after a couple of pints. 'I'd been doing this court case about a dog that had developed a liking for the local postman's trousers. Must be the blue serge or something. Anyway, one day it managed to sink its teeth into the poor chap's thigh and he had to have ten stitches. The dog's owners were charged with failing to keep the animal under proper control. So, I filed the story and guess what bright idea the news editor immediately came up with?'

Kate herself loathed covering court cases. In her very first week she'd walked into Bowland Magistrates Court and, uncertain where to sit, had plonked herself down on a bench with an excellent view of the proceedings, right at the front. To her horror she'd immediately been turfed out by the snooty-looking Crown Prosecution Service solicitor. 'The press bench is back there,' he'd told her and the whole court had laughed uproariously. She'd never quite got over this embarrassment and was a bag of nerves every time she was subsequently sent to court.

'Come on Ben, spill the beans,' said one of the other reporters, a pretty dark-haired girl called Rebecca Wilson, who always hung on Ben's every word.

Ben had barely been able to speak through the gales of laughter.

'He ordered me to get friendly with the bloody dog's owners and move in with them for the week. To see if the animal was really vicious – or whether it just had a thing about the Royal Mail!'

'How did it go?' asked Rebecca, gazing adoringly at Ben.

'Look at this,' instructed Ben and pulled his trouser leg up to the knee to reveal a muscular calf and three large bite marks. 'I'd only been in the house for ninety minutes when I got the first one. And to think I came into newspapers because I fancied doing something more cerebral than reciting GCSE set texts round the class.'

'Have you written a story about your deeply traumatic experience, then?' teased Kate.

'Bloody hell, you're worse than my news editor,' chuckled Ben. 'He made me write a thousand words before he'd let me out to the hospital for my tetanus booster. You know, thinking about it, I'm sure the old stage epithet must apply to newspapers. Never work with children or animals.'

Ben was great, thought Kate. It wasn't that she fancied him or anything like that, though he was undeniably attractive – tall and broad, with sandy-coloured hair curling over his collar and brown eyes that didn't seem to miss a trick. No, he was just good company, always ready with a sympathetic quip and the offer of another drink when one of them had cocked up yet another story.

'. . . And that draws this afternoon's proceedings to a close,' burbled the chairman. 'I look forward to seeing you all at the same time next week.'

Kate consulted her watch in panic. It was four pm and she hadn't taken anything down at all for at least the last hour, not since the Porters' application to build a conservatory in their back garden. She flicked through her notebook with mounting horror. No. There was virtually nothing there at all.

'Shit,' she said out loud, then glanced up to see the committee clerk bearing down on her.

'I wanted to have a word with you, Miss, er . . .'

'Grant,' said Kate helpfully and, standing up, offered him her hand. 'Kate Grant.'

The clerk looked at her hand disdainfully, as if it was the most unsavoury object he'd ever been presented with. He kept his own hand stiffly by his side.

'I understand that you're from London and not acquainted with reporting on complex local issues,' he said, placing great emphasis on the words 'complex' and 'local'.

'Well, it's not exactly difficult to understand,' said Kate with a ready smile. 'It's only people wanting to put dormer windows in their attics and tack ensuite bathrooms on to the back of their houses, isn't it?'

The clerk's face turned pink and, realising that she had gone too far, Kate said hastily, 'I was only joking. I didn't mean . . .'

The clerk grew even more agitated.

'My point precisely,' he hissed. 'You clearly don't understand complex local issues. Now, to get to the specifics of the matter, the whole planning committee is absolutely outraged by your behaviour. We've never come across anything like it. This afternoon you have sucked sweets, you have laughed out loud at the most inappropriate moments, you have treated the whole proceedings as though it were a game. And I can assure you that it most definitely isn't a game. I shall, of course, be writing a letter of complaint to your editor. And as for your clothes . . .'

He paused and Kate looked down in puzzlement at the cropped navy cardigan and shocking pink velvet drainpipes that she was wearing.

'What's wrong with my clothes?' she demanded, totally mystified. At home people were always complimenting her on her sense of style.

The clerk glanced at her ensemble again and shuddered.

'Your clothes may be considered suitable in the

south but let me assure you, Miss Grant, they cut no ice in the north,' he said coldly. 'No ice whatsoever. And I shall of course be drawing your editor's attention to your complete disregard for Bowland District Council forthwith.'

A shiver of dread ran down Kate's spine as she stomped up the stairs and pushed open the newsroom door. It had taken her fifteen minutes to walk back to the office and she knew that that would have given the pompous prat at the council plenty of time to bend Thorndike's ear.

She sidled over to her desk and tried to take her place as unobtrusively as possible. This was a tricky manoeuvre as someone had shoved her desk right up against the wall and she had to heave it out again in order to sit down. The table legs squeaked loudly on the ancient linoleum as she did so, alerting Thorndike, who'd been deep in conversation on the phone, to her return.

'Kate Grant,' he said, swivelling his chair round to face her. 'I've been waiting for you to get back.'

Kate's heart beat faster and faster. Thorndike was going to fire her, she knew it. He had been waiting for her to trip up for weeks now and she'd finally given him the perfect excuse to get rid of her. Poor old Scar had been booted out after the balls-up on her first day and it was obvious to everyone that she was next in line for the chop.

Thorndike was such a miserable old sod, reflected Kate. He somehow seemed to take a perverse pleasure in other people's cock-ups. Right now he was probably champing at the bit at the prospect of telling her how useless she was and ordering her out of the building.

Much to her surprise, however, Thorndike almost seemed to be smiling at her. It was more of a leer than a smile, admittedly, and his pointy teeth looked distinctly fang-like, but he didn't seem *quite* so sour as usual.

'Now,' he said. 'How did you get on with the planning meeting?'

Kate hesitated for a second before replying, then decided to try and bluff it out. She was pretty sure that the old codgers on the planning committee hadn't discussed anything of any consequence. They never did.

'Er, fine. Absolutely fine.'

'Good,' leered Thorndike.

'Shall I type out a couple of shorts on the more interesting applications?' asked Kate. Even though her heart wasn't in it, she might as well appear willing.

'You can do better than that, love,' said Thorndike. 'A little birdie's just rung to tell me that you've got a belter of a story up your sleeve.'

'I have?' said Kate, a note of uncertainty creeping into her voice.

'Come on, love, don't play games with me. Just file me five hundred words on the planning committee giving Mike Elton's flash new health club scheme the green light and I'll be well pleased. You might even get the splash again this week if you do a decent job. There'll be loads of people gnashing their teeth at the prospect of a massive new development on a green field site.'

'There will?' said Kate. She didn't have a clue what Thorndike was on about.

'So what do you reckon is the best line from the health club story?'

Kate stared at him in astonishment. Despite her

growing panic, it struck her forcibly that for the first time in seven weeks he was actually asking for her opinion.

'Er, I'm afraid I'd better come clean,' she began tentatively. 'There's a bit of a problem on this one.'

Thorndike sighed theatrically.

'Shut up whingeing will you? Give me five hundred words and you can get off home.'

Kate put her head in her hands. What did she have to do to get the bloody man to listen to her? At that moment, however, Thorndike's phone rang and he switched his attention to the call.

'Really?' she heard him saying, and then, 'yes I agree her dress sense leaves a little to be desired.'

Five minutes later he slammed the telephone down hard and stormed over to her desk, his face thunderous.

'I don't send you down to the council for you to get bloody Bertwhistle's knickers in a twist. He's a pain at the best of times so just don't wind him up in future will you?'

Kate twiddled with her earrings. When Thorndike heard what she was about to tell him, she was pretty certain she wouldn't *have* a future.

Chapter Seven

It was almost the middle of the morning by the time Kate dragged herself out of bed. She'd wanted to be absolutely sure that Danny and the others had left for work before she ventured out of her room. She couldn't face their knowing looks and false sympathy right now.

What the hell was she supposed to do now she had lost her job? There were just two options. Either stay in Bowland and find a job as a barmaid or something, an unappealing prospect to say the least. Or creep home with her tail between her legs and beg her father to resuscitate that post as ghastly Gordon Osprey's secretary. No, that was an even less attractive proposition.

On the spur of the moment Kate picked up the phone to ring Laura. She'd been feeling guilty about her sister for weeks. Apart from sending a hastily scrawled postcard of a wild-looking moorland sheep when she'd first arrived in Bowland, Kate had barely given her a second thought. Now she had time to make amends on that score, at least.

Five minutes later she was regaling Laura with all the grisly details of her demise at the *Bugle*.

'Kate, you're absolutely mad,' said Laura, exasperated at the mess Kate had made of her new career. 'After all that trouble you went to to get that job as well. Why did you have to go and rock the boat like that? Why didn't you just try and keep a low profile?'

'You're absolutely right of course – as usual,' agreed Kate ruefully. Looking back on the unpleasant scene with Thorndike yesterday, she couldn't help wishing that she hadn't let rip at him in the way she had. She shuddered at the names she'd called him. God, why couldn't she be more like Laura – calm and reflective and sensible? Laura had always had her head screwed on, even when they were children. She never let things get to her like Kate did. She had even coped better with their mother's disappearance. While Kate had broken down and cried on her sister's shoulder night after night when they were little, wailing about how much she missed her mum and how much she wanted her back, Laura was always so much more stoical, so much more in control.

'Couldn't you go and beg him for your job back?' suggested Laura. 'Just kind of bow and scrape and tell him you'll behave yourself from now on?'

'Er, that could be a little bit tricky.'

'Why?' said Laura. 'What on earth did you say to him?'

Kate swallowed. In the cold light of day she could hardly bear to think about it. The words 'toerag' and 'scumbag' floated unbidden into her mind. She recalled Thorndike roaring that she'd never make a reporter in a million years, not when she couldn't even recognise a splash at a hundred paces. To which she had shrieked, 'You can stuff your bloody job – the *Bugle*'s a crap newspaper anyway.'

Laura fell silent as Kate admitted what she had shouted at Thorndike.

'Are you still there, Laura?' asked Kate. There was

something about Laura's voice that wasn't quite right. She sounded more detached, more withdrawn than usual.

'What? Oh I'm fine. Just had a few late nights, that's all.' Laura shuddered inwardly. Her late nights weren't quite the sort of late nights Kate would be imagining.

'Out on the town with Alexa again? Honestly, you two. I wish there was a decent club in Bowland. The only night out I've had in the last few weeks is at this gruesome pub called the White Elephant. It's dingy and dirty and full of old men throwing up. You'd absolutely hate it.'

Now it was Laura's turn to feel uncomfortable. She hadn't set eyes on Alexa since their night out at the Seven Sisters. Nor on Robert, either. The moment he'd spotted Alexa watching them smooching on the dance floor, he'd let go of her like a shot and rushed back to Alexa's side like an obedient puppy. God knew what he'd told her. Laura had quietly disappeared out of a side door and hailed a taxi home. In the early hours she'd stuffed herself with all the most revolting things she could lay her hands on. She'd grabbed four choc ices from the freezer and devoured them one after the other. Upstairs in her bedroom she'd gorged herself on a whole packet of digestive biscuits, two pizzas and half a loaf of bread, thickly smothered with butter and apricot jam. Replete and more disgusted with herself than ever, she'd spent the rest of the night vomiting her insides out in a desperate attempt to purge herself.

'Sorry, I was miles away,' she told her sister now. 'What did you say?'

'I asked if you'd been seeing a lot of Alexa. She's got a new man, hasn't she?'

'Yes,' replied Laura flatly. 'I mean no, I've hardly

seen Alexa at all. But she's so absorbed with her painting these days. She's got a new exhibition coming up soon and she's very bound up with that.'

'How's Daddy?' asked Kate, sensing Laura's reluctance to talk about Alexa.

'Working too hard, as usual. He's definitely up to something. I haven't a clue what it is but he slams the phone down whenever I walk into his study. You know how secretive he is.'

'What do you think he's doing? Is he trying to take over another newspaper group or something? He's so keen to expand the business. He sees himself as the Rupert Murdoch of local newspapers.'

'Who knows?' said Laura wearily. Unlike Kate, she'd never been that interested in her father's deals.

'He *is* all right, isn't he?' said Kate. 'There isn't something you're not letting on about?'

Laura sighed heavily.

'Everyone's absolutely fine, Kate. If you could drag yourself down here sometime you could see for yourself. I'm fine, Daddy's fine and Dodo's fine. End of story.'

Laura paused for a moment. She would have loved to talk to Kate properly, confide in her about Robert and everything else but somehow she just couldn't. Not on the telephone and not in the office, not with her new boss charging past every two minutes like a bull in a china shop and the other secretaries earwigging like mad. Anyway it was all too humiliating. She wasn't sure she could ever bring herself to tell Kate the truth about her late nights. *She* would never have got herself into a mess like this.

When she'd put the phone down Kate made herself a

cup of black coffee and stumbled back to bed with it. She couldn't put her finger on exactly what the problem was but there was definitely something wrong with Laura.

They were a totally dysfunctional family, she reflected. Why had they turned out like this? You would have thought that Clare's disappearance would have bound them closer together, not pushed them further apart.

Kate took a sip of coffee, almost scalding her mouth as she did so. What would she and Laura have been like, she wondered, if Clare had always been there to bring them up? More important than that, what would it have been like to have a mother around to help and guide you, to give you a hug when you felt down and a look of pride when you'd achieved something great in your life? Oh, HH had tried his best, she knew that. And so had Dodo. But – and she'd never dream of admitting this to either of their faces – it somehow just wasn't the same.

The sound of someone pounding on the front door interrupted Kate's muddled thoughts. She put her coffee down hurriedly, spilling some on herself in the process, and thundered down the stairs.

'Hold your horses,' she shouted as the banging on the door began again. 'You'll knock the door down if you're not careful.'

When she opened the door she could hardly believe her eyes. There, standing on the doorstep clutching a small drooping bunch of clashing, multicoloured freesias and looking as if this was the last place on earth he wanted to be, was Thorndike. He was wearing the same shabby tweed jacket and brown corduroy trousers that he always wore and he clearly hadn't shaved for a couple of days.

'Oh,' she said coldly. 'It's you.'

'Can I come in?' said Thorndike. 'I've bought you these to cheer you up.'

Kate regarded them with suspicion. She'd never seen such a pathetic bunch of flowers. Thorndike had either grabbed them straight out of someone's garden or bought them at the local garage. No, that was highly unlikely. Thorndike was notoriously tight-fisted.

'What do you want?' said Kate. 'I assumed we'd both said all we wanted to say last night. You certainly didn't mince your words.'

'Come on, cut the bullshit,' said Thorndike gruffly. 'Let me in.'

Kate stood aside and let Thorndike come through. She felt much more comfortable now that he was being his usual bloody self. Thorndike with a false smile and a bunch of flowers was just too creepy for words. She led him down the dingy passageway into the kitchen and gestured to him to take a seat. He slammed the flowers on the table, clearly desperate to get rid of the damn things, and turned to face her again.

As he looked her up and down, Kate was acutely aware of her bare legs and tousled hair. In her haste to get to the front door she hadn't even thought to grab a dressing gown.

'What do you want then?' she said, keen to get shot of him as fast as possible. 'If it's the office key I never had one. You were obviously pretty sure right from the start that I wouldn't be staying long.'

'Look,' said Thorndike, finally sitting down on one of the mismatched wooden chairs. He put his elbows on the table, as if to show that he meant business. 'I know we haven't exactly seen eye to eye and I've had to bawl you out on several occasions, but that doesn't mean you haven't got potential. I lost my rag with you last night, I admit that, but I think even you probably agree that I had good cause. Now, I've been mulling things over and I've come round here to offer you a second chance. What do you reckon?'

Kate looked at him warily. Just as she'd sensed that Laura was keeping something from her earlier on, she was pretty certain that Thorndike wasn't giving her the whole story now. But for once she decided to hold her tongue and hear him out.

'OK,' said Kate. Deep down she was over the moon that he was giving her her old job back but she was damned if she was going to let Thorndike know that. It would be too uncool for words.

Thorndike's eyes narrowed slightly. He'd expected a little gratitude, at least.

'Is it all right if I take the rest of the day off and come back in tomorrow?' asked Kate. 'There doesn't seem to be much point in coming in now, does there?'

'Don't push your luck,' ordered Thorndike, banging the table with his fist. 'You'll get back to work this minute. I've got a job that I want you to get on with right now. It's Wednesday, remember, so we're going to press tonight. I'll wait here while you fling some clothes on. And make sure it's nothing flashy. There isn't a minute to waste.'

Twenty minutes later, Kate was standing outside Bert and Violet Rawlinson's door, wondering how she could ever find the courage to confront them.

She cursed bloody Thorndike again. It was perfectly obvious now why he had been so desperate to get her back to work. All that bullshit about her having potential when the only thing he was really interested in was getting the splash for tomorrow's paper.

'Nicky Rawlinson's been found,' he'd told her.

Kate squirmed with discomfort now as she recalled her reaction to the news. Naïve, to say the least.

'That's fantastic,' she'd smiled, genuinely pleased. 'Is she back with her mum and dad? They'll be so relieved that she's OK.'

Thorndike had stared at her as if she was a complete imbecile.

'You'll never make a bloody reporter if you jump to conclusions all the time,' he'd bellowed. 'Watch my lips. Listen to what I am actually saying. Did I tell you that Nicky Rawlinson was as right as rain and tucking into a bowl of cornflakes back at home? Hmmm? No, I bloody didn't. The girl's dead and probably has been for weeks. A couple of walkers found her body under some bushes up on the moors. Looks as if she's been sexually assaulted, then strangled and dumped on the tops. I want you to get the parents. Right? Pam's tried her luck down there and been blown out. They told her that they won't talk to anyone except you.'

Kate dug her fingernails hard into the palms of her hands now, bracing herself to ring the Rawlinsons' doorbell. With luck they might still be down at the police station and then she wouldn't have to face them. It was all very well casually popping in now and again to check how they were coping – as she'd done at Thorndike's behest over the past few weeks – but the thought of confronting them now that their only daughter had been found brutally murdered was something entirely different. She was completely out of her depth.

She pressed the buzzer as lightly as she could, willing there to be no one inside.

Within seconds, however, the door was wrenched open, almost flying off its hinges in the process.

In front of her stood Bert and Violet's eldest son Dave, a huge bear of a man, wearing a grimy white vest and a pair of jeans that looked as if they hadn't been washed for months. His eyes were red and swollen, as if he'd been crying. Kate had met him at the house once before, and he hadn't exactly laid out the red carpet then. She dreaded to think how he would react to her now that Nicky was dead.

'I've, I've just come round to tell you how terribly sorry I am,' Kate stuttered. 'About Nicky, I mean.' Unsure what to say next, she felt as if she was stumbling around in the dark, trying to find the right way forward.

'I had a long chat with your mum and dad a few weeks back and they were so certain that she'd come back eventually. I know how all of you must be feeling now.'

'Do you now?' spat Dave harshly. 'And how would that be then?'

Kate blushed. What a stupid bloody thing to say, she thought. His kid sister had just been murdered and here she was telling him she knew what he was going through, when of course she didn't have a clue.

'Who is it, Dave?' shouted a man's voice from the back of the house and suddenly Bert Rawlinson appeared. Bert looked like a shadow of the man Kate had first met. He'd been scraggy before, but he must have lost at least another couple of stone. His cheekbones protruded from his ravaged face and his hair, previously a kind of mousy brown, had now turned white.

Kate gulped nervously. She was going to be as welcome at this house as a Seventh Day Adventist.

'Oh, hello love,' said Bert, a ghost of a smile crossing his face when he saw Kate. 'I'm pleased to see you, really I am. Come in. I'm just making a brew for the wife.'

'Are you sure, Dad?' said Dave, putting his arm round the older man's narrow shoulders.

'Course I'm sure. She's the only one of them I trust, that's for certain. I don't know why she understands but she just does.'

Following the pair of them into the kitchen, one large and muscly, the other stooped and pitifully thin, Kate wondered what on earth she thought she was doing. She should be leaving the Rawlinsons to do their grieving in peace, not bombarding them with intrusive questions about how poor Nicky had died.

'Don't be stupid, love,' snapped Bert when she voiced these thoughts out loud. 'So long as you're gentle and don't go throwing your weight around like that old tart your paper sent down here earlier, we're pleased to have you. I want you to do us a favour, in fact.'

'Me?' asked Kate. She was astonished at his magnanimity. 'What can I do for you now, when the only thing you really hoped and prayed for isn't going to happen, is it?'

'No, it isn't,' said Bert, his eyes glistening with tears. 'All me and the wife wanted was for Nicky to barge through that door like she always did, pinching all the best biscuits from the tin and switching that blasted music of hers on at top volume. But, no, it isn't going to happen now.'

'So how can I help you?'

Bert stared at her blankly.

'Vi and me, we're just ordinary folk, but we want everyone to know how special Nicky is, I mean was,' he said softly. 'We want you to explain what she was like. A kind of tribute to her, really. It would mean a lot to us, love, if you could show everyone what we've lost.'

Two hours later, Kate was back in the office, hammering out her story on the word processor as though her whole life depended on it. She must have learned something over the past few weeks, she thought, because the words flowed far more easily than they ever had before. Then again, perhaps it was because she just couldn't let Bert and Vi down. She had to do justice to them. And to Nicky's memory.

Once the paper had finally been put to bed everyone stumbled round the corner to the White Elephant for a quick pint. As Kate took a slug of her glass of warm sweet Liebfraumilch – the only wine the pub ever served – she couldn't help marvelling at the change in her fortunes over the last twenty-four hours. Thorndike had actually told her she'd made a reasonable stab at the Rawlinson interview, Danny had gone into raptures over the pictures of Nicky that Bert and Vi had lent to her and even Pam had grudgingly bought her a drink. Maybe things were looking up at last.

Chapter Eight

By the end of the week, Kate sensed that she was beginning to be accepted at the *Bugle*. Against all the odds, Thorndike was almost being civil to her and Pam Newbold seemed to be bending over backwards to become her new best friend. At her weekly training session in Preston she'd finally passed the one hundred words per minute shorthand test at her third attempt and the intricacies of the laws of contempt had suddenly started to make sense. On Friday afternoon, when the group congregated in the Greyhound, the ugly modern pub opposite the college, she'd regaled them all with the story of her spectacular firing and rehiring.

'You are a fool, Kate,' snapped Rebecca Wilson as, amid raucous laughter from everyone else, Kate reached the denouement of her story. 'You'll have to take your career a bit more seriously than that if you're going to get anywhere. But maybe the *Bowland Bugle* is the pinnacle of your ambition? What do you think, Ben?'

Kate glanced quickly at Ben Maguire. As usual he and Rebecca were sitting next to each other, their knees a mere whisker away from touching. Kate was pretty sure that there must be something going on between them. As far as she knew no one else in the group had paired off so far, and she couldn't help feeling slightly sick that a man like Ben had been stupid enough to fall for Rebecca's dubious charms. Rebecca was stunning, even Kate had to admit that, but there was a coldness about her. Maybe she would end up as a Fleet Street superstar but right now it was hard to imagine some poor old sod like Bert Rawlinson unburdening his soul to her. She'd eat him for breakfast and spit him out afterwards.

They all fell silent, waiting for Ben's response. He was universally acknowledged as the leader of the group, due to both his age and the fact that he'd already spent five years working as a teacher. Kate reckoned the rest of them must seem like spotty adolescents to him; all the time they'd been at university or college he'd been out grafting in a tough inner-city comprehensive.

Ben stared intently at Kate for a few seconds. Wondering what on earth he was going to say, Kate shifted uncomfortably in her seat and took another sip of her disgusting white wine. What was it about all the pubs around here? Why couldn't any of them serve a decent Chardonnay?

'I think Kate takes her career very seriously already,' Ben said finally. 'I'm sure she's going to surprise us all. Aren't you, Kate?'

Kate was taken aback by Ben's odd choice of words. He'd never shown the slightest interest in anything she did before. What the hell was he on about?

'That's right, Ben,' she laughed, trying to hide her discomfiture. 'I've got more ambition in my little finger than the rest of you have got put together.'

At this the others all protested noisily. They'd got in

81

at least four rounds of drinks by this time so Harvey Collins started burbling drunkenly about how he was going to be the first reporter to file from the moon, while Thea Beale reckoned she'd be the first woman tabloid editor in her twenties.

'You'd better get your act together then,' chuckled Ben. 'Fascinating as they undoubtedly are, you're not going to get very far writing little parish council reports for the *Accrington Standard*.'

It was nine pm by the time they all drifted out of the pub. A few trainees, Ben and Rebecca among them, decided to go off clubbing but Kate declined the offer and headed back towards the station. She must get her act together and buy a car, she thought. She was sick of being at the mercy of the ropey train service back to Bowland. It stopped at virtually every village station in the whole of Lancashire along the way.

After five minutes or so, the streets grew more deserted and the street lamps few and far between. Kate tried not to think about the heavy footsteps thudding behind her. She quickened her pace, all too conscious of being a woman alone in a dark, unfamiliar town. But the thudding speeded up too and suddenly, terrifyingly, a pair of large hands grabbed her from behind.

'There's no need to run away,' said a man's voice and he spun her round to face him.

'G-G-God, you scared the living daylights of me,' stammered Kate when she saw who it was. 'You don't make a habit of doing that, do you?'

'Oh Kate, I'm sorry,' said Ben sheepishly. 'I'm a complete idiot. I never thought . . .'

To Kate's surprise, though, he didn't take his arms

away. Instead, he tightened his grip around her and, intoxicated by the nearness of her, suddenly kissed her long and hard on the lips.

Kate could hear her heart thumping as slowly her arms crept around him and she began kissing him back. He felt solid and warm and, after all the weeks of living on her wits on the *Bugle*, it was nice just to be held.

She had no idea how long it was before they drew apart and smiled shyly at each other. For the first time since she'd met him, Ben looked ridiculously young and very unsure of himself.

'Kate,' he murmured finally. 'You have no idea how long I've wanted to do that. All those weeks of sitting through interminable lectures on boring local government and committal proceedings and all I could think about was touching you. I had to sit as far away as possible to make sure I didn't. I've wanted you so much, I thought I'd go out of my mind.'

He smoothed her hair back from her face with infinite gentleness and began kissing her all over again.

'We can't stand here all night,' whispered Kate. 'Can we go back to your place?'

'Sweetheart,' sighed Ben. 'I thought you'd never ask.'

'Oh my God, what time is it,' shrieked Kate when she woke the next morning. For a moment she couldn't fathom where the hell she was but when she saw Ben lying naked beside her she smiled beatifically.

'Where are you going?' he mumbled sleepily.

'I've got to get to work. Thorndike's only just coming round to thinking that I'm all right. I can't ruin it all now by being hours late.'

'Come here,' said Ben, and, winding his arms tightly around her, planted a kiss on her lips. Somehow one thing led to another and it was half an hour before they surfaced for air.

'I'll definitely get the sack now,' groaned Kate.

'Definitely,' agreed Ben with a grin.

'It's not funny. Thorndike relented once but he won't do it twice. I know he won't.'

'Absolutely,' said Ben, trying to keep a straight face. 'Was it worth it, though?'

'Was what worth it?'

'Bloody hell, sweetheart, you're dense sometimes. Was last night worth losing your job for?'

Kate turned and yawned lazily at him.

'You bet it was,' she said. 'Given the same choice, I'd do exactly the same thing all over again.'

'Come here, then . . .'

'I can't,' giggled Kate. She dragged herself out of Ben's bed and began picking off the floor the clothes she'd discarded so recklessly last night. 'I must go.'

Ben propped his head on his elbow and watched her. A wave of tenderness swept through his whole body. There was something so vulnerable about Kate, he reflected. On the surface she seemed so confident and impulsive – indeed the first couple of times he'd met her, he'd written her off as a scatty little rich girl who was simply playing at being a reporter – but underneath she was crying out to be loved.

'You do know it's Saturday, don't you?' said Ben, his voice casual.

'What?'

'It's Saturday.'

Kate stopped doing up the flies of her trousers and stood, naked from the waist up, to face him. Christ, she was beautiful, thought Ben. He ached to touch those breasts again.

'You knew all along, didn't you?' she said.

'Maybe.'

'Right,' she said, throwing herself on the bed next to him again. 'I'm going to have to do something about you.'

'I wish you would,' said Ben softly.

It was five in the afternoon before they finally dragged themselves out of bed. They'd lain among the rumpled sheets for hours, just touching and talking and making love all over again.

Kate admitted that she'd been positive that he was only interested in Rebecca Wilson.

'Never,' said Ben. 'She might have been interested in me and I confess she looked sensational in those leather trousers of hers, but I'm afraid my heart was already taken.'

Ben told Kate of the years he'd spent teaching at a Southwark comprehensive, his increasing disillusionment and the assault by a fifteen-year-old pupil that had finally made him quit. In turn, Kate described the day her mother had walked out and the sense of desolation she'd felt ever since.

So that was it, thought Ben to himself. He'd sensed right from the outset that there was something desperate, something needy, about Kate, something that all her outer charm and confidence couldn't quite mask.

'You poor darling,' he said softly and gently touched her cheek. 'Have you ever tried to find her?'

'I've thought about it, yes,' whispered Kate. 'But I've always stopped short of doing anything about it.'

'Why?'

Kate paused for a moment. Unused to confiding in

anyone, not even Laura or Dodo and certainly not HH, about her feelings towards her mother, she found it difficult to put it into words.

'I suppose it's because of my father,' she said. 'I don't know what went on between them before she left and in a way I'm not sure that I want to know. He's always gone to such lengths to avoid talking about it all. What if I start digging around like Sherlock Holmes and stumble across something horrific? He might even have killed her for all I know.'

Ben stared at her. As one of four children from a close-knit, uncomplicated farming family he found it difficult to comprehend what Kate was saying.

'You don't really think that, do you?'

'Oh no,' said Kate hurriedly. 'Daddy's a tough man, that's why he's got where he is, but he's not the violent type. At least I don't think so . . .'

Her voice trailed away miserably. She knew that one day she was going to have to confront what had happened in the past, but not right now. Not now, when she'd just found Ben.

The recent financial performance of Leadington Newspapers made grim reading, thought HH, as he made his way down the columns of figures that Gordon Osprey had brought in.

'I wouldn't touch this group with a bargepole, Hubert,' Gordon had said scathingly. 'It's small fry as far as we're concerned. Leadington only has a paltry twelve papers in its stable and the most successful of the lot sells the princely sum of twelve thousand papers a week. There's nothing in it for us, HH. It's barely breaking even.'

'Thank you, Gordon, but you'll let me be the judge

of that, won't you,' HH had told him sharply. He knew full well, however, that his longstanding deputy had an irritating habit of almost always being right.

The wind and rain lashed the moors so ferociously that Kate found it virtually impossible to put one foot in front of the other.

'Whose bright idea was this?' she mouthed at Ben, who was making almost as little headway as she was.

'Yours,' shouted Ben and, despite the storm, they grinned at each other. It was a relief to smile, thought Kate. Her throat ached with sadness at the thought of what poor Nicky Rawlinson must have suffered up here.

'I'm desperate for a cup of tea,' she yelled. 'Shall we go back to your car?'

They'd only been walking for about half an hour but at least she had accomplished what she'd set out to do – and that was to lay flowers at the spot where Nicky's battered body had eventually been discovered.

'I know you'll think I'm completely mad,' she'd said quietly when Ben brought up the subject of how they were going to spend Sunday. 'I know reporters aren't supposed to get involved or anything but it's just something I feel I have to do.'

'Do you know where she was actually found?' Ben had asked.

To be honest Kate wasn't entirely sure, but when they got up to the tops it became all too clear. Someone – and Kate was certain that despite his poor health it must have been Nicky's father Bert – had got there before them and covered the small area next to a clump of bushes with scores of yellow and white carnations.

On the ground close by lay the tatty remains of a piece of blue and white police marker tape.

'What a terrible place to die,' whispered Kate as she placed her bunch of white lilies next to Bert's flowers. Her voice quavered. 'It's so desolate here. And Nicky was only fourteen. She must have been so frightened.'

'Come on,' said Ben, his arm tightening around her shoulders. 'You've done what you came to do. You can't do any more. I'll buy you that cup of tea now.'

Half an hour later they were sitting next to a roaring fire in a quaint sixteenth-century tea room. Kate knew she should just relax and enjoy being with Ben but somehow she couldn't shake off her melancholy. She didn't know why, but Nicky Rawlinson's fate had got to her. She couldn't get the dead schoolgirl out of her mind.

'You never met her,' said Ben gently, 'so why is she bothering you so much?'

Kate looked at him. They'd both discarded their soaking wet coats and boots, which lay steaming in front of the fire in a tangled heap, but Ben still looked drenched.

'Why?' he repeated, and as he did so he leaned across and tenderly cupped her face in his hands.

Kate swallowed hard. She thought she was going to cry.

'It's something to do with losing someone,' she began. 'When Bert said he yearned for Nicky to walk back in as if nothing had happened, it, it just struck a chord with me. I mean, I'm proud of my father and everything – he's achieved more than anyone I know and I love him, I really do. But when it comes down to it I don't really need him and he doesn't need me.

He isn't the one I want. I know I'm twenty-two years old now and I should be able to cope on my own, but I just wish my mother would come back.'

'Go on,' said Ben.

'I thought it would have got better by now but it hasn't. It gets worse all the time. With every year that goes by I keep wondering how she could have done it. For ages Laura kept saying that the reason that she went was simply because we weren't good enough. If the two of us had been better she might have had more of a reason to stay. For all I know, Laura still believes that.'

'But that's absolutely ridiculous, isn't it? You know that.'

'Oh, I do now,' said Kate vehemently. 'But I didn't back then. Laura and I turned into such good little girls after she went. We did everything we were told. Butter wouldn't melt in our mouths. We really thought that we could make her come back simply by being good.'

'But you couldn't,' prompted Ben gently.

'No,' said Kate. 'And she never will come back now. I suppose I've just got to learn to live with it.'

They sat without saying anything for a couple of minutes, each wondering what on earth had possessed an apparently devoted mother to walk out on her two young children. Ben was the first to break the silence.

'You know what you said about your father?'

'Sorry, I was miles away,' said Kate. 'What about my father?'

'You said that he'd achieved so much in his life. What did you mean? Is he well-known or something?'

Kate regarded Ben steadily. In the two months she'd

been in Lancashire she'd told no one about her father. She'd immersed herself in her new identity so completely that for days on end she forgot that he even existed. She was so immersed in her new life as Kate Grant that she often forgot that Kate Hollingberry even existed.

'Can I trust you?' she said hesitantly.

To her surprise Ben threw back his head and laughed.

'Kate, we've just spent twenty-four hours in bed together making wild, passionate love. And now you ask if you can trust me?'

All of a sudden his smile faded and he looked deeply hurt.

'I don't know how you can ask me that. If you aren't sure by now whether you can trust me or not then you'll never know it.'

Kate reached for his hand across the table, wanting desperately to reassure him.

'Of course I know. I just get screwed up about anything to do with my parents. It's all right on the surface but when I think about the past and how they always seemed to put themselves before Laura and me, I get in a state. I do trust you, Ben. I completely trust you.'

'So tell me,' he said.

Kate took a deep breath and smoothed damp tendrils of hair back from her face. She looked no more than a child like that, thought Ben. He wanted to grab her and hold her tight, never let her go.

'I'm not really Kate Grant at all,' she said. She was so desperate to get the words out before she lost her nerve that they tumbled out in a rush.

'I knew it,' said Ben dramatically. 'You are an industrial spy. You've been sent on a mission to prise the innermost secrets of the *Preston Gazette* out of me. What do they call this sort of thing? You've enticed me into a honey trap.'

Kate couldn't help giggling.

'Come on, be serious,' she laughed. 'No. My father's Hubert Hollingberry. As in Hollingberry Holdings, I mean. The biggest regional newspaper group in the country? I don't know why but I've always had this obsession about getting into journalism on my own merits. I couldn't bear it if everyone assumed that my father was just pulling strings for me.'

'But he's hardly Rupert Murdoch, is he?' said Ben. 'Honestly, sweetheart, I do think you've slightly got things out of proportion.'

'Haven't you heard of him then?' asked Kate. Ben made her father sound so inconsequential. Perhaps he was right. Maybe no one would bat an eyelid about him.

'Oh, you know, vaguely,' said Ben, waving his hands dismissively. 'Actually, he owns the *Preston Gazette*.'

'Oh God,' muttered Kate, burying her head in her hands. 'He's got so many papers all over the place that I can hardly keep track of them these days. So he's your boss.'

Ben immediately lifted her chin up and gazed at her with exasperation.

'Sweetheart, don't be so stupid. Of course he's not my boss. I've got as much chance of bumping into your father behind the filing cabinet as you've got of being the next Prime Minister.'

'I want to be the next Prime Minister,' said Kate obstinately.

'What the hell does it matter if your father's my

boss or not?' said Ben. 'I'm crazy about you and you never know, if I play my cards right, you might end up being crazy about me. So who bloody cares about your father? Eh?'

Kate tried to smile but couldn't. She wished she'd never started this conversation.

'But you promise you won't tell anyone?'

'On one condition,' said Ben softly.

'What's that?'

'As long as you come straight back to bed with me for the rest of the afternoon. Yes?'

Kate slowly nodded her head. Perhaps Ben was right. She was getting her knickers in a twist over nothing. It was time she stopped worrying about who her father was and got on with her own life.

Chapter Nine

Laura stared at herself critically in the mirror. There was no doubt about it: she was looking terrible these days. Her hair was lank and in need of a decent cut and her skin had a translucent, almost ghostly, sheen to it. It was hardly surprising that Robert had given her a wide berth. No man in his right mind could possibly be interested in someone so hideous.

Astonishingly, even HH had commented on his elder daughter's appearance. Most of the time he was so bound up in his own affairs that he scarcely noticed Laura. Even though the two of them occupied the same house they could go for days on end without bumping into each other.

But this morning Laura had been up earlier than usual. She'd binged till late the night before and then, revolted by what she had done, had spent the early hours of the morning throwing up. After that, she couldn't get back to sleep at all and had dragged herself out of bed at six to have a bath and pull herself together before crawling into work.

'Bloody hell, Laura, you look like a shadow of yourself.' Those had been HH's first words at breakfast. As usual he was tucking into a hearty bowl of porridge, topped with a profusion of cream and brown sugar. Laura nursed a mug of weak camomile tea – all she could face after last night – and felt slightly nauseous again.

'Is there anything the matter, darling? Anything you want to talk about?'

Laura looked up from her tea in astonishment. HH's tone, usually so brusque, had been unexpectedly gentle. She shook her head dismissively nevertheless. She couldn't face discussing it with anyone. Least of all with her father. He wasn't exactly renowned for his tea and sympathy.

'I'm fine, honestly. There's some sort of virus going round the office so I'm probably next in line. That's all.'

Her casual words had sent a shiver of alarm down HH's spine. He'd hurriedly finished his breakfast and made a dash for the door, popping one of his new vitamin tablets as he went. A workaholic with distinct hypochondriacal tendencies, he was appalled at the prospect of catching whatever it was that was afflicting his elder daughter.

Now Laura carefully plastered on a thick layer of foundation in an attempt to hide her pallor. She added face powder and blusher, taking care not to overdo it. If she looked *too* rosy-cheeked, she knew she'd draw even more attention to herself.

A couple of hours later she was sitting in front of her boss's desk, trying to concentrate on the letters he was dictating. Like HH, Hugo Bentley was far too preoccupied to take much interest in anyone apart from himself. A tall, dark-haired bachelor in his early thirties, he was so obsessed with his own career at the merchant bank that the ups and downs of other people's lives tended to pass him by completely.

Laura had been his secretary for three months now but beyond the fact that he was a stickler for spelling and grammar, that he took two sugars in his coffee and that he liked to work late, she knew very little about him. She avoided gossiping with the other secretaries at the bank as a rule, but, as far as she knew, none of them had gleaned anything much about Hugo Bentley either.

Likewise, Hugo had made little effort to befriend Laura. She was quiet, efficient and had rather good legs; he reckoned that that was about as much as he needed to know.

'. . . I would like to thank you for expressing your interest and shall be pleased to retain your details on file should further suitable opportunities arise. Yours sincerely . . .'

Laura tried to concentrate on what Hugo was saying. Usually her pen sped across her shorthand notebook almost as fast as he spoke, but today her brain felt like glue. She was at least two sentences behind him now. What was that he'd said about 'expressing interest?' She was going to have to ask him to run through the letter again, starting at the top.

'Sorry, could you . . .' she said tentatively as he swivelled his chair round to study his computer screen once more.

Unfortunately Laura never managed to complete her sentence.

As Hugo dragged his eyes reluctantly away from the screen, irritated at the interruption, his secretary slid off her chair and crumpled into a pathetic heap on the floor.

Hugo clicked his teeth with annoyance. He was snowed under with work; he didn't have time for any kind of histrionics right now. Why couldn't these bloody girls ever keep their boyfriend troubles and menstrual cycles out of the office? He'd rather do without a secretary altogether than have to cope with problems like this.

He stepped gingerly over Laura's body, noting again in passing what great legs she had, and yelled for one of the other secretaries to come and help him.

Almost immediately, Allison Taylor and her boss, Michael Portland, came running. While Hugo looked on helplessly, Allison held Laura's hand and gently stroked the side of her pale cheek. After a couple of minutes, when Laura seemed to be coming round, Michael carefully lifted her into a sitting position.

'Fetch her a glass of water, Hugo, for God's sake,' hissed Michael under his breath. The head of the bank's venture-capital arm, Michael had never had much time for Hugo. And right now he felt intensely irritated at the way Hugo was just standing languidly by on the sidelines, still glancing periodically at his computer screen and doing absolutely bugger all to help Laura.

Supported by Allison and Michael, Laura took a small sip of water and forced herself to gulp it back.

'I'm so sorry, I don't know what came over me. It's terribly hot in here – I'm sure that it just got a bit overpowering.'

Allison and Michael glanced at each other doubtfully. In fact the Moneyflair office, with its state-of-the-art air-conditioning system, was anything but hot. Allison, a down-to-earth woman in her forties, had noticed Laura's sickly white face and the dark circles under her eyes in the Ladies earlier on and wondered if the girl was pregnant or something. She suspected that there was much more to this than met the eye.

'I'll be able to get on with my work now,' murmured Laura, desperate to escape Allison's watchful gaze.

'Great,' replied Hugo breezily, helping Laura to her feet. 'I knew you'd be as right as rain in no time.'

Michael Portland was horrified. He'd always reckoned that Hugo Bentley was a cold fish but this was the limit. Anyone with an ounce of compassion in them could see that Laura Hollingberry was in no fit state to carry on working. She barely had the strength to stand up, let alone stagger back to her word processor and continue as if nothing had happened.

'You'll do no such thing,' said Michael sternly, pulling rank on Hugo and taking matters into his own hands. 'Allison will collect all your things together and then Hugo will escort you home in a taxi. I'll ask reception to get one organised right away.'

Laura nodded wearily. She didn't have the strength to argue.

'And you, my girl,' continued Michael, wagging his forefinger at her, 'will stay at home until you've recovered. You look as if you need to take better care of yourself. Do you understand?'

Again Laura acquiesced. She felt too feeble to do anything else. It struck her forcibly, however, that it was quite nice when someone else took over for a change and told her what to do.

Hugo barely uttered a word on the journey from the City to Chelsea. As the black cab sped effortlessly through the unusually light mid-morning traffic, he clenched his fists repeatedly to contain his irritation. How dare Michael Portland interfere in his business? He should be getting on with the task of preparing a bid defence for his most important client, not playing nursemaid to his secretary. He glanced sideways at

Laura. She was sitting as far away as possible from him, her head thrown back and her eyes closed. She did look ill, he conceded. Her face had a greyish tinge to it now and she was clearly exhausted. For a moment or so he felt rather sorry for her. Then he slapped his knee with annoyance. He had far more important things on his mind than worrying about a sickly secretary.

When the taxi drew up outside HH's house, however, with its four storeys, imposing white stucco pillars and glossy black front door, Hugo couldn't hide his surprise.

'Are you quite sure that this is where you live?' he asked kindly. Perhaps Laura was hallucinating or something. This couldn't be the right place. He'd been expecting to drop her off at a shabby bedsit somewhere near World's End. Not outside this huge house in the heart of the most expensive bit of Chelsea.

Laura smiled wanly.

'I'm not so ill that I've forgotten where I live, Hugo,' she said.

Hugo glanced at her quickly. She'd never called him Hugo before. In fact, come to think of it, she'd never called him *anything* before.

'You do know who she is, don't you?'

The instant he got back to the office, a full two hours after his idiotic secretary had tumbled off her chair, Hugo had stormed straight into Michael Portland's office. Infuriated at the peremptory manner in which Michael had taken charge, he was determined to have things out with him.

But Michael had completely taken the wind out of his sails by offering him a chair, fetching him a cup of coffee and asking solicitously after Laura. And now this extraordinary remark.

'What do you mean "do I know who she is?"' growled Hugo. He'd taken his horn-rimmed spectacles off and was polishing them absent-mindedly with his handkerchief. He looked much younger, almost schoolboyish, without them.

'Well, do you?' repeated Michael.

'She's my goddam secretary, of course. What else do I need to know? Her favourite colour, her middle name, her bra size?'

'Ah, but you do know her surname, don't you?'

Hugo spluttered with exasperation.

'Of course I bloody know her surname. It's Hollingberry. Laura Hollingberry.'

As he repeated the name, the light slowly began to dawn in Hugo's brain. All of a sudden, everything was falling into place. The grand house in Chelsea, Laura's peculiar lack of deference towards him, Michael Portland's concern when she fell ill.

'She's not related to, to Hubert Hollingberry, is she?'

'Well done, Hugo, go to the top of the class,' said Michael with heavy sarcasm. 'You've obviously made a real effort to get to know your secretary. How long did you say that Laura has been working for you? Tell me. I've forgotten.'

It was more than two weeks before Laura recovered sufficiently to return to work. For the first week, she had lain in bed all day long, forcing herself to swallow the hearty meals that Dodo insisted on serving up like clockwork three times a day. She hated someone else being in control of her diet like this.

When Dodo had first set eyes on her elder niece, she'd been appalled by her appearance. She could have kicked herself for not noticing before this how awful Laura looked. She was consumed with guilt. How could she have been so blind? In fact Dodo was, as usual, being ultra-hard on herself. Now the girls were off her hands, she had finally moved back to her own flat and begun to think of herself for the first time in her life. Apart from her weekly visit to see HH and Laura, she passed her days by walking her dog, a skittish black poodle called Fenella, going out to bridge parties and raising money for good causes.

Laura had laughed off Dodo's concern by convincing her that she was only sick because she'd developed a wheat allergy. The family doctor hadn't been quite so gullible, however, and sternly warned her that if she didn't sort out her eating habits once and for all she risked becoming really ill.

'But you won't tell Daddy and Dodo, will you,' pleaded Laura.

'No, not unless you give me permission to,' said Dr Barratt. He'd seen Laura through a number of similar scares in the past and knew how paranoid she was about her family finding out about her bulimia. Privately he was surprised by the recurrence of Laura's illness. He'd helped her seek psychological help for her problem three years ago, and Laura had seemed to emerge so much stronger and more positive. He'd been confident that she had come to terms with the past and knocked the bulimia on the head for good.

'But it would help if you could talk to someone again. If not your aunt or your father, how about Kate? You've always been close. I'm sure she'd be supportive.'

'She's not here,' snapped Laura. 'And anyway, I'm over it now. Dodo's moved back in to look after me and I've been eating like a horse over the last couple of weeks. And more important, I've been keeping it all down, I promise.'

Ted Barratt regarded her steadily. It was true, she did look a lot better than she had a few days earlier. Her hair had a lustrous sheen to it once more and her skin seemed slightly rosier but then again, he'd given her the benefit of the doubt before and look what had happened. And no matter how much she protested about how great she was feeling, she couldn't hide the dullness in her eyes.

'And you'll carry on eating well?'

'I promise,' said Laura. She was quite happy to promise anything as long as he stopped asking questions and left her alone.

As he'd turned to leave, still not one hundred per cent convinced by her insistence that she was all right, Dodo had tapped lightly on the bedroom door and peeped in.

'Sorry to interrupt, darling, but you've got a visitor. It's a man,' she mouthed theatrically.

For a moment Laura's heart leapt. It must be Robert. Somehow he had heard that she was ill and he'd dropped everything to come rushing to her bedside.

The first thing she saw was an enormous bouquet of white lilies advancing through the door. The bunch was so massive that it completely obscured the person behind it. Laura noticed, however, that the mystery man had excessively polished brogues, black socks and pinstriped trousers and her heart sank. It couldn't be Robert after all. Combat trousers and scruffy trainers were more his style.

When the bouquet was laid gently on her lap, the identity of Laura's mystery visitor was finally revealed. Laura was astonished to see that it was her boss. Apart from a short note wishing her well, she hadn't heard hide nor hair of Hugo Bentley since he'd brought her home that day. The rest of the office had sent flowers and chocolates but from him there had been absolutely nothing.

Away from the office, Hugo Bentley looked younger and more unsure of himself. He wasn't wearing his glasses either and for the first time it struck Laura that he was actually quite good-looking – in a studious sort of way.

'Hugo,' she murmured with a smile. 'How sweet of you to bring me some flowers. Lilies are my absolute favourite. They smell heavenly. Why don't you sit down?'

Hugo Bentley lowered himself nervously onto the chair beside Laura's bed. He'd been agonising all morning over whether to come and see her. If he was honest with himself – which he wasn't usually – Michael Portland's revelation that she was Hubert Hollingberry's daughter had cast her in a completely different light. Whereas before he had thought of her as a reasonably competent secretary, but nothing more, he had now succeeded in building her up into the woman of his dreams. She was attractive, personable – and, most important of all, seriously rich.

Chapter Ten

The alarm, set for the unearthly hour of five am, almost made Kate jump out of her skin when it went off.

'Oh my God, it's the middle of the night,' she cursed, then turned over grumpily and tried to go back to sleep. It seemed no time at all before Ben was bringing her a cup of Earl Grey tea and kissing her goodbye.

'What time is it now?' she mumbled.

'Five thirty,' said Ben, sitting on the side of the bed. 'If I don't get off soon I'll get stuck in the rush-hour traffic around Birmingham. It's always hell around Spaghetti Junction. All those sad commuters listening to Terry Wogan with their noses pressed against the windscreen. Give me the north any time.'

It was a week before Christmas, and after months of trying to persuade his parents to take a holiday from their Wiltshire farm Ben and his younger sisters had finally got them to agree – on the proviso that they ran the place in their absence.

'I wish you didn't have to go,' said Kate, sitting up and ruffling her hair. She took a slurp of tea. 'You won't forget me, will you?'

'Sweetheart, I'm only going away for a couple of weeks. You make it sound like a lifetime.'

'It's going to feel like a lifetime,' grumbled Kate.

'Especially with all the boring Christmas specials Thorndike has put me down for. Village pantos, nativity plays, Christmas fairs, the lot – it sounds absolutely gruesome. And anyway, how did you get out of doing all this crap for your paper?'

'Ah, that would be telling,' laughed Ben. He gave her a last, long, lingering kiss, and, finding it almost impossible to tear himself away from her, his hand touched her breast lingeringly. Kate couldn't bear it. She groaned and pulled him down beside her once more.

'This is the hardest thing but I must, must, go,' he murmured. 'I just wish you were coming too.' He disentangled himself from her embrace and walked backwards out of the door, blowing kisses till he was out of sight.

'I really love that man,' whispered Kate to herself as she snuggled down into the warm sheets again. Meeting Ben had changed everything immeasurably. They'd been together for exactly two weeks and two days now and she'd never been so happy in her life.

Covering an OAPs' Christmas coffee morning was the last thing Kate felt like first thing on a Monday, but Thorndike had put his foot down, so she didn't have any choice in the matter. After her bungling start on the *Bugle* she'd been trying to keep her nose to the grindstone. In fact she'd volunteered for so many of the tedious jobs over the past few weeks – and there were lots of them, golden weddings, funerals, parish council annual meetings, you name it – that she was rapidly becoming the most popular person in the office.

'I actually get some evenings at home with the

wife and kids because of you,' Rob Bennett had told her approvingly. At thirty-eight, he'd been on the *Bugle* far longer than anyone else and, even though he didn't have the title, he considered himself to be chief reporter in all but name. Predictably, Pam Newbold disputed this and the pair of them were forever at daggers drawn. In recent weeks Pam had even started styling herself 'chief correspondent', just to bug Rob. It had clearly worked because Rob was constantly bending Thorndike's ear, threatening to walk out if he wasn't given both the title he reckoned he was due *and* a pay rise.

'That man is such a well-balanced individual,' Pam Newbold had murmured one day as Rob could be heard pleading his cause to Thorndike yet again.

Kate had looked up, startled to hear Pam saying anything remotely complimentary about Rob.

'Why do you say that?' she'd asked.

'Can't you see, sweetie?' Pam had chortled. 'Look. He's got chips on both shoulders.'

Now Kate glanced around the shabby scout hut where the Bowland OAPs' Christmas bash was being held this year. Far from being the quiet, civilised affair she had been expecting, it was turning out to be a complete bunfight. When word filtered through that a *Bugle* reporter was there, the old people descended on Kate like flies, all clamouring for her to include their names in the paper. Even Prince Charles himself couldn't have been more sought after by this lot. Kate dutifully took down all their names, checking whether Isabel was spelt with an 'a' or an 'o' and whether Alastair had an 'a' or an 'i' in the middle. She'd taken to heart Thorndike's advice to her soon after she'd joined the *Bugle*. 'Whack in as many names as possible in every piece you write,' he'd instructed. 'Everyone you mention immediately rushes out and buys a copy so it ups our sales. And cor blimey, do we need our sales upping.'

It was eleven thirty am by the time Kate had eaten her fill of soggy homemade flapjacks and rock cakes and admired the snaps many of the pensioners proudly produced of their grandchildren. Feeling a bit guilty, she stammered a polite apology and crept away before anyone could grab her again and bore her rigid with tales of how youngsters today didn't know they were born.

When she finally got back to the office half an hour later, desperate to get her teeth into a decent job for a change, the place, usually a mêlée of argumentative banter, instantly went silent.

'Have I tucked my skirt into my knickers by mistake?' joked Kate merrily as she made her way to her seat. After the council clerk's scathing remarks about her outlandish dress sense, she'd been making an effort to dress ultra-conservatively of late, something which didn't come entirely naturally to her. Today she was wearing a knee-length navy skirt, matching jacket and plain white T-shirt. She couldn't quite bring herself to buy a pair of American Tan tights, however, and in her own inimitable style had set the whole outfit off with eye-catching scarlet stockings and a chunky silver bracelet.

There was still no reply. Assuming that she must have smeared flapjack crumbs all over her chin or something, Kate plonked herself down on her chair and consulted a tiny make-up mirror just to check. No. No problem there. What the hell was going on?

'Is anyone going to tell me what I've done? Why

have you all sent me to Coventry? It's just like being back at boarding school again.'

Kate glanced at Thorndike but he too averted his gaze and stared back at his computer screen, stony-faced. Kate was now becoming seriously rattled. Even at moments of supreme crisis, Thorndike could always be relied upon to make some deeply insulting remark. What on earth could she have done wrong now? It must be something unspeakable if Thorndike wouldn't tell her. He liked nothing better than giving someone a good bollocking.

She caught Rob Bennett's eye suddenly and, feeling sorry for her, he silently pushed a copy of that morning's *Daily News* across the desk. Kate glanced at it curiously. It was open at the City page, a part of the paper that she rarely even looked at.

'What am I supposed—' she began. And then she saw it.

'*Hollingberry snaps up ailing news group*' declared the headline in big bold letters above the narrow left-hand column. Kate's blood ran cold at the mere mention of her father but she gritted her teeth and forced herself to read the piece below.

'*Newspaper chief Hubert Hollingberry last night confounded the City by buying a small unprofitable newspaper group based in the north-west. Hollingberry, who is tipped for a knighthood in the New Year's Honours list, already owns several papers in the area and has now added Leadington Newspapers, a group of twelve paid-for weeklies, to his stable. It is not yet known how much he paid for Leadington or precisely why he wanted its papers in the first place. Perhaps the only clue is that his younger daughter Kate, 22, is a trainee reporter on the company's smallest newspaper, the Bowland Bugle.*'

Kate swallowed hard and continued reading. The piece went on to detail the way Clare had mysteriously walked out on her husband nearly twenty years before, leaving Hubert to bring up their two young daughters.

'Clare Hollingberry's whereabouts remain a mystery concluded the piece. 'Hubert Hollingberry has always refused to discuss his wife.'

Unused to reading about her mother in a cold, detached newspaper report, Kate gulped back a tear and put her head in her hands. When she looked up again thirty seconds later, though, she was clear-eyed. She was damned if she was going to show any of this lot how upset she really felt.

The newsroom was still hushed and it was a couple of minutes before Kate trusted herself sufficiently to utter a word without breaking down.

'Well, now you know,' she said. She made a concerted effort to sound as bright and breezy as she could. 'And I'm sure you can understand why I changed my name. Kate Hollingberry is such a mouthful. Anyone in their right minds would choose something else, wouldn't they?'

Her upfront approach must have worked because first Pam, then Danny and the others slowly crossed the office. Pam gave her a big hug, the rest of them simply touched her on the shoulder to show their support. Eventually the only person left sitting at his desk was Thorndike. As hard-faced as ever, he barely gave a clue as to what he thought about the extraordinary revelation in the *Daily News*.

'Well, I suppose being owned by Hollingberry could mean that there'll be more money in the kitty,' he said finally, his voice just as gruff as usual. 'But if you bloody think you're going to get special treatment just because your father's top brass you've got another think coming.'

In the days that followed Kate tried to get on with her work as efficiently as she could. Thankfully, there was little or no change in the way the rest of the office treated her. Thorndike was grumpier than ever and Rob Bennett still expected her to take on all his night jobs. The only person who tried to ingratiate herself was Pam Newbold, but the others poked such fun at her for constantly offering to buy Kate drinks and inviting her round for endless meals at her house that even she soon gave up.

In bed at night, however, there was one thing that bugged Kate more than anything else. There was no way her father would have told his own papers that she was working on the *Bowland Bugle*, let alone confided in a rival rag like the *Daily News*. Pathologically secret about family matters, he never mentioned Clare or his daughters to anyone outside his inner circle. No, there was only one other person in the entire world who knew that Kate Grant wasn't her real name and that was Ben. She'd trusted him with things that she'd never told another living soul – her true feelings about her mother, for instance, *and* her real identity – and what had he done? He had completely betrayed her.

Chapter Eleven

HH pushed his empty plate across the table, sat back in his chair contentedly and took a long sip of the excellent burgundy that he'd selected from the cellar for Christmas lunch. He was seated at the head of the dining table at home in Chelsea, with Dodo opposite him, Laura on his right and Kate on his left. Dodo had even persuaded HH to bring out the Hollingberry family silver in honour of the occasion. He usually kept it locked up in the safe, claiming that it was far too precious to actually use.

'It's wonderful to have both my girls here for Christmas,' HH beamed, putting one hand on Laura's and the other on Kate's. 'Isn't it, Dodo?'

His elder sister, wearing her best blue silk dress in honour of the occasion, gave a tentative smile. She was delighted to have both the girls home for Christmas, of course she was, but privately she felt worried about them both. She'd been anxious about Laura for some time, ever since she'd collapsed at the office. Admittedly she looked a different person now. She'd gained some much-needed colour in her cheeks and her skin glowed with vitality. Over lunch she'd been far merrier than she'd been in a long time. But Dodo wasn't a fool. Living with Laura was like

110

being on a roller coaster. Sometimes she was up, while at other times she seemed almost clinically depressed.

And then there was Kate. She was usually the happy-go-lucky one, the one who took life in her stride and didn't let things get her down. She'd sailed through school and university without any problems at all. So what on earth had happened to her now? Before she'd left for Lancashire, Kate had been so brimming with life, so excited about starting her new career. Dodo had spoken to her on the phone several times during her first weeks on the paper and she had been absolutely fine. Now Kate, who could almost always be relied upon to be the life and soul of the party, was quiet and listless. She hadn't arrived home till late on Christmas Eve so Dodo hadn't had much of a chance to talk to her yet. But it was pretty clear that something was wrong. While the rest of them, even, it had to be said, Laura, had tucked into the delicious turkey with alacrity, Kate had just picked at her vegetarian casserole and refused to try any Christmas pudding at all.

HH, true to form, didn't even seem to have noticed that there was anything amiss. As usual, he'd dominated the conversation all through lunch, regaling them with tales from the boardroom and the golf club – he'd recently taken up golf in a belated attempt to shed some of his excess weight – and never drawing breath for long enough to listen to anyone else. If she hadn't been so fond of her brother, Dodo would have felt like wringing his bloody neck. Talk about self-obsessed. He was so caught up in his own affairs that he never stopped for a minute to consider how Laura and Kate were getting on.

Now HH placed his linen napkin on the table and cleared his throat noisily.

'Ahem, there's something important that I must tell you. Something I've been meaning to tell you all for a while.'

The three women glanced at each other nervously. For a split second the same thought crossed all their minds. Was HH about to mention Clare's name? After all these years? Kate, the youngest and most streetwise, immediately feared the worst. Perhaps he was going to tell them that she was dead. A shiver of alarm ran down her spine.

'Is it something awful, Daddy?' she began. 'Because if it is, I don't think this is quite the right occasion.'

'Awful?' repeated HH. 'Of course it's nothing awful. It's so rare that we're all together these days, I wouldn't let something awful blight it, would I? I was just about to fill everyone's glass and tell you some news. Some very good news indeed.'

Kate watched her father as he slowly made his way round the table. He was getting old, she thought, and, despite her exasperation with him, she couldn't help feeling a little bit protective. His hair was starting to recede now, and, despite his concerted effort to get fit, his face still had an unhealthy bluish tinge to it.

Finally HH finished pouring the wine and sank back into his chair again.

'The news is that I'm getting a knighthood in the New Year's Honours List. It's all confidential till New Year's Eve, of course, but I wanted the three of you to know before anyone else.'

Dodo, Laura and Kate each breathed an inward sigh of relief, thankful that HH's announcement hadn't been the controversial one they'd all been dreading. There was a moment's hesitation before first Dodo and then Laura got up to congratulate him.

'I'm so proud of you, Hubert,' said Dodo tearfully. Never completely comfortable with physical shows of affection, she gave him a swift hug. 'I only wish Mother had been alive to see it.'

'Come on, you silly old thing,' said HH. He couldn't help feeling touched by Dodo's reaction. 'I always forget how sentimental you are. It was only a matter of time before it was my turn, you know. We just had to be patient.'

Laura dropped a light kiss on his cheek and whispered a quick 'well done, Daddy' in his ear. A strong whiff of alcohol enveloped her as she did so and she wondered, not for the first time, exactly how much HH was drinking these days.

Kate was the only one who remained in her seat. She hadn't uttered a word.

'Aren't you going to say anything, Kate?' asked HH. He felt mildly hurt that she seemed so uninterested in his announcement. Of the three of them, he'd thought she would have been the most impressed. She'd always taken more interest in the business than Laura.

'Yep, it's great,' said Kate half-heartedly. 'Whose palm did you have to grease?'

HH's eyes widened with astonishment. Was he hearing things? Had his younger daughter really meant to insult him? Or was she just cracking a joke that hadn't quite come off? But, reluctant to dampen the Christmas spirit which he'd thought was alive and kicking just a few seconds earlier, he decided to give her the benefit of the doubt.

'Very funny, Kate. What's the matter? Don't you approve of the honours list?'

'Well, it is a bit like getting a gold star from the teacher, isn't it?' murmured Kate. 'And you don't usually get a knighthood without giving something in return, do you?'

HH glowered at her. He'd never have dreamed that Kate could be so sour.

'Now look here, young lady,' he retorted, waggling a large forefinger at her menacingly. 'You don't speak to your father like—'

This was the moment when Dodo hurriedly intervened. Anxious to avoid a showdown between HH and Kate, especially today of all days, she noisily clashed a few silver spoons and forks together and started collecting the pudding plates.

'Come and help me make some coffee, Kate, will you?' she instructed, and judging by the look in Dodo's eyes Kate knew that she didn't have any choice in the matter.

When they got down to the kitchen the usually placid Dodo turned on her niece.

'I know how completely impossible your father can be,' she hissed in a loud whisper. 'I know that more than anyone. But if you're holding some grievance against him you'd better get it over with in private. And *not today*. Right, my girl?'

Kate held Dodo's stern gaze for as long as she could, then looked away. Dodo didn't get cross very often but when she did it wasn't a pleasant experience.

'Right,' she murmured.

Deep down, Kate was still simmering with resentment at HH's takeover of Leadington Newspapers behind her back. She knew for a fact that he wouldn't

114

have touched the group with a bargepole if she hadn't been working there. For God's sake, hadn't she had to put up with him bossing her about, vetting her friends and laying down the law for long enough already? And even now she was grown-up he was *still* doing it. Why couldn't he just let her get on with her own life? He was a complete control freak. All that he'd succeeded in doing was make her days at the *Bugle* a million times more difficult than they had been before.

Upstairs, Laura, desperate to avoid any more unpleasant confrontations, was doing her best to lighten the tension by making polite conversation with HH.

'Actually, Daddy, I've got some good news of my own,' she said shyly.

HH, still incensed by Kate's scathing remarks, was miles away.

'Oh yes,' he mumbled, clearly not in the least interested. 'What's that?'

Laura wondered whether this was the right moment to tell him. She'd planned to wait until this evening, but something inside told her that her revelation might defuse the icy atmosphere between Kate and their father.

'It's Hugo and me,' she said. 'We're getting married.'

For a few seconds Laura wondered whether her father had heard her. He stared at her with incomprehension.

'Who the hell's Hugo?' he said finally.

Now it was Laura's turn to look hurt. He *must* know who Hugo was. She'd introduced the two of them a few nights earlier when Hugo arrived to take her out to dinner. HH had seemed a little distracted at the time, it was true, but he *must* remember Hugo. How could he have forgotten him already?

In fact HH knew exactly who Hugo was. He was

Laura's boss, that tall gangly City chap who had called for her on the night he clinched the Leadington deal. HH had been so tickled pink that he'd snapped up the group Kate was working for, and for such a song, that he really hadn't taken much notice of the man. Hugo Bentley had seemed reasonably presentable, but apart from that HH hadn't given him a second thought.

'You could at least show a little bit of interest,' Laura said bitterly. 'Anyway, I thought you'd be pleased. You'll be getting me off your hands at last.'

Looking at the miserable expression on her face, HH was suddenly reminded of Clare. A shiver of pain surged across his chest and he visibly winced. He tried to keep Clare out of his mind as much as possible but there were moments, usually in the dead of night, when she haunted him with her pale blonde hair and luminous beauty. He'd never particularly noticed it before now but Laura had grown uncannily like her mother. Kate had a look of her too, of course, but she was a bit taller and altogether more robust.

'I'm sorry, darling,' he said, squeezing her hand tightly. 'Of course I'm pleased. It's wonderful news. It really is. I'm going to go and find a bottle of bubbly to celebrate.'

Left on her own, Laura felt curiously deflated. She'd been hugging her news to herself for the last couple of days, thinking that announcing her engagement at Christmas would be the icing on the cake. But now HH and Kate had had a row, Dodo was furious with Kate and HH couldn't even be bothered to ask a single question about Hugo. She was suddenly aware that if her mother had been here, it would have all been so very different.

*   *   *

Kate was pole-axed by Laura's announcement. More than anything, it brought home to her with a jolt how far apart they had grown. At one time Laura wouldn't have been able to change her knickers without Kate knowing about it. Now Laura was getting married and Kate hadn't even been aware that she was seeing this Hugo chap. She'd never even heard her sister mention his name before today.

'So what's he like?' Kate asked Laura later on. Christmas Day was almost over and HH and Dodo had both retired to bed. The sisters were lying side by side on the hearthrug in the drawing room, enjoying the dying embers of the fire.

Laura giggled.

'He's tall, dark and . . .'

'. . . handsome?' suggested Kate.

Laura considered the matter for a moment, then shook her head vehemently.

'No, not exactly handsome,' she reflected, trying hard to conjure up Hugo's face in her mind. 'More . . . pleasing.'

'Mmm . . . pleasing,' repeated Kate thoughtfully. Considering that Laura had just agreed to marry this man, she would have expected her to come up with a slightly more passionate adjective than 'pleasing'.

'Are you in love with him?' she asked bluntly.

Once again Laura giggled.

'What a question. Of course I am. We're getting married aren't we? Of course I'm in love with him.'

'Of course you are,' said Kate hurriedly. 'Now come on, tell me all the gory details. How long have you known him and how did he propose? Was it all terribly romantic? Did he go down on one knee?'

Laura's thoughts wandered back to Hugo's proposal the Sunday before. It had come like a bolt out of the blue, certainly, but she couldn't exactly claim that it had been heart-stoppingly romantic. He'd invited her out to lunch at the Caprice with one of his business associates, a man whom he'd clearly been desperate to impress. Hugo had made much of the fact that Laura's father was the legendary Hubert Hollingberry – which had made Laura feel slightly uncomfortable – and then proceeded to outline in minute detail some of the deals he himself had pulled off over the years. It was only after the man had finally left that Hugo had become softer and gentier again and suggested taking a walk together in Green Park. It had been a bitterly cold day and as Laura hurried along to try and keep up with Hugo's long stride she had dug her hands deep into her coat pockets to get warm. She had been beginning to wonder whether their relationship was going anywhere. In the office Hugo always made a point of being friendly but distant. No one would have suspected for a moment that they ever saw each other outside work. Perhaps the only reason he kept inviting her out to dinner was because he felt sorry for her, thought Laura sadly. And, if that was the case, it certainly didn't do much for her self-esteem.

'You look freezing,' Hugo had said suddenly. 'Here, have my gloves.'

He had stopped and taken Laura's hands in his, carefully transferring his black woollen gloves onto her freezing fingers. It struck Laura forcibly all of a sudden that this was the first time that Hugo had actually touched her. On every occasion they'd been out together over the past few weeks he had seemed to studiously avoid having any physical contact with her at all. Once or twice Laura had even caught herself thinking wistfully of Robert. So he obviously hadn't given a damn about her, just used her for sex really, but there had been a passion about him that seemed strangely lacking in Hugo.

As if he could read her thoughts, Hugo kept hold of Laura's hand and they continued walking.

'I think a lot of you, you know,' he said quietly.

Astonished, Laura glanced at him. Coming from the reserved Hugo, this was high praise indeed.

'I'm glad,' she smiled softly.

'Aren't you going to say anything else?' said Hugo. 'Like whether you have any feelings for me?'

'I thought it was just me,' said Laura, her words all coming out in a rush. 'I didn't think you felt the same way. You're always so aloof and serious in the office. I thought that maybe you only wanted to be kind to me after I was ill.'

Hugo cleared his throat noisily. He'd been thinking about this for several days now, and now seemed as good a time as any to say it.

'I wasn't just being kind at all,' he said, his voice gentle. 'I really do think an awful lot of you, Laura. An awful lot of you. I don't know how to say this really but I think that we would make a very good team. Would you do me the honour of marrying me?'

Chapter Twelve

Ben tapped the steering wheel impatiently as he waited for the traffic lights to change. Everything seemed so much slower up north, he thought, and couldn't help feeling irritated. The post always arrived later, most of the shops still closed for a half day in the middle of the week, even the seasons seemed to lag behind the rest of the country. When he'd left his parents' Wiltshire farm at six am this morning he'd spotted a few early snowdrops peeping out of the grass, and his heart had lifted at the prospect of spring. Up in Lancashire, however, there was no sign at all that milder weather might be imminent. It had snowed heavily in the night and now the main roads through Preston were a mass of brown slush. He reckoned that if it hadn't been for Kate he might have been tempted to stay down south and try his luck getting some shifts on the London papers. Doing casual shifts had long been the best way of getting onto papers like the *Daily News*. Young journalists fresh from the provinces tended to start by working night shifts, progressed to days if they did well, and if they really excelled they might stand a chance of eventually being offered a contract, or, better still, a staff job.

Kate. For the first fifty miles of his drive north Ben

had concentrated on listening to an ill-tempered phone-in about fox-hunting on the radio, and through sheer force of will had managed to avoid thinking about her. But then the news had come on and with it the announcement that Kate's father had received a knighthood in the New Year's Honours List. Hubert Hollingberry's mellifluous tones filled the car as he described his pride at receiving such an honour and all Ben's resolve instantly crumbled. For the rest of the journey he couldn't banish Kate from his mind. His thoughts flitted back and forth from Clare Hollingberry's mysterious disappearance to Kate's fierce determination to lay flowers in memory of Nicky Rawlinson, from her dazzling smile to the way she looked at him when they were making love. Ben was far from being a sentimental man – in the past he'd moved smoothly from one woman to another without the slightest qualm – but now he felt sick with apprehension at the prospect of seeing Kate again. He knew in his gut that something had gone horribly wrong in the two and a half weeks since he'd last seen her. When he'd left she'd been trying to drag him back into bed again. But since then . . . for God's sake, he hadn't even been able to reach her on the phone. He'd left countless messages in the office before Christmas and she'd never rung back. Not once. He'd rung her at home after Christmas and the bloody answerphone was always on, with her bloody father's voice droning on about how he could be contacted at bloody Hollingberry Holdings if the message was urgent.

Now it was New Year's Eve and Ben was still none the wiser as to what the hell was going on. If it had been any woman other than Kate who had been giving him the runaround like this he would have told them to bugger off and got on the phone like a shot to ask Rebecca Wilson out. But Kate was different. He wished he could tell *her* to bugger off but he simply couldn't. In the two weeks they'd been together she'd got to him like no one ever had before.

'. . . *Bowland businessman Mike Elton's face was all smiles this week as he laid the first stone of his new £500,000 leisure complex . . .*'

Kate tapped the words out aimlessly. She couldn't have cared less if Mike Elton was building a sodding space station in the Forest of Bowland.

This was going to be the most miserable New Year's Eve ever. There'd only been two of them in the office all day for a start, just her and Rob Bennett, and Rob had scuttled sheep-faced back to his wife and kids immediately after lunch, leaving her completely on her own. At this rate she'd be celebrating the New Year alone in her bedroom with a bottle of gin and Clive James on the telly.

Kate had been back at work since the day after Boxing Day, but, apart from a flying visit to put this week's paper to bed, Thorndike and Pam Newbold had barely been near the place. Bowland itself was completely dead too; the post-Christmas *Bugle* had been embarrassingly thin. Thorndike had been so desperate for a front-page lead that he'd been forced to splash with an account of the two babies born in Bowland's maternity unit on Christmas Day. He'd filled the rest of the paper with rubbish about school nativity plays, details of works' dos and countless pictures of the mayor switching on the Christmas lights.

'What the hell am I doing in this dump?' Kate asked herself for the hundredth time. Things hadn't been so bad when she'd been preoccupied with the Nicky Rawlinson story. And then, just as Thorndike decided to stop treating her like the office bimbo and start taking her seriously at last, her father had had to go and stick his oar in. But all that was nothing compared to the pain of what Ben had done. Why, when she was falling head over heels in love with the man, had he had to go and kick her in the teeth like that?

Kate felt sick at the very thought of Ben. Now she couldn't believe she'd ever confided in him in the way she had. She, of all people. In recent years she'd been reluctant to confide her true fears about her mother even to Laura or Dodo. So why the hell had she said anything to a man who was almost a complete stranger? She should have enjoyed the sex – a ripple of pleasure ran through her as she remembered their nights together – and then told him to sod off.

Kate put her head in her hands. Except Ben hadn't been a stranger, had he? He'd really seemed to care. Everything he'd done had seemed to show he cared. The way he'd asked her what gave her the most pleasure, the way he'd propped his head up with his hand and studied her face after they'd made love, the way he'd always slept with his body twined around hers, one hand cupped around her breast.

Suddenly it was all too much for Kate. She laid her head down on her desk and wept.

Kate had no idea how long she'd been slumped over her desk when the sound of footsteps clattering up the stairs and a door slamming behind her almost made her jump out of her skin.

'Bloody hell, Kate, what are you doing here all on your own?' yelled Danny. He strode jauntily across to her desk, plonked his ubiquitous camera bag on top of her keyboard and drew a chair up next to her. The force of the bag must have hit the delete button or something, because letter by letter the account of Mike Elton's colourful past that Kate had spent all afternoon writing disappeared from the screen before her very eyes. Kate didn't know whether to laugh or burst into tears again.

'Haven't you got a home to go to?' said Danny good-naturedly, completely oblivious to the havoc he'd just caused.

Kate stared at him blankly, unable to believe what Danny had done. It had taken her hours to come up with that intro, let alone the rest of it.

'Are you seeing the New Year in with Ben?'

At the sound of Ben's name, Kate flinched. But, mustering all her powers of self-control, she sank her fingernails into the palms of her hands and stared at Danny.

'No, I'm bloody not.'

'Aren't you two together any more then?' asked Danny in a flash of perceptiveness. Danny and the art of sensitivity didn't usually go hand in hand.

'No, we're not,' glared Kate. Something in her expression warned Danny that it would be extremely unwise to carry on with this line of questioning.

'That's great,' he shrugged, running his hands awkwardly across his bare head. The barber down the road had given him a fearsome number-one haircut the day before and his scalp looked even more exposed than usual. If he hadn't had such a merry disposition he would have appeared utterly terrifying. As it was, he looked about six years old.

'What do you mean by that?' demanded Kate. She

wasn't in the mood for smart-arse cracks from Danny Simpson.

'Er, nothing. I didn't mean anything at all.'

'Good,' grunted Kate. 'Anyway why did you come into the office in the first place? You can see how dead it is. If it's to tell me it's my turn to clean out the fridge at home I'll clock you one.'

'Needed some rolls of film,' said Danny, jumping off the desk and rummaging around in the photographic cupboard in the corner. 'I'm off up to the tops to do some snow scenes. It's all turned to slush in town but I know it'll be sensational up there. If I get some good snaps one of the nationals might be interested. Want to come?'

The prospect of escaping from the office and breathing some fresh air into her lungs instantly caught Kate's imagination. The chip-fryer must have been on overtime downstairs because the smell of greasy fish and chips had somehow managed to permeate the entire *Bugle* newsroom. Even her hair felt suffused with chip fat, she thought with disgust. Ben probably wouldn't touch her with a bargepole even if she gave him the chance. Which she wouldn't, of course.

An hour later Kate and Danny were throwing snow-balls at each other with all the exhilaration of school-children half their age. Kate had never seen such a breathtaking landscape in her entire life. Every inch of the fells was white, and even when she screwed up her eyes and looked hard she couldn't quite work out where the earth stopped and the sky began. For the first time in two weeks she'd almost managed to put Ben and his deception out of her mind.

'You're really a country girl at heart, aren't you?' remarked Danny as they paused for breath.

'What makes you say that?' said Kate. Born and bred within spitting distance of Sloane Square, in the past she had always assumed she was a townie through and through. Her school years had been spent in a leafy Home Counties suburb and then she'd lived in Manchester for three years while she was at university. This was the first time in her life that she'd had anything whatsoever to do with life in the country.

'You just seem to be in your element when you're up here. On top of the world somehow. Don't ask me why, you just are.'

And in a flash it suddenly dawned on Kate that Danny was absolutely right. Forget the trials and tribulations of the *Bugle* and the hurt that Ben had caused her, she *did* feel at home up here. Her skin glowed and she felt invigorated for the first time since before Christmas. It was as if she belonged here somehow. She was *meant* to be here.

By eleven pm Kate's earlier melancholy had completely lifted, and thanks to six consecutive glasses of wine at the White Elephant she felt much more in the party mood. Barney, the notoriously tight-fisted pub landlord, had gone mad for once and booked a local band to liven up the usually dead atmosphere in the place. The band were surprisingly good, though Danny and Kate burst into fits of giggles when the lights went up at the end of their first set to reveal four pimply-looking schoolboys. They had all the gear all right, the electric guitars and synthesisers, but the lyrics they'd been bellowing about sex and life and rock and roll were completely at odds with their skinny frames and young faces.

'They look as if they should all be in short trousers,' chuckled Danny.

'I wonder if their mums are happy about them being out this late?' giggled Kate, swallowing the dregs of her seventh glass of Barney's revolting Liebfraumilch in one gulp. Just then the band launched into their next set and, springing to her feet, she grabbed Danny's arm and pulled him drunkenly onto the dance floor.

Five minutes before midnight the pair of them were still dancing, their energies fuelled mostly by the vast quantities of alcohol that they had each drunk. The pub had filled up by now and with the onset of midnight the atmosphere was getting more and more raucous.

Barney switched on the huge TV set above the bar, usually reserved solely for his twin passions of racing and football, and almost immediately Big Ben began to chime. Overcome by Kate's nearness, Danny pulled her to him and planted a huge smacker of a kiss on her surprised lips. If she hadn't been so plastered, she thought later, she would have told him to where to go, but at the time she snuggled closer into his arms and snogged him back.

'Happy New Year,' Kate told him drunkenly as, unable to believe his luck, Danny pulled her back to the bench where they'd been sitting. Eager to carry on exploring her gorgeous body, he took another slurp of beer and turned to face Kate again. He could have wept with disappointment. Far from staring at him with desire in her eyes, Kate suddenly slumped in a heap against his chest, completely out for the count.

It was precisely at this moment that the doors of the pub flew open and a tall man with sandy-coloured hair and broad shoulders strode up to the bar.

Ben still couldn't quite believe he was doing this, but

his desire to be with Kate had become too overpowering to ignore any longer. He'd been battling against it all evening, sitting in his grotty flat in Preston with a crappy paperback and a bottle of warm beer. But finally he couldn't bear it. He'd grabbed his car keys and set off in search of her, going first to her house and then, when he found the place shrouded in darkness, to the only other place he could think of, the White Elephant.

Now, his eyes darted around the pub like those of a madman, desperate to seek her out. In the dim light he couldn't make out anyone he knew at first but finally his eyes alighted on Danny Simpson, sitting by the far wall. The snapper, wearing his usual battered leather jacket, seemed to be stroking the hair of some blonde lying across him. Sensing that someone was staring at them, the woman lifted her head from Danny's lap and gazed bleary-eyed at Ben. Her face looked glazed with drink and she gave no hint whatsoever that she'd ever in her life set eyes on him before.

Furious with himself for pursuing Kate like this – she obviously hadn't wasted much time picking up someone else while he'd been away – Ben roughly pushed through the crowd to where Danny was sitting.

'Wotcha mate,' said Danny amiably. He knew he recognised the face but in his drunken state he couldn't quite put a name to the man standing in front of him.

'Don't you bloody "wotcha" me,' shouted Ben, jabbing his finger furiously at Danny. 'What the hell do you think you're doing with my girlfriend?'

For a moment Danny looked bewildered, but then the fog cleared and he realised who Ben was.

'She says she's not.'

'Not what?' demanded Ben.

'Not your girlfriend, mate.'

For a split second a pained expression crossed Ben's face. Then he grabbed hold of the lapels of Danny's jacket and brought his face to within an inch of the photographer's.

'Then tell her something for me when she wakes up from her drunken stupor, will you?' he said.

Danny nodded nervously. He didn't fancy getting into a fight with this man.

'Just tell her . . .' Ben stopped for a moment, overcome with grief at Kate's betrayal. 'Just tell her that I didn't bloody want her any more anyway. Tell her that.'

Chapter Thirteen

Taking a deep breath to steady her nerves, Kate pushed open the heavy wooden door of the coroner's court. She'd never covered an inquest before and even though Thorndike had warned her that today's proceedings would be just a formality, an opening and adjournment, she couldn't help feeling apprehensive. Thea Beale, one of the other Leadington trainees, had admitted that she'd actually fainted at her first inquest.

'This poor man had died in a motorway pile-up,' she'd told Kate at the first training session of the new year. 'I was absolutely fine, scribbling away in my notebook, until the pathologist started to give evidence. I could never stand the sight of blood and when he started going into horrendous detail about the post-mortem and all the injuries this man suffered I just couldn't help it. God, it was so embarrassing. The coroner had to adjourn the whole thing while they got me out of the place. My news editor went blooming berserk.'

Kate hadn't paid much attention to Thea's words at the time. Her head had still been reeling at the news that Ben had abruptly upped and left his newspaper out of the blue.

It was Rebecca Wilson, of course, who'd put the word about, delighted that it had been her in whom Ben had confided and not Kate.

'I can't say that I was at all surprised,' she'd gloated. 'After all, Ben was so clearly destined for better things. He must have felt he was wasting his time up here. He's already done a few shifts on one of the nationals in London. He got a byline in the *Daily News* the other day. Did you see it?'

'But what made him disappear so suddenly?' Thea had quizzed Rebecca, puzzled by the suddenness of Ben's departure. 'Without saying goodbye to any of us.'

'He said goodbye to me,' said Rebecca smoothly, stealing a sly glance at Kate to gauge her reaction. But Kate had refused to give Rebecca the pleasure of seeing how upset she really was and swiftly changed the subject.

Now, as she tiptoed across to the press bench, she remembered Thea's experience in front of the coroner and crossed her fingers that she would be able to cope with hearing the terrible details of Nicky Rawlinson's injuries. Then she checked herself angrily. Of course she could cope. If Bert and Vi Rawlinson were strong enough to hear what some evil monster had done to their daughter, then *she* certainly could. She was only here to do her job, after all; Nicky had been Bert and Vi's *life*.

Bert Rawlinson grabbed Kate's hand briefly as she walked past his chair, and squeezed it reassuringly. Touched by his gesture, Kate felt a surge of affection for the man. Having exhausted all possible leads, the police had now begun to scale down the hunt for Nicky's murderer. The *Bugle* had carried precious little about the story in recent weeks either, but Bert hadn't given up hope that the killer would be caught one day. Kate still visited the Rawlinsons almost every week and always marvelled at their fortitude.

'Hello again,' whispered a male voice as she took her seat on the press bench. Startled, Kate glanced up. She recognised the man immediately. It was Charley Stone, the reporter from the *Evening Clarion* whom she'd spilled coffee down all those months ago. He looked as immaculate as ever. His dark hair had been cropped short and his clothes had London stamped all over them.

'What on earth are you doing here?' she enquired.

'Same as you, I should think,' said Charley smoothly.

'OK, point taken,' smiled Kate. 'But I didn't think you'd bother with this. It'll be months before the full inquest.'

Charley grinned, giving Kate the benefit of his ultra-white teeth. 'I couldn't resist seeing you again, could I?'

Kate elbowed him in the ribs, causing Charley to double up in apparent agony. For a moment she was fooled and felt mortified. She couldn't think what on earth had come over her. Then, much to her relief, Charley sat up straight again and winked at her good-naturedly.

Suddenly Kate caught the eye of the coroner. Dr William Macaulay-Scott, the highly regarded barrister who had been coroner for the Bowland area for more than twenty-five years, was glaring at her sternly. Kate flushed bright scarlet and after that, despite Charley Stone's best attempts to distract her, made a point of keeping her head down for the rest of the proceedings. She noted down every single one of the coroner's words, desperate to be seen to be conscientious. She couldn't risk another complaint about her attitude. Charley, however, didn't bother to take out his notebook at all. Much to her discomfort, he just sat watching her scribbling.

'The inquest into the death of Bowland schoolgirl Nicky Rawlinson was this week opened and adjourned until a date to be fixed,' recited Charley at the end of the proceedings. *'Nicky, 14, was found strangled on the moors above the town last year but her killer has still not been found . . .'*

'What on earth are you going on about?' asked Kate, stuffing her notebook in her bag and pulling on her short crimson mac.

'You've been noting everything down like a madwoman all afternoon,' he chuckled. 'God knows why. The story will only merit a couple of paragraphs at the most, even in your joke of a rag. I've just drafted your story for you. And now you've got that out of the way you can come and have a drink with me instead.'

Kate stared at him in astonishment. The man's arrogance was quite breathtaking.

'Who says I want to?' she said, gathering all her belongings together.

'I do,' beamed Charley.

He put his arm around Kate's shoulders and tried to propel her out of the door. For a few seconds she went along with it but then something in her rebelled. What the hell was she thinking of? She wasn't going to risk her job again by going for a drink in the middle of the afternoon with a man she barely knew when she should be back at the office filing her story. And anyway, she'd had it with men for the time being.

Ben had let her down and now bloody Danny kept following her round like a lovesick schoolboy, hoping for a repeat performance of New Year. She shivered involuntarily as she remembered the narrow escape she'd had with Danny. Smooching drunkenly on the dance floor had been one thing but as for anything else, ugh. Definitely not. Ben, Danny and now Charley. No. She didn't want anything to do with any of them.

Chapter Fourteen

'God, you look totally ridiculous,' Kate told herself as she gazed sulkily at her reflection in HH's floor-length mirror.

Kate had always prided herself on having a style all of her own, yet here she was wearing an unflattering calf-length dress that made her look like a lumpy thirteen-year-old. The frock had been fashioned out of heavy cream silk and finished off with a wide primrose sash that made her waist look absolutely enormous. Even an ultra-slender model like Jodie Kidd couldn't have carried it off. The crowning glory was a girlish headdress of tiny cream roses. Kate still couldn't quite believe that she'd let Laura talk her into wearing an outfit like this. And court shoes, for God's sake. She wouldn't normally be seen dead wearing a pair of court shoes.

Kate secretly reckoned that Dodo must have had a hand in all this. Even though the two sisters were now in their twenties, Dodo still had a tendency to treat them both as if they were about ten years old. She was always buying them outfits from places like Laura Ashley and Peter Jones and had long been looking forward to the day when one of them walked down the aisle in a cloud of white tulle.

Now, of course, that day had arrived, though Kate wasn't at all sure that Dodo completely approved of Hugo Bentley. And, for what it was worth, *she* certainly didn't.

Kate flopped onto the substantial leather armchair in HH's dressing room and reflected on her prospective brother-in-law. She'd only met him twice, it was true, but he'd struck her as cold-blooded and humourless.

Deep down, Kate was pretty sure that Laura had only agreed to marry Hugo in a misguided attempt to put the past behind her and start a new life of her own. Laura was simply crying out to be loved. Anyone could see that. Yet whether Hugo was capable of loving anyone apart from himself seemed doubtful. He reminded Kate of a leech, somehow. Once he'd drained Laura of all her energy and her money and her contacts, he'd drop her like a hot brick. Kate was certain of that. She'd tried to broach the subject with Laura on several occasions, tried to warn her sister that she was marrying Hugo Bentley for all the wrong reasons. But each time Laura had pursed her lips, told her how sweet Hugo was and huffily changed the subject. Whether it was through some misguided loyalty to Hugo or a desperation to believe that their marriage really *would* be like a fairy tale, she simply wouldn't hear a word against him. She went all starry-eyed each time he walked into the room, waited on him hand and foot and seemed pathetically grateful that he should want to have anything to do with her.

No, all Kate could do for now was let her sister get on with it and hope that Laura didn't get too damaged in the process.

HH was in his element. Resplendent in his morning

suit – if he was honest even he had to admit that it fitted just a fraction more snugly than it had a few months before – he was regaling his 250 guests with tales of the bride's childhood.

'I am indeed blessed to have two such wonderful daughters,' he said, beaming around the massive strawberry-pink marquee that had been erected in his garden, which was surprisingly large for Chelsea. 'And they are, of course, two such distinct characters, Kate so lively and exuberant, Laura so conscientious and . . .'

'. . . dull,' thought Laura forlornly. She felt a lump in her throat. Even today of all days, when she should be the undisputed star of the show, the beautiful bride, she was a dismal failure. She'd clammed up several times when HH's acquaintances and business associates – who accounted for most of the guest list – attempted to congratulate her. And she knew that the huge meringue of a wedding dress she'd gone for had turned out to be a disastrous choice for her tiny frame. Kate had tried to steer her away from all the froth and frills and leg-of-mutton sleeves and towards a long elegant column of a dress that she insisted would flatter her sister's delicate beauty. But Laura had refused to have any of it; it was her wedding and for once in her life she was going to do things her way.

Now her pale face flushed at the thought of her obstinacy. She and Kate hardly ever rowed and she absolutely hated it when they did.

Laura looked up suddenly and caught Kate's eye. With a grin Kate nodded towards HH, who was still burbling on, more about himself than about Laura, and then mimed a theatrical yawn at her sister. Laura would have never dared to do such a thing in a million years, but she couldn't help smiling back all the same.

Just then she felt a sharp kick on her ankle underneath the table.

'Ssssh,' hissed her new husband under his breath. 'You're making a spectacle of yourself.'

Stung by the reproving look in his eyes, Laura stared down into her lap. Hugo was quite right of course, she thought, as she fiddled nervously with her wedding ring. It had been altered especially in the weeks before the ceremony to fit her slender fourth finger but now it seemed far too big again. She slid the gold band absent-mindedly up and down her finger. She would have loved Hugo to have worn a wedding ring too but he had laughed out loud at the very idea, telling her that only wimps wore rings. And because he was almost a decade older than her and so much cleverer, she had meekly acquiesced.

HH hadn't built Hollingberry Holdings into such a successful empire by being profligate with his money, but he'd certainly pushed the boat out for Laura's wedding. After the ceremony at St Olave's, a pretty flower-filled church in an elegant Chelsea square, the guests had strolled round the corner for an exquisite lunch prepared by one of London's smartest party organisers. It was a bright but chilly March day and the guests were greeted at the gate by a band of devastatingly handsome waiters who wore long white aprons and proffered glasses of Bollinger as if it were going out of fashion. Laura's teeth were chattering so much with nerves by this time that she could hardly get her lips to her glass to drink, but Hugo downed his first glass in one swig and immediately leaned forward for another.

Standing in the receiving line, Hugo barely uttered a word to Laura. All his charm, Kate observed wryly, seemed to be reserved for the most influential of HH's acquaintances – some middle-ranking politicians, the deputy chairman of the Bank of England, a few stock-brokers from the most prestigious firms.

'It's his wedding day, the happiest day of his life, and what's bloody Hugo Bentley doing?' Kate muttered under her breath. 'He's bloody networking.' She could only hope that Laura hadn't noticed what he was up to.

Laura was indeed oblivious to the rapt attention Hugo was showing to some wedding guests and the cavalier fashion in which he was treating others. Sand-wiched between the tall figures of her husband and her father, it was all she could do to remain upright. And uppermost in her mind were her shameful actions of the night before.

In the three months since Hugo had asked her to marry him, Laura had been certain that she'd got her eating habits under control at long last. With her confidence boosted by Hugo's attentions and all the excitement of planning the wedding, she had seemed to blossom. She'd begun to eat normally for the first time in ages, her health had improved and she'd even managed to patch things up with Alexa, laughing off her 'flirtation' with Robert as 'a moment of madness'. Alexa's own relationship with him had subsequently fallen apart – due largely to her obsession with a statuesque black model called Lenny who'd posed for her at one of her life drawing classes – so she was more than happy to kiss and make up with Laura.

She'd drawn the line, however, at being one of Laura's bridesmaids.

'Darling, I'd do anything in the world for you, you know that, but I'm twice your size. I'd look totally ridiculous in a bridesmaid's outfit,' she'd guffawed. 'Let me and Lenny come as special guests.'

'And what about Robert? Should I invite him?' Laura had forced herself to utter his name for the first time in months. She'd almost succeeded in putting him out of her mind once she and Hugo were engaged, but the way he'd treated her still hurt.

'Oh, fuck Robert,' said Alexa. 'He's ancient history.'

For one awful moment, as the jazz band swung into action and the bride and groom processed into the centre of the flower-filled marquee to take their places for lunch, Laura thought she was going to be sick. Hugo, at her side, strode ahead forcefully, completely unaware of his wife's growing alarm. Laura clutched onto his arm and tried her utmost to put the overpowering smell of the dressed crab out of her mind.

'Are you all right?' whispered Kate as Laura took her place at the table. Her elder sister had suddenly turned deathly pale – her face almost matched her dress – and she looked as though she was about to faint.

'I'm fine,' said Laura in a clipped sort of voice, clinging onto the back of the gilded chair for support. Hugo, busy talking to Gordon Osprey, didn't seem to have noticed that anything was amiss.

And miraculously, when Laura sat down, she *did* feel fine. She forced herself to put the excesses of the night before – a family-sized tin of baked beans, a whole baguette, a packet of Mars bars and a carton of chocolate ice cream – out of her head, and began to pick tentatively at the first course. Next to her, Hugo was tucking in heartily; from the moment they'd exchanged wedding vows in church to now, he hadn't shown any sign of nerves at all.

When HH finally got to the end of his speech, it was Hugo's turn to rise to his feet and address the guests. He thanked HH for his lavish hospitality and praised Kate for taking care of Laura.

'That's something that will stick in his throat,' thought Kate wryly. She and Hugo were hardly soul-mates. As far as she was concerned, he was a ruthless fortune-hunter who wasn't in the least bit interested in her sister, he thought she was silly and feckless, an unfortunate influence on Laura.

As it turned out, Hugo kept his words about Kate to an absolute minimum. He muttered a few half-hearted phrases about what a support she'd been to Laura and how pretty she looked – 'yuck,' thought Kate, making a face – but the main thrust of his speech seemed to be about how similar marriage was to business.

'They both require a lot of thought, compromise and due diligence,' he informed the wedding guests. 'Neither of them are easy but when successfully executed they both bring unmatched rewards.'

'I bet they do,' murmured Kate under her breath, noting caustically that at no point in his speech had Hugo mentioned anything about love or passion or what a gem he'd found in Laura.

The rest of the afternoon passed by in a whirl. Once Laura had managed to eat something *and* keep it down, a touch of colour returned to her cheeks and she started to enjoy herself. After she and Hugo had cut the cake, an elaborate tower of white icing arranged in huge circular tiers, and posed for more photographs, they made their way, hand in hand, around the twenty or so tables. Laura surprised herself by how easily she managed to make polite conversation, even with the substantial number of guests on whom she had never clapped eyes before. But it was still a relief when they reached the table where Alexa and Lenny were sitting.

'Darling, you look absolutely sensational,' cried Alexa. She leapt to her feet and took Laura's small hand in her own much larger one.

'So do you,' giggled Laura, gazing with admiration at Alexa's magenta velvet frock coat and matching drainpipe trousers. The vivid colour clashed alarmingly with Alexa's bright red hair but her friend managed to carry it off with her usual panache. Next to her, Lenny looked positively ordinary in his grey morning suit.

'Has Hugo made you very happy?' she whispered to Laura while Hugo's back was turned.

Startled by the bluntness of Alexa's question, for a moment Laura couldn't think what to say.

'D . . . d . . . don't be silly,' she stammered eventually. 'Of course he has. I've never been so happy in my whole life. I feel like a real person at last.'

By the time they left for their honeymoon Laura had begun to wilt again. She wasn't a gregarious person by nature and the effort of being on show and talking to so many people had completely exhausted her. Hugo had booked them a room at the Ritz for the first night of their honeymoon and they were due to fly out to Paris the following day. When they'd first discussed it, Laura had naïvely assumed that they'd be in France for two weeks, but Hugo had insisted that he couldn't possibly be away from the office for more than a week.

'I'm sorry, Laura, I'd love it to have been longer,' he'd said, 'but I've just got too much on at the moment. We'll make up for it later in the year, I promise.'

Now they were finally on their own, Hugo put his arms around Laura and kissed her softly on the forehead. Laura snuggled happily into his embrace and, anticipating a more intimate kiss at long last, lifted her face up towards his. This was what being a couple was all about. Just her and Hugo, and what was it Mrs Patrick Campbell had said so memorably about marriage? 'The deep, deep peace of the double bed after the hurly-burly of the chaise longue.'

Not that there had been much hurly-burly on the chaise longue with Hugo, thought Laura ruefully. He had kept physical contact to the absolute minimum, kissing her chastely on the cheek when they met and just very occasionally putting his arm around her to guide her along the street. They'd never really talked about it, but Laura had simply assumed that he was of the old school and believed that sex should be confined to marriage. In retrospect, she reckoned she'd been wise not to tell him about Robert.

Just as Laura's lips were within a whisker of touching his own, Hugo abruptly drew back and looked away.

'Sweetheart, you must be absolutely whacked,' he said awkwardly. 'We've got the rest of our lives for this sort of thing. I think we should both have an early night tonight. Don't you?'

Chapter Fifteen

Charley Stone put his feet up on his desk and took a sip of strong black coffee. He studied the wedding picture on the front of the first edition of the *Clarion* with interest. Bloody Drew Thompson, he thought sneeringly. He was the most clueless editor he'd ever worked for. Anyone with half a brain could have told him that putting the boss's daughter's wedding on page one would endear you to nobody. And it wasn't as if the girl was a looker either, she was far too scrawny.

'*HH's daughter weds City high-flyer,*' ran the caption underneath. '*Clarion chairman Hubert Hollingberry beamed with pride yesterday as his elder daughter Laura married top merchant banker Hugo Bentley. His younger daughter Kate, who has followed her father into the newspaper business, acted as bridesmaid . . .*'

'Bloody hell,' muttered Charley. 'Who wrote this shit? They should be shot.'

He forced himself to plough through the tedious story about corruption in the civil service that Drew Thompson had inexplicably decided to splash on. But for some reason his eyes kept straying back to that wedding picture and in particular to HH's younger daughter. She was small and pretty and blonde and, although everyone else in the picture was smiling broadly at the camera, she had a scowl of defiance on her face. Probably because her dress was so unspeakably awful, grinned Charley. There was something so familiar about her . . .

All of a sudden the truth hit him like a tidal wave and he banged his head with his fist in irritation. He must be going soft in his old age. Of course he bloody recognised her . . . Why the bloody hell hadn't he clicked straight away? It was that reporter, what was her name? Kate Grant, the girl at the inquest. He'd sensed that there was something different about her the very first time he met her. She'd seemed far too cosmopolitan for a place like Bowland.

Charley threw down the paper and began hammering away at his keyboard like a man possessed. Within seconds a list of Hollingberry cuttings appeared as if by magic on his computer screen. He scrolled through them impatiently. There was loads of boring City-page stuff about HH's newspaper empire, a lot of it dating back to the Sixties, when HH had taken over the helm from his late father. But for some reason there were surprisingly few cuttings about HH's family background. The most recent profiles, published when HH was awarded his knighthood, detailed his business achievements, his grand house in Chelsea, his obvious pride in his two daughters and his passion for good food and golf. Only one piece mentioned anything at all about HH's wife, and that was a *Daily News* story from the mid-Seventies. Charley sped through the short article with growing interest. When he'd finished it, he pressed the print button.

'Here Jonty, do you know anything about this story?'

Charley passed the printout across to Jonty Miller, the *Clarion*'s longest-serving news reporter, who occupied the desk opposite him. At sixty-one, he was counting the days till his retirement, all too aware that reporting had become a young person's game. He'd made it quite clear long ago that there was no way he was going to be hauled out of bed at three in the morning and sent to doorstep some poxy South London drug-dealer, or ordered out of the office to infiltrate a dodgy security outfit. Despite his bolshiness, Jonty had managed to stay at the *Clarion* for thirty years, a feat that was almost unequalled by anyone else. A handful of his contemporaries had criss-crossed between different newspapers, steadily climbing the executive ladder, but a whole lot more had suffered the ignominy of redundancy. Now Jonty was seen as a safe pair of hands, able to churn out anything from a tirade about the minuscule length of Caprice's skirt to an in-depth analysis of the state of the armed services. And what was more, he did it all on time and without the kind of histrionics to which some of the more junior members of the *Clarion*'s staff were prone.

Jonty skimmed through the article with a bored look on his face. As a rule, he took no interest whatsoever in office politics or what the rest of the reporters were up to. He couldn't care less, just so long as he got out for his usual pint at lunchtime and was on the 6.42 train back to St Albans at night.

'*The mystery disappearance of HH's wife,*' proclaimed the strapline. '*The wife of well-known newspaper proprietor Hubert Hollingberry walked out on her husband and two young daughters a week ago and hasn't been seen since. Clare Hollingberry, 28, married her husband, who is ten years older than her, eight years ago and there had been no*

146

hint before that the couple, who live in a stylish Chelsea townhouse, were unhappy together.

'Hollingberry, 38, refused to discuss the matter last night. A statement released by his solicitor, Mr Oliver Brown, said: "This is a private family matter but I can confirm that Mr and Mrs Hollingberry have agreed to part. Mr Hollingberry will have custody of their two daughters."'

'So?' Jonty said finally.

'So do you know anything about what happened to HH's wife, of course?' said Charley impatiently. 'I'd always assumed he was a widower.'

'Never assume anything in this business, dear boy,' said Jonty. 'You should know that. But now you mention it, I do remember something about HH's wife walking out on him. It was all hushed up though. HH wouldn't have a word of it printed in any of his own papers so we never covered it at all. I haven't a clue what happened to Clare Hollingberry. She probably just pushed off. I'm sure it wasn't anything sinister.'

'Did you ever get to meet her?'

'Mmmm,' said Jonty thoughtfully. 'She came into the office a few times. She was a pretty little thing. Much younger than HH of course, and quite clearly out of her depth.'

'And that's all you know?'

''Fraid so, dear boy. Why? Is it important?'

Charley considered the matter for a moment. Was it important? It was a cracking story, of course it was, but even he was shrewd enough to realise that it wasn't one for him. It had all happened nearly twenty years ago, for a start. And if he was in the least bit interested in hanging onto his job on the *Clarion* – or in getting to know HH's daughter better – it would definitely not be advisable to go delving into the murky recesses of the boss's past.

'No, not really. I was just curious, that's all.'

But somehow he couldn't bring himself to forget the matter altogether. Half an hour later he lifted his phone and punched out the number of his pal on the *Daily Recorder* diary.

'Jake?' he whispered into the mouthpiece. 'I've got a story for you. Interested?'

Tipping a rival newspaper off about a potential story was a cardinal sin in newspapers but that didn't deter Charley in the least. He'd pocketed an easy £100 on a number of occasions and he hadn't the slightest qualm about doing it again.

He quickly outlined the details of Kate's humble existence on the *Bowland Bugle*, adding a little colour to spice it up.

'Sorry mate,' said Jake Horner matter-of-factly. 'It's an old story. The *News* mentioned something about HH's daughter being a trainee hack a couple of months back.'

He mulled the matter over in his head for a few seconds.

'Oh, what the hell. I'll do a short on it. She wears crazy clothes, you say? And she's close to the father of that murdered girl? I like the sound of that. Give me a bit more background and I'll probably use a couple of paragraphs tomorrow.'

Kate thought she was going to throw up. She stared miserably at the newspaper Pam Newbold had just slid across her desk. After a while the words on the page all merged into one meaningless mass. She couldn't believe that Ben was doing this to her. Why

148

couldn't he just leave her alone? Not content with tormenting her the first time, now he'd gone and done it again.

She skimmed through the spiteful diary item once more.

'*The daughter of wealthy newspaper tycoon Hubert Hollingberry is slumming it on one of his least successful rags. Unconventional Kate Hollingberry has become a trainee reporter on the risible* Bowland Bugle – *the paper sells a distinctly unimpressive 10,000 copies a week and according to local sources wouldn't spot a decent story if it landed straight in its lap. She has also become close to the father of local child-murder victim Nicky Rawlinson. She visits Bert Rawlinson several times a week to comfort him.*

'*Kate, whose glamorous mother Clare mysteriously walked out on the family twenty years ago, uses her mother's maiden name of Grant. She is well known for her outlandish clothes, which have lately brought her into conflict with the local council as well as with her boss. Why Kate, 22, bothers to work at all, and especially on a paper like the* Bugle, *is puzzling. HH would no doubt be more than happy to give her a job in London and one day she will inherit a large chunk of his multi-million-pound fortune.*'

'Come on, Kate, keep your chin up,' said Thorndike, handing her a chipped mug with a picture of the Queen's Jubilee on it. Kate glanced up at him quickly, unable to believe what she had just heard. Not only had Thorndike actually said something kind, but he'd also made her a coffee. And he never made coffee. Everyone in the office always joked that he didn't know how to.

'But, but, aren't you livid about all this?'

'Why should I be?' said Thorndike, shrugging his shoulders.

Kate stared at him again.

'Well, for a start, they say the *Bugle* is "risible" and for another they've got our circulation figures completely wrong. It's so unprofessional.'

'So?' said Thorndike. 'It's no skin off my nose. If you're going to get your knickers in a twist every time someone is a wee bit critical of you then you're in the wrong job, love. You should have heard what people have said about me in the past.'

'I suppose so,' said Kate. She rubbed her nose ruefully. 'Anyway, why are you in such a good mood? Have your lottery numbers come up?'

Thorndike stared back at her in amusement. No one else in the office would ever dare say anything like that. All of them, well maybe not the brassy Pam Newbold, were scared shitless of him. But Kate was made of sterner stuff. He could see that. There was no doubt that Pam could have made it to Fleet Street if she hadn't been quite so idle and had been a little less inclined to spend all her time fluttering her eyelashes at coppers. Rob Bennett wouldn't stand a cat in hell's chance – he was a pipe-and-slippers man through and through. But Kate was a different kettle of fish. She was definitely worth keeping an eye on.

'Mmmm, something like that,' muttered Thorndike. Then, raising his voice to his usual bellow, he yelled, 'I know you lazy good-for nothings will do anything for a free drink. Get down to the Elephant at one thirty pm and I'll buy you all a beer.'

'Tell me I'm hearing things,' whispered Pam to Kate. 'Thorndike must be starting the male menopause or something. Either that or he's gone off his rocker.'

Wandering down to the Elephant at lunchtime with

the rest of the *Bugle* staff, Kate felt a sudden surge of affection for them all. They were a motley crew, that was for sure, but, after six months on the paper, she was quite fond of them. So Thorndike could be a bully at times and George Gibbs, the chief sub, was a bit of an old bore the way he went on and on about his passion for DIY, but they were all right. After the revelations about her father and his inexplicable takeover of Leadington, they could quite easily have toadied around her or, even worse, frozen her out altogether. But they hadn't. And for that she was supremely grateful.

When all six of them had a glass in their hand – Kate had finally given up on Barney's vile white wine and was now drinking lager – Thorndike got to his feet and cleared his throat noisily.

'Christ,' groaned Pam. 'Something must be up. Thorndike's going to make a speech.'

'Right,' said Thorndike. 'I won't beat about the bush. I'm off to pastures new. I've been offered a job on the *Daily Chronicle* and I'm moving down south. Tomorrow.'

'What's the job?' asked Rob Bennett quickly, wondering whether he might be in line for Thorndike's old one. He'd kick up a real stink if they tried to give it to Pam and not him.

'Deputy news editor.'

'What's the money?' yelled Pam and everyone laughed.

'Better than here,' shouted back Thorndike. 'But that wouldn't be difficult, would it?'

'Can you get me a job too?' said Danny in his most grovelling voice.

'No bloody chance,' snorted Thorndike, draining the

last of his pint. 'Now if you'll excuse me, I've got to get going.'

And with that he was up and gone.

The woman stared longingly at the photograph in the newspaper. Her daughters were so beautiful, more beautiful than she'd ever dreamed. She drew her fingers to her lips and then carefully touched the face of each in turn. She ached to fold them into her arms and tell them how much they were loved. How much they had always been loved. And how sorry she was. After all that had happened, neither of them had found happiness. She could see it in their faces. And with a flash of insight she knew that there was one person to blame for that. One person and one alone.

Chapter Sixteen

The atmosphere at the *Bugle* was subdued the following morning. Not only were most of them suffering monumental hangovers from Thorndike's piss-up the day before, but they were all deeply apprehensive about his successor. Thorndike had been an out-and-out bastard to work for, they were absolutely agreed on that, but at least he'd been a known quantity. And he'd known what he was doing. He'd never failed to get the paper to bed on time and in reasonable shape. Now the whole place felt like a ship without its captain.

Kate tried to concentrate on the parish-council report she was writing. Getting a line out of the tedious annual meeting Thorndike had ordered her to show up to a couple of nights earlier was proving almost impossible. The most contentious discussion of the evening had focused on the type of flowers to be planted in the hanging baskets outside the village hall. Somehow Kate didn't think she'd be getting the splash with this one.

The rest of the office had virtually given up on work altogether. Rob Bennett was writing a letter of application for Thorndike's old job although he couldn't work out who on earth to send it to. Pam

Newbold was busy filing her nails and looking up her stars in the *Daily News*. *'An exciting new opportunity is on the horizon,'* she read. *'Make sure that you seize it with both hands.'* George Gibbs reckoned that as the member of staff who'd been on the paper the longest, he was the man for the job. And if he got it he'd certainly shake things up. He'd bring in a DIY page and a four-day week for a start. Fridays were always an absolute wash-out on the *Bugle* – he could use the time far more constructively on his home improvement projects.

Kate deleted her sixth intro from the screen with a sigh of frustration and started on a seventh version. She wondered how Laura was enjoying her honeymoon. Paris in springtime sounded wonderfully romantic, but then again, Paris in springtime with Hugo probably wasn't such a great proposition. She hoped that Hugo was at least making an effort to behave like a besotted husband, even if he wasn't one.

The *Bugle* staff were all on the verge of calling it a day and adjourning to the Elephant for a hair-of-the-dog session when the office door creaked open and Laurie Laing shuffled in, coughing and wheezing more than ever. Everyone gaped at his appearance. He'd never been Arnold Schwarzenegger, it was true, but he had aged alarmingly over the past few months. His face, which now had a yellowish tinge to it, was even more lined and he was walking, if you could call it walking, with a stick. Typically, though, and despite all the dire warnings from his exasperated doctor, he still had a fag in his hand.

George was the first person to come to his senses.

'Laurie, old chap,' he cried, jumping to his feet and rushing to get the old man a wooden chair to sit on. 'It's wonderful to see you looking so well.'

Laurie looked at George with a flicker of contempt in his eyes.

'Yes, isn't it?' he said, lowering himself carefully onto the chair. 'Especially when you were all assuming you'd seen the last of me, too. Now, I should imagine that you're all wondering why I'm here. Eh?'

No one spoke. He was perfectly right, however; they were all dying to know. Surely he couldn't possibly be thinking of coming back to work again? Not in his condition. The stairs would kill him, even if the smoking didn't.

'I'm sure that you were all as shocked as I was by Thorndike's defection to London,' he croaked. 'After all that the *Bugle* has done for him I would have thought that he could at least have worked out his notice. But staff seem to possess no sense of loyalty these—'

Suddenly Laurie Laing was overcome by another terrible coughing fit. George and Rob looked at each other in consternation, each wondering whether they should slap him on the back or something. But within a couple of minutes Laurie had got over it and carried on with what he'd been saying.

'I would love to return to work as soon as possible but as you know, I am on long-term sick leave.' He began coughing again. 'We intend, of course, to advertise Thorndike's position and I'm sure it will be highly sought after. But in the meantime we shall have to appoint an acting news editor to fill the breach.'

Rob instantly stood to attention like an army major inspecting the troops. It was quite obvious that he was the only choice for the job.

'After giving the matter a lot of thought I have finally reached my decision,' continued Laurie. 'I didn't want to foist someone completely unknown on you . . .'

Pam picked up her emery board again and began filing her nails expectantly, utterly confident that she was about to be made the new acting news editor.

'. . . So I'm sure you'll all be absolutely delighted when I bring him in.'

Pam's head shot up. '*Him*'? She must be mistaken. Surely Laurie Laing hadn't just said '*him*'?

Slowly the door creaked open once more and a burly young man with thinning hair and a bright red face ambled clumsily over the threshold. The entire staff gasped with astonishment. It was Scar.

In the few months since he'd been booted out of the *Bugle*, Scar hadn't changed very much. He'd lost a little bit more hair and, thanks to the extra time he'd had to spend working out at the gym, had developed a few more muscles. But apart from that he was pretty much the same old Scar. Awkward, unconfident and still hopelessly enamoured of Pam Newbold.

As he stood in the doorway, watching his uncle's every move and trying desperately hard to avoid Pam's eye, Kate couldn't help feeling sorry for him. It wasn't Scar's fault that he was such a dumbwit, she thought. But what the hell did Laurie Laing think he was playing at, foisting his blithering idiot of a nephew on them? He couldn't organise a piss-up in a brewery, let alone produce a half-decent newspaper. And the *Bugle* went to press tomorrow.

'Now eh oop, Steven lad,' said Laurie, turning to Scar. 'If you'd like to say a few words to the staff before I go.'

Scar flushed again. He wished he was capable of telling his uncle where to stick his bloody job. If he hadn't been so desperate for work and so anxious to keep up the payments on his beloved Ford Escort he would have done exactly that. He might not be Brain of Britain but it was pretty clear to him why Laurie had come up with this latest wheeze. His uncle was fed up to the back teeth of being treated like shit by Thorndike and had been determined to appoint someone whom he could order about. And as far as he was concerned Scar was the ideal candidate.

'Yep,' mumbled Scar. 'Just that I'm delighted to be back among old pals. And I'm certain that we're going to make a real go of this paper—'

Scar stopped in his tracks. Pam Newbold had glanced up from her nail-filing and was looking him straight in the eye. Mesmerised by her nearness, his mind went completely blank and he couldn't think of another word to say.

'So I'll see you all bright and early tomorrow,' he uttered finally. And then, suddenly unearthing one of Thorndike's favourite lines from the recesses of his brain, he added, 'And make sure that one of you has a splash tucked away in your bottom drawer.'

When the sound of Laurie Laing's shuffling and Scar's heavy footsteps had died away, the *Bugle* staff all burst out laughing. Despite their individual outrage, even Rob, Pam and George joined in, unable to believe that even Laurie Laing could be quite this stupid.

'There's only one thing for it,' guffawed George. 'Let's all go and drown our sorrows. You coming, Kate?'

Kate grinned at her colleagues. She could read them like a book. No matter how depressed they were, the prospect of a few pints at the Elephant always did the trick.

'I'll catch you up,' she said. 'I'll go crazy if I don't

get these parish-council reports done. Get me a lager in, will you?'

'You'll probably get the splash with the hanging baskets story,' joked George. 'Scar couldn't spot a real story if it hit him smack in the chops.'

Once they'd all clattered out, Kate tried to concentrate on her work. Now that the office was quiet and the tension about who would be the new boss had been defused by Laurie Laing's lunatic announcement, she polished off five stories in no time. She was just switching off her computer and looking for her coat, intending to join the others, when the door opened and Scar crept back in again. He stared at the empty room with a look of astonishment, then consulted his watch just to make sure he wasn't going mad.

'It's only four pm,' he said. 'Where is everyone?'

'Pub,' said Kate bluntly. They'd all be half-cut by now so it was no use trying to cover up for them. Even Scar wasn't gullible enough to believe that they'd gone out mob-handed on the story of the decade. Not quite, anyway.

'Bloody hell,' grunted Scar. 'And just when I've brought in the splash too. Oh well. I know you're not very experienced but we haven't got time to waste. *You'll* have to take it on board.'

Kate stared at Scar. Blooming cheek. And he'd only been gone an hour or so. What pathetic pretence of a story could he have drummed up in that short space of time?

'What is it?' she asked wearily.

Ten minutes later she was haring out of the chippie as fast as her legs would carry her. Scar had offered to come with her but she'd firmly dissuaded him, mindful of the last time they'd worked together. He would be nothing but a liability on a matter as sensitive as this.

Kate had listened with growing alarm to Scar's garbled account of his conversation with a chap down at the gym. Overcome with fright at the prospect of having to sort out his tricky ex-colleagues *and* produce a decent-looking paper by six pm the next day, Scar had popped into the health club to do a quick workout while he still had the chance. He'd been pedalling away on one of the machines when he'd got chatting to a bloke called Tony who was going hammer and tongs next to him. He'd seen him several times before but had never realised he was a copper.

'You look as if you're trying to give yourself a heart attack,' Scar had remarked idly.

'Bad day at work,' grunted Tony.

'What happened?'

'I thought I'd seen everything,' said Tony. A wintry smile appeared on his sweaty face. 'But this one beats the lot.'

'What do you mean?'

'We've nailed Nicky Rawlinson's killer.' Tony thought for a moment, then revised his words. 'Well, we haven't exactly nailed him, but we've got someone in the frame. I'm pretty sure he's about to be charged.'

'And who is it?' asked Scar casually, taking care not to sound *too* interested.

'The brother,' said Tony flatly. He paused for a moment, then went on. 'You just can't credit it, can you? There he was, as cool as cucumber for all those months. Living in the same house as his mum and dad, day in, day out, and all the while making out that he didn't have a clue what had happened to Nicky. When all the time—'

'Which brother?' interrupted Scar.

Tony looked up sharply, suddenly acutely aware that he shouldn't really be talking about matters that were about to become *sub judice*.

'Why? Do you know them?'

Scar began to back-pedal furiously.

'Never set eyes on them but I remember seeing in the paper that the girl had a couple of older brothers.'

'Three,' said Tony. 'It's Dave, the eldest, who's going to be charged.'

'So why the hell did he kill his kid sister?' asked Scar, still unable to get his head around the horror of it all.

'He's always had a screw loose, that one,' said Tony. 'He's been in and out of jail for a few years but it's always been burglary and petty theft before. Nothing like this. It seems Nicky had found out he'd been nicking stuff from his dad and selling it to earn a few bob. She threatened to tell Bert and Dave went bloody bonkers. He bumped into her on the way to school – accidentally on purpose – and persuaded her to go up to the tops with him. And then . . .'

At this point, even Tony was unable to go on. He'd thought he was completely hardened to the horrors he'd seen over the last sixteen years during the course of his job, but the depravity of this attack had stunned even him.

Now, as Kate sped breathlessly through the maze of streets leading to Moor View, she could feel her heart beating wildly. Surely Scar must have got the wrong end of the stick? It just couldn't be true. Bert and Vi were the salt of the earth; it was hard to take in the possibility that they had somehow reared a monster capable of assaulting his own sister and then

160

battering her to death. But, as the prim middle-class streets with their immaculate front lawns and redbrick garages tacked on the side gave way to rows and rows of back-to-back terraces, she began to think about Dave Rawlinson. Bert's eldest son had often been at the house when she'd visited, a glowering presence slumped in the corner of the kitchen, more often than not swigging back bitter straight from the can. Kate had convinced herself that he was just being protective of Bert and Vi, but now she wasn't so sure. He'd never once uttered a word of sorrow about his little sister; he'd swiftly taken over her room and the only time she'd heard him speak in recent months had been to ask Vi for a fiver to go out boozing.

When Kate finally turned the corner into Moor View she had to steel herself to carry on walking. Beyond the untidy line of houses, with their front doors opening straight onto the pavement, the moors rose up majestically. 'The kids used to treat the tops as their very own back garden when they were nippers,' Bert had told her once. 'They all knew the moors like the backs of their hands.' So perhaps it was no wonder that Dave had been able to dump Nicky in a place that had gone undiscovered for so long.

Today it was Vi who opened the front door. She had never looked so frail and so old. Her eyes were dry but they were red-rimmed and it was clear that she'd been crying. When she saw that it was Kate standing there, her bottom lip started trembling and she kept wiping her hands uselessly on her faded floral apron.

'I didn't think you'd be bothering with us any more,' she said, her voice little more than a whisper.

Kate didn't know why but she instinctively reached

out and touched the side of Vi's tired face with her hand.

'Why do you say that?' she murmured. 'You and Bert are my friends. I'll *always* bother with you.'

A tear trickled down Vi's cheek and she wiped it away roughly. 'But only so long as we can be of some use to you,' she said angrily. 'Only when you want something from us.'

'That's not true,' protested Kate. 'Well, I know it was in the beginning. I felt so sad for you but yes, I was just doing my job. Then Thorndike, I mean my old boss, told me to stay in contact with you, just in case, just in case there were any new developments, so I did. But after a while I realised I wasn't coming here because *he* said I should. I was coming here because *I* wanted to come.'

Vi stared at her uncomprehendingly. 'You'd better come inside,' she said wearily and led Kate along the narrow dark hall, past the door to the bathroom and into the kitchen at the back. Not for the first time, the room's dinginess struck her forcibly. The one tiny window faced a brick wall, so there was little natural light. Most of the time Vi kept the overhead light on but today the room was shrouded in darkness.

'Bert's not here,' Vi announced matter-of-factly once they'd sat down.

'Where's he gone?'

'He's down at the police station,' said Vi. 'This is going to break him, you know. I thought he was on the verge of giving up once our Nicky had gone but now this. He won't be able to bear it. It's, it's too much for him. He'll never get over this. It'll break his heart.'

Kate stared at Vi, unable to grasp what the older woman was going through. To lose a daughter like they had was too much for any parent to endure. But to discover that the monster responsible was their own son . . . it was impossible to see how Vi and Bert could ever come to terms with this.

'I'll make you a cup of tea,' said Vi. She picked nervously at the peeling Formica table.

Kate shook her head. 'No, Vi, *I'm* going to make *you* one. And I'm going to sit with you until Bert comes back.'

'But I don't have the faintest idea how long he'll be. And I've still got to tell our Thomas and our Peter.'

Vi covered her face with her hands, unable to bear the thought of breaking the news to her younger sons.

'Do you know where they are?' asked Kate gently.

'They're both on the afternoon shift at Bowland Cement. They don't usually get in till gone eight pm.'

'Do you want me to ring the company for you and ask them to come home?'

Vi looked at Kate.

'Could you do that?'

'Of course I could,' said Kate. 'Now you sit there while I make you a cup of tea and then I'll nip down to the phone box at the end of the street.'

'You won't say what's happened, will you?' pleaded Vi. 'It's got to come from me or their dad.'

'No, of course I won't. I'll, I'll just say that there's been a family crisis and they are both needed at home urgently.'

Looking back, Kate had no idea how any of them got through that night. Images of the shattered faces of Tom and Pete Rawlinson when their mother sat them down and told them what their own brother had done to their little sister came back to haunt her again and again. But neither of the boys questioned whether the police had got the right man. God knew what Dave Rawlinson had done in the past but there didn't seem any doubt in any of their minds that he was quite capable of such evil.

Then at eleven fifteen pm Bert had stumbled in, wide-eyed with shock and incomprehension. He'd barely said anything, just hugged Vi, Tom and Pete and nodded wordlessly to Kate.

'They've charged him,' he'd said finally and it was only then that he'd broken down and wept in Vi's arms.

Chapter Seventeen

'What do you mean you can't write anything?' screeched Scar first thing the next morning.

Despite her lack of sleep, Kate wanted to laugh at his reaction. Scar had only been in the job for five minutes and already he was doing a pretty passable imitation of Thorndike. The only difference between the pair of them was that Scar didn't intimidate her in the slightest. It was a bit like being bawled out by a whiny three-year-old – in other words, totally ineffective.

Kate willed herself not to lose her temper.

'You're the *acting* news editor of this newspaper,' she said, putting as much emphasis as she could on the word 'acting'. 'I really think you should swot up a bit on your *Essential Law for Journalists*.'

'What's that when it's at home?' said Scar obstinately.

'My point precisely,' said Kate. She rifled through her desk drawer, overflowing with old notebooks and scraps of paper, and handed him a battered green textbook.

'Read this,' she instructed. 'It'll tell you everything you need to know about how the law works. But the most important thing for now is that Dave Rawlinson has been charged with Nicky's murder and we just have to report the bare facts. We can't publish any background stuff about him.'

'Why not?' said Scar. It seemed a waste when they had such a cracking lot of material.

Kate groaned. 'Because . . .' She was just about to call Scar a 'fuckwit' when she suddenly remembered that, preposterous as it seemed, he was her new boss.

'Because,' she repeated, trying her utmost to remain calm. 'Because he hasn't been tried yet and you might prejudice the trial.'

Scar looked even more terrified when Kate told him that editors had gone to jail in the past for ignoring the laws of contempt.

'Right,' he said nervously. 'I'll hand this one over to you now. But we'll still get the splash with it, won't we?'

'Of course we will,' Kate told him reassuringly. 'Dave Rawlinson's making his first appearance in court this morning so we can peg the whole story on that. You're really lucky all this has happened this week. You've got a ready-made splash.'

After all her attempts to explain the finer points of the English legal system to her new boss, Kate was outraged when Scar decided to send Pam down to the Magistrates Court with her to cover the story.

'Doesn't he think I'm up to it or something?' she complained as the pair of them strolled into the court-house together.

'Oh forget it, love,' said Pam, teetering along beside her on her highest leopard-skin stilettos. 'It gets us both out of the office, doesn't it? And if Nicky's parents are there you can talk to them afterwards while I have a word with the coppers.'

'I suppose so,' said Kate. After the anguish of

the night before she wasn't particularly relishing the thought of facing Bert and Vi again so soon. Judging by the state they'd been in last night she couldn't think how on earth they were going to cope with the ordeal of seeing Dave in the dock.

But for some reason Bert and Vi didn't turn up at all and Kate couldn't help feeling relieved. She and Pam had to sit through several minor driving offences before the magistrates turned their attention to Dave Rawlinson. As the more junior of the two of them, Kate dutifully took notes while Pam sat back and tried to work out who was the best-looking man in court.

'I think you've made a hit with someone over there,' she whispered loudly to Kate as the Crown Prosecution Service solicitor ran through the case against some unfortunate man who'd knocked down a police-station bollard when he'd had one too many to drink.

'Don't be ridiculous,' said Kate, trying to concentrate on her impossibly squiggly shorthand.

'I'm not,' whispered Pam. 'Look. Over there.'

'Oh bugger,' said Kate as she realised she was losing the battle to keep up with the CPS solicitor.

'Calm down,' said Pam, putting her hand on Kate's. 'This driving offence stuff will only make a couple of pars, you know. You don't need every cough and spit. Just the name, address, age, charge and outcome. And if there's anything you've missed we'll check it with the clerk afterwards. Now, Kate, will you tell me who that gorgeous man who can't take his eyes off you is?'

Kate glanced towards the public gallery at the back of the court, where Pam was pointing. Despite the fact that Dave Rawlinson hadn't been charged until late last night, the press bench was packed to overflowing with reporters. The latecomers had obviously spilled into the public gallery because there, sitting in the middle of them looking pleased as punch with himself as usual, was Charley Stone.

'D'you mean the flash-looking git in a pinstriped suit?' whispered Kate.

'Of course I do,' giggled Pam, carefully smoothing her hair. 'He's in a different league to the others, isn't he?'

Looking around the court, Kate had to agree with her. Compared to the local press and radio reporters, with their shabby tweed jackets and fraying shirts, Charley Stone looked like some strange exotic creature that had suddenly landed from outer space. While the reporters sitting either side of him, both of whom Kate knew, scribbled feverishly in their notebooks, Charley sprawled casually in his seat, his hands clasped behind his head. Yet again, Kate wondered why on earth he was taking such a keen interest in this story. It was a tragic case, she appreciated that more than anyone, but murders were two a penny in London. Why had Charley Stone travelled all the way up here just for a remand?

'He's called Charley Stone,' she murmured under her breath to Pam. 'He works for the *Evening Clarion*. I met him a few—'

Kate stopped in mid-flow as the chairman of the magistrates, another mousy-looking man in a tweed jacket, suddenly announced Dave Rawlinson's case.

An involuntary shiver of alarm ran down her spine as Dave Rawlinson was led into court. On the face of it he looked pretty much the same as usual, that is, large, sweaty and unprepossessing. He was wearing his habitual grimy tracksuit and trainers and his lank, shoulder-length hair had been scraped back into a ponytail with an elastic band. The only thing that was different was that he was handcuffed to a burly police officer.

Dave Rawlinson's appearance in court was remarkably brief. He spoke only twice, grunting a swift 'yes' to his name and address, before being remanded in custody for a week.

'Well, that's not going to set the front page on fire, is it?' moaned Pam as Rawlinson was led out of court. 'I'll just collar one of the coppers though. See if I can get anything out of them. I'll catch you back in the office.'

Kate grinned at her. What was it about Pam and coppers? She'd been having a fling with a sergeant from CID on and off for months, everyone knew that, but she just couldn't resist the opportunity to chat up some of his mates. It was pretty obvious that writing the splash was going to be down to Kate. And then if Pam was running true to form, she'd flounce back into the newsroom this afternoon and bold as brass put her byline in front of Kate's. If Pam wasn't such a laugh to be with, Kate could quite cheerfully have throttled her.

Kate was on her way out of the courthouse by the time Charley Stone finally caught up with her.

'Hey, what's the rush?' he said, grabbing her arm. 'Aren't you pleased to see me?'

Kate smiled back at him. He was almost as incorrigible as Pam.

'It's probably escaped your notice but I've got a story to write. We go to press this evening.'

'We go to press . . .' Charley Stone consulted a flashy-looking Rolex '. . . in thirty-five minutes.'

'So what are you hanging around here for then?' said Kate.

Charley stared at her in amazement. He wasn't used to women playing hard to get.

'Because,' he said, his eyes boring into hers, 'because before I file, I want the prettiest girl in court to agree to have a drink with me tonight.'

Completely taken aback by this, Kate burst out laughing. Most of the men she'd met in Lancashire preferred the less fancy approach. But she had to admit that after the shitty way in which Ben had treated her, it was quite flattering to have someone as good-looking as Charley Stone asking her out.

'And you came all the way up to Lancashire to ask me that? What if I say no?'

'Then you'll break my heart,' joked Charley. He sensed he might be getting somewhere with her at last. 'I'll weep all the way back to London.'

'Looks as though I'll have to put you out of your misery then, won't I?' said Kate good-humouredly. 'I'll see you in the Elephant at eight, shall I?'

When Charley wandered into the pub that night, a studied ten minutes late, he still wasn't entirely sure *why* he was pursuing Kate Grant so keenly. So she was bright, and pretty, but then he'd had lorryloads of girlfriends in the past who'd been just as bright and just as pretty. No, he couldn't work out whether he was interested in her a) because it looked as though this case would bring him to Bowland quite a bit over the coming months, b) because her dad was a stinking-rich newspaper tycoon, or c) whether he was just interested in her full stop.

As he positioned himself at the bar, he grimaced

involuntarily. This really wasn't his sort of place at all. He might have grown up in one of the rougher bits of Blackburn but that didn't mean that he wanted to have anything to do with that sort of life now. He'd got rid of both his broad Lancashire accent and his propensity to call a cup of tea 'a brew' and a pair of trousers 'yer kecks' a very long time ago. These days he preferred the more refined surroundings of places like Quaglino's or the Groucho Club to pubs as scummy as the Elephant. He and Kate would have one drink here at the very most, he resolved. Then they'd drive out to somewhere a lot more salubrious.

Twenty minutes later, he was sweating with indignation. How dare some lowly cub reporter like Kate Grant keep *him*, a star writer on the *Evening Clarion*, hanging around in a dive like this? If anyone was going to stand someone up, it should be bloody *him* standing *her* up.

Suddenly he was tapped sharply on the shoulder from behind.

'And about fucking time too,' he said as he swung round, then stopped abruptly. Kate had arrived all right but she wasn't on her own. Standing by her side, looking inordinately pleased with herself, was a large brassy woman with dangly gold earrings that even Bet Lynch would have rejected as too flashy. She must have been at least forty but her substantial bosom had been poured into a skintight black top and she was wearing a short pink skirt that barely covered her knickers. Charley didn't know whether to say 'phwoar' or crack up laughing. This woman looked as if she'd be more at home on the streets of Soho than sleepy old Bowland.

'Charley, this is Pam Newbold, one of the other

reporters on the *Bugle*,' said Kate with a knowing smile. 'I didn't think you'd mind if I brought her along.'

It struck Charley forcibly that alongside Pam Newbold, Kate, with her shiny blonde hair and bohemian clothes – tonight she was wearing a denim jacket, diaphanous Indian skirt and a pair of Doc Martens – looked innocent, fresh-faced and absurdly young. You'd never put the two of them together in a million years.

'Chief reporter actually, Kate,' Pam corrected her smoothly.

'What do you mean?' demanded Kate. 'Has Scar told you something that he hasn't told the rest of us?'

'Not exactly, no,' purred Pam. 'But don't worry. I'm sure he'll get round to it in due course.'

Kate didn't believe a word of this. For a start Scar hardly dared even open his mouth when Pam was around. And he was far too gormless to have appointed a chief reporter so soon.

'There's nothing like a friendly bit of rivalry, girls, is there?' said Charley. 'But never mind, Kate, I'm sure your time will come.'

A look of horror crossed Pam's face as he spoke.

'Oh no, Charley, you've got it all wrong. Kate's just a trainee. Didn't she tell you? It'll be years before she gets to be a senior reporter like me.'

Inside, Kate was seething. Bloody Pam. She'd begged to come along and be introduced to Charley Stone. In fact the only reason they'd been so late was because Pam had taken so bloody long to put her warpaint on. And now they were here, all Pam could do was pull rank and slag her off.

'Is that so?' said Charley smoothly. 'I'm sure if you work hard enough, Kate, you might make it to the upper echelons of the *Bugle*. Just like your friend. Pat, wasn't it?'

'Pam,' said Pam and Kate simultaneously, though Kate couldn't help feeling pleased that Pam hadn't made a big enough impression on Charley for him to get her name right.

'Now what can I get you ladies to drink?'

The two women's choices of drink said everything about them, thought Charley, as he placed a lager in front of Kate and a Bacardi and Coke before Pam. He couldn't help wondering why Kate had brought Pam along in the first place. Was it for protection – although, for all her youth, Kate seemed pretty streetwise – or maybe Pam was such a man-eater that she couldn't resist the chance to muscle in on Kate's date. As Pam fluttered her eyelashes at him prettily and continued to flaunt her extraordinary chest at every conceivable opportunity, he suspected that it was probably the latter.

Half an hour later, when Pam had ignored several whopping hints to leave the pair of them in peace, Charley was forced to take desperate measures. He stood up and put his jacket on.

'I'm afraid it's about time we made a move, Kate. It's been wonderful meeting you of course, Pat, but if we don't get a move on they'll give our table to someone else.'

Kate looked at him sharply. He hadn't mentioned anything about having dinner before. It had just been a casual drink. What was he on about?

This hint, however, was obvious enough even for the thick-skinned Pam. She too rose to her feet, giving Charley one last flash of her cleavage as she bent to retrieve her bag, and giggled girlishly.

'Silly me, look at the time. I promised the new inspector down at the nick that I'd have a drink with him tonight. I hate having to tear myself away but I must dash.'

When she'd finally gone, Kate caught Charley's eye and they both burst out laughing.

'That was really mean of you,' she said when she'd stopped chortling enough to get a few words out.

'*Moi*?' said Charley, trying to look as if he didn't have a clue what she was on about.

'Yes, you,' said Kate. 'You made it pretty obvious that you didn't want her around. She'll be absolutely poisonous to me tomorrow. I'll really suffer for it.'

Charley shrugged his shoulders nonchalantly.

'Serve her bloody well right if you ask me. The silly bitch shouldn't have gatecrashed like that.'

'How do you know she did gatecrash?' asked Kate. 'Maybe I invited her to come along.'

'Well, did you?'

'Well, not exactly, no,' admitted Kate and she couldn't help giggling again.

'Come on,' said Charley, grabbing her by the hand and pulling her to her feet. 'I've got a hire car outside. Do you fancy dinner in a fantastic country pub I know?'

An hour later, they were tucking into the most delicious dinner Kate had eaten since her arrival in Lancashire. In most places that she'd visited with Ben, the landlords had looked puzzled when she'd announced that she was a vegetarian. Then if she'd been lucky they'd just about managed to rustle up a baked potato or a tired-looking bowl of ratatouille. On this menu, however, there were loads of things to choose from.

'This is wonderful,' said Kate, gazing around at the tiny candlelit tables and old-fashioned wooden bar with appreciation. 'I've never heard of this place before. And it's so peaceful. I thought all the pubs round here were like the Elephant.'

'All cloth caps and whippets and racing on the telly, you mean?' grinned Charley.

'No, not exactly,' said Kate, before admitting, 'well yes, maybe.'

'Do you like it up here?' he asked.

Kate thought for a moment. She remembered how she'd told Ben that being in Bowland was like coming home at last. At the time she'd instinctively felt he understood. But all that seemed a lifetime ago. Now she couldn't be sure of anything. She glanced up at Charley's inquisitive face. No. She wasn't going to risk pouring her heart out to a man for a second time.

'It's all right,' she said casually in between mouthfuls of mushroom risotto.

'That good?' said Charley.

'Yep,' said Kate. Charley was good fun and she was enjoying herself. But she wasn't entirely sure she could trust him. Not quite yet, anyway.

Chapter Eighteen

Laura groaned lazily and slid her hand over to the other side of the bed to touch Hugo. She opened her eyes in puzzlement. There was no one there; just a cool flattened pillow where Hugo's head had been. She glanced at the alarm clock on his bedside table. The luminous dial confirmed that it was only six forty-five am So where on earth was he?

She rolled out of bed and wandered through the flat in a daze. She really must do something about this place. It looked so austere and unlived-in, a neglected bachelor pad that gave precious little away about its owner. Unprepossessing venetian blinds hung in every single room, the walls were totally devoid of pictures and the only signs that anyone ever used the kitchen were a packet of breakfast tea left lying by the kettle and a large tin of Marvel on the side. The oven was so spanking new and spotless that Laura suspected it had never been used for as much as an Indian takeaway.

Perhaps Hugo had gone for a run in the park, she thought hopefully. Battersea Park was just over the road, and on the flight back from Paris last night he'd told her of his determination to get fit. What a sweetie he was. He must have made a real effort not to wake her.

Laura had a quick shower then propped her mirror against the kettle to put her make-up on. It was their first day back at work and she was determined to look as glamorous as possible, make Hugo really proud of her. An hour later, dressed in a bright fuchsia suit – it had a much shorter skirt than she usually dared wear – and with her hair pulled back into an elegant chignon, Laura was growing increasingly alarmed. Hugo was such a stickler for punctuality. He wouldn't want to be late, not on his first day back. Perhaps he'd had an accident or something. Surely he couldn't still be out jogging?

As the clock in the hall approached eight am the truth gradually dawned on her. Hugo's overcoat wasn't hanging on the hook where he usually left it. And his briefcase wasn't there either. A sliver of hurt sliced through her. Here was she, envisaging a cosy drive into work together now that they were married, when all the time he'd simply got up and left by himself.

It was nine thirty by the time Laura staggered into the office. She'd completely underestimated the length of time it would take to travel in from Battersea. First there had been the walk over Albert Bridge and up almost the entire length of the King's Road to Sloane Square. This had taken twenty-five minutes, during which she'd got drenched to the skin. Then the horrendous experience of being packed onto the tube like a sardine. Laura, her hair now hanging down her neck like rats' tails, had thought wistfully of the days when HH had given her a lift in his chauffeur-driven Mercedes.

But worse was to come. When she finally arrived at her desk she'd thought she must be seeing things.

There, sitting in *her* chair, was a woman she'd never set eyes on before, wearing a dark business suit. Her long brown hair was caught up at the back with a large tortoiseshell clip.

'What are you doing in my seat?' asked Laura shyly, her resolve to be more purposeful now that she was married completely forgotten.

'It's *my* seat,' said the woman without taking her eyes from her computer screen. 'Anyway, who are you?'

'Hugo Bentley's secretary,' mumbled Laura. 'And his *wife*.'

Instantly, the woman swung round, a look of deep embarrassment crossing her face.

'Oh dear. Hasn't he told you? I thought married couples usually told each other everything.'

When the woman saw Laura's wobbly mouth and the tears welling in her eyes, she instantly regretted her jokey tone.

'Oh God, I'm sorry,' she cried, jumping to her feet. 'I was only kidding you. I didn't mean anything by it. Honest. Here, have a tissue.'

Laura smiled wanly at her. She looked nice, she thought. Friendly. But she was clearly older than Laura had first assumed. Her forehead had the faint lines of early middle age. She was definitely nearer forty than thirty.

'I'm all right. Really I am,' said Laura, wiping her nose. 'It's just been one of those mornings. But I still don't understand why you are sitting in my chair.'

'You sound like Goldilocks and the Three Bears. I'm Joanna King, by the way.'

'And I'm Laura,' said Laura, taking Joanna's hand.

'Laura Bentley,' she added proudly. Even after one week of marriage, the fact that she now bore Hugo's name still gave her a thrill.

At that moment Hugo's office door opened and Hugo himself strode out with a sheaf of papers in his hand.

'Jo, have you finished that re—'

He stopped in his tracks when he saw Laura.

'Laura. What are you doing here?'

Stung by his coolness, especially when she compared it with the friendly way in which he'd greeted Joanna, Laura instinctively cowered.

'What do you mean, Hugo? I . . . I work here.'

'I've been meaning to talk to you about that,' said Hugo quietly.

'I . . . I don't understand what you're saying.'

Joanna shifted uncomfortably in her seat. As a temp who had moved from department to department at the bank over the last few months, she'd leapt at this job with alacrity when she'd been offered it half an hour ago. She'd heard on the grapevine what a tricky bastard Hugo Bentley could be, but the prospect of a decent salary, health insurance and six weeks holiday a year was simply too good an opportunity to turn down.

'Look,' she said awkwardly. 'Why don't I make you both a coffee and you can go and discuss all this in private?'

'Thanks, Jo. I'd be grateful,' said Hugo. He hated his private life impinging on work like this, but he needed to sort this out with as little fuss as possible. 'Give us five minutes, will you? But we must crack on with that report after that. I've got a few changes I want you to incorporate.'

Laura followed Hugo meekly into his office and sat down opposite him. Perhaps he'd say something loving now that they were alone.

Hugo, however, was too bound up with the piles of paperwork he had to catch up with to waste time making small talk.

'It's my fault. I should have discussed it with you before,' he began brusquely.

'Told me what before?' said Laura, at a complete loss as to what was going on.

Hugo sighed heavily.

'I should have told you that you can't possibly work for me any more. Come on, Laura, you know that. We're married now. I earn plenty of money for the pair of us and anyway, you're rich in your own right. You don't need to work.'

'But I *like* coming to work,' protested Laura. 'I don't know what I'd do with myself if I didn't.'

Hugo could have kicked himself for not tackling all this earlier. Why had he been so bloody dense? He'd never in a million years imagined that Laura would want to continue working as his secretary after the wedding. He'd assumed that she'd do what all his colleagues' wives did – take painting classes, go out to coffee mornings, look for a house in the country.

'I'm sorry, Laura,' he said, his tone more gentle. 'I really am, but we must keep our work and our home life separate. Surely you can see that?'

'Perhaps I could get a transfer,' said Laura hopefully. 'Maybe it wouldn't be a good idea for us to work in such close proximity, but I'm sure I could move to another department. Or to another bank even.'

Hugo got up and walked round his desk to where Laura was sitting. He ruffled her hair, rather like he would that of a child, then crouched down so that his head was on a level with hers.

'You know that's impossible, darling. It would only compromise both of us. We couldn't talk freely about anything if you were working for another bank.'

None of Hugo's words were making any sense as far as Laura was concerned. Why was it such a big deal *where* she worked? She was hardly a high-flyer. But then again, she and Hugo had only been married for just over a week. She didn't want to rock the boat over something as trivial as this. Perhaps it would be best to give him the benefit of the doubt. He was so much cleverer than her, after all.

'All right,' she said with a nervous smile. 'I'll go and tell personnel.'

She kissed him swiftly on the cheek and hurried towards the door.

'Just one more thing,' called Hugo, not bothering to look up from his report as she disappeared out of the office. 'I'm not being critical or anything but don't wear such a short skirt again, will you, darling? It makes you look a bit cheap.'

Joanna King seethed inwardly when she heard Hugo Bentley's last admonition to his wife. It merely served to confirm what she had suspected all morning – that her new boss was a complete pillock. Laura Bentley looked like a bag of nerves, to put it mildly, and all Hugo seemed intent on doing was eroding her confidence even further. It wasn't really any of her business, she was well aware of that, but she knew whose side she was on.

When Joanna took Hugo the report she'd typed for him, however, he was charm itself. The insensitivity that he'd shown towards his wife had totally evaporated. If she hadn't been so appalled by his behaviour she might have thought she'd imagined the whole incident. Now he seemed kind, attentive and deeply appreciative.

'I hope your wife wasn't too upset,' said Joanna. She was damned if she was going to pretend that nothing had happened.

'Oh don't worry about her,' said Hugo with a smile. 'She's just a little bit highly strung. And she doesn't like being ticked off.'

'Who does?' murmured Joanna. She had the distinct feeling that it wouldn't be long before she and Hugo Bentley came to blows. But what the hell, the job would pay the mortgage for the time being and with her experience she was quite capable of getting another one when she and Hugo parted company.

'Now,' continued Hugo. 'I want to ask you to get out the file on a company I'm interested in. I don't need to remind you that everything we discuss between these four walls must remain absolutely confidential. If I ever hear you breathing a word about any of my work it will be a disciplinary matter. I'm sure I'm making myself clear.'

After the embarrassing scene at the office, Laura felt deeply apprehensive about Hugo's return home. She'd whiled away the morning by wandering aimlessly around Harrods and Harvey Nichols, treated herself to an armful of glossy magazines and ordered several metres of stunning violet silk from a posh interior-design shop to make new curtains for Hugo's – she meant their – bedroom. By the time she heard Hugo's key in the lock she was dreading what kind of mood he was going to be in. Everything had been her fault, she completely accepted that, but all afternoon her mind had been racing with ideas about how best to please him. She'd prepared a complicated dinner from a Robert Carrier cookery book, meticulously tidied and cleaned the flat and even consigned the offending pink suit to a pile of clothes she'd decided to pass on to Kate.

But when Hugo swept through the door just after eight pm he was full of the joys of spring.

'Darling,' he said as she stood uncertainly in the hall. 'It's so wonderful to have you to come home to.' He swept her into his arms and kissed her more passionately than he ever had in their entire relationship.

'You look gorgeous enough to eat,' he whispered. 'I'm going to have a bath. Will you come and talk to me?'

Laura could scarcely hide her astonishment. She'd been trying to convince herself for more than a week now that there was nothing abnormal about it, but she still couldn't get her head around why she and Hugo hadn't yet made love. During their time in Paris he'd constantly managed to evade the issue, either claiming that they were both too tired or that he wanted to stay up and watch a late-night movie. He hadn't shown the slightest interest in touching her or seeing her naked body, and after a few nights of being rebuffed like this Laura had given up sleeping in the nude and taken to wearing her virginal long white nightie in bed again. She never for one moment suspected that Hugo might have hang-ups about sex. The reason he wasn't interested in her was obvious. She simply wasn't good enough for him.

Chapter Nineteen

'Do you want to come in for a coffee?'

Charley Stone didn't hesitate. He'd been working up to this all evening.

'I'd love to,' he said, glancing up and down at the startlingly hideous Thirties semi that appeared to be Kate's home. He'd imagined she might live somewhere a little bit classier than this dump.

'What's the matter?' asked Kate. 'I won't be offended if you don't really want to. Have you got an early start tomorrow?'

Charley flashed another megawatt smile at Kate.

'I'd adore a coffee.'

Kate opened the door and led him down a dark narrow hall into the kitchen. Along with his many other faults, Charley Stone was an out and out design snob. He'd recently employed an interior designer to revamp his small Notting Hill flat and, despite the staggering bill at the end of it all, considered it money well spent. Now the place was painted white throughout, with a stunning ash floor and carefully chosen items of furniture from the Conran Shop. He couldn't help wrinkling his nose with distaste at Kate's house. It reminded him of his mother's place in Blackburn. The hall was covered in peeling beige wallpaper for a start, and ugh, the smell. It was as if something had died in there.

'Sorry about the pong,' apologised Kate. 'We think it's probably Joe's socks. His personal hygiene leaves rather a lot to be desired.'

'And who exactly is Joe when he's at home?' enquired Charley, as Kate switched on the kitchen light.

'Bloody hell,' he groaned without waiting for an answer. The overhead strip lighting was so dazzling that it almost brought tears to his eyes.

'It's a bit of a shock, isn't it,' laughed Kate. 'I defy even Cindy Crawford to look good in this light.'

Charley blinked for a few seconds, a bit like a rabbit caught in a car's headlights, before continuing.

'You were going to tell me about Joe,' he reminded her.

Kate had filled the kettle and was now busy hunting for a jar of coffee. Judging by the state of the place, Charley knew that it would be pointless asking her if she had any freshly ground.

'Got it,' she cried triumphantly as she unearthed something from the back of a scummy-looking cupboard. 'Sorry Charley. You were asking about Joe. Well, Danny Simpson, you know, the photographer on the *Bugle*, is the main tenant and Joe is his younger brother. He's studying design in Preston and he's a bit of a slob.'

'Anyone else live here?'

'Yep,' said Kate, spooning coffee granules into a couple of mugs. 'A solicitor called Jules.'

'Male or female?' enquired Charley.

'Male,' said Kate.

'So you live with three blokes,' said Charley. As the evening went on he was just beginning to appreciate that there was more to Kate than first met the eye. Prior to this he would have imagined her living in a picturesque village outside Bowland with a couple of jolly girls and a rota for doing the chores. Not in this hellhole.

Just as Kate was pouring hot water into the mugs, there was an almighty crash directly overhead. It sounded like the entire ceiling was about to cave in. Charley, not usually a man to suffer problems with his nerves, almost leapt out of his seat with fright. Kate, however, barely turned a hair.

'What the hell was that?' demanded Charley.

'What's the time?' asked Kate without even bothering to turn round.

'Half past twelve.'

'Must be Joe then,' said Kate matter-of-factly.

'Doing what exactly?'

'Poor Joe,' said Kate. 'He's a tormented artist. He's incredibly bound up in his work and when he gets back here at night all he's fit for is hurling himself into bed and trying to get some sleep. The only trouble is that he thrashes around so much that he falls out of bed every other night. His room's just above, you see.'

'Bloody maniac,' grunted Charley. 'I thought I was about to have a heart attack.'

Without thinking, Kate suddenly put her coffee cup down and walked round to the back of Charley's chair. Before he was even aware of what she was doing, she was sliding her hand inside his shirt. Her closeness was intoxicating, thought Charley, enjoying the touch of her cool palm against his chest. He'd fully assumed that she would be painfully inexperienced and shy, that if he wanted to take things further he'd have to move mind-numbingly slowly. But now here she was, seizing the initiative before he'd even thought of how to go about making the first move.

'You're not as hard as you like to make out, are you, Charley Stone?' she whispered in his ear.

'Oh I think you'll find that I am, darling,' murmured Charley, sliding her hand down towards his crotch.

Kate groaned appreciatively.

'So I see,' she said. 'We'll have to do something about that then, won't we?'

'I wish you would,' muttered Charley. He got to his feet and took her roughly in his arms. Slowly his tongue began exploring her mouth and just as Kate thought she was going to die with anticipation he drew back, took off her jacket and one by one undid all the tiny pearl buttons down the front of her shirt. When he'd finished he saw to his surprise that she wasn't wearing a bra. She stood, naked from the waist up, smiling back at him. Instantly he reached forward and caressed each breast in turn. Her nipples were surprisingly large and rosy and hard. God, he wanted her badly.

George Gibbs elbowed Rob Bennett sharply in the ribs.

'You can see what that pair have been up to,' he chuckled. 'They've got it written all over their faces.'

Rob pursed his lips in disapproval. George was such a nosy so-and-so. He spent half his days peering out of that bloody window. It was a shame he didn't show the same application when it came to laying out pages. But all the same Rob couldn't resist taking a surreptitious peek to see who George was talking about this time. He immediately clocked Kate Grant walking along the pavement arm in arm with that poncey-looking reporter from the *Evening Clarion* who'd been sniffing around Bowland for a while.

Rob tried to look uninterested. He was the most strait-laced person in the office – with the added burden of being married to a born-again Christian – and did his best to avoid salacious comments.

'Kate's not that sort of girl,' he said hurriedly. 'All she's interested in is keeping her head down, working hard and getting her indentures. And she's got far too much sense to be taken in by some smart alec from London.'

He rubbed his nose ruefully. To be honest, he had a vested interest in Kate remaining single. If she *had* found herself a new boyfriend – and he hoped desperately that she *hadn't* – she might not be quite so enthusiastic about taking on his night jobs. Life had become an awful lot more pleasant since he had passed his entire load of parish-council meetings on to Kate. June, his wife, had stopped nagging now he got home on time every night and even the kids seemed more settled.

George looked dubious. Rob clearly didn't have a clue about women. He was pretty sure that Kate Grant and Charley Stone were an item now. Since the break-up with Ben Maguire he'd been on at her constantly to find someone new.

'It's not natural, a girl like you being on her own,' he'd kept telling her. 'You'd be a lot happier if you found yourself a new chap.'

'Why? Got anyone in mind?' Kate had teased. 'Do you reckon Scar might be interested?'

Rob had had enough of talking about Kate's love life by now and had turned back to his desk to start making the usual morning calls to the emergency services –

police, ambulance and fire station. It was about time he picked up a decent story, he reflected. Pam Newbold had nabbed the splash for the last three weeks on the trot now. Mind you, he reckoned this week's didn't count because she'd shared a byline with Kate.

Bored to tears by the school soccer report he was supposed to be subbing, George glanced out of the window again and wolf-whistled loudly. Kate and Charley Stone, their bodies entwined around each other, were now kissing passionately on the pavement below.

'What was that you said about keeping her head down, Rob?' muttered George. 'Keeping her tongue down that bloke's throat more like.'

When Kate finally managed to tear herself away from Charley and dashed up to the office she was faced with a stream of ribbing from George. But in a way she felt almost grateful that he was speaking to her; the rest of the office seemed to be giving her the cold shoulder. Just as she'd predicted, Pam was making her suffer for her date with Charley the night before, while Rob, she couldn't think why, kept shooting disapproving glances at her. Scar, following Pam's lead as usual, had first bollocked her for being late and then ordered her out to interview an old woman who'd rung in claiming that she was Princess Anastasia, long-lost daughter of the last Tsar of Russia.

'You *are* joking, aren't you?' Kate had said grumpily. 'What the hell would she be doing living in Bowland for God's sake?'

Scar, however, had shaken his head and told her not to be so defeatist.

It was amazing, thought Kate, as she stomped huffily down the office stairs. Scar should be grateful to her, not just for writing this week's splash, but for helping him out of a hole *and* explaining the finer points of the English legal system to him. But look at him; power had clearly gone to his head. He was behaving like a prat.

In fact Scar was enjoying himself hugely. If he said it himself, this week's *Bugle* didn't look half bad. His uncle Laurie, never one to throw compliments around even at the best of times, had actually rung to congratulate him.

'I knew you had it in you, lad,' he'd said. 'Keep up the good work.'

Scar had flushed bright scarlet with pleasure. He had found his vocation at last.

As he sat doodling in his notebook, trying to work out the best strategy for inviting Pam Newbold out, the office door opened and two men walked in. They were both wearing immaculately cut charcoal suits and had an air of importance about them. One was carrying a bulging alligator briefcase; the other clutched a slim leather envelope under his arm. It was a few seconds, however, before either of them spoke. They stood gaping at the *Bugle* newsroom as if the place was something straight out of the ark.

'Where can we find Mr Laurence Laing?' enquired the elder of the pair eventually. He was tall and slim, with jet-black hair that looked as though it owed a lot to Grecian 2000, and a distinctly southern accent.

'Er, who is it that wants him?' asked Scar nervously.

'I do,' said the older man.

Scar shut up for a few seconds, somehow sensing – and rightly so – that these two were way out of his league.

'And y . . . y . . . you are?' stammered Scar.

By this time everyone in the office had stopped what they were doing, all enjoying Scar's discomfiture.

The older man stepped forward and flashed a humourless smile at him. His teeth were a work of art, thought Pam Newbold admiringly. So even. And so dazzlingly white. For a few seconds she toyed with the notion of getting her own capped, then reluctantly dismissed the idea. The salary she earned on the *Bugle* was so pitiful that it barely kept her in Colgate.

'Gordon Osprey, deputy chairman of Hollingberry Holdings,' said the older man smoothly, stretching out a well-manicured hand to Scar. 'And this is my assistant, Tim Jefferson.' He paused for a moment to allow for the usual deferential reaction he got from lowly newspaper staff.

Scar, running true to form, looked deeply puzzled by Gordon Osprey's introduction. He sat silent for a moment, trying to get his head around what it meant, before opting for the upfront approach.

'What the fuck's Hollingberry Holdings when it's at home?' he said finally.

From the rest of the staff there was a collective intake of breath. Little did Scar know it, thought George Gibbs ruefully, but he had just sealed his fate. And he could hardly have made a better job of it if he had jumped in his own coffin and banged the lid down on himself.

'Can anyone here please enlighten their colleague?' enquired Gordon Osprey. 'Or are you all as utterly ignorant as he is?'

Scar's face turned puce at the man's insulting remark. He was half-inclined to headbutt him and be done with it. As if reading his mind, George Gibbs laid a restraining hand on Scar's arm.

'Hollingberry Holdings owns Leadington Newspapers,' hissed George under his breath. Then, as if to force the point home, he added, 'And Leadington owns the *Bugle*. Geddit?'

Scar did indeed get it at last and initiated a belated attempt to charm his two visitors. George groaned inwardly. It was a little like launching a ropey lifeboat the day after the *Titanic* had sunk.

'Er, er, I'm Steve Scarsdale, the news editor of the *Bugle*,' stumbled Scar, scrambling hastily to his feet. 'I am so, so, completely delighted to welcome you to the *Bugle*. Laurie Laing is my uncle but I'm afraid he's on long-term sick leave so I'm in charge.'

Gordon Osprey's eyes gleamed with interest.

'Is he, indeed? And from what I've seen of his work record he's still receiving full pay, isn't he? Tim, I think you'd appreciate a full and frank talk with Mr Laing and his nephew. Wouldn't you?'

Tim Jefferson threw his head back and laughed sycophantically.

'Absolutely, Gordon. Now, Mr Scarsdale, perhaps we can start with you? Shall we have our chat in here or is there somewhere a little more private we can go?'

It was a subdued Scar who emerged from the advertising rep's office twenty minutes later. So much for his hopes of building a sparkling new career on the *Bugle*. His head drooped dejectedly. He'd been kidding himself all along. He was an out and out loser. He was never going to make it now.

Gordon Osprey was still finding it hard to work out

what he was doing in this northern backwater. It wasn't his sort of place at all. The moors had looked spectacular from the car, even he could appreciate that, but he just wasn't a country-lover at heart. He was at his happiest closeted in his office in the City, poring over sales figures, looking at possible acquisitions and attempting to keep HH's crazier schemes in check. Gordon was rapidly coming round to the opinion that the knighthood had gone to HH's head. The man had been absolutely impossible to deal with over the last few months. Ordering Gordon around as if he were some junior errand boy. Treating him as if he was half-witted. And why the hell he'd ever bought Leadington in the first place was completely beyond him. He'd warned HH to keep his eye on the big picture, but know-it-all HH had disregarded him as usual and snapped up the ailing group for what HH insisted was a bargain and he himself thought was completely over the top. It was turning out to be such a shambles that they probably couldn't give it away now.

And as if all that wasn't enough, HH had despatched him up to Lancashire to take a look at Leadington for himself. Gordon had protested furiously at the idea when HH came up with it. He was the deputy chairman, after all. He should be working on corporate strategy, not trawling round the countryside looking at penny rags like the *Accrington Standard* and the *Bowland Bugle*. The circulation of the entire Leadington group was piteously low. If he had his way, he'd close the whole damn lot of them down, sell off the premises and have done with it.

'It'll do you good to get out on the ground, Gordon,' HH had instructed. 'You spend far too much time in the office. It'll give you an overview. You'll thank me for it in six months' time, you'll see.'

So here he was, closeted in this squalid office above a fish-and-chip shop of all places, chatting to the useless band of no-hopers who constituted the *Bugle* staff.

Except that there seemed to be one very important person missing. Kate. And when it came down to it, Gordon was pretty sure that *she* was the real reason why bloody HH had sent him up here in the first place. HH simply hadn't had the balls to come up and see Kate's workplace for himself. So he'd concocted this crazy cock and bull scheme to send *him*, his number two, on a fact-finding tour – when all he really wanted was a bit of feedback about what the hell his younger daughter was getting up to in the far frozen north.

Gordon sighed wearily. He took a sip of the disgusting-looking coffee Pam Newbold had just put in front of him, then noticed the chipped mug and hastily put it down again. God knew what he might catch here.

Gordon Osprey was a fastidious man. He always paid great attention to his appearance, wearing bespoke suits from Savile Row, neat gold cufflinks and highly polished brogues from Church's. He hated anything remotely grimy and if he could have got away with it he would probably have preferred to have as little as possible to do with the rest of the human race. He'd been married once, a very long time ago, but Josephine had upped and left him within six months of their wedding, unable to cope for a second longer with his pernickety ways.

'I'm sorry, love,' said Pam, who'd watched the way he'd dropped his coffee mug as swiftly as a red-hot poker. 'Do you take sugar? I forgot to ask.'

Gordon glanced up from the copy of the *Bugle* that

he'd been flicking through. It was deeply unimpressive, he'd decided. Page after page of turgid parish-council reports, few features and, most depressing of all, hardly any advertising. No wonder it didn't make any money.

'No, I don't take sugar,' he said curtly.

'Silly me,' Pam giggled flirtatiously. 'I should have known you don't. You're slim as a whippet. I bet you never have to watch your waistline, do you?'

Gordon met her gaze coldly. He couldn't stand open-plan offices. Stupid people burbling in your ear all day long when you were trying to get on with your work.

'Where's Kate today?' he asked suddenly.

Pam was slightly taken aback by this question. Kate's family background wasn't a secret any more but she still tended to think of her as a young, slightly green trainee who had a lot to learn.

'She's been sent out on a job. Why? Do you know her?'

'I obviously work with her father,' said Gordon curtly. He was damned if he was going to discuss HH and Kate with a stranger. 'Now, if you don't mind, I've got a lot to get through this morning. I'd like to see each of the staff in turn to discuss the future.'

'What bloody future?' muttered George under his breath. It was pretty clear what was coming. He'd seen it all before. Gordon Osprey and his sidekick hadn't travelled all the way up here to admire the scenery. No, it would be a case of firing half the staff, slashing the costs, and then they'd be speeding back down south by tomorrow morning. That was if the *Bugle* was lucky. It was entirely possible that Gordon Osprey intended to shut the paper down altogether.

'Who do you want first?' asked Pam, smoothing her hair and wishing that she'd paid more attention to her appearance this morning rather than flinging on this boring red trouser suit.

Gordon Osprey consulted his list of employees. 'George Gibbs, Steven Scarsdale – no, he's been dealt with already – Rob Bennett, Danny Simpson, Pam Newbold. In that order please. And the rest of you can wait outside until I call you in.'

Pam's face brightened. At least she'd have time to put her make-up on properly now. She wondered briefly whether it was worth going home to change into something a little more eye-catching, but on second thoughts decided that there probably wasn't a lot of point. Gordon Osprey didn't look the susceptible type. He seemed more interested in sales figures than figures of any other sort.

When Pam strolled back into the office later that afternoon she was bearing a glossy black carrier bag from Bowland's one and only designer clothes shop and was beaming from ear to ear. The newsroom was virtually empty, apart from George Gibbs, who was tinkering with the new DIY column he had bludgeoned Scar into running. Everyone else had buggered off home. Even Kate, usually the last to leave, had been and gone, half-appalled that the ghastly Gordon Osprey had shown his face, half-amused when she heard that he'd promptly sacked Scar.

'You look like the cat that's got the cream,' remarked George, taking in Pam's bright eyes and flushed cheeks.

'Meow,' laughed Pam, walking over to George's desk by the window. 'Do you know, George, I think

I'll sit here from now on. It's definitely the best desk in the office, isn't it?'

'Like hell you will,' said George, furious at her nerve. 'I've sat at that desk for nearly twenty years and I'm not moving for anyone.'

'Which is why,' said Pam, plonking her bag down proprietorially on top of George's papers, 'it's my turn now.'

George stared at her in amazement. Pam had never been a pushover, that was true, but she didn't usually go out of her way to pick a fight. Not with him, anyway. What did she think she was playing at?

'Come on, Pam,' he said, his voice sounding weary. 'You'd better tell me what's going on.'

Pam grinned at him. Her pleasure was palpable.

'Are you sure you really want to know?'

''Course I want to know,' grunted George. 'I wouldn't be asking if I didn't, would I?'

Pam's eyes glittered with excitement. She was going to flaming burst if she didn't tell someone soon.

'He's made me the new editor.'

'Who has?'

'He has. Gordon Osprey, I mean.'

'What? You can't be serious.' George could hardly believe what he was hearing. Pam had only been on the paper for five years. How could Gordon Osprey possibly put her in charge? For God's sake, Scar had been bad enough, but at least he'd been malleable. During Scar's absurdly brief tenure, George had only had to drop a few suggestions into his ear and they'd been as good as done. The forthright Pam Newbold was a different kettle of fish altogether.

'Promise you won't tell anyone else till tomorrow?'

'All right,' said George in a surly voice. He was

pretty sure he knew what was coming. The *Bugle* had been overstaffed for years. Everyone knew that. And it had only been a matter of time before Hollingberry Holdings cottoned on.

'There's good news and bad news,' said Pam, although she for one didn't look too bothered by the latter.

'Go on,' said George gruffly.

'The good news is that your job is safe. You'll carry on as chief sub, just as before.'

'Osprey's told me that already,' grunted George. 'What's the bad news?'

'The bad news is that Gordon says the *Bugle* is ridiculously over budget and needs to cut costs. So he's slashing the staff by half. You and I stay, so does Danny and so does Kate.'

'Well, *she* would, wouldn't she?' said George bitterly.

'Yes, of course she would,' said Pam briskly. 'But she earns next to nothing and you've got to hand it to her, she isn't afraid of hard work. She'll earn her keep.'

'I s'pose so,' said George. 'So tell me who's out on their ear.'

'Laurie Laing, Scar – obviously – but they're no great loss, are they? We're better off without them. Oh, and Rob.'

George slumped onto his chair without saying anything. He had never been Rob Bennett's biggest fan, but he wasn't bad at his job. This news would devastate him. He had a young family to look after, for God's sake, and reporters' jobs hardly grew on trees in this neck of the woods.

'Does he know yet?'

'No,' said Pam and her voice went quiet. 'I've got to ring him in a minute.'

'I don't envy you that.'

It wasn't a task that Pam was particularly looking forward to, either. Gordon Osprey had spent no more than fifteen minutes with each of them, running through their roles on the paper, their experience and their current salaries. Rob had clearly got his back up in some way because he was in and out in less than ten minutes. Pam, however, had played her cards cleverly. For once in her life she'd ignored the temptation to flirt and had concentrated on outlining her ideas about how she could improve the paper and spend less.

'Right,' Gordon had pronounced bluntly at the end of her presentation. 'I'm going to put you in charge. I'll pay you a grand more and give you the editor's title but if you haven't sorted the paper out in three months you'll be out of a job too.'

In her heart of hearts Pam was certain that Gordon Osprey's decision to slash the staff in half was the right one. The *Bugle* had been losing money hand over fist for months, and it was obvious that if nothing was done about it soon the entire paper would end up at the knacker's yard. She couldn't wait to get stuck into editing it. She'd be the first to admit that she hadn't exactly pulled her weight over the last few months, but now that she was assuming overall responsibility her head was buzzing with ideas. She intended to inject more features about local characters, less worthy council stuff. More humour and warmth, fewer wordy reports about dog fouling and planning policies. Even though there would only be four editorial staff in future she reckoned that Gordon Osprey had chosen the right team. She and Kate could easily handle all the reporting between them, George, if a little on the lazy side, was a bloody good sub, and Danny would

199

carry on as photographer as before. Pam gritted her teeth and picked up the telephone to break the news to Rob. She was determined to show Gordon Osprey that she could make a go of the *Bugle*. Despite his cool, detached manner she had the distinct feeling that he might well prove to be a very useful ally indeed. And the clandestine way his eyes kept darting down her cleavage hadn't escaped her notice, either. Perhaps he wasn't quite as holier-than-thou as he liked to make out. If she kept her head down and succeeded in turning the *Bugle* around she might even get her teeth into something bigger and better before very long.

Chapter Twenty

'You should watch that Charley Stone, you know,' Pam remarked idly as she flicked through the morning post. She chucked half of it in the already overflowing waste-paper bin and groaned. 'Bloody PRs. I wish they'd get their brains in gear before they send out all this rubbish. What good is a press release about Safe Swimming Week when Bowland hasn't even got a bloody swimming pool?'

Kate glanced up from her desk. Pam was always getting a bee in her bonnet about publicists.

'It's not their fault if they've got the *Bugle* on their database,' she said. 'And you'd be livid if they didn't send us stuff, wouldn't you?'

'Oh, all right, Goody Two Shoes,' grinned Pam. 'Have you finished the amateur dramatics review yet? And without being too scathing about it?'

'Yep,' said Kate, pressing a button on her keyboard to send her copy over to Pam. 'Their performance of *The Wizard of Oz* was absolutely excruciating but I've managed to restrain myself from being too rude, I promise. Anyway, what did you mean about watching Charley?'

Pam stared at Kate. There was definitely something different about her. Something she couldn't quite put her finger on. Her usually glowing skin looked pallid and dull and this morning she'd dragged her hair back into a particularly unflattering plait. Kate wouldn't normally be seen dead looking like that.

It was two months since Pam had taken charge of the *Bugle*, and, even if she said it herself, things were going pretty well. The paper looked cleaner and more professional and while she hadn't been so stupid as to drop all the irritating Women's Institute reports and tedious lists of school exam results, it actually had some decent stories inside for a change. The circulation figures hadn't exactly shot up – it would take a bomb dropping on Bowland to cause that – but they'd put on five hundred or so and the new managing director of Leadington was pleased with her. Gordon Osprey hadn't commented at all but Pam wasn't too bothered. She was pretty sure that he'd come out of the woodwork, given time.

No, the hardest thing about Pam's new role had been having to deal with Rob Bennett. The man had been utterly unable to accept that he'd lost his job and for the first couple of weeks after his sacking had turned up for work each morning as if absolutely bugger all had happened. Despite Pam's entreaties to him to get his act together and start hunting for something else he'd insisted on making the police calls and had even turned in a couple of half decent news stories. But she'd written him a glowing reference and three weeks ago, thank God, he'd got himself a job in the council press office. Now, despite all the trauma, he seemed happier than he had been for years. He was on a good pension scheme, was never asked to work nights and since he no longer considered Pam his arch-rival they had started to get on much better. The bloody cheek of it, reflected Pam wryly, was that he'd even put a quiet word in her ear that if she ever fancied a move, *he* might be able to wangle *her* a job at the council.

So what was the matter with Kate? She'd been on the paper for more than eight months now and was rapidly turning into a reasonable reporter. She had a good eye for detail, could turn a story around pretty fast and was, on the whole, fair and accurate. There'd been a minor spot of bother when she'd written a story about a brand new keep-fit group for fatties called 'Big, Beautiful and Thick'. George, who subbed all the copy, hadn't picked up on it for some reason and Pam had been inundated with letters of complaint. 'We're called "Big, Beautiful and *Fit*," not "Big, Beautiful and Thick",' the group leader had shrieked down the telephone at her. There had been threats of litigation and all sorts, but the row had been defused by Kate offering to sit in a pair of stocks at the health club and face a barrage of custard pies being chucked at her. This event had made great front-page pictures for the *Bugle*, of course.

But that had all been weeks ago. Now Kate seemed like a shadow of her former self. Besides looking deathly white, she had huge black rings round her eyes and while she had never been overweight at the best of times, she was alarmingly thin.

'Come on,' persisted Kate. 'What did you mean about Charley?'

Pam stared back at her. She wasn't entirely sure *what* she had meant by her comment. There was just something innately untrustworthy about him. She sensed somehow that Charley wasn't so much interested in Kate for herself as for who her father was. Pam had grown fond of Kate and she hoped against hope that she was wrong.

'Oh, nothing,' muttered Pam dismissively. 'He's just so smooth, isn't he? And I'd hate to see you getting hurt.'

If Kate hadn't been feeling so ghastly, she would have laughed out loud. Was this really Pam Newbold, the greatest man-eater of all time, talking? Now she sounded more like her mum than her boss. Suddenly Kate felt a lump in her throat and tears sprang to her eyes. What on earth was the matter with her? She'd got over her mother a long time ago, she knew she had; it wasn't like her to get all tearful about everything now.

But if she was honest with herself, Kate knew exactly what was wrong. She could hardly bear to contemplate it but deep down she knew what the matter was, all right. It was May now, and – she counted the weeks quickly on her fingers – she had been seeing Charley for just about nine weeks. And now she was bloody pregnant.

Kate was still surprised by the speed with which her relationship with Charley had developed. She hadn't even thought of him in that way at all until the night she'd invited him into the house for a coffee. But he'd looked so sleek and glamorous sitting in Danny's hideous dump of a kitchen and all of a sudden, she wasn't quite sure why, she had ached to touch him. Perhaps it was because she missed the feel of Ben's skin against hers so much, perhaps she simply needed someone to hold her, but one moment they were talking casually about Danny's brother and work and art and the next they were frenziedly ripping each other's clothes off.

And the sex *had* been fantastic, thought Kate dreamily. When they'd both stumbled out of her bed the following morning, she could still feel the imprint of his mouth over her entire body. Charley kept groaning that he could barely walk.

But what had possessed her to be so careless that first time? And why on earth had she come off the Pill after Ben? By the time she met up with Charley again at a Manchester hotel two weeks later she'd made sure she was back on it again, but – little did she know it at the time – it was already too late. The damage was done.

So far Kate had done a total of ten pregnancy tests in the hope that she might be wrong. She smiled grimly as she thought of them all. She must have bought a pregnancy kit in every single chemist's shop in Bowland by now. But if she'd been hoping for a different result, it had been to no avail. Each time the indicator had turned bright blue almost instantly. There was no doubt whatsoever. She was *definitely* pregnant.

She still hadn't told anyone, either. Not even Laura. And God only knew what Charley was going to say. He was good fun to be with, all right, and sensational in bed, but there was no way that he was the type to be contemplating settling down with anyone, let alone her. And he definitely wasn't the love of *her* life. *He wasn't Ben.*

Kate dropped her head into her hands. If only this had been Ben's baby growing inside her she would have felt entirely different. She wouldn't have minded giving up everything, her work, her family, yes *everything*, to live in a hovel with Ben and their baby. And she wouldn't have been nervous about telling him, either. She was certain that he would have been just as excited as she was.

Kate clamped her teeth together tightly to stop herself crying. It was no good thinking about Ben any more. He was out of her life for good. They had no future together now.

It was over two months before Kate managed to break the news to Charley. For weeks she had comforted herself with the excuse that there had been precious little opportunity to tell him anyway. In June he'd taken a three-week holiday in Australia with a mate from work. Well, he'd claimed it was a mate from work and Kate didn't have the heart to cross-question him. Then he'd only been back for a week when the office had sent him to New York to cover for the bureau chief out there who'd been rushed into hospital with a perforated lung. By the time Charley was back in London again it was nearly August and Kate was dreading seeing him.

'You've either found someone else,' teased Charley over the phone one day, 'or you only wanted me for my body and now you've had me you're not interested any more.'

'That's not true,' laughed Kate hollowly. 'You know—'

Suddenly she broke off what she was saying. She was certain she'd just felt the baby move for the first time. It was a quick fluttering movement, a bit like a butterfly, and she'd hardly had time to register it before it was gone again.

'Are you still there, Kate? Or have you nodded off with boredom? I really am losing my touch, aren't I? I'm going to have to do something about this, you know. Remind you of what you've been missing.'

'Don't be silly,' said Kate and her voice was brisk. 'Of course you're not. Losing your touch, I mean.'

'So when am I going to see you then?'

Kate hesitated again. She was getting on for nineteen weeks pregnant now, and even though the large baggy jackets she'd started wearing had covered her bump so far she was well aware that she wasn't going to be able to hide her pregnancy for much longer. Pam had been giving her a lot of funny looks too, especially during those early weeks when she'd kept retching violently and dashing to the loo at every available opportunity. Why hadn't anyone ever told her that it wasn't the food itself that made you feel sick in the first three months of pregnancy, but the smell of it? Even the way the inside of the fridge smelled turned her stomach and she could hardly bear to set foot in Danny's revolting kitchen.

What was she going to do about Charley? He would be aghast at the prospect of fatherhood. He seemed so resolutely single, so set on having a good time. They'd been to bed a handful of times and yet they hardly knew each other at all. They'd barely even discussed what type of music they each liked or their favourite movie, let alone whether either of them ever wanted to have children. And if so, who with. But she *had* to do it. She *had* to summon up the guts to break the news to him. And soon. Very soon.

As things turned out, though, the decision of exactly when she should break the news was taken out of her hands. She was sitting slumped over her keyboard the following Friday morning, trying to ignore the smell of frying cod wafting up from below, when he rang her.

'I've been sent on my dream job,' he bellowed down his mobile. 'The desk has had a tip that Darren Gordon and his new bit of stuff have booked into this amazing country house hotel in the Yorkshire Dales for the weekend. The soccer season starts next week and he should be turning out for a friendly over the weekend but the office reckons he's done a bunk. Do you fancy coming over for the ride? It's not very far from you.'

Kate's heart sank at the prospect. Darren Gordon was an up and coming football star with whom all the tabloids were obsessed. He had corkscrew curls down to his shoulders, a permanent suntan and a predilection for young busty blondes. As a result the press were constantly hot on his heels, chasing him up and down the country in their quest to discover whom he was currently screwing. The word was that he had now turned his attentions to Denise Virtue, the new presenter of a downmarket satellite breakfast show, a girl who was stunning, admittedly, but barely capable of stringing together words of more than two syllables. Kate wasn't a football fan and couldn't have been less interested in Darren Gordon, but she couldn't go on avoiding Charley for the rest of her life. Even if he did a runner the instant she told him, he had a right to know that she was expecting his child.

In the second trimester of her pregnancy Kate was feeling as grim as ever. All the books she'd bought (and hidden away from Pam's beady gaze) insisted that she was bound to be glowing with health and vitality by this stage. What a joke. Kate only just about managed to drag herself out of bed each morning and she always felt as if she needed at least another four hours' sleep. Worse than that, she could still face only the plainest of food, couldn't eat anything at all after six pm and was constantly on the verge of bursting into tears.

'I'd love to,' murmured Kate into the phone, hoping

that she sounded a little more enthusiastic than she actually felt.

When she arrived at the Greengage Hotel soon after eight that night Kate took one look at the lavish decor in reception and the heavy velvet drapes at the windows and her heart sank. She'd spent countless weekends in places like this as a child. HH had always been useless at taking holidays from work but every few months or so, Dodo would reprimand him sharply for not seeing enough of his daughters and cajole him into taking them all away for the weekend. The trips had never been a success, reflected Kate sadly. Although HH had always started off with good intentions of spending 'quality time' with his daughters, he would soon be sniping at their 'appalling' table manners and ordering them to 'sit up straight' when he was talking to them. He rapidly grew bored of their company and retreated to his paperwork, just like he did at home. The girls ended up playing with poor old Dodo as usual. As their aunt was unable to drive in those days they did endless jigsaws, learned to crochet and, if they were lucky and the weather permitted it, embarked on the odd nature ramble. The hotels tended to be so stuffy and old and filled with doddery guests that there were rarely any other children to play with. Worst of all, Kate and Laura had to tiptoe about like mice so as not to disturb any of the other residents.

'Can I help you, dear?'

Startled, Kate whirled around to face a kindly-looking man of about fifty-five. He was wearing an olive green uniform, a comical bellboy cap and a brass badge that said 'Reception'.

'I'm sorry,' she said. 'I was miles away. I'm looking for Mr Stone, Charley Stone.'

'Ah yes,' said the man knowledgeably. 'And you must be Mrs Stone.'

Kate's jaw dropped for a moment. This place must be even more old-fashioned than she'd given it credit for.

'Yes, yes, I am,' she agreed.

'I'm afraid Mr Stone has been unavoidably detained. He left a message for you saying that he would be back at about eleven pm and that if you arrived before his return you were to make yourself comfortable in your room.'

A feeling of relief swept over Kate. She had three hours on her own to collapse on a bed and relax. What utter bliss. Forget the idea of a wild weekend in bed with Charley; she couldn't think of anything more appealing than sleep. Glorious sleep.

It was after midnight by the time Charley crawled back into the hotel. He'd carefully worded his message to Kate to make it sound as though he was out working but in fact he'd been on the piss with Johnnie Groom, the *Clarion* photographer who'd accompanied him up to Yorkshire from London. By early evening Charley had seriously begun to doubt whether the news desk's tip had been a reliable one. The entire hotel staff – right down to the lowliest porter, who in Charley's experience could usually be relied upon to spill the beans if the backhander was sufficiently generous enough – had denied all knowledge of the soccer player. Bob Wrigley, his mate on the sports desk, was sceptical too, insisting that there was absolutely no way Darren Gordon would duck out of his team's pre-season friendly against Manchester United the following day. So when Johnnie suggested a swift pint in the village pub to drown their sorrows Charley had agreed with alacrity. One swift pint had turned into quite a few and they'd rounded off the evening with several games of pool.

Charley turned his key in the lock and stumbled into the bedroom. Bloody hell, he mumbled drunkenly. If he'd been hoping that Kate would be sitting up stark naked in bed with a glass of champagne to welcome him, then he was clearly doomed to disappointment. The place was pitch black. Perhaps she hadn't even bloody bothered to turn up after all. He fumbled for the light switch and the room was instantly bathed in light. Charley smiled. She was there all right, tucked up in the ornate four-poster in the middle of the room, waiting for him. The only trouble was that she looked dead to the world.

For a moment Charley stood there, gazing down at Kate. She was just as pretty as ever, he thought, though on closer examination her face looked a little more gaunt than he remembered. He lifted the heavy woollen blankets and fine cotton sheet that covered her body and smiled ruefully when he saw that she was wearing old-fashioned blue and white striped pyjamas, the sort his dad used to wear. So much for the night of passion he'd been anticipating, he thought, leaning forward to cover her up again. Suddenly his whole body went rigid. He could hardly believe what he was seeing. Lying on her side, the gentle swell of Kate's middle was unmistakable. Her stomach had been as flat as a washboard the last time they had made love. Charley remembered it distinctly. Several times that weekend he had traced his fingers from the top of her head right down to the tips of her toes, and marvelled at the smooth delicacy of her skin. There had been no bump at all then. *Definitely no bump.*

As if sensing Charley's sharp scrutiny, Kate began to stir. She moaned lazily, enjoying the last residues of deep sleep. When she opened her eyes, however, and realised that Charley was standing there looking at her, she sat up with a start.

'Hello,' she said shyly. He looked almost too handsome to be true, she thought with a curious sense of detachment. So ridiculously healthy and tanned and alive, the complete opposite to the way she felt these days.

'We need to talk,' he said tersely, flopping down onto the bed with a thud.

'What? Now?' said Kate.

'Yes, now,' said Charley. He undid the laces of his shoes and threw them across the room so hard that they bounced off the wall.

'Wh . . . what about?' asked Kate nervously. She'd never seen Charley in this sort of mood before. There was something unpredictable about him, menacing even.

Charley glared at her.

'I think you know what about.'

Kate's brain was working overtime, trying frantically to understand why he was being so cold, so distant. This wasn't the way she had planned to break the news to him at all.

'Come on. Tell me,' he ordered.

Charley leaned forward and placed his hands under her chin. He stared into her eyes so long and hard that Kate, unused to being under the spotlight like this, began to shift uncomfortably. 'If you let go of me, I will,' she said in a quiet voice.

Charley dropped his hands abruptly and took a deep breath, as if willing himself to remain calm.

'I'm pregnant,' whispered Kate. Her voice was now so soft that Charley had to lean forward to catch what she was saying.

'Is it mine?' he said quickly.

Kate's face flinched. She'd known all along that Charley was unlikely to be ecstatic at her news, but his words struck her as callous and cruel.

'Why? Don't you want it to be?' She asked.

Charley flopped back onto the bed. Despite the quantity of alcohol he'd drunk he suddenly felt stone cold sober.

'I . . . I just don't know.'

'Well it is,' said Kate sharply. 'I've been trying to pluck up the courage to tell you for weeks but you were never there. I'm sorry if it's a shock but don't worry, I'm perfectly capable of managing without you. You don't ever have to have anything to do with me again. Or the baby. We don't need you.'

Charley lay staring up at the hotel ceiling. It was a few minutes before he spoke. He was more appalled than he could possibly say. All these years of leaping into girls' beds without a qualm and he'd never been caught out before. He cursed under his breath. What the hell was he going to do?

'You're not telling me you're going to bloody keep it?'

Kate stared at Charley in disbelief.

'I'm nineteen weeks pregnant,' she said coldly. 'Don't you think that I would have done something about it before if I didn't want it?'

Even Charley felt a pang of guilt at this. Kate looked so absurdly young sitting there. It struck him forcibly all of a sudden that she had had to live with the knowledge that she was pregnant for months now. All the time that he had been gadding around the world, having a great time screwing whoever took his fancy, she had been slogging back and forth to the *Bowland Bugle* and wondering what to do for the best.

His tone softened.

'How have you been feeling?' he asked, sitting up again.

'Bloody awful,' said Kate stonily. 'But why should you care about that?'

Overcome with a rare attack of contrition, Charley wrapped his arms around Kate and buried his face in her neck. She tried to pull away but he was too strong for her.

'Because I do care,' he said. 'Because it's our baby and I do care.'

Charley squeezed Kate's hand across the breakfast table. Maybe this would turn out to be the best thing that had ever happened to him, he told himself. Settling down and having children hadn't exactly been at the top of his wish list, but ending up with the daughter of Hubert Hollingberry might well have its advantages. And being with Kate was certainly no hardship. She was pretty and bright and when she was on form she was great company, there was no doubt about that.

'How are you feeling this morning?' he asked, his voice sounding more sympathetic than last night.

Kate smiled at him wanly. In truth she was feeling like death, but that wasn't what Charley wanted to hear right now. Despite his initial horror at her news, he seemed to be making a concerted effort to be supportive this morning. She wouldn't call it tender, loving care exactly, but at least it was a start.

'Pretty good,' she replied, trying hard not to look at

the rashers of fatty bacon and slab of sunshine-yellow congealed egg on Charley's plate.

'I'm glad,' said Charley and squeezed her hand again.

If Kate hadn't been feeling so nauseous she would have burst out laughing. Charley seemed hell-bent on treating her with kid gloves today; she felt more like his ninety-year-old maiden aunt than his girlfriend.

Charley was halfway through a long and involved story about his stay in New York when he froze in mid-sentence. Kate, sitting with her back to the door, immediately turned her head to see who he was staring at with such utter fascination.

There, standing in the doorway to the packed dining room, was a stocky, bronzed man in his mid-twenties with wild blond curls and a scowl on his face. He looked exotic enough in the rarefied confines of the Greengage Hotel, but alongside his companion he almost paled into insignificance. The woman was probably nearer thirty and was dressed in an outfit that even Naomi Campbell herself would have had trouble carrying off. She wore a tiny leopard-skin crop top – it was so tight that her substantial breasts looked in danger of popping out altogether – scarlet knee-length pedal pushers and a pair of patent leather mules with spiky six-inch heels. Her long blonde hair had been scraped right back from her face and was held in place by a large pair of dark glasses. The Greengage Hotel couldn't have seen anything as startling as this apparition in its entire existence, thought Kate with a grin.

'Oh my God,' said Charley, his voice barely audible. 'It's *them*. It's bloody Darren and Denise. They did turn up after all.'

Darren Gordon was clearly having a contretemps of some sort with one of the waiters because he was waving his arms around and gesticulating wildly. The odd 'fucking cunt' and 'we'll see about that, mate' could be heard above the general breakfast clatter but eventually the footballer must have begun to calm down, because he and his girlfriend could be seen following the waiter across the dining room.

'Bloody hell,' mouthed Charley across the table, scarcely able to contain his excitement. 'I don't believe it. Don't look now but they're heading in our direction.'

Charley gave Kate a second-by-second commentary on the pair's progress as they drew closer and closer, eventually coming to a half right next to their own table.

'I'm sorry to disturb you sir,' said the waiter in a thick Yorkshire accent. 'Please accept my profuse apologies but we seem to be overbooked for breakfast this morning. As you have a table for four would you possibly mind sharing your table with Mr and Mrs, er . . .'

'Beckham,' grunted Darren Gordon. A smirk appeared on his face as he mischievously gave the waiter the name of his deadly rival.

'Of course we don't mind,' spluttered Charley, unable to believe his luck. 'We're absolutely delighted that you can join us. Do sit down.'

Darren gave Charley a dubious look and then plonked himself down on one of the red velvet-covered chairs. Denise took things a little more slowly, first placing her patent clutch bag on the starched white linen tablecloth and then lowering herself gingerly onto her seat. Kate couldn't help grinning as she did so. She was sure that if Denise moved too quickly she ran the risk of splitting her trousers.

'So what brings you two here? A romantic weekend in the Dales?' enquired Charley chattily, ramming his fork into the middle of his fried egg.

Kate gulped nervously as the bright yellow yolk burst open. She held her breath and tried to think of something else, anything else. For a moment she thought she was going to get away with it but then suddenly, suddenly her insides couldn't cope any longer. She could feel her stomach churning wildly and the contents welling back up through her throat . . .

'Oh my God,' she shrieked in panic. 'I'm going to be sick.'

Charley could only watch in dismay as Kate collapsed across the table and vomited the entire contents of her stomach all over the tablecloth and down the front of Denise Virtue's leopard-skin crop top. He wasn't entirely sure whether he was going to laugh or cry as the remains of Kate's muesli dripped down the TV girl's cleavage and onto the swirly hotel carpet. In the end he couldn't help chuckling and once his mouth had started to twitch he found that he couldn't stop.

For a few seconds Darren and Denise sat rooted to the spot, paralysed with horror at what had just happened. Then, as if desperate to do something to get rid of the vomit, Darren emptied the milk jug down his girlfriend's front. This was clearly the final straw for Denise. She leapt to her feet in tears and dashed towards the door as fast as her six-inch heels would carry her, closely followed by Darren.

When he realised that he'd just missed what would probably be his only opportunity to get a talk with the most notorious soccer player in the country, Charley instantly stopped chuckling. He suddenly couldn't see the funny side any more.

'Thanks so bloody much,' he hissed at Kate, who sat white-faced with shock at what she'd just done. 'Bang goes my exclusive with the lovebirds. You certainly pick your moments, don't you?'

Chapter Twenty-One

'Come on darling,' bellowed Hugo through the bathroom door. 'We're going to be terribly late if you don't get a move on.'

Laura stared at herself in the mirror. She didn't look *too* bad, she thought, adjusting her wide-brimmed pink straw hat for the umpteenth time so that it sat properly on her head. She wondered what on earth Kate would be wearing today; hiding a six-month pregnancy wasn't going to be easy, and yet she'd refused point-blank to let Laura go shopping with her.

Laura felt a sharp pang of envy each time she thought about Kate's pregnancy. She'd tried so hard not to feel jealous but it was impossible. She kept telling herself that Kate's life had turned out disastrously over the past few months – first the break-up with the man she'd been so crazy about, now the ignominious end to her career and the prospect of having a baby with someone none of them, not even HH, had ever met. Even so, Laura would have given anything to be in her sister's shoes right at this moment. She desperately wanted a child of her own. And now that she'd given up her job and Hugo had become so much more interested in sex there didn't seem to be any reason why she shouldn't have one. Why hadn't it happened so far?

Hugo's interest in sex had soared dramatically the moment he'd laid down the law and ordered Laura to stop work. From a distinct reluctance to touch her at all in the first weeks of their marriage, he had now gone to the opposite extreme. He demanded sex the instant he woke up in the morning and very often when he walked through the door in the evening. Their lovemaking wasn't exactly adventurous – there was rarely any foreplay or tender caresses or words of love from Hugo – but at least he wanted her and for that she was grateful.

On the couple of occasions that Laura had attempted to talk to Hugo about the abrupt transformation in his attitude he had clammed up like an oyster shell and refused to discuss it. She'd soon given up trying to fathom him out and now simply prayed that she got pregnant sooner rather than later. She couldn't wait to have a baby of her own to love, someone on whom she could lavish all the care and attention that she'd missed out on during her own childhood.

Kate's bombshell had come completely out of the blue. Laura hadn't even seen her younger sister since her own wedding in the spring. Kate hadn't bothered to come down to London at all over the summer, and each time Laura had tentatively suggested visiting her up north Kate had managed to put her off with some feeble excuse or other. Laura felt deeply hurt. It was blatantly clear that her sister was so taken up with her exciting new life that she didn't have time for her any longer.

Laura daringly applied a little more fuchsia lipstick

to her pale lips and thought back to Kate's phone call a couple of weeks earlier.

'Are you around on the 13th?' her sister had asked breathlessly, as if she was in a huge hurry.

'Which 13th?'

'The 13th of September, silly,' Kate had retorted. 'It's in two weeks' time. A Thursday.'

'I think so,' said Laura, fully aware that the pages of her diary were almost a complete blank for the rest of the year but feeling too proud to tell her sister how empty her life really was. In truth, now that she'd given up her job and stopped seeing Alexa – Hugo deeply disapproved of Alexa – she had her work cut out to fill her days at all. There was only so much shopping and cooking and cleaning she could do, and she was seriously considering enrolling on an art course.

'Good,' said Kate. 'You'll be able to come to the wedding then.'

'Whose wedding?' said Laura, puzzled. 'I don't know anyone who's getting married.'

'You idiot,' laughed Kate, only she didn't sound as if she found it that funny. 'It's mine. Charley and I are getting married.'

'Charley who? I didn't even know you were seeing anyone.'

Kate sighed as if her sister was a complete imbecile.

'He's called Charley Stone, he's a reporter on the *Evening Clarion*, we've been seeing each other for a few months and we're having a baby at Christmas. OK?'

If Laura hadn't been in such a state of shock she might have taken offence at the coolness of Kate's tone. But as it was, her head was spinning at Kate's announcement. The news of Charley and the wedding was staggering enough, but it paled into insignificance alongside Kate's final statement.

Laura had sat down abruptly, unable to take the news in properly. A baby. Kate was having a baby. Her sister was having a baby with a man none of them had clapped eyes on. Laura did the sums quickly on her fingers. She must be five or six months pregnant already and yet she hadn't even bothered to tell her own sister. Why couldn't her family ever be open with one another?

'H-h-have you told Daddy?' Laura had asked nervously. She could hardly bear to think how he would react to the news. Kate was so young for a start, and the apple of their father's eye. Not only had HH hoped that Kate would one day follow him into the family business but he'd always predicted that Kate would marry someone of note. Certainly not some scummy reporter on one of his own newspapers.

'Laura,' bellowed Hugo again. 'If you don't come right now they'll be on their honeymoon before we get there. *Come on.*'

Laura added a touch more blusher to both cheeks and then hurried into the hall. She stopped briefly and did a childish twirl to show off her ensemble to her husband.

'Darling, you look good enough to . . .'

'What?' asked Laura half-coquettishly.

Hugo didn't bother to answer. He took her arm firmly and led her out of the flat as if she were a small child and he was her father. All the same, she couldn't help feeling pleased. Hugo didn't proffer compliments very often and she'd picked out this pale pink Jasper Conran suit with him in mind. She knew that he hated anything too flashy, or too revealing, but the moment she'd set eyes on this outfit, with its boxy jacket and floaty skirt just above the knee, she'd been confident that it would meet with his approval.

By the time they reached Chelsea Register Office the wedding party had indeed gone inside. Laura couldn't help feeling relieved. She'd much rather face them all once the wedding was over.

Half an hour later the small group of guests assembled awkwardly on the steps of the register office. They were a motley crew, thought Laura with a wry smile. Kate admittedly looked radiant in a short white shift, bare legs and high strappy sandals, but there was no hiding her pregnancy. Her bump was clearly visible now and she was drawing attention to it even more by the way she kept smoothing her dress over it. Standing beside her in a plain dark suit, Charley Stone was making a supreme effort to charm everyone. He'd clearly done his homework because he'd known exactly who they all were without having to be introduced. He'd got Dodo eating out of his hand by raving about the works of Wagner and had even managed to win Hugo over – no mean feat, reflected Laura – by launching into a debate about mergers and acquisitions. He'd charmed Laura herself by kissing her on the hand and complimenting on her outfit. The only person whom Charley had so far steered clear of was HH.

Laura stared hard at her father. He was being far less ebullient and domineering than usual. Where he would usually be at the centre of any gathering, now he seemed to be on the sidelines. He didn't look at all well, either. At her wedding he'd told half the guests how he had decided to cut down on his workload and to play more golf. Judging by his appearance, Laura doubted that he had done either. His complexion was even more florid than before, and, far from losing weight, HH had clearly piled on a few more pounds in recent weeks. She couldn't help feeling a bit sorry for him. Everyone else seemed to be in deep conversation while he looked totally alone. On the spur of the moment she edged over to her father and slipped her arm through his.

'It's a happy day, isn't it,' said Laura, smiling up at him.

HH's expression was grim.

'How do you make that out exactly?'

Laura drew back nervously. Always anxious to avoid confrontations of any kind, she definitely did not want to be treated to a monologue on HH's poor opinion of his new son-in-law and the fact that the man had managed to get his younger daughter pregnant months before the wedding day.

HH took a large white handkerchief out of his waistcoat pocket and mopped his glistening brow.

'Anyway, it should be you having a baby, not her,' he mumbled breathlessly, apropos of nothing.

'Why do you say that?'

'Kate's supposed to be the career girl. You're the one who got married first and gave up your job, God knows why. I thought you'd be the first one to give me a grandchild. But you haven't had any success in that department yet, have you?'

Laura's face went pale. All her life she'd felt a complete failure compared to the rest of them. Kate and HH had always been the high-achieving, successful ones, the ones who were going to set the world on fire. What had she done? Just trundled along in their wake. Now it was perfectly obvious that she couldn't do anything right in her father's eyes. She never had been able to and she never would.

There were hardly any other guests at the wedding. Just Charley's mother Elsie, a tired-looking widow who'd travelled down on the overnight coach from Blackburn, his air-hostess sister Melanie, who had flown in from Miami with a sensational tan and a handsome American toyboy in tow and Charley's best pal, a gossip writer from the *Daily Recorder* called Jake Horner.

Much to Charley and Kate's embarrassment, HH had arranged for a photographer from the *Clarion* to come and do pictures on the steps of the register office. The fact that it had turned out to be Gus Jones made it even worse. The man was well-known for his mischief-making and Charley could predict the laughter back in the office when they pored over Gus's pictures and saw how far gone Kate was.

For once in his life, however, Gus managed to turn up trumps. Realising full well that the picture wouldn't make the paper at all – not if HH had anything to do with it – if Kate looked like a galleon in full sail, he whispered a few timely words of advice in her ear as he expertly arranged the wedding group.

'If you stand on the middle steps, sweetheart, I'll put your father and your aunt behind you and everyone else in front. Just keep holding your flowers in front of you and remember, *smile*. This is supposed to be the happiest day of your life. *Isn't it?*'

When Kate looked back at Gus's pictures in later years she could almost convince herself that she'd been happy that day. She was beaming in every single shot and even Charley looked as though he was head over heels in love with her. The only people who didn't seem quite so enamoured of the whole charade were Laura, who had a pinched, worried expression on her face, and HH, who grimaced menacingly throughout the entire proceedings.

After Gus had finished the pictures he rushed back to the office with his film and the wedding party moved on to the Ritz for the reception. Despite his horror at Kate's marriage, HH hadn't been able to bring himself to deprive her of a celebratory lunch. Laura had had the works so it seemed only fitting that Kate should have the same. But whether this particular marriage would last or not, he somehow felt extremely doubtful.

'. . . And now will you raise your glasses to the bride and groom,' roared Jake Horner with relish. 'To Kate and Charley.'

'Kate and Charley,' repeated the guests and held their champagne glasses aloft.

This was turning out to be a rum do, reflected Jake as he sat down and knocked back his sixth glass of Bollinger. Charley was usually the life and soul of any party but today he looked as if he had had all the stuffing knocked out of him. It was almost as if he knew he was making a huge mistake and just wanted to get the whole thing over with as quickly and as painlessly as possible. Jake had never met Kate before – as far as he knew Charley hadn't bothered to introduce her to any of his pals, in fact he hadn't even invited the rest of them along at all – but she too seemed curiously detached, as if she was on autopilot. Come to think of it, the pair of them had hardly uttered a word to each other all day. They seemed like total strangers, thought Jake, a bit like that couple in Birmingham who'd won a wedding contest run by a radio station and met for the first time seconds before the ceremony itself. How the hell Charley and Kate were going to cope in three months' time when the baby was born didn't even bear thinking about.

Jake and Charley had known each other for more than ten years, since the days when they'd both worked as trainee reporters in Blackburn. Their backgrounds couldn't have been more different. Jake was the son of a GP and had grown up in the leafy suburbs of Princes Risborough. He'd progressed smoothly from public school to university and then won a place on a prestigious newspaper training scheme which had promptly sent him up to the Lancashire mill town in a bid to 'toughen him up'. Charley, on the other hand, was a local lad. His dad had buggered off when he was ten, leaving Charley's careworn mum to bring him and his younger sister up on her own. Charley freely admitted that he had been a handful, cheeking his mum and his teachers and forever bunking off school to go shoplifting with his mates. He'd jacked in school altogether at sixteen and dossed around for two years before realising with a blinding flash that his life was going precisely nowhere and that the only way out was to go to college and get some GCSEs. He'd astonished both himself and everyone else by discovering that he was far brighter than anyone had ever given him credit for, and at twenty he'd started work on the *Hyndburn Gazette* alongside Jake.

The pair of them hadn't had any time for each other at all in the early days, grinned Jake to himself now. Charley had been a rough diamond, ever ready with a cutting remark about Jake's 'snotty southern accent' and 'poncey clothes'. Jake would rather have died than admitted it then, but he'd actually been more than a little afraid of Charley. He had always seemed so worldly wise for a boy so young, so full of cheek and so dead cool. Nothing ever seemed to bother him. Even now Jake vividly remembered the day their old news editor had despatched him to interview a couple whose son had been knocked down and killed in a hit-and-run accident. Charley had approached the whole thing without seeming to turn a hair, filing a story that was both moving and sensitive to the family's grief and rightfully earning himself the splash in that week's paper. When Jake's first death-knock came a few weeks later he'd been shitting himself with nerves. As a consequence he'd uttered something so boorish and inappropriate to the poor woman who'd just lost her husband in a factory accident that he'd immediately got the door slammed in his face. His story, cobbled together from the police and the ambulance service, made precisely one paragraph in the paper.

It was a whole year before Jake and Charley had patched up their differences. One day Jake had lent Charley a fiver and Charley had returned the favour the next by giving Jake a prized list of contacts at Blackburn Rovers. Their friendship didn't exactly blossom overnight but little by little they each began to realise that, as the most junior hacks in an office of old codgers, they could have more fun by uniting rather than fighting. Slowly Charley had had the edges knocked off him and Jake had begun to unbutton a bit. By the time they decided to try their luck in London a couple of years later they'd become firm friends. They found a flat together in East Dulwich (Jake's dad stumped up most of the rent) and both started doing shifts on national papers.

Looking at Charley now, thought Jake, you'd never dream the sort of background he came from. He'd lost his Lancashire accent, developed a taste for expensive designer clothes and had bought a swanky flat in Notting Hill. It was all in complete contrast to the tiny terraced house he'd grown up in. Jake hadn't set foot inside Elsie Stone's house for years but he'd never forgotten how run-down it was. Charley's mum had just about managed to make ends meet by working back-breaking hours as a factory machinist, and Charley always handed over a large cut of his wages, but the house still had an outside toilet and for years Charley's mum had shared a bed with his sister Melanie.

Jake was sure that it was the grinding poverty of Charley's upbringing that had made him so upwardly mobile in his later life. But one thing was for certain. Now that he'd married Hubert Hollingberry's daughter he wouldn't ever have to worry about money again.

Chapter Twenty-Two

Kate lay in bed and stared disconsolately out of the window. The tiny white stars on the Christmas tree in the flat opposite twinkled tastefully at her – anyone who was stylish enough to live in Notting Hill wouldn't be seen dead buying gaudy multicoloured ones. Kate herself hadn't even bothered to get a tree at all this year, convinced that she'd either be in hospital having the baby over Christmas or up to her eyeballs in nappies and Babygros.

It was a week past her due date and Kate couldn't think of anything in the world that she could face doing. Or, for that matter, anyone that she could face seeing. She was so huge now that she hadn't even set eyes on her toes for weeks.

The fact that it was New Year's Eve and she was all alone added salt to the wound. The *Clarion* was only publishing two editions today (rather than the usual four), yet Charley had disappeared off to work as usual at the crack of dawn. He'd promised to be back to celebrate the New Year with her, but by the time it got to ten thirty Kate had given up waiting and gone to bed. She knew beyond any shadow of a doubt that she'd be seeing it in alone.

Now that she knew him a little better Kate had

begun to appreciate that Charley was a party animal at heart. He was like some faded old showgirl who couldn't resist the roar of the crowd and the smell of the greasepaint. He only had to get wind of a knees-up and in a flash he was in the thick of it. No doubt that was what had happened tonight. He'd have joined some of the other reporters for a few beers down at the Antelope, the *Clarion*'s local, as usual. Then someone would have mentioned going on to some party or a club and Charley, being Charley, would have found it impossible to turn down the invitation. That was the usual scenario.

In many ways Kate wasn't *that* bothered. She'd moved into Charley's flat the week after their wedding – Charley had already taken so many holidays this year that the office had turned down his request for more time off, even for his honeymoon. The flat was undeniably stunning, with a pale wooden floor throughout and modern art hung on dead white walls, but it was far too small for two, let alone three. Charley had secretly been hoping that HH might treat them to a spacious new flat as a wedding present, but he'd had to be content with a pair of ornate silver candlesticks instead. When the two of them were both in the flat Kate felt cramped and hemmed in. Charley liked everything to look absolutely perfect; he couldn't bear it if she so much as left a teaspoon lying on the draining board or a shampoo bottle by the sink. And if she left any of her clothes out he heaped them all into the washing basket whether they were dirty or not. So to have the place to herself tonight wasn't exactly a hardship – though she still couldn't help wondering where he was, who he was with and what the hell he thought he was playing at.

A few minutes before midnight Kate changed her mind and decided she couldn't simply ignore New Year altogether. She hadn't slept through it since she was about twelve. She staggered out of bed and grabbed a lone bottle of Moët et Chandon out of Charley's massive American fridge. Surely one small glass of champagne couldn't harm the baby?

Switching on the television, she grimaced at the grinning crowd of B-grade celebrities clamouring to be centre-stage, and uncorked the champagne. The cork burst out of the bottle like a rocket, firing straight into one of Charley's prized halogen lights from the Conran Shop. The bulb shattered, sending tiny shards of glass splintering over the floor. Kate slumped heavily on the immaculate cream sofa in dismay. What on earth was Charley going to say? After a few anxious seconds, however, hysterical laughter set in. Damn Charley and his light, she thought, taking a quick swig from the bottle. She'd barely touched a drop of alcohol since discovering that she was pregnant and the fizz went instantly to her head. She felt strangely dizzy and light-headed, as though her head was completely detached from her body.

Suddenly she stopped in her tracks and clutched her stomach. It was as if a rope was being drawn tightly around her pelvis, held there for a few seconds and then slowly released. Kate put the bottle of champagne down in panic and wondered if she should do anything and if so, what. When after a few minutes nothing more had happened, she relaxed again and stroked her bump reassuringly. Then the pain came again.

Fingers shaking, she grabbed the telephone and punched out the numbers of Charley's mobile.

'The number you have dialled is not available,' spouted the operator in her usual smug voice.

Kate put her head in her hands. Damn Charley, she thought. How could he do this to her? How could he switch his mobile off? Tonight of all nights. He knew the baby was due any day and yet he'd still gone out on the piss with his mates from work. In reality, she knew the answer to her question only too well. Because he was bloody selfish, that was how he could do it.

Clutching onto the side of the sofa in agony by now, Kate tried the *Clarion* news desk. It took ten or so rings before anyone answered.

'Hello. News desk. Can I help you?' said a weary male voice. He'd clearly drawn the short straw tonight.

'Where's Charley Stone?' yelled Kate, her sense of desperation mounting.

'Why? Who wants him?'

'His wife. That's who bloody wants him . . . Oh God.'

Kate dropped the receiver as yet another contraction ripped through her body. She knew from the few ante-natal classes she'd got round to attending (alone, of course; Charley had been far too busy) that she should be timing them, but by this time her brain seemed to have turned into spaghetti. Finally, her sense of urgency mounting, she dialled the number of the one person she knew she could rely on absolutely. The one person who never let her down. Laura.

Once again the telephone rang nine, ten, eleven times, and it suddenly struck Kate that it was bloody New Year's Eve. Of course Laura wouldn't be there. She'd be out enjoying herself at some swanky New Year's Eve party.

'Come on, come on,' she urged, drumming her fingernails on the receiver.

Big Ben had begun to chime on the TV and Kate was just about to hang up when Hugo's voice (sounding astonishingly sober) answered.

'Who is it?' her brother-in-law asked tersely. The New Year's Eve spirit clearly hadn't filtered through to him.

'It's Kate,' moaned Kate. By this time she was squatting on the floor in an effort to alleviate the pain.

'Can't it wait?' said Hugo. 'We've got guests for dinner. I'll get her to ring you in the morning.'

'Get her *now*,' wailed Kate into the receiver. '*NOW*. It can't bloody wait. It can't. Get her *NOW*.'

It seemed like an eternity before Laura came to the phone. In reality it was probably only about twenty seconds.

'Can you hang on a bit longer, darling?' said Laura. Her voice sounded warm and loving and she didn't waste time by asking stupid questions. Like where was Charley when his wife needed him so desperately.

'I . . . I think so.' Just hearing Laura's voice made her feel stronger and infinitely more able to cope.

'Right. I'm on my way now. I'll be with you in fifteen minutes. Try and stay calm and I'll get you to the hospital in no time at all. You and the baby are going to be fine.'

Charley thrust into the girl's body with all his might. God, this felt amazing, he thought. He'd forgotten how amazing it felt. He and Kate hadn't had sex for weeks. She was so vast for a start, so big that even she didn't feel comfortable with the idea of sex. And as for him, he felt a tiny bit guilty about

234

it, but he just didn't fancy her very much at the moment.

'Happy New Year Charley,' said the girl softly as he suddenly came with a massive groan of pleasure. 'You needed that, didn't you?'

Afterwards Charley rolled off her roughly and took the girl in his arms. She was devastatingly pretty, small and dark with a mass of dark brown curls tumbling down her back. She had just started doing shifts on the *Clarion* and all the male reporters had been taking bets on who would be the first to get her into bed. As a newly-wed and with a baby on the way, Charley hadn't figured highly in the stakes; most reporters had been putting their money on Charley's photographer friend Johnnie Groom. Not only was he young, free and single, but most women had only to see his shoulder-length blond hair and shy smile and they were hooked. But as far as Charley was concerned, old habits died hard. He'd got chatting to the girl in the Antelope and when some of the other hacks had moved on to a club it had only seemed natural that they should both go along too.

'You're sensational. What did you say your name was?' he whispered into her ear. To her his words sounded deliciously flirtatious and teasing. In fact they were utterly genuine. Someone, he wasn't entirely sure who now, had introduced them at the pub but for the life of him Charley couldn't remember what the hell she was called.

'Rebecca,' murmured the girl, her face nuzzling into the warmth of his neck.

'Rebecca,' murmured Charley with appreciation. He closed his eyes and drifted off into a delicious post-coital doze.

When he awoke half an hour later, Charley had no idea where on earth he was. He glanced down at the girl in his arms and had to think hard to recall how he'd got there. The room was in darkness but when his eyes grew accustomed to it he could see that it was tiny, with only a single bed, a standard lamp and a makeshift clothes rail overloaded with clothes.

'Is this your place?' he asked suddenly.

'I share it with another girl,' said Rebecca softly. 'Annie Brooks. She's a reporter too. She's just got a six-month contract on the *News*.'

Rebecca propped her chin upon her hand and gazed at him.

'Do you think I stand a chance?' she asked, suddenly more serious than before.

A sense of alarm swept through Charley. For God's sake, surely she knew that this was a one-night stand? The sex had been mind-blowing, there was no doubt about that, but as for anything more, it was impossible. Out of the question. he knew he might not behave like it but he was a married man now, with a kid on the way. The thought of Kate and the baby hadn't crossed his mind all night long but now, in the cold light of dawn, he instantly came to his senses. He felt like a drunk who had stepped out of the pub and been blasted in the face with a bucket of ice-cold water.

'Do you?' persisted Rebecca.

Charley ran his fingers through his hair distractedly. What the hell did he think he was doing? Now he was starting to sober up he distinctly remembered telling Kate that he'd be home to celebrate New Year's Eve. Now look at him. It was nearly twenty-four hours since he'd uttered those words and here he was, lying next to some bird he'd picked up in the pub.

'Do I what?' muttered Charley in a daze. He jumped out of bed and began pulling his clothes on. In his desperation to screw Rebecca he'd scattered them all over the bedroom floor. Bloody hell, even his brand new Hugo Boss jacket.

'Do you think I stand a chance of getting a contract on the *Clarion*?'

'What? Oh, God knows. You'll have to talk to the news desk.'

Charley grabbed his socks and sat down on the end of the bed to put them on.

'Where are we, by the way?' he asked.

'I take it you're off,' said Rebecca coolly.

'Er, yes,' said Charley, slightly embarrassed now he had got all his clothes back on. 'I'm afraid I have to dash. But I can't remember how we got here or where you live.'

'Nice to know I made such an impact on you. And you're in Bayswater, by the way.'

A huge sense of relief washed over Charley. Bayswater. He'd been dreading her breaking the news that he was in Willesden or Ealing or somewhere he'd never heard of, miles away in the back of beyond. But Bayswater. That was just down the road from Notting Hill. He'd be home in twenty minutes if he ran for it.

Charley had never been in such a hurry to get out of a place in his life. He picked up the rest of his stuff like a man possessed and tore out of Rebecca's first-floor flat without a backward glance. It was only when the front door banged loudly behind him that he realised that he hadn't even bothered to say goodbye.

As he walked briskly along the Bayswater Road it began to rain. Charley was so deep in thought that at first he didn't really notice. What a bloody terrible start to the New Year. He and Kate had only been married for three months and despite all his good intentions he'd already screwed someone else. Worse than that, he'd been screwing that someone else when he should have been at home with Kate.

Thinking about it now, Charley still wasn't totally sure how he felt about Kate. What had seemed like a pleasant diversion while he was stuck up north on the Nicky Rawlinson story had somehow turned into something far more serious than he had ever planned. Not that it was such a hardship being with Kate. It wasn't. She was good company and pretty and even though they had never talked about her father in any great detail, the fact that she was Hubert Hollingberry's daughter undoubtedly had its compensations. It was pretty obvious that she and Laura were bound to inherit the business one day; Charley would never have to go back to the poverty he'd known as a child. But despite all that, he seemed unable to shrug off the feeling of intense boredom that had descended on him since the wedding. Kate was hardly the type to cross-question him on what he got up to, but even so he loathed the fact that he was now inextricably linked with someone else. He hated not being able to take off to New York for the weekend on a whim any more, or book a week's skiing with some mates without telling her first. And soon there'd be the baby to think about, too. That would pull the noose even tighter around his neck.

Charley shivered involuntarily as he hurried along Notting Hill Gate, and turned the collar of his jacket up. It was pouring with rain by now and he was soaked to the skin. The street, littered with beer cans and discarded pizza wrappings from the night before, was completely deserted. It looked pretty much like he was feeling, as if it was suffering from the excesses of a hard night's partying. Charley thought of the strong black coffee that he was going to treat himself to when he got back home and his mood brightened. Perhaps Kate had gone to bed early last night. Perhaps she'd been so tired that she hadn't even noticed his absence at all.

Chapter Twenty-Three

Laura peered into the plastic crib parked next to Kate's bed and smiled beatifically. She reached down and wriggled her fingers into the baby's tiny pink fist. Instantly, and gratifyingly, the baby's grasp tightened around them.

'Isn't she gorgeous,' marvelled Laura.

'What? Oh yes. Gorgeous,' agreed Kate wearily.

'Do you want to hold her?'

Kate closed her eyes. She had never felt so tired in her entire life. All she wanted to do was sleep. Sleep for a hundred years.

'She's all right where she is for now, isn't she?' she murmured. 'I think I'll just have a little doze. Just until the midwife comes back.'

Within seconds Kate was sound asleep. Laura hadn't had any rest all night either but she simply couldn't tear her eyes away from the baby. She was a good weight, well over eight pounds, but she seemed so tiny, so vulnerable. How on earth could Kate bear to turn over and go to sleep now? She hadn't even decided on her daughter's name yet, let alone tried feeding her.

Laura glanced across at her sister, cocooned beneath the hospital's crisp white sheets, and then back to her niece. The baby looked so angelic lying there flat on her back, her blue eyes staring up towards the ceiling. Surely Kate wouldn't mind if she picked her up for a quick cuddle? Laura's arms just ached to hold her.

Laura had no idea how long she sat cradling her niece on her lap. She knew that she ought to go and telephone Hugo and tell him that everything was fine but she simply couldn't bring herself to let go of her.

It was nearly eight am now, more than seven hours since she'd got Kate to the hospital. Laura smiled fleetingly. They must have looked a right pair when they'd arrived. Kate's contractions had been getting more and more frequent yet it had been Laura herself who'd been the anxious one, the one fussing about and shaking with nerves. They'd been directed up to the maternity unit on the second floor, and the instant they'd got inside the lift and the doors had slid shut behind them Kate had let out the most almighty scream of pain. The whole hospital must have heard it. For one awful moment Laura had been truly terrified that Kate was going to give birth on the floor of the lift right there and then. Thankfully, the contraction had passed, but they'd been so relieved that when the lift doors opened again on the second floor they'd literally tumbled into the arms of the midwife waiting to greet them.

In the event it had been another two hours before the baby was born. But even so, the cheerful Irish midwife had told Laura, the birth was amazingly quick and straightforward, especially for a first baby.

'Thank your lucky stars, sweetheart,' she'd said, placing Kate's blonde-haired daughter in her arms. 'You could have been going for another twenty-four hours.'

Laura had suggested getting in touch with Charley to break the fantastic news, but each time she attempted to leave Kate's side her sister grabbed hold of her arm and implored her to stay with her. It struck Laura forcibly that their roles had inexplicably reversed once more. It was as if they were little girls in Chelsea again. All those long nights when she'd had to get out of bed to soothe Kate's brow and assure her that everything was going to be all right. But, somewhere along the line, Laura couldn't work out quite how or why it had happened, all that had changed. Kate had somehow metamorphosed into a strong young woman able to cope with everything life threw at her, while she, Laura, had turned into the needy one, the hopeless, inadequate one who was no good at anything.

'But you definitely won't be like that, will you?' whispered Laura softly to the warm bundle in her arms.

'Won't be like what?' murmured Kate.

Laura looked up, startled. Kate had woken up and was lying on her side smiling at the pair of them.

'Oh nothing,' muttered Laura. 'I was talking to myself, that's all.'

Kate stared hard at Laura, trying to work out what was going on in her mind. Laura never gave much away.

'When are you going to have a baby?' she asked suddenly. 'You'd be a brilliant mother, you know. You look so right sitting there with her in your arms.'

Laura's face flushed a vivid shade of red. Flustered, she got to her feet, carried the baby across to her sister and carefully placed her in Kate's arms.

'It's not as simple as that,' said Laura briskly.

'I don't know about that,' said Kate, gazing down at

her daughter in wonderment. She still couldn't quite believe that the baby, *her baby*, was actually here at last. 'I mean, look at me. I got pregnant practically the first time Charley came anywhere near me. If you ask me it was all a bit *too* blooming easy.'

Laura didn't reply and when Kate glanced up again she realised that her sister was crying. Huge fat tears were coursing down her cheeks and in her haste to wipe them away she'd rubbed her eyes so hard that they'd gone all red and puffy.

'Laura,' said Kate softly. 'What's the matter? What's happened?'

Laura rubbed her eyes again. She couldn't bear to talk about it, not even to Kate. Today wasn't the right time anyway, not when Kate's baby was barely a few hours old.

'It's nothing,' she said in a shaky voice. 'I'm just being silly, that's all. Let's talk about something else. When are you going to feed the baby? She must be starving, poor little lamb.'

At that moment one of the midwives bustled in and took charge. Laura relaxed into the background, grateful to escape Kate's all-too searching questions. Perhaps it was something to do with Kate's journalistic training, but her sister possessed the uncanny knack of bringing up subjects that she would rather bury under the carpet. Like babies and why there was no sign of her and Hugo having any. And it wasn't as if they weren't trying. Completely the opposite. They'd never used any kind of contraception at all and, if anything, Hugo's appetite for sex seemed to be on the increase.

Laura sighed heavily and looked down at her lap. She and Hugo had never talked about it – they didn't talk about much of any consequence – but she'd had this awful feeling for a while. A growing sense that as usual she was the one at fault. Dr Barratt had warned her repeatedly over the years that if she didn't sort her diet out once and for all it would have dire consequences one day. She'd see-sawed between binge-eating and near-starvation for so long that her periods had stopped altogether before she met Hugo. Even now they were pretty irregular. Deep down she feared that she'd never manage to conceive.

'Ouch, that's bloody agony,' shrieked Kate. 'I thought this was supposed to be the most natural thing in the world.'

Laura glanced anxiously at Kate. The midwife seemed to be trying to position the baby at her breast, ready for her first feed. But, judging by the look on Kate's face, the whole thing was a little bit more tricky than she'd been expecting.

'Just relax,' soothed the midwife. 'Let her take her time. Fix her on well, with your breast deep in her mouth, and then she'll latch on and start sucking. Keep cuddling her close to you and you'll both be fine.'

Within a few minutes Kate seemed to calm down and, although she still kept protesting that the baby wasn't latched on properly, they both seemed to be getting the hang of things. Kate couldn't take her eyes off her daughter, marvelling at how perfect she was.

'I'll never ever leave you,' she whispered softly. 'Never. Whatever happens.'

Perhaps it was the wonder of holding her own child in her arms, but for the first time in months Kate's thoughts strayed to her own mother. The intense love she felt for her baby, this was what Clare must have felt for both her and Laura when they were born. So how on earth could she have ever abandoned them?

How could she have walked out and never got in touch again? Gazing at her baby, Kate knew that she could never do such a terrible thing. It was utterly unthinkable.

Suddenly the curtain screening Kate's bed from the rest of the ward was swept aside and Charley burst in.

'Why didn't you tell me you were in—' he began and then stopped dead in his tracks.

'Oh my God. You've had the baby. You've had the baby already. And I wasn't even here. Darling I can't bear it. I'm sorry. I never dreamed . . .'

'Ssssh, you'll disturb her if you carry on like that,' said Kate softly. Laura had been expecting her to go ballistic but her sister was completely calm. 'It doesn't matter now. We're both fine. Come on. Come and meet your daughter.'

Laura felt a lump in her throat as Charley edged nervously over to Kate's bedside and stood gazing down at his baby daughter. Her brother-in-law looked absolutely terrible, she thought, as if he hadn't had a wink of sleep all night. Usually so immaculate, today Charley hadn't got round to shaving and his clothes looked as if they'd been screwed up in a ball and chucked on the floor. But then again, despite his bedraggled appearance, nothing could detract from the look of joy all over his face. Laura still had grave suspicions about Charley Stone – a playboy through and through, in her opinion – and his reasons for marrying her sister, but there was no doubting his pride in his new daughter.

'She's so beautiful,' he whispered, reaching out hesitantly to touch her downy head. 'What are we going to call her?'

Kate stared at him. Not only could she smell beer on Charley's breath, but there was something else too, something she couldn't quite work out. The moment passed, however, and she pushed her nipple back inside the baby's mouth. She reckoned that she was beginning to get the hang of this breastfeeding lark.

'She's called Daisy,' said Kate firmly.

'Oh but I thought . . .'

'She's called Daisy,' repeated Kate. 'Daisy Angelica Clare.'

Charley shut his mouth again. They'd only discussed names a couple of times and he'd been keen on Isabella for a girl and Edward for a boy. But, suffused with guilt from last night, he wasn't going to risk sparking off an argument.

'Daisy,' he repeated. 'That's lovely. It really suits her.'

Kate raised her eyebrow slightly. It wasn't like Charley to agree to something quite so readily but she simply didn't have the energy to think about it now.

It was four days before Kate and Daisy were discharged from the hospital. Daisy had developed a touch of jaundice when she was two days old and the midwives wanted to keep an eye on her.

'She looks as if she's just had a wonderful holiday in the Caribbean,' Charley had smiled lovingly. 'Did you have a fantastic time out there, darling?'

Kate was still astonished by the change in Charley's attitude towards her. Since Daisy arrived, he had suddenly turned into an attentive, considerate husband. It wasn't that he'd been awful to her before but he certainly hadn't been like this. Nothing seemed to be too much trouble right now. He walked down to

Marks and Spencer's every day to get sandwiches for her because she couldn't stand the hospital food, he bought her two stunning new Janet Reger nighties and he even seemed positively enthusiastic about changing Daisy's nappy.

'I'd never have thought it in a million years but he's far better at it than I am,' Kate had giggled to Laura. 'Maybe I should go back to work and leave the pair of them to it.'

The only blot on the horizon had been HH's absence from the hospital. Dodo had visited several times, bringing with her old-fashioned bootees and matinée jackets that she'd knitted specially and tickling Daisy under her chubby chin, but for some reason HH had stayed away. If Kate was hurt she'd tried not to show it. In the dead of night, however, during the few hours when the ward was quiet, she'd puzzled over it. The one thing that she'd been sure of all along was that HH would be a completely besotted grandfather. What on earth had she done to offend him?

Now, as Charley drove up Kensington Church Street – very slowly, as if he had a priceless cargo in the back, which of course he had – Kate could scarcely contain her excitement. She'd been away from home for less than a week, but after the confines of the maternity ward the outside world seemed tantalisingly glamorous. The Christmas lights were still up everywhere, a fitting welcome, thought Kate, for Daisy's first venture into the outside world, and the street bustled with life. It wasn't that she'd minded being in hospital – she hadn't, apart from the unspeakable food. There had been midwives on hand to show her how to give Daisy a bath and advise on everything from feeding to sleeping positions, but she'd been longing for some

247

peace and quiet. The woman in the next bed had insisted on having the TV blaring out at all hours and the ward had constantly been packed with visitors.

'Er . . . you might be a bit surprised when you see the flat,' said Charley tentatively as he drew up outside.

Kate smiled at him. She was so desperate to get home that she wouldn't have cared if he'd painted the whole place vermilion with lime green spots.

'Why's that?' she said.

'It's a bit full,' said Charley.

When Charley opened the door into the flat, Kate, following behind with Daisy in her arms, gasped out loud. Charley's, she meant *their*, ultra-stylish flat was completely unrecognisable. The sitting room, once the epitome of urban, minimalist chic, had been utterly transformed. It now resembled a chaotic nursery. Piles of nappies, linen and baby clothes spilled from every conceivable surface, while in the middle of the room stood a huge old-fashioned pram with a navy blue cover.

'I've been doing a bit of shopping while you were in hospital,' said Charley sheepishly.

For a few seconds Kate was so overwhelmed she couldn't think what to say. So far she and Charley had avoided discussing New Year's Eve and what had been so important that he'd completely missed Daisy being born, but all this . . . this *showed* that his heart was in the right place. She'd been so superstitious about the baby that she'd bought virtually nothing at all before the birth, apart from a jaunty red and white striped Babygro that she'd spotted on a stall at Covent Garden and couldn't resist. But all the time she'd been in hospital Charley had been secretly amassing everything Daisy could possibly need. Even more touching, the baby paraphernalia had completely ruined the look of his flat and yet he didn't seem to care a hoot.

'Come here,' said Kate, laying Daisy carefully down in the posh new pram.

'Why?' said Charley.

'Because I want to give you a huge hug, that's why,' said Kate. 'I can't believe that you've done all this for us. It's fantastic.'

Charley wrapped his arms around her tightly.

'I know I've been a bit of a shit in the past,' he mumbled into her neck. 'I know I've got a funny way of showing it sometimes but I just wanted you to know that I do care. I really do.'

Kate swallowed hard to stop herself from weeping. Despite the ignominious start to their relationship, Daisy had been born safe and well and now Charley seemed to have turned over a completely new leaf. At the rate he was going, he was well on his way to becoming the world's proudest father. Perhaps the three of them were going to be all right after all.

Chapter Twenty-Four

Four miles away in Chelsea, HH sat at his study desk and stared gloomily into the sediment lurking at the bottom of his claret. He was on his own, as he increasingly tended to be these days. Kate and Laura had flown the nest now, and even Dodo, with her classical music concerts and her bridge and Fenella, her ridiculous toy poodle, seemed to have built up a new life that no longer included him. Up until a few months ago, Dodo had regularly dropped round two or three times a week to cook him supper and to (frequently) bore the pants off him. But now she seemed too taken up with new friends to bother much with him, and somehow he couldn't help missing her inane chatter.

Despite his melancholy, HH knew that when it came down to it the solitary state that he found himself in was all his own fault. Thinking about it now, he'd been so taken up with the business over the years that he'd neglected those closest to him. And he was still doing it. He hadn't even got round to sending Kate a congratulatory card yet, let alone bothered to visit his new baby granddaughter. He wasn't entirely sure why he hadn't. It wasn't as if he hadn't had the time. His fleeting passion for golf had passed (gone the way of all the other hobbies he'd taken up over the years) and he rarely dropped into his club, with its men-only bars and stuffy rules. In fact he no longer did anything very much apart from going to the office. And even that didn't seem particularly appealing any more. Where he would once have worked fourteen hours on the trot and thought nothing of it, these days he'd increasingly had enough by lunchtime. The will to work – or to do anything else for that matter – seemed to be rapidly deserting him.

At fifty-seven, HH was a disappointed man. So he'd made a huge success of the family business, built it up from a mediocre ragbag of failing papers to the thriving group it was today *and* earned himself a knighthood in the process, but at what cost personally? His emotional life was a complete mess. Not only had his marriage collapsed years ago (in circumstances that he couldn't bear to think about) but – and it pained him to admit this – his daughters were virtual strangers to him. More worrying still as far as he was concerned, neither of them was involved in Hollingberry Holdings. He had once dreamed that in time Kate would learn enough about the business to play a key role in its future. She'd spent several summers working in the office while she was at university, and HH had been pinning his hopes on her. But then what had the headstrong girl gone and done? Only thrown all his wise advice back in his face, run off to join some failing rag up north and got herself bloody pregnant in the process.

HH poured himself another glass of claret. Perhaps, he reflected, *that* was why he hadn't yet been to see Kate and the baby. Simply because he couldn't accept that she had a new life now. She was a wife and mother first and *his* daughter second. All his hopes that he could mould her into the heir apparent of Hollingberry Holdings, the person who would guide the family business into the twenty-first century, had come to bugger all.

The question of who should succeed him as chairman of the company had been troubling HH for the past few months. He had no intention of letting go of the reins for a good few years yet, but, pragmatist that he was, he knew that it was vital to give the matter some thought sooner rather than later. It was about time that he began grooming his successor. The value of the company would start to plummet if he didn't get cracking. The City didn't like companies that appeared to be too dependent on one individual. And a couple of his key financial advisers had been urging him to get the executive hierarchy of Hollingberry Holdings sorted out once and for all.

So what were his options? With Kate and Laura out of the picture (well, Laura had hardly been in it in the first place), that left few possibilities. Gordon Osprey was the obvious choice. He was astute, thorough, had worked for HH for nearly thirty years and knew the business like the back of his hand.

HH frowned as he thought about his number two. There was something about the bloody man that stuck in his throat. It probably always had, but up until recently HH had tried not to think about it. The truth was that Gordon was just a bit *too* smug, a bit *too* pleased with himself and his abilities. Fair enough, he was pretty damn good with figures (he had a flair for creative accounting that had pulled Hollingberry Holdings out of a tight spot on several occasions) and a bloody hard worker. With no one to go home to at night, he was often in the office till well after ten pm. HH couldn't fault him on that score. No, he reflected, the truth was that he simply didn't like the man. He'd rather die than give Gordon Osprey the satisfaction of assuming that everything HH had slaved away for was going to be his one day.

Leaning back in his leather armchair, HH quickly ran through the other internal candidates. One by one, he ruled them out. Some were too doddery and set in their ways; others were simply too inexperienced and cavalier in their approach. Take Tim Jefferson, for instance, Gordon Osprey's slimy sidekick. He wouldn't trust him as far as he could throw him. The other option was to poach someone from the upper echelons of his competitors. But there again, there was no one who caught his imagination.

With a heavy sigh, HH reached across the desk and picked up the silver frame containing Kate's wedding photograph. There they all were, the members of his family, captured faithfully on film by the *Clarion* photographer Gus Jones. HH peered at each of them one by one. Laura, pretty in pink, but with the usual worried expression on her face, Dodo with tears streaming down her cheeks – why *did* his sister always get so emotional? – and the best man looking as if he'd had one too many the night before. And then there was Kate. Kate, who had simply outshone them all. She had looked – HH fumbled for the right word to describe her – radiant. HH felt a lump in his throat. He hadn't been able to show it somehow, but nothing could eclipse his pride in her that day. Overcome by the strength of his feelings, he hurriedly turned his attention to his two new sons-in-law. Hugo Bentley, so serious and sedate, though undoubtedly highly regarded in

City circles, and Charley Stone, the roguish charmer who'd progressed steadily though unspectacularly up the *Clarion* ladder.

As he stared at the colour photograph, taken just three months before, a thought suddenly occurred to HH. He banged his hand on his forehead in frustration. *Of course.* Why the bloody hell hadn't he thought of it before? It was staring him in the face. He'd just hit on the perfect way to secure the future of Hollingberry Holdings once and for all. And what was even more satisfying, it would also put Gordon Osprey's snotty nose seriously out of joint in the process.

'We'll give it ten minutes or so and then if he's not there we'll go and grab some breakfast down the road,' Charley told Johnnie Groom, the snapper who had accompanied him on the early morning job. 'And make sure you stand well back. Let me do all the talking.'

Doing his best to stifle a large yawn, Charley banged the tasteless-looking knocker on the livid pink front door. Trust Darren Gordon to live somewhere like this. With all the loot that the young soccer player had stashed away during his career he could have snapped up a beautiful four-storey Georgian house in a leafy Islington square. And what had the no-mark gone and chosen? This glorified executive home, with iron gates at the end of a short driveway, a couple of Victorian-style street lamps and a swimming pool in the shape of a football. It was vulgar, vulgar, vulgar, as Lord Charteris had once said so memorably of the Duchess of York.

Charley glanced again at the drawn curtains, then at the four pints of gold top standing forlornly on the doorstep, and wished, not for the first time in his life, that he worked on a morning paper rather than an evening one. Take his mate Jake Horner for instance. Jake was perfectly at liberty to wander into the *Daily Recorder* office at around ten-thirty am, a good four hours after Charley and the rest of the *Clarion* reporters started work and a whole hour after the *Clarion*'s first edition had been put to bed. Charley had been on the *Evening Clarion* for six years and everyone assumed that he must have got used to the paper's killer hours by now. But he hadn't. If anything, they had got worse. And now that Daisy was keeping him up half the night with her yelling he usually felt like something that the cat had dragged in.

At the thought of Daisy, however, his face softened. She was four weeks old now, his darling girl with soft blonde down on her head and little chubby cheeks. Charley had never so much as held a baby in his arms before Daisy was born, but now he was completely besotted with her. If he was honest with himself, and *that* was a tall order, he'd never felt this much for anyone in his life.

Nevertheless, despite his devotion, he was still pretty grateful to get out of the house every day and escape to the *Clarion* office. Work seemed surprisingly easy compared to the challenge of tending to the demands of a one-month-old baby. That was what Kate kept telling him as well. She was up at least two or three times every night to feed Daisy and was so attentive to her needs during the day that she often didn't find the time to get dressed, let alone buy anything for supper.

But apart from the utter chaos at home – Daisy's baby equipment was still swamping the flat – Charley felt surprisingly content. He'd even made a resolution to avoid the pub after work so that he could rush home and see 'his two girls'.

No, there was only one fly in the ointment right now. And that was bloody Rebecca Wilson, the young casual he'd been stupid enough to screw on New Year's Eve. In the first couple of weeks after Daisy's birth Charley had been so taken up with the baby that he'd pretty much forgotten about Rebecca's existence. The fling had meant nothing whatsoever to him and he'd wiped it from his memory accordingly. His life was complete now and he had absolutely no intention of repeating the experience with Rebecca.

But Rebecca evidently assumed otherwise. She'd made that much clear by the way she'd sidled up to his desk a couple of weeks after New Year and dropped a light kiss on the back of his neck.

Charley had swung round from his computer screen in shock, hoping that the beady-eyed Jonty Miller, hammering away diligently at his keyboard opposite him, hadn't noticed anything. The last thing he needed right now was a word of this getting back to Kate, or, far worse, to her father.

'What the bloody hell do you think you are playing at?' he had reacted angrily.

But if he'd thought that his hostile reaction might scare her off, he was mistaken.

'I just wanted to remind you what you've been missing,' she said, flicking her dark ponytail over her shoulder and walking off.

Charley had stared at her back view with astonishment. She couldn't be more than twenty-four, about Kate's age in fact, but she was remarkably cool and self-possessed. Most young casuals hardly even dared to utter a word to the staff reporters, yet she exuded confidence from every pore. Whether she was any good at her job was another matter. She must have done a dozen or so shifts so far but she'd had next to nothing in the paper.

'I'd keep an eye on that one if I were you,' Jonty had piped up from his computer terminal. 'She's got danger written all over her pretty little face.'

'Bugger off, Jonty,' Charley had snapped. 'It's none of your business.'

'Suit yourself, pal,' said Jonty and returned to his teenage pregnancy story.

Now, as he stood on Darren Gordon's fancy doorstep, Charley cursed himself yet again for ever being stupid enough to get involved with Rebecca Wilson. He had the uneasy feeling that she might be harder to shake off than he'd previously assumed.

At that moment the bright pink door swung open to reveal Darren Gordon himself in a minuscule pair of scarlet Y-fronts and nothing else. His trademark curls were completely awry and he was rubbing the sleep from his eyes.

'What d'ya want?' he bellowed at Charley. 'It's the only fucking day this week that I haven't got training and I was looking forward to having a lie-in.'

In a trice Charley had pulled himself together. It was no good dwelling on bloody Rebecca and the trouble she might cause now. He had a story to get on with.

'Charley Stone from the *Evening Clarion*,' he said, flashing an out-of-date Metropolitan Police press card at the soccer star. 'We've heard on the grapevine that you and Denise have split up,' he added hurriedly. 'I wondered if you'd like to comment.'

Darren's eyes flashed angrily.

'Did you now?' he said, the menace in his voice all too apparent. 'Here, haven't I seen you somewhere before?'

Charley groaned inwardly. He definitely didn't want a rehash of events at the Greengage Hotel all those months ago, when Kate had vomited her guts all over him and Denise. Neither did he feel in the mood for the footballer playing clever Dicks with him.

'No, I don't think so. I must have a common sort of face or something.'

'Who is it, Darrie?' called a woman's voice from somewhere deep inside the house. 'Hurry up, can't you? I've got something I want to show you.'

'I bet you have,' thought Charley, trying to keep a straight face.

Now Darren shifted awkwardly, clearly uncertain what to do next.

'Yep, me and Denise have split up,' he said furtively.

'Anyone else involved?' enquired Charley, trying to sound as relaxed as possible.

Darren shot a guilty look behind him and then whispered, 'No. No one else involved.'

Once again Charley attempted to stifle a chuckle and asked Darren what had precipitated the break-up with Denise.

'What do you mean by "precipitate?"' asked Darren.

These bloody footballers, thought Charley to himself. They might be earning twenty grand a week with their feet but their brains were always filled with sawdust.

'Why did you finish with Denise?' he said helpfully.

Darren, who was hardly Brain of Britain material,

still looked confused. He was in two minds. If he told Charley Stone to bugger off, the paper would only send another lot down to pester him again tomorrow and he could do without that. At least if he spilled the beans now it would all be out in the open and they might leave him alone for a bit.

'We never saw each other, that was the problem,' grunted the soccer star, finally deciding on the latter option. 'She had to be up at four for breakfast telly and I, I'm not an early riser by nature. Now, if you don't mind . . .'

As Darren stepped aside to close the door, a young girl suddenly appeared from nowhere, naked apart from a tiny white towel that barely covered her bottom.

'Oh,' she giggled. 'I thought you lot had gone.'

Despite his new-found devotion to his wife and daughter, Charley couldn't help gasping with appreciation at the apparition in front of him. The girl was no more than nineteen or twenty but she was an absolute knockout. White-blonde hair down to her waist, smooth, lightly tanned shoulders and legs up to her armpits. She made Denise Virtue look like an ageing drag queen.

'Happy now?' grunted Darren.

'Just tell me your name, age and what you do for a living and I will be,' said Charley smoothly to the girl. He knew he was pushing his luck but this story would be worthless without her name.

Darren glared at the girl, willing her not to speak, but she didn't take a blind bit of notice. She had her own career to think of.

'Ally,' she said in a soft cockney accent. 'Ally Nicholson. I'm a model.'

'That somehow doesn't surprise me in the least,'

smiled Charley, gesticulating wildly behind his back to Johnnie Groom, the photographer. He was pretty sure that neither Darren nor Ally had spotted the snapper skulking in the bushes, and if Johnnie could just capture the pair together right now they could well be in with a chance of getting the front page.

Right on cue, Johnnie stepped forward and snapped Darren and Ally. He moved so fast that neither of them had time to either kick up a fuss or slam the door in the journalists' faces.

'Thanks,' said Charley briskly. 'Now we'll leave you to get on with, er, whatever it was you were busy with before.'

Kate was on the verge of taking huge offence at her father's failure to come and see Daisy when he unexpectedly turned up out of the blue, laden down with toys, baby clothes and an appealing honey-coloured teddy bearing a Harrods label. He apologised so profusely about not visiting his first grandchild earlier that Kate decided that she might just give him another chance. It was only after he'd gone that it struck her how out of character his behaviour had been. The most extraordinary thing of all had been his sudden interest in Charley and his career on the *Clarion*. Whereas he'd barely grunted more than a few words to Charley since their wedding, he now appeared fascinated to hear about the stories he'd been working on recently.

'Didn't you think my father was behaving slightly strangely?'

Charley, cooing at Daisy in her baby chair, looked up in puzzlement.

'I'm not with you, sweetheart.'

'Oh come on, you know how self-obsessed he usually is. He's only ever interested in what's going on at Hollingberry Holdings and all Gordon Osprey's little idiosyncrasies. He's never been your number one fan either and suddenly he's all over you like a bad rash.'

Mulling this over, it struck Charley that she might have a point. HH had spent a couple of minutes at most admiring Daisy and asking Kate how she was. He'd then proceeded to grill him for more than an hour and a half about his career on the *Clarion*, his views on how the paper was doing and his ambitions for the future.

'Maybe he's just realised that I'm not all bad,' said Charley with a chuckle.

'Not *all* bad, I suppose,' agreed Kate.

'But you have got something, you know. Your father did seem a bit keener on me than usual. Not that that would be difficult. *And* he's asked me to have lunch with him at the Savoy Grill next week.'

Chapter Twenty-Five

Kate glanced at her reflection in the mirror. She didn't look *too* gross. Not considering that she'd only just had a baby. Still half a stone overweight, maybe, and a little bit pale (she quickly added more blusher to rectify that), but overall not *too* shaming.

The extra effort she was making with her appearance was all down to Charley's phone call of half an hour earlier. These days she simply picked yesterday's clothes off the bedroom floor, smoothed them out a bit and then shoved them straight back on again. Ironing was a luxury she simply didn't have time for. But judging by what Charley had just told her, that wouldn't be good enough today.

'Sweetheart, can you help me out on something?' he had pleaded in his most appealing voice.

'I expect so.' Bogged down with domestic details these days, Kate immediately assumed he must want her to collect one of his suits from the dry-cleaners. 'What is it?'

'Don't laugh but Joe Harris, the features editor, heard me droning on to Jonty this morning about being exhausted. I was telling him how I've been losing half a night's sleep getting up with Daisy. I'm so tired right now that I'm having to prop my eyelids open with bloody matchsticks to stay awake.'

Kate had felt a wave of irritation waft over her. Talk about rewriting the facts. There was no doubt that Charley was devoted to Daisy but when it came to lack of sleep Charley didn't even know he was born. And it was total crap about him getting up in the night to help with her. He'd changed Daisy's nappy on the odd occasion since leaving hospital and never let her forget it.

'So?' she said.

'So Joe thought it would be a great idea if I wrote a piece on the stresses and strains of being a new father. Everyone always goes on about how hard it is for mums but no one ever talks about the effect having a baby has on the father.'

'That's because it doesn't have any effect at all,' snorted Kate, trying hard not to lose her temper. '*I'm* the one who has to feed her, *I'm* the one who has to cart her around in a baby sling all day because she doesn't like being put down and *I'm* the one who gets up to feed her every three hours during the night. You just carry on as normal.'

'Oh come on, sweetheart, it's not quite like that.'

'Isn't it?' retorted Kate. 'Look. I love looking after Daisy but I'd definitely say that it was more demanding for me than it is for you. And anyway, what has this gem of an idea got to do with me? Can't you just get on with it? You don't usually have to run it by me first.'

'I was on the point of coming to that, sweetheart. They're planning to use it over a double-page spread so they want to do some pictures of the three of us playing happy families. That won't be too difficult, will it? And there's another thing. My piece is going to be the main piece of course, but they're keen to use a few words from you as well.'

For a second Kate panicked. She hadn't written so much as a shopping list in the last four months, not since the day she'd left the *Bowland Bugle*.

'I can't,' she wailed.

'Don't be ridiculous,' said Charley, clearly irritated. 'Of course you can. All you have to do is sit at the keyboard and type out what you tell me every night when I get in. How you've had to feed Daisy virtually all day, how you only managed to get dressed by one o'clock, how you'll go potty if she's sick down her outfit again when you've only just changed it.'

'It sounds like real Nobel Prize-winner stuff,' said Kate dryly.

'So are you going to come into the office and do it or not?'

'Yep,' said Kate. 'I'll come. As it's you.'

Charley hesitated for a second. He wasn't sure whether it would be diplomatic to say anything about Kate's appearance or not. But then again, he didn't want her to turn up at his office looking like a bohemian ragbag.

'And you'll make sure you look your best, won't you? I'd hate people to think that . . .' He broke off, not wanting to offend her.

'You'd hate people to think that you're married to an old dog,' said Kate, finishing off his sentence for him. 'Don't worry. We won't let you down.'

By the time Kate had found the one outfit that not only looked half-decent but also didn't have possets of baby milk regurgitated all over the shoulder it was lunchtime and Daisy was due for a feed. Bugger it, if she didn't leave the flat now she'd never get out at all.

She'd just have to take a cab to the *Clarion* office and feed the baby on the way.

It was only when the pair of them were speeding past Marble Arch that it dawned on Kate that she was wearing the worst possible outfit in which to breastfeed Daisy. She'd chosen a long black jersey dress that skimmed flatteringly over her rounded tummy and yet was low-cut enough to show off her newly developed bosom to perfection. Even Charley had told her how sexy she looked in it and he wasn't exactly lavish with his compliments these days. Over the top she'd thrown an old leather jacket and armfuls of her trademark beads. She'd been pretty pleased with the combination at home but now, as the cab crawled along Park Lane in the familiar February drizzle, she wondered how the hell she was going to manage this. There was no way that she could wait until she arrived at the *Clarion*'s Docklands office and nip into the Ladies; Daisy was already whingeing loudly and refusing to be fobbed off with the rattle that Kate kept waving in front of her nose.

To hell with it, thought Kate, as Daisy's face grew redder and redder and her crying began to reach fever pitch. Praying that the cab driver wasn't looking too closely in his rear-view mirror, she hitched her dress up to her armpits and stuffed Daisy underneath. Instantly Daisy went quiet and began to chomp on her breast with a determination that belied her tender age. Kate made a concerted effort to avoid catching the cab driver's eye, trying to look as if sitting in the back of a cab with her dress around her shoulders and her boobs and knickers on full display to the whole of London was the most natural thing in the world.

By the time the taxi finally got to Docklands Kate's

265

own face was bright scarlet. Itching for the journey to end, she detached Daisy from her breast – with a loud squawk of protest from Daisy – and paid the driver without looking at him. No doubt he'd be having a real laugh with his mates at her expense later on but for now (and much to his credit, thought Kate), he didn't comment on her attire or lack of it.

Kate had been hoping that she'd at least have time to brush her hair and touch up her make-up when she arrived. But as she strolled into the *Clarion*'s grand marble entrance hall Charley was pacing up and down waiting for her.

'Where the hell have you been?' he demanded irritably.

'Where do you think I've been?' retorted Kate. 'You can't just get up and go with a four-week-old baby, you know. We both needed clean clothes and then I had to sort out nappies and stuff for Daisy.'

'Hello darling,' cooed Charley to Daisy, although Kate couldn't help noticing that he refrained from taking her in his arms. He probably didn't want to risk her being sick down his immaculate linen suit.

'Anyway, what's the problem?' asked Kate. 'There's no rush, is there?'

'There is, I'm afraid,' said Charley, striding ahead of them so fast that Kate, her arms laden down with Daisy and her packed changing bag, had to run to keep up. 'Joe Harris mentioned the idea at morning conference and the editor liked it so much that he wants it for tomorrow's paper. I've done my piece but they need the pictures and your stuff by three pm at the latest. It's going on an early page.'

Looking back later, Kate had no idea how on earth she managed to write her piece about the trials and tribulations of new motherhood. And if she'd assumed that Charley would be on hand to help out, she was to be sadly mistaken. After Gus Jones had finished doing his pictures, Charley found her an empty desk, gave her a cursory lesson on how to use the *Clarion* computer system and then promptly left her to it, telling her he had loads of urgent phone calls to make. Kate laid Daisy across her lap and stared blankly at the screen. She reckoned that she probably had about twenty minutes before Daisy started bellowing.

In the end Kate managed to churn out about four hundred words of utter drivel. Some nonsense about how in the aftermath of childbirth, her body looked like an overripe peach, her brain had turned to jelly and her hair resembled Cruella de Vil's because she hadn't had time to get her highlights done since the baby was born. Talk about trivial, she muttered shamefacedly to herself. And her piece was going to look even more embarrassing next to Charley's highly polished prose.

'Yep. That's great, Kate,' said Joe Harris, scanning Kate's copy over her shoulder.

Kate stared at him in astonishment.

'You're not just saying that?'

"Course I'm not just saying that,' said Joe. 'We're pretty ruthless round here, you know. We'd spike it if it wasn't up to scratch. And do you know something?'

Joe Harris glanced furtively behind him.

'What?' asked Kate, lifting Daisy upright now so that she could see what was going on.

'Your piece is much funnier than Charley's,' he whispered. '*Much* funnier. It's exactly what we wanted.'

Joe's words sent a warm glow through Kate. Gorgeous

though Daisy undoubtedly was, she still felt a pang of regret at having had to leave the *Bugle* halfway through her indentures. Pam Newbold had been sweet about it – she'd even promised to have Kate back after the baby was born – but in her heart of hearts she'd known that Kate wouldn't ever return. The *Bowland Bugle* wasn't exactly the *Sunday Times*.

As Kate sat in the *Clarion* newsroom cuddling Daisy and enjoying the noisy bustle of reporters scrambling to finish their stories for the last edition of the day, she mulled over the idea of starting work again. Maybe she could do some freelance feature-writing, keep her hand in that way. Suddenly her eyes met those of a pretty, dark-haired girl sitting on the far side of the room and she froze. She'd have known that cool gaze anywhere. It was Rebecca Wilson, the girl from the training course, the girl who'd followed Ben Maguire around like some fluffy lapdog. What the hell was she doing here?

At the other end of the newsroom, pretty much the same thoughts were going through Rebecca's head. As far as she was concerned, Kate Grant had been nothing but a pain in the arse up in Preston. And eighteen months on, Rebecca still couldn't understand what on earth Ben Maguire had ever seen in her. Kate wasn't exactly God's gift – right now she looked a complete shambles – so what was it about her that had cut him up so badly?

Rebecca had assumed that she'd seen the last of Kate when she chucked in the towel and left Lancashire, but now the bloody woman had turned up at the *Clarion*. And with a tiny baby in tow. Rebecca frowned. The baby certainly couldn't be Ben's because she still saw him from time to time and he hadn't mentioned anything about starting up with Kate again. In fact Ben was so snowed under with work these days that he scarcely had time to eat, let alone have sex with anyone. Least of all with her – he'd made it quite plain on numerous occasions that he wasn't interested. Rebecca had been doing shifts for several national papers too, but whereas she'd scarcely had any bylines at all (she'd rarely even been sent out of the office), Ben seemed to be making quite a name for himself. He'd got the splash in the *Daily Recorder* this morning with an exclusive about soccer hooligans. At this rate she reckoned he was well on his way to being offered a six-month contract there, if not a job.

It was funny, thought Rebecca, how few of the twelve journalists on the training scheme had lasted the course. They'd all been contracted to stay on their papers up there for at least two years, learning the vagaries of newspaper law, local government, interview techniques and shorthand. But first Ben had dropped out. Then Rebecca had got fed up with living in the frozen north and left. And now it turned out that Kate had followed suit too.

Irritated with herself for wasting time thinking about Kate, Rebecca turned her back ostentatiously and picked up the battered-looking telephone on her desk. She hadn't been given a story to work on all day and she didn't have a clue who she was going to ring, but it was crucial to give the impression that she was fiendishly busy.

Chapter Twenty-Six

'. . . And we are delighted to welcome Ben Maguire, the *Daily Recorder*'s star reporter, to the studio today.'

Pete Fleet, host of the morning chat show on Highwave Radio, nodded cheerily towards Ben as he ran through his introduction.

'Now, Ben, perhaps you could tell us how you managed to infiltrate this gang of football hooligans. They sound a nasty piece of work. I see you've gone and got the crew cut but you don't exactly come across as your average lager lout yourself.'

Ben ran his fingers across his shorn head and laughed dutifully at Pete Fleet's joke. This was the last place on earth he wanted to be right now, trapped in a dingy basement studio with a pair of headphones clamped to his ears and a microphone stuck up his nose. He was a lowly freelance reporter, for God's sake – he hadn't even made it onto the *Recorder*'s staff yet. He should be out covering the news, not being interviewed about himself. He was due at the ITN studios in Gray's Inn Road later and after that half a dozen local radio stations wanted to talk to him.

This whole charade had begun after an ugly pitch invasion at a Premier Division match in East London a couple of weeks earlier. A gang of youths, fuelled by the number of pints they'd downed before the match and frustrated by their team's inability to score by half-time, had started hurling beer bottles at the rival supporters. There hadn't been any trouble on this scale for years and, caught on the hop, the two managers had foolishly sent out a couple of their star players to plead with the louts to see sense and stop before someone got hurt. Not surprisingly, this plan had totally backfired. Darren Gordon, Bermondsey United's star striker, had been hit on the shoulder by flying glass and carted off to hospital on a stretcher, bleeding profusely. He was doing fine now, although there was still grave concern that he might never play soccer at top level again.

The story had been running for two days when Ed Topcliffe, news editor at the *Daily Recorder*, had come up with the bright idea of tracking down the gang responsible and finding out what made them tick. 'Are they soccer fans or young louts fired up by hate?' he'd demanded of Ben, who'd drawn the short straw. 'Have they got jobs? Are they married with kids? Is there a political agenda? I want every cough and spit, every last detail about their lives.'

Now Ben leaned forward in his chair and spoke directly into the microphone.

'The *Daily Recorder* takes the issue of football hooliganism very seriously indeed,' he said in his gravest voice. 'Once we realised that this was a problem that is still prevalent in pockets of London we felt that we should try and find out what motivates young lads to commit acts of such appalling violence at football matches. Soccer is supposed to be our national game. Every weekend thousands of parents take their kids to watch their heroes play like angels and yet this mindless minority are set on spoiling it for the enthusiastic majority.'

Ben paused for breath. He was pretty sure that he sounded like a pompous ass. And it was total crap to say that the *Recorder* was concerned about football hooliganism. The only thing that the *Recorder* was interested in was putting on circulation. The reasons why he had been sent to cover the story rather than anyone else were fiendishly simple.

a) He was the right sex (the hooligans were so bloody sexist that there was no way a woman could ever worm her way in)

b) he was the right age

c) he didn't happen to be tied up on another story at the time.

It was no use explaining on air the finer points of the news desk's shambolic methods of sending reporters out on stories, however, so Ben ploughed manfully on. He clearly struck a chord with listeners because a few minutes later the switchboard had lit up like a beacon. Calls about violence at soccer grounds were coming in so thick and fast that even the producer emerged out of his glass-fronted cubicle behind the studio and asked Ben to stay on and continue the discussion.

'We'll just break for the news on the half-hour and then we'll be right back to star reporter Ben Maguire,' announced Pete Fleet, giving Ben a wink.

Ben rolled his eyes. If anyone happened to be listening to this back in the *Recorder* newsroom they'd be killing themselves laughing.

'I've just got to nip down the corridor for a pee,' whispered Pete Fleet, dropping his headphones – a much swankier set than Ben's – onto the desk. 'Help yourself to a coffee and there's a pile of this morning's papers if you haven't seen them all yet. Oh, and the first edition of the *Clarion* has arrived too.'

Ben riffled through the red tops. The *Recorder* had splashed the follow-up to his hooliganism story – an interview with the stunned parents of the lout who'd been arrested for the attack on Darren Gordon. But all the other papers seemed to be far more interested in the exploits of an ageing pop star who had just left his third wife for his pregnant teenage mistress. Ben sighed heavily; he'd been freelancing for the tabloids for well over a year now, but he knew in his heart of hearts that this wasn't the job for him. It was about time that he got his act together and approached one of the heavy papers, set about doing something a bit more serious. He hadn't given up teaching to spend his days pursuing lager louts with IQs the size of postage stamps and writing rubbish about the love lives of the soap stars.

As he mused on the shortcomings of the *Recorder* and its competitors, Ben's attention was suddenly caught by the centre spread of the *Evening Clarion.*

The spread was dominated by a huge colour picture of a young couple holding their tiny daughter. The baby, in a pink Liberty-print dress, looked adorable, yet splashed across the top was the headline: 'The stresses and strains of new parenthood'. Ben's eyes flicked through the intro. The baby's father had written the text to the left of the picture while the longer piece, to the right of the picture, was by her mum.

This was exactly the soppy sort of women's-page bilge that Ben would normally have bunged straight in the bin. He couldn't abide nonsense like this at the best of times. During his first few weeks at the *Recorder* the (female) features editor had asked him to write a piece entitled 'Meet the New Men,' about men in their late twenties and early thirties who were footloose, fancy-free *and* desperate to settle down and have kids. Ben had refused point-blank. He didn't give a fuck if it ruined his chances at the *Recorder*; he was *not* going to write crap like that.

The piece in today's *Clarion* was in pretty much the same kind of vein. The father was complaining how his wife thrust the baby at him the moment he walked tired and hungry through the door at night, with the words 'it's your turn to look after her now.' The mother told how she'd been transformed from a journalist with a promising career ahead of her into a stay-at-home drudge.

If it had been anyone else in the picture Ben would have groaned out loud and told the couple to get a life. But, alone in the dungeon-like studio, all he could do was sit and gaze at Kate and marvel at the change in her. It was quite plainly her but she looked a completely different woman from the one he'd fallen in love with in Lancashire. It didn't matter how bitter he felt about her now; she had fizzed with warmth and vitality back then. But in this picture she simply looked disappointed, weary and a little overweight, as if she'd just discovered that marriage and motherhood weren't all they'd been cracked up to be.

Once Ben had got over the shock of seeing Kate, he turned his attention to her husband. Who was the man who'd succeeded where he'd failed? He couldn't believe his eyes when he saw the name at the bottom of the piece. He'd never met Charley Stone on a job or anything but he knew him by reputation all right. The other hacks on the *Recorder* were always talking about Charley Stone and his amazing conquests. What the hell was someone like Kate doing with a Lothario like him? She must have changed. She couldn't be the same girl who'd broken his heart.

On the other side of London, Rebecca Wilson was also reading the *Clarion* spread. And, if anything, she was even more stunned by it. She'd been mildly taken aback by Kate's unexpected appearance in the newsroom the day before, admittedly, but she'd never in a million years dreamed that Kate was there because she was married to Charley Stone. She'd known all along that Charley was married but hadn't had a clue who to. Now, as she sat on the bed in her grotty Bayswater flat, she stared at the picture in disbelief. As far as she was concerned, Charley and Kate looked like the most mismatched couple in the world. Charley looked gorgeous and glamorous as usual, while Kate appeared frumpy and dull.

Things weren't going smoothly for Rebecca. John Fry, the *Clarion*'s news editor, had warned all the casual reporters a few days earlier that with the end of the financial year looming, he was going to have to cut costs. He'd put a stop to most non-essential foreign trips already, had slashed reporters' expenses to the bone and now he was going to have to let most of the freelances go. Deep down Rebecca knew that when it came to it she would be first in line for the chop. The other freelances were all far more experienced than her. She wasn't even qualified. She could compose a three-line picture caption and write a decent weather report but she panicked like crazy at the mere whiff of a major story breaking.

The only question was – what was she going to do when the shifts at the *Clarion* dried up? She'd hawked her CV and pitifully thin envelope of cuttings round most of the other papers already and had barely got her foot in the door. Perhaps it was about time she called in a few favours.

Charley was lying full-length in a peppermint-scented bath at home. Crazy as he was about Daisy – she'd even given him her first gummy smile this morning – it felt wonderful to have the place to himself for a change. Kate, her confidence boosted by Joe Harris's complimentary remarks about her piece, had taken the baby round to see Dodo and was then planning to have lunch with Laura at the Oyster Bar.

Charley chucked Daisy's yellow plastic duck out of the bath. He wasn't entirely sure how he felt about Joe's enthusiastic response to Kate's writing. The features editor hadn't uttered a word about his own contribution; he'd just droned on and on about how amusing Kate's had been and how he'd love her to do more. Bloody hell. If Charley didn't watch his step it would be *him* sitting at home childminding Daisy and *Kate* working all hours at the *Clarion*.

This was why lunch with HH was going to be vitally important. A good performance today could stand him in good stead for the future.

At thirty-one, Charley knew that he was a decent reporter. He was equally well aware that he was never going to be a great one. He'd never make a James Cameron or a John Pilger. He didn't have the right temperament, for a start. And most stories bored him rigid these days. Once upon a time he might have got excited about the prospect of covering Darren Gordon's love life or the latest drugs raid; now he could barely stifle a yawn when the news desk doled the stories out. The same stories came round with such monotonous regularity too. Soon it would be spring and with it all the usual set pieces. The Chelsea Flower Show (*Clarion* angle – which celeb has had a rose named after them?), Henley (*Clarion* angle – will short skirts be allowed in this year?), Ascot (*Clarion* angle – find the guest with the largest, craziest hat), Wimbledon (*Clarion* angle – should female players be allowed to stuff balls up their knickers?)

No, Charley knew that it was about time he changed tack, began building for the future. He certainly didn't want to be sitting in the newsroom at the age of sixty-two, like Jonty Miller. He had his sights set on greater things.

And if one man held the key to Charley's ambitions it was undoubtedly HH. Charley was fed up running around the country for the princely sum of £45,000 a year. What was the point of being married to Kate after all if he couldn't pull a few strings and wangle himself a better job? If he could just convince his father-in-law that he was much more than a jobbing news reporter he'd be set up for life.

Two hours later Charley followed HH dutifully into the Savoy Grill. He couldn't help noticing how HH, who was looking even more portly and out of breath than he had the previous week, nodded discreetly to a couple of government ministers lunching with a well-known newspaper editor.

It wasn't until they were seated at HH's usual table in the corner of the restaurant, however, that HH got down to business.

'I've got a proposition to make to you,' he said. He peered at Charley over the top of his menu.

Charley's brain ran riot. HH had cross-questioned

him last week about the changes he would make at the *Clarion* if he were in charge. Surely HH wasn't going to offer him the editorship?

'Er, what's that, sir?' said Charley, doing his utmost to sound as deferential as possible.

'I won't pretend that you were exactly the son-in-law that I had in mind for Kate. And I must admit that I had hoped that she would wait until she was a little bit older before she settled down and had a child. But it's done now and so we must make the best of it. You're happy together, I take it?'

'Blissfully,' said Charley. He succeeded in putting the minor disagreement he'd had with Kate earlier that morning out of his head.

'Good,' said HH approvingly. 'Now, what was I saying?'

'Something about a proposition you wanted to make?' prompted Charley.

'Quite,' said HH. 'Now. I'm sure you are aware that Hollingberry Holdings is a family business. I hold forty per cent of the shares – they'll go to Kate and Laura when I'm gone – but the rest are owned by Gordon Osprey and a few others, mainly institutions.'

'Er, yes,' said Charley. In fact this was all news to him. Kate had never said a word to him about inheriting shares in the company one day. She always abruptly changed the subject when he tried to talk to her about Hollingberry Holdings.

'At the moment I am trying my damnedest to secure the company's future. I once hoped that Kate might be up to the job but I can see now that I was wrong. She used to adore talking about the business when she was younger but she's much too taken up with you and the baby at the moment to get involved now. So, after a lot of thought, I've decided that I should like you, as her husband, to get more involved. Put reporting to one side, I mean, and move across to the management side.'

It took all Charley's strength of will to stop himself leaping to his feet in the middle of the Savoy Grill and punching the air in triumph. This was the break that he'd been praying for.

'I won't let you down, sir,' he said. He hoped that he sounded suitably humble.

'Good,' said HH. 'Now, what I am proposing is this. I want you to spend at least six months in each of our key departments. And I'm not going to throw you in at the deep end straight away. You need to learn the business and I need to see what you are made of. The first job I'd like you to take on is that of deputy managing director at the *Clarion*. I'm sure that you are more than capable of that.'

Charley's face fell. Talk about the lowest of the low. At least being a reporter meant that he managed to escape the confines of the office from time to time. He could just envisage what his new role would entail – sorting out car-park passes and checking that reporters' expenses weren't too fanciful. He couldn't cope with the excitement of it all.

'Thank you sir,' said Charley glumly. 'I'll make sure that I do a fantastic job.'

Chapter Twenty-Seven

Laura lay flat on her back on the narrow NHS bed and stared up at the baby-shaped crack in the ceiling. She'd tried so hard to be positive over the last few months, tried so hard not to become consumed with jealousy when Daisy was born. But where had all this effort got her? It had got her to precisely here. To this tiny, airless cubbyhole of a room just off the maternity unit, the same one, ironically, where Daisy had emerged into the world two months ago. And it was here that a chinless young doctor straight out of medical school had just informed her that it looked extremely unlikely that she'd ever have children.

A sob rose in Laura's throat again when she remembered the expression on his face as he'd broken the news to her. She'd never forget it. He'd looked like a frightened rabbit. She'd half expected him to make a bolt for it; it was quite clear that nothing he'd ever been taught in his student days had prepared him for distress on this scale.

'Is there anyone that we can ring for you?' he had asked gently.

Unable to speak and with tears still streaming down her face, Laura had hugged her knees to her chin and shaken her head vehemently. She didn't want anyone at all. No one. Not Kate. Not Dodo. And certainly not Hugo. Not when she'd failed him so badly. In the back of her mind she'd always known that he wanted children some day. He'd been dropping the words 'when we have a baby' into his conversation for quite a while, as if it were all a foregone conclusion. As far as he was concerned, the two of them would simply decide *when* they wanted a baby and hey presto, that was what would happen. Just like dialling up a pizza.

Laura covered her face with her hands. How come she had made such a mess of her life? How come she loathed herself so much that she'd spent so much time sitting alone stuffing her face with food and then throwing it all back up again? All those years when friends at school had been tiptoeing along the corridor for an illicit drink and a fag and she'd been tiptoeing along the corridor to vomit the contents of her stomach down the loo. At her worst she'd felt so inadequate and worthless that she'd consumed laxatives by the packet and even starved herself for long periods, but apart from Alexa and Dr Barratt no one knew the true scale of her problem. Sometimes she'd get up in the mornings and discover that she weighed pounds less than she had the night before.

She was convinced beyond any shadow of a doubt that her eating disorder and infrequent periods were the real reasons for her inability to conceive. The doctor had suggested that there could be other factors, like the fibroids in the cavity of her womb and the fact that one of her Fallopian tubes was damaged, but Laura didn't believe a word of this.

It was two hours before she'd stopped sobbing and the nurses decided she was strong enough to drive home. On her way back to Battersea, she took a detour past the supermarket to collect bread and milk for Hugo's breakfast the following day. Pushing the trolley half-heartedly up and down the aisles, she felt as if she was in a trance. For some reason her body seemed to be operating quite separately from her head. Her head was instructing her to pick the usual things off the shelves, fruit, vegetables, wholemeal bread, fish, chicken, all the healthy stuff that Hugo always insisted upon. But when she glanced into the trolley at the checkout, it was inexplicably filled to overflowing with the complete opposite – chocolate biscuits, ice cream, profiteroles, pizzas, three loaves of white processed bread, a bumper packet of Mars bars.

Laura paid the bill as if she was on autopilot, loaded the shopping into the car and drove home. It was after six pm by the time she staggered into the flat, but she reckoned that there was just about time to do the thing she craved most in the world. Plonking the groaning carrier bags on the kitchen table, she set about cramming as much food as she could into her mouth as fast as possible. She was so intent on stuffing everything in that she barely tasted any of it. It was only when she was replete that she finally sat down, exhausted and bloated, on one of the kitchen stools. She had no idea how long she sat there, but when she consulted her watch again it was seven thirty. Immediately she panicked. Hugo would be back at any moment, and everything was bad enough already without the unbearable shame of his finding out about this hateful secret too. Leaving the remains of her impromptu feast on the table, she rushed into the bathroom, rammed her fingers down her throat and set about bringing it all back up again as swiftly as she could before Hugo walked in.

She was so absorbed in her gruesome task that she didn't hear the front door slam and Hugo call out for her.

'Darling, I'm back,' he shouted. He hadn't told Laura in advance but he'd had lunch with HH at the Savoy Grill and he was feeling on top of the world. Not only had HH complimented him on how well he was doing at the merchant bank, but he had also asked him to step in and handle a couple of potential acquisitions on behalf of Hollingberry Holdings. And about bloody time too, Hugo had thought, though he couldn't help feeling pleased all the same.

Puzzled by Laura's silence – she usually came dashing to greet him the instant his key turned in the lock – Hugo peeped first into the drawing room and then into the kitchen. When he saw the chaos there – the biscuit wrappings, the empty family-sized tub of ice cream dripping all over the floor, the remains of a large white loaf – he was at a complete loss to understand what was going on. Laura hadn't mentioned anything about having anyone round.

At the sound of groaning from the bathroom he instantly assumed the worst. Laura sounded in total agony, as if she was dying or something.

As Hugo peered tentatively round the door he saw Laura on her knees with her head bent over the lavatory bowl. When it dawned on him that she was only being sick, he sighed with relief.

'Darling,' he said and his voice sounded infinitely gentle. 'Are you ill or something?'

At the sight of him Laura's face went even paler than before. She couldn't bear the humiliation of him finding her like this. He'd hate her for ever if he found out the truth.

'What is it? Is it something you've eaten?'

Laura smiled wanly.

'What? Oh yes. It must have been that sole I cooked for supper last night. I, I, don't think it agreed with me.'

Hugo's face went ashen. If the sole had had this effect on Laura then the chances were that he would be next in line. And he couldn't possibly afford to be ill now. He had a crucial meeting tomorrow.

'Are *you* all right, Hugo?' said Laura, staggering weakly to her knees like a newborn foal.

'Er, I'm not sure,' said Hugo. 'Now you mention it, I don't feel exactly . . .'

'Why don't you go and sit in the drawing room with the paper and I'll bring you a cup of tea,' suggested Laura, half-hoping that Hugo would insist that she should be the one to go and sit down and not him.

Hugo stared at her.

'Do you know what? That's not a bad idea at all. I've been on the go all day. And you're all right now, aren't you darling?'

Laura nodded at him.

'Yes, Hugo. I'm perfectly all right now.'

When she got up the following day Laura was in a far more positive frame of mind. She had finally resolved to do something she should have done years ago. She was going to go and talk to Dodo about the past. She'd always yearned to talk to someone about Clare and the reasons for her walking out, but it was a subject that she'd never dared to bring up with HH. Her father had avoided mentioning Clare's name for so long now that it had become a habit with all of them. But in the dead of night, as she'd lain in bed beside Hugo, listening to his snuffling and snoring and reflecting on all her hang-ups and neuroses, Laura had suddenly come to the conclusion that half her problems probably dated back to the day her mother had walked out.

Laura couldn't bring herself to talk to her father, she absolutely couldn't. But for the first time in her adult life it had suddenly dawned on her that Dodo must know far more about her parents' marriage than she'd ever let on. In the months before Clare left, Dodo had frequently been round at the house to take her and Kate to the park or whisk them upstairs for a quick game of snakes and ladders. Looking back now, Laura wondered whether her parents had used Dodo as a decoy – someone who could keep her and Kate occupied while HH and Clare were trying to sort out their troubled marriage. At the thought of her mother, Laura gulped back the tears again. Eighteen years on, she could barely remember what Clare even looked like. The only picture she possessed of her was a tiny, grainy snapshot of Clare squinting into the sun in the garden at Chelsea. The black and white photograph had been taken from so far away that all Laura could see was that her mother's hair had been fair, like hers and Kate's, and that she was small and slight. Apart from that, her mother was a complete stranger to her. For all Laura knew, she could have walked past Clare in the street every day for the last year and been none the wiser.

Dodo's face turned ashen at Laura's request. True, it was a simple enough demand, but after all this time it still came as a huge shock. Clare's name hadn't been uttered by any of them for so long now that for long periods she succeeded in forgetting about her existence entirely.

'What's brought all this on, darling?' asked Dodo gently. She'd known from the instant she'd opened the door and seen Laura's pale, tear-stained face that something was very wrong. She'd seen it coming, in a way. Laura hadn't been right for years. There had been a brief period of happiness around the time she and Hugo got married – the melancholy that engulfed her had seemed to lift momentarily – but now Laura appeared more wretched than ever.

'I want you to tell me everything you know about Mummy,' said Laura, her words tumbling out in a nervous rush.

The word 'Mummy' sent a jolt through Dodo. She hadn't heard Laura refer to 'Mummy' since she was about eight or nine, and even then it had been rare. It sounded very odd indeed now, especially coming from a grown woman of twenty-six. It had the effect of making Laura seem more childlike than ever.

Dodo led Laura into her drawing room. As usual, her heart lifted at the view across the park from her fourth-floor flat, and she could tell from Laura's quiet sigh of delight that she appreciated it too. It was spring now and the cherry blossom was just coming into bloom. A gang of skateboarders were doing extraordinary leaps and twirls on one of the paths criss-crossing the park and Laura and Dodo watched them in silence for a few minutes. It was a bit like having their own private theatre box on the world outside.

Dodo was the first to break the spell.

'What sort of things do you want to know?' she murmured.

Laura turned to face Dodo.

'You mean you'll tell me?' she said breathlessly.

Dodo took her elder niece's hand in hers. It felt tiny and fragile, like a small child's.

'Of course I will, darling. I'll tell you anything you want. So long as I can remember, that is. My memory isn't what it used to be.'

Laura's face lit up.

'You've got the best memory in the whole family. I bet you can even remember what I wore for my tenth birthday party . . .'

'. . . Pink dress with white polka dots, puffed sleeves and a very wide sash,' smiled Dodo. 'Or was that the one I made for your ninth?'

The two women laughed together and suddenly Laura felt very glad that she had come. Just being with Dodo made her feel warm and loved and more secure than she'd been for months.

'I just think that if I could make sense of what happened with Mummy, why things got so bad that she walked away from us, it would help me a lot,' began Laura tentatively.

'So you want to know why she went?' said Dodo.

'Yes, I do.'

Dodo looked thoughtful for a moment.

'You do realise that it's really your father that you ought to be having this conversation with, don't you darling?'

'I know,' said Laura awkwardly. 'But you know exactly what he'd say, don't you?'

'Mmmm,' agreed Dodo and her voice sounded thoughtful. 'He'd start off by giving you a lecture about the importance of looking to the future rather than dwelling on the past.'

'Yes. And then he'd ruffle my hair and tell me not to worry my pretty little head about things that happened such a long time ago.'

Not for the first time in her life, Dodo felt completely exasperated with her brother. Hubert was absolutely impossible. He spent as much time ducking and diving in his family life as he did in his business dealings. The only trouble was that when he did it with Laura and Kate it was Dodo who was left to pick up the pieces.

'Is there any particular reason why you want to talk about all this now?' asked Dodo as casually as possible. She scooped Fenella, her little black poodle, off the floor, and began to stroke her.

Laura hesitated for a moment.

'Yes,' she said quietly. 'It's, it's difficult to talk about it but I went to see the gynaecologist yesterday and he told me that I may never be able to have a baby.'

Stunned by this sudden announcement, Dodo immediately shooed a none-too-pleased Fenella off her knee and put her arms around Laura's slim shoulders.

'Darling, I'm so so sorry. What did he say to you?'

Laura bit her lip hard to stop herself from bursting into tears.

'He, he tried to be kind but he just said that there's nothing much that he can do. I never told you this but I've never . . .' Laura gulped and forced herself to continue. 'I've never had regular periods and . . . oh, there are other problems too. He said that it might happen but it would be a miracle if it did. He's going to do some more tests but I could tell that he definitely wouldn't take bets on me ever conceiving.'

Suddenly the strain of the last twenty-four hours all became too much for Laura and she burst into floods of tears.

Dodo plonked a very indignant Fenella back on her lap again and thought hard. It must have been the shock of hearing that she might never have children of her own that had set Laura thinking about Clare. It was at times like this that children, no matter how old they were, desperately needed their mothers. Dodo vividly remembered the way she had felt when Oliver Brown, HH's solicitor and the only man she had ever loved, had jilted her and run off with a plain girl called Irene with legs the shape of milk bottles. The only person Dodo had wanted at that horribly painful moment was her mother. HH, just as oblivious to other people's feelings then as he was now, hadn't even noticed that she was upset. He'd blithely carried on using the services of Oliver's law firm and for many years afterwards Dodo had had to cope with the annual ordeal of greeting Oliver and the ghastly Irene at the Hollingberry Holdings Christmas party. But time had healed the hurt and now Dodo didn't give a damn about seeing them. She grinned to herself. It helped too that Oliver's once lustrous brown hair had turned completely white and that Irene had put on so much weight that she increasingly resembled a beer barrel.

On the spur of the moment, Dodo tucked Fenella under her arm and stood up.

'Come on,' she told Laura.

'What do you mean?' asked Laura, startled by Dodo's sudden firmness.

'You need a good dollop of fresh air. It's the very best thing when you feel low. The two of us are going to have a hearty walk around Battersea Park and on the way I'm going to tell you every single thing I remember about your mother.'

Ten minutes later the pair of them were strolling

companionably along the river, arm in arm. Much to Fenella's intense displeasure, the little poodle had been kept on the lead but every so often she'd sniff the scent of a rabbit or squirrel and tug Dodo along the path in dogged pursuit.

'The first time I met Clare I couldn't believe how pretty she was,' began Dodo. 'She was tiny and blonde. You're so very like her, you know. And when she smiled, her face absolutely lit up, just like yours does.'

'Does it?' asked Laura quietly.

'Yes, it does. You should try and do it more often.'

'Where did they meet?' prompted Laura.

Dodo looked vague.

'Oh, at some student party or other. Your mother was studying art at the Royal College, you know. She was a very promising artist, just like you were, but she gave it all up after she met your father. I'm sure she probably regretted it later but Hubert was always so unfair, so dismissive of her paintings, that I think she lost heart. He's never had any aesthetic sense, has he? Clare did these marvellous abstracts – so detailed, with great swathes of colour – but Hubert was always on at her to explain what they *meant*. That's him all over, isn't it? He can't just enjoy things for what they are.'

'She took one of my paintings with her when she went,' said Laura.

'Did she? I don't remember at all.'

Laura stared across the river. The sun had come out from behind the clouds now and with it the first of the pleasure boats, loaded with sightseers. It was strange, she thought all of a sudden, how HH had treated her mother's painting like her own. She remembered the time she'd told him of her ambition to go to art school. Instead of encouraging her and expressing enthusiasm, her father had completely poured scorn on the idea and urged her to get 'a proper job'.

'It was a picture of our house in Chelsea, with me and Kate peeping out of the two top windows. I did it at school and Mummy stuck it up on the kitchen wall. She rolled it up and stuffed it under her arm when she left.'

Dodo swallowed hard. Here was yet another detail from the past that she had completely forgotten.

'I shouldn't really say this but Hubert and Clare seemed so unsuited right from the start. Hubert was such a bully. I mean I'm very fond of him, you know that, and I'm sure he doesn't mean to be cruel – but he simply can't bear not getting his own way. He's like some huge JCB bulldozing his way through everyone's lives. Clare was sensitive and vulnerable and she simply couldn't stand up to him.'

'So what happened between them?' asked Laura. 'If they were so unsuited why did they ever get married in the first place?'

'I think they were quite happy in the early days,' said Dodo. 'Your mother was an only child. Not only that, but she'd lost her parents in a car crash when she was a teenager and in a way Hubert became like a second father to her. She was only twenty when they got married and she must have felt that it was a chance to create a new family of her own. She was absolutely ecstatic when you were born. And Kate too. I still can't understand quite why she . . . she . . .'

'Abandoned us?' said Laura brusquely.

Dodo rubbed her forehead. The effort of trying to recall the events of the past was making her weary.

'Don't say that,' she said, her voice sounding unexpectedly fierce. 'Clare loved you and Kate with all her heart. And whatever happens in the future, Laura, you must remember one very important thing. She would never have left you without good reason. She just wouldn't.'

'But we're grown-up now,' said Laura. 'Surely it's time she got in touch and told us the truth.'

Chapter Twenty-Eight

Charley couldn't help it. He'd been trying to pretend otherwise for the past few weeks but the truth was that he was bored out of his skull. As he sat in his minuscule office, sifting through the scores of dog-eared garage receipts lying in an untidy heap on his desk, he kept trying to tell himself that tedious as his new job seemed, it was bound to lead to greater things in due course. But he wasn't entirely convinced. For a start he still didn't trust his father-in-law an inch. HH might have hinted that Charley had a promising career in management ahead of him, but it was hard to work out quite what checking the repair bill for Johnnie Groom's latest company car prang had to do with it.

The worst thing of all, reflected Charley, was how isolated he felt. His new office was on the floor above the *Clarion* newsroom but it could have been a hundred miles away. Even Charley had been surprised by how much he missed the atmosphere down below. Up here he was on his own virtually all day. Tim Jefferson popped in every now and again to dump yet more boring paperwork on his desk but apart from that he rarely saw anyone. There was no gossip, no joshing about John Fry, the news editor, and his terrible news judgement, none of the buzz that filled the newsroom when a major story was breaking. And worse than that, all Charley's old pals seemed to be steering well clear of him now that he'd moved up to management. They'd never dream of inviting him to join them for a pint in the Antelope after work these days. It was as if he had the plague or something.

The only person who seemed completely happy with the situation was Kate, largely because Charley was home on the dot of six thirty pm for the first time in their married life. Not only that, but Joe Harris had finally offered her the chance to write a weekly column about new motherhood. She was so desperate to make a good job of it that the moment Charley walked through the door at night Kate handed Daisy over to him and rushed into the bedroom to write.

Charley looked at his Rolex hopefully. His spirits dropped when he saw that it was still only four pm. Bloody hell, another two hours before clocking-off time. At that moment there was a soft knock on the door. Charley's heart jumped with excitement. He didn't care who it was, he was just desperate to see *someone*. As long as it was someone to talk to, Gordon Osprey, Tim Jefferson, the cleaning lady, anyone, he would welcome them in with open arms.

'Come in,' he shouted, trying not to sound too eager.

Slowly the door opened and Rebecca Wilson sidled through the gap. It struck Charley forcibly that if this had been two months ago, he would have instantly told her to bugger off and leave him alone. But right now, he felt so pissed off with everything that he even felt pleased to see her. And there was no denying that she looked pretty good too. He couldn't help contrasting her appearance to Kate's. While Kate spent most of her time slopping around in a horrendous pair of black leggings – he loathed leggings – and a shapeless T-shirt, Rebecca was wearing a short red skirt and low-cut black body that clung in all the right places.

'Rebecca,' he said, just a shade too heartily. 'What exactly can I do for you?'

'I'll have to have a little think about that,' smiled Rebecca. Pleased that he hadn't – as she'd feared – chucked her out, she advanced further into the office and sat down on the chair facing him.

Charley got a satisfying flash of cleavage as she bent forward to pull her chair nearer to his desk.

'Well?' he said, leaning back on his own seat and resting the back of his head on his hands.

'John Fry's just told me he can't offer me more than one or two shifts a week from now on,' said Rebecca despondently.

Deep down, Charley couldn't say that he was at all surprised. If he'd been Rebecca Wilson's careers adviser he would have told her to change tack and go into something like retail management long ago. She simply wasn't cut out for reporting. She couldn't write, for a start – he'd read some of her copy onscreen a while back and it was little short of useless – and her news sense was pretty non-existent too.

'I'm sorry to hear that,' said Charley. 'But I'm afraid that there's nothing much I can do about it from up here.'

'I've been wondering about that,' she said.

Charley was immediately on his guard.

'What do you mean?' he said, just a shade too quickly.

Rebecca picked a stray paper clip off Charley's desk and prised it open with her fingers.

'Oh, nothing much. But you know the way everyone in the newsroom gossips. They've never got a good word to say about anyone. And I'm afraid you're no exception.'

Cut off from the newsroom banter for the past few weeks, Charley's curiosity was aroused.

'What *are* they saying about me?'

Rebecca put the paper clip down again and tucked her hair behind her ears.

'Do you really want to know?' she said coyly.

'I wouldn't ask if I didn't, would I?' grunted Charley.

Rebecca giggled.

'No. I suppose not. Anyway, they're all saying that the only reason that you've been given this flash new job in management is because you're Hubert Hollingberry's son-in-law.'

'That's fairly predictable,' mused Charley, 'although I wouldn't exactly call this job "flash" myself. Just between ourselves, I can honestly say that I've never been so frigging fed up to the back teeth in my entire life. If I have to go through one more of Gus Jones's utterly fictitious expense claims I'll go stark raving bonkers. I thought *I* tried it on when I was a hack, but his are such a joke that he should be writing comedy scripts. He was on a story about a lion that had escaped from a circus a couple of weeks back and he's only gone and put in a claim for a rope to catch the damned thing. A *rope*. I bloody ask you. I suppose if I give him enough of one he might go and bloody hang himself with it.'

'So you wouldn't say no to a commiseration drink then?' said Rebecca.

'We're a right fucking pair, aren't we?' chuckled Charley. 'I'm not sure who should be commiserating with whom.'

He mulled it over for a moment, well aware that he would be completely mad to take Rebecca up on her offer, then jumped to his feet.

'Oh bugger it. Why not? Come on, if you follow me down the back stairs no one will ever know.'

Half an hour later, Charley and Rebecca were already halfway through their second bottle of champagne. Thanks to his elevated new status Charley had finally got his hands on a company credit card the day before and he was keen to christen it.

They were sitting in a wine bar a couple of streets away from the office. Rebecca didn't give a damn about being seen with Charley, but he wasn't quite so rash as to suggest drinking in the Antelope in the middle of the afternoon.

'Tell me a bit more about yourself,' said Charley, filling Rebecca's glass for the unpteenth time.

'What do you want to know?'

'Anything you want to tell me,' said Charley amiably. The champagne was starting to take effect and he felt better already.

'I was born in Oxford, studied History and Politics at Exeter University and then did my newspaper training up in Preston. That's about all there is to tell really.'

'Preston,' repeated Charley thoughtfully. 'My wife was on a local paper up in that neck of the woods too.'

'Yeah, I know,' said Rebecca. 'Well, I didn't before but I do now. After that sickly sweet his-and-hers thing you did the other week.'

Charley rolled his eyes. He couldn't help but agree.

'It *was* pretty stomach-churning, wasn't it? But Joe Harris was over the moon. He's even offered Kate a regular column on the back of it. The first one's going in the paper next week.'

Rebecca seethed inwardly. She felt sick to the back teeth with jealousy. What was it with Kate Grant? Not only must she be absolutely loaded but she always nabbed exactly what Rebecca wanted. First she'd got her claws into Ben Maguire. Then she'd managed to snap up the divine Charley Stone. And now, to cap it all, she'd been given her own column in the *Clarion*. What had she, Rebecca, accomplished in all this time? A few one-night stands, a grotty rented flat in Bayswater and the bloody run-around from the *Clarion* newsroom. Great.

Despite the animosity she felt towards Kate, however, she realised the importance of choosing her words carefully now.

'I suppose she's got a built-in advantage though, hasn't she?' she said casually.

Charley looked up from his glass. His head hurt and he was definitely beginning to feel the worse for wear.

'What do you mean?'

'Well, I know she doesn't use her father's name for work but everybody knows who she is, don't they?'

Charley took his last swig of champagne and considered what Rebecca had just said. After a few seconds' thought, he got to his feet abruptly. It was as if Rebecca's acid words about Kate had suddenly brought him to his senses. What the hell did he think he was doing drinking with a tart like Rebecca? He'd been married for less than a year, had a darling baby daughter and if he kept his nose clean might one day have a lucrative career in management. So he'd had an off day today; that didn't mean he had to take up where he left off with the poisonous Rebecca Wilson.

'You should watch your step, you know,' he said coldly, putting his jacket back on. 'HH didn't have anything whatsoever to do with Kate getting her column. If I were you and I'd just been chucked out of the *Clarion* on my ear I'd be very careful about insinuating things like that. Especially to me, you bloody cow.'

Despite his impromptu drinking session, Charley was still back home by seven that evening. He'd made another desultory attempt to tackle the mountain of paper on his desk, then decided to call it a day, fully expecting to face the usual scene of unmitigated chaos at the flat.

But when he stumbled through the door, prepared to greet a grumpy Kate and colicky baby, he almost did a double take. For the first time in months the flat looked immaculate and calm. Kate was sitting on the sofa, wearing an elegant grey silk trouser suit he'd never seen before and reading a book, while for some reason Daisy was conspicuous by her absence.

'Where the fuck—' began Charley but Kate held a finger to her lips.

'Sssh, she's just gone to sleep,' she whispered.

Hearing this, Charley felt mixed emotions. On the one hand he felt oddly disappointed at not being able to take his baby daughter in his arms and hold her tight; on the other, the thought of having a normal grown-up conversation with Kate without constant squawks from Daisy was more appealing than he would have imagined. This was definitely a first, he reckoned. Kate had kept reassuring him that Daisy would start going to sleep at a more reasonable hour soon, but he'd taken her words with a pinch of salt. Daisy had never been to sleep before midnight in her life so far – he'd been utterly convinced that his daughter was destined to be the It girl of the new millennium, living it up until the early hours and then sleeping in until lunchtime the next day.

'What sort of day have you had?' asked Kate, presenting Charley with a chilled glass of white burgundy.

'Not bad,' said Charley. He took a slurp of his wine, anxious not to let on that he'd already drunk at least a whole bottle of champagne.

Kate poured herself a glass and then came and snuggled up next to him on the sofa.

'What's brought all this on?' said Charley. The most he could usually look forward to these days was a quick peck on the cheek before they both crashed out.

'I've been thinking,' said Kate.

'Sounds dangerous,' said Charley, stroking her hair absent-mindedly. 'What have you been thinking?'

'I've been thinking that we ought to make more of an effort with each other.'

Charley loosened his tie from its stranglehold around his neck and raised his eyebrows quizzically.

'What sort of effort?'

Kate smiled at him and slid her hand underneath his shirt. Worn down by both lack of sleep and the constant demands of breastfeeding, she hadn't felt like making love for months, not since well before Daisy was born. But now, feeling the warmth of his chest against her hand and his breath on her neck, she was suddenly filled with desire.

'This sort of effort,' she murmured and slowly began to undo his trousers.

*　　*　　*

Dodo's hand shook uncontrollably as she read the postcard for the umpteenth time. Her heart was beating just as wildly now as it had when the card had dropped through the letter box six hours earlier. Her first reaction on picking it off the doormat had been to smile appreciatively at the idyllic scene of a row of grey stone cottages overlooking a shallow stream. A typical Lancashire village, it said on the other side. Other than that, there were no clues as to the identity of the place. The words on the back, however, soon wiped the smile from her face and sent a shiver of concern down her spine.

For the rest of the day, Dodo had paced frantically round the flat, totally at a loss as to what to do for the best. Fenella had trotted back and forth at her heels, puzzled as to why she hadn't yet been taken for her daily stroll round the park.

Now Dodo checked the postmark once more. The card had been posted in Bowland, Lancashire, a couple of days before. Considering the heart-to-heart she'd had with Laura the other day, the timing seemed extraordinary. Why on earth had it been sent now? After all these years? And how had the sender known where she lived?

Slowly Dodo reread the oddly familiar italic script once again. She'd scanned the words so often by this time that she was almost able to recite them off by heart.

'Dodo. How are my girls? I miss them more with every passing day. How can I ever make it up to them? C.'

301

Chapter Twenty-Nine

A large gaggle of ducks flocked around Laura's ankles as she sat on the bench by the stream. As they waddled closer and closer, she couldn't prevent a gurgle of laughter escaping from her lips. When their beaks began to nudge at her shins she threw up her hands to show that she didn't have anything remotely edible for them. That didn't work so she clambered hurriedly onto the seat. They didn't exactly *look* hungry, she thought. Far from it; some of them were so fat that they could barely move. And the man in the pub had told her that visitors swarmed to the tiny village of Longshott all through the summer months, so the ducks never went short of a crust or two.

Laura lifted her face up to the May sun, enjoying the warmth on her pale skin. Summer had taken an age to come this year but now it seemed to have arrived with a vengeance. The Lancashire hedgerows were lush and green and clouds of cow parsley filled the village lanes.

Considering that she had never set foot in this corner of England in her life, it was strange how at home Laura felt here. Like Kate, she'd always thought of herself as a Londoner through and through but she knew that she was going to feel bereft when she left this place. After a couple of days in Longshott she felt calmer and more at peace than she had for months. A weekend here had done her more good than Hugo's recent suggestion of a week at a health farm would ever do.

Right from the start Laura had kept telling herself that this trip of hers and Dodo's was probably a complete wild goose chase. Deep down, neither of them had truly expected to find Clare living in the village pictured on the postcard she'd sent so totally out of the blue. But then again, they had agreed that they had to at least *try* and find her. So they'd travelled up to Bowland, where Clare's card had been posted, asked around and discovered that the village in the picture was Longshott.

Still stranded on the bench, Laura sighed heavily. This could be the closest she ever got to finding her mother.

Suddenly her reverie was interrupted by a man shouting at her from the other side of the brook.

'What?' she yelled back, unable to hear anything above the ducks' cacophony.

'I said "are you all right?"'

Laura gaped at the man. She'd never set eyes on him in her life before but he was now rolling his trousers up to his knees and wading across the stream towards her.

'I . . . I'm fine,' began Laura uncertainly. She couldn't help feeling a tiny bit nervous. Dodo had disappeared up to the post office to ask if anyone there knew of Clare and there was no one else around. What did this huge bear of a man, with hair shorn terrifyingly close to his scalp, a stud in his ear and a bright red face, want with her?

When he had climbed out of the stream, his feet dripping wet and covered with bits of algae, he began riffling through the voluminous pockets of his combat trousers. He clearly couldn't find what he wanted in his side pockets but after delving into the ones at the back he gave a grunt of triumph.

'There,' he said, producing a brown paper bag. 'I knew I had some in there somewhere.'

He took out the heel of a white loaf and proceeded to tear it up into tiny pieces. Waving some of it tantalisingly in front of the ducks he then hurled it upstream.

'Good shot,' called Laura as the bread flew through the air in a perfect arc and landed in the water. The ducks, however, were infinitely more interested in the bread than in the man's fine overarm technique and made an instant scramble for it.

The man blushed at the compliment and stuffed the bag back into his pocket.

'They're greedy beggars, the Longshott ducks,' he mumbled shyly in a broad Lancashire accent. 'But it'll give you a chance to climb down now, any road.'

'Thanks,' said Laura, flashing him a beaming smile and jumping down to the ground. 'I thought I was going to be trapped up there for the rest of the day.'

The man stared back at her, clearly uncertain quite what to say.

'What's the temperature like?' asked Laura impetuously.

'You what?'

'The temperature. Of the water. Is it freezing?'

'What? Oh yep. Freezing.'

Laura took off one of her sandals and dipped a toe gingerly into the water. She grimaced. He was right. It was positively icy.

It dawned on Laura all of a sudden that the man standing in front of her with dripping feet was just as shy and awkward as she was. His size and bulk gave him a menacing appearance but he seemed barely capable of saying boo to a goose.

'Do you live round here?' she asked.

'Yep,' he replied. 'In one of them cottages the other side of the bridge.'

Laura glanced at the row of pretty stone houses he was pointing at. They were tiny, with ivy-clad walls, and looked as though they hadn't changed in the last two hundred years. Despite the onset of summer, their owners had obviously lit their fires because smoke was pouring out of every chimney.

'Lucky you,' said Laura.

The man looked at her quizzically. He couldn't help thinking that there was something strangely familiar about her, something he couldn't quite put his finger on. He wondered if she was on the telly, then dismissed that idea. She was well-spoken all right but she seemed too timid for anything showy.

'Where do you live then?' he asked.

'London,' replied Laura.

'You up here on holiday, then?'

'Sort of,' said Laura. She didn't want to go into details, and certainly not to a stranger. She hadn't even told Hugo the real reason for this visit. As far as he was concerned, Laura was simply having a quiet few days away with Dodo.

'Been up here before, have you?'

'No,' said Laura, 'though I can't think why. It's so beautiful. My sister used to work round here and she was mad about it. I always thought the north was all industrial wasteland and dark satanic mills before.'

'You what?' said the man.

'Never mind,' said Laura.

'Where did your sister work?'

'On the local paper. The *Bowland Bugle*. She wasn't here for very long though, just a few months or so. She left to have a baby.'

Suddenly the confused look on the man's face cleared and he gave Laura a disarming grin.

'Of course,' he said, slapping his substantial thigh. 'I should have realised before. I know exactly who you are now.'

'Do you?' said Laura.

'Yep. I knew there was something about you. It's not that you look exactly like her. You're smaller and slighter – and I hope you don't mind me saying this, you're not so sure of yourself, are you? But there's definitely a family resemblance. I'm Steve Scarsdale by the way, but everyone calls me Scar. I used to work at the *Bugle* with Kate.'

Scar offered Laura a large and rather sweaty hand. Laura took it gingerly. She'd come all this way to try and find her mother and yet the only person she'd stumbled on was this bumbling giant who, hard as it was to imagine, was an old colleague of Kate's.

'Laura Bentley,' she said quietly. 'Do you still work for the paper?'

The friendly grin on Scar's face instantly vanished.

'Er no,' he mumbled. 'The powers that be, they, um, sacked me a while back.'

'And what do you do now?' asked Laura.

'Bouncer,' muttered Scar under his breath, as if it pained him to admit it.

'Where?'

'Snazzy Kecks nightclub in Bowland. It's a bit of a hellhole but it's just for now, mind. Just until I can find something more suited to my talents.'

Looking at Scar's discomfiture, Laura couldn't help feeling a bit sorry for him. In many ways he seemed as much an outsider as she was. She was just about to ask him more about Kate's time on the *Bugle*, when Dodo came into view. She had Fenella on the lead but the little dog was straining so far ahead of her that it looked as though Fenella was taking Dodo for a walk rather than the other way round.

'Hello,' she puffed when she reached Laura and Scar. She took out a large white handkerchief and mopped her brow. 'Walking up that hill and back has completely done for me, I'm afraid. I'm not quite as fit as I thought.'

Laura couldn't help giggling. Dodo, with her penchant for cream cakes and knickerbocker glories, was the least fit person she knew.

'Any luck?' asked Laura.

'I'm afraid not, darling. But they suggested asking around in some of the pubs and shops in Bowland.'

'Dodo, this is Scar,' said Laura. 'He rescued me from a flock of marauding ducks and it turns out that he used to work with Kate on the local paper.'

'How lovely to meet you,' said Dodo in her most charming voice. Privately she was wondering what on earth had possessed Laura to get talking to such a lout, but she kept her thoughts to herself. 'But I can't possibly call you Scar. What's your real name?'

'Steve Scarsdale,' mumbled Scar. Under Dodo's steady gaze, he felt like a small boy being cross-examined by his teacher. 'I mean, Steven Scarsdale.'

'That's more like it, Steven,' said Dodo. 'I suppose you must know virtually everyone around here. Have you lived here all your life?'

'Yep,' said Scar. 'Since I was a nipper.'

Dodo looked at Scar disarmingly.

'In that case,' she said, slipping her arm conspiratorially through Laura's, 'perhaps you might be able to help us.'

Sitting in his usual place at the head of the mahogany boardroom table, HH surveyed the far wall and wondered how much longer Gordon Osprey was intending to drone on for. This monthly business review with his deputy had been going on for two hours now and he felt like banging the man's self-satisfied head against the table. So far he'd sat through half an hour of boring minutes from last month's meeting. A ludicrous argument (rejected out of hand by HH on cost grounds alone) about whether they should move the company headquarters from downmarket Docklands back into a swanky City office. And a bad-tempered discussion about whether the performance of the Leadington group was now so dismal that they should ditch it altogether (HH never liked to admit failure, even on a small scale, but finally agreed to consider it). Then, to cap it all, Gordon Osprey had had the nerve to launch into a spiteful tirade about Charley Stone and what the hell HH thought he was doing appointing him as deputy managing director of the *Clarion*.

'I'm told that he was a decent enough reporter when he put his mind to it but a senior executive he certainly is not and never will be,' stormed Gordon, thumping his fist down on the table. 'Tim Jefferson says that he can barely add up and instead of going through all the editorial expenses with a fine-tooth comb, he signs ninety-nine per cent of them without even bothering to read them properly. We've agreed that we've got to cut costs substantially this year, HH, and this sort of thing simply can't go on. You and I both know that. You must send him back to the newsroom. That's where he belongs.'

In his heart of hearts HH was a little inclined to agree with his number two. From what he himself had seen, in his first eight weeks as an executive Charley had proved to be sloppy, inconsistent and yes, downright lazy. As far as he could ascertain, his son-in-law's only real redeeming feature was the ease and speed with which he had managed to get up Gordon Osprey's nose.

'And who is the chairman of this company?' asked HH coldly. He'd been happy enough to let Gordon have his say but he'd definitely gone too far now. It was time to remind him who was in charge.

HH sat up straight and put his elbows on the table to show that he meant business.

'You are,' said Gordon quietly, meeting HH's gaze.

'Yes, and it's a fact that you seem to forget a lot of the time,' said HH. 'I'd be grateful if you remembered it the next time you open your big mouth and start rubbishing members of my family.'

Gordon stared at HH in amazement. HH had been bloody appalled when Kate had announced she was marrying the idle Charley Stone – he'd as good as told him of his horror. What was he playing at now? Gordon had worked with him for long enough to know that as a rule HH couldn't stand smart-arses like Charley Stone, with their Hugo Boss suits, laptop computers and mobile phones. Something was definitely up. After all these years in business with him, Gordon could read HH like a book.

'And while we are on the subject of my family,' continued HH smoothly, 'there's something else that I think I'd better tell you. My other son-in-law, as I am sure even you are aware, is the highly regarded merchant banker Hugo Bentley.'

Gordon Osprey murmured politely. He was tempted to remind HH that he'd been at Hugo's bloody wedding but he realised that it was time for a bit of brown-nosing. He'd already gone as far as was wise on the subject of Charley Stone for one day

'Good,' said HH, clearing his throat noisily. 'And I'm sure you will all be pleased to know that Hugo is going to start giving us the benefit of his considerable expertise. I have asked him to handle a couple of potential acquisitions for Hollingberry Holdings and he has kindly agreed. I'm certain that you will enjoy working with him. Both now and in the future.'

Gordon looked up sharply from the picture of a brick wall he'd been doodling on his copy of the board papers. Why was HH bringing Hugo Bentley in? There was definitely more to this than met the eye. He'd have to collar HH when he was in a better mood and quiz him further.

Dodo glanced around the bar and shuddered inwardly. She'd never set foot in a place like this in her life and judging by what she'd found she had no intention of ever doing so again. The bar was covered with greasy rim marks, the ancient linoleum on the floor was filled with gaping holes and some sleazy wrestling match was blasting out from the enormous television screen suspended from the ceiling. Even Fenella had turned her nose up at the place and had retreated underneath Dodo's seat.

It had been Dodo's suggestion that they meet Scar for a drink at the pub where all the *Bugle* staff drank. Goodness knows what had come over her, thought

310

Laura. It was all well and good sounding Scar out about Clare, but why they had to do it in a dive like this was completely beyond her. The place smelled atrocious too, of beer and sweat and something else that she would rather not think about.

Beside her, Dodo sipped cautiously at her glass of sherry. By the look on the barman's face when Dodo had ordered two glasses of dry sherry you would have thought that he had never even heard of the stuff. It had taken ten minutes of rooting around in the back before he'd produced an unlabelled bottle of brown liquid which he assured her was dry sherry. Privately, Dodo had her doubts.

'Are you sure this is such a good idea?' whispered Laura under her breath.

Dodo stared back at her niece with a puzzled look on her face.

'What do you mean? We're only going to show him this old picture of Clare and ask him if he knows her. It can't do any harm. Can it? We've shown it to enough people over the last couple of days, after all. I should think the whole of Lancashire knows we're looking for her by now.'

'But what if he tells everyone? He used to work for a newspaper, didn't he? He may be the world's biggest blabbermouth for all we know.'

Dodo took Laura's hand and sandwiched it between her own.

'Darling, that's a risk we are going to have to take. Do you or don't you want to try and find your mother?'

Laura nodded vehemently.

'You know that that's what I want more than any-thing in the whole world.'

'Good,' said Dodo. 'Now that means we're going to have to take a few risks. You've spent far too long bottling everything up. Fearing that anything you do is going to offend your father. You're twenty-six years old now and it's time you started sorting your life out. What will happen if the worst comes to the worst and Steven tells the world you're trying to find Clare? Hmm? Which I'm sure he won't, although that's by the by. Will the world come to an end?'

Laura shook her head violently.

'No, but Daddy would be so cross.'

'Oh, your father can go and boil his head,' said Dodo vehemently. 'Who cares what he thinks? We've all bent over backwards to try and appease him for far too long. It's time we started pleasing ourselves for a change.'

Laura's eyes widened in astonishment. She couldn't think what on earth had come over her aunt recently. Dodo had always been such a staunch ally of HH, ever ready to remind both her and Kate that their father was only doing his best for them. Now here she was telling her to forget about him and to start thinking about what *they* wanted.

At that moment the hulking figure of Scar appeared in the pub doorway. He'd clearly made an effort to smarten himself up because he had shaved and was now wearing a brown tweed suit that looked at least two sizes too small for him. Laura couldn't help giggling at his appearance. She much preferred the scruffy version. Somehow he didn't look himself dressed up like this.

'We're over here,' cried Dodo, waving a handkerchief jauntily in his direction.

The other three or four drinkers in the pub, all of them men, elbowed each other in the ribs as Scar smiled bashfully and headed towards the women. Scar's mystery assignation would be all round Bowland by the time the evening was out.

'Er, good evening ladies,' he said shyly. 'Can I buy you both a drink?'

'Absolutely not, Steven,' said Dodo. 'I insist on buying you one. As a thank-you for rescuing my niece from the ducks this afternoon. What would you like?'

Uncertain about what to order – he didn't quite feel comfortable asking for a pint in Dodo and Laura's company – Scar glanced at the tiny thimbles of brown liquid they were both drinking. 'Er, what have you got?' he enquired.

'Dry sherry,' barked Dodo. 'Will you have the same?'

Scar nodded awkwardly. It was a warm evening and, swathed in stifling tweed, he could feel himself beginning to sweat profusely. Why hadn't he just come as he was before? And he was going to look a right plonker dressed like this on the door at Snazzy Kecks later on.

Dodo placed a thimbleful of sherry in front of him and sat down heavily.

'As I said this afternoon, you obviously know everyone round here, Steven,' she said.

Scar nodded dutifully and drank half his sherry in one slurp.

'Good,' said Dodo. She leaned forward conspiratorially.

'Laura and I need some help,' she murmured, 'in tracking down Laura's mother.'

Scar listened attentively as Dodo related a simplified version of the events leading up to Clare's disappearance.

'So you see none of us have heard a word since she left eighteen years ago,' said Dodo. 'She could be dead for all we know.'

At this Scar glanced across at Laura. He saw that her eyes had filled up with tears and her mouth had begun to wobble precariously. Even to his untutored gaze, she looked as if she was on the edge of a nervous breakdown. She needed feeding up, too. The girl was as thin as a rake.

'Have you got a picture you can show me?' he asked tentatively.

When Laura handed over the precious black and white photograph of Clare that she'd kept by her bedside for so long, Scar almost did a double take.

'But, but it's you,' he spluttered. 'You could be sisters. She's the spitting image of you.'

Instantly Laura grabbed the picture back from him and studied it closely again. It was funny, she thought. She had gazed at this picture so often – it was amazing that it was still in one piece really – and yet for some reason the resemblance had never struck her before. But Scar was absolutely right. She *did* look uncannily like Clare.

'When was it taken?'

'I think it was about a year before she went,' said Laura, looking at Dodo for confirmation. 'So Clare would have been about twenty-seven.'

'Only just a little bit older than you are now, darling,' said Dodo, squeezing her hand again. 'So what do you think, Steven? Have you ever seen her round here?'

It seemed an eternity before Scar replied. He kept looking from the picture to Laura and back to the picture again, as if he couldn't quite separate the two.

'No,' he said finally. 'I wish I could say that she lives down the road from here but I've never for the life of me set eyes on her before.'

Laura's face plummeted with disappointment. Ever since Dodo had first suggested this trip she'd kept telling herself that she mustn't get her hopes up. Not expect too much. But now she had to face the truth. They'd shown Clare's picture to loads of people in Bowland and Longshott, and no one had shown a flicker of recognition. The likelihood was that Clare had just been passing through Lancashire when she posted the card and was miles away by now.

Laura tried to smile at Scar. She'd tried to find her mother and failed. Now she had to put the past behind her and concentrate on the future. Her and Hugo's future.

Chapter Thirty

By the time Daisy was six months old, Kate felt more contented than she'd ever been in her life. For all the tricky first months of constant breastfeeding on demand and loud screeches of protest whenever she was put down, Daisy had grown into a chubby, merry-natured baby who could now sit up by herself and beamed gratifyingly at virtually everyone who looked at her. Kate's column in the *Clarion* – a snapshot of what being a new mother was *really* like, sleepless nights, leaking breasts and all, seemed to be attracting loads of approving comments from readers and Joe Harris had promised her more work whenever she felt ready for it.

Best of all, after the months of treating her as if she was his boring kid sister, Charley seemed to be turned on by her once more. These days, they could barely keep their hands off each other. It was like the first few months of their relationship all over again. The only thing that was different was the fear that Daisy, asleep in her cot next door, might wake up and interrupt their love-making. But that just made it all the more exciting, reflected Kate. It was like being a teenager a second time round, worrying that her father might hear and come storming in to break it all up.

Apart from the improvement in his sex life, Charley wasn't quite so happy with his lot. He hadn't admitted as much to Kate, but it was slowly beginning to dawn on him that working in management wasn't all that it was cracked up to be. In many ways it was akin to walking barefoot across a floor littered with drawing pins. Between them, Gordon Osprey and Tim Jefferson seemed to take extraordinary pleasure in making him look as absurd as possible. He didn't seem to be able to do anything right. Just a couple of weeks back he had sent a memo round all the *Clarion* staff warning that the number of company cars was going to be slashed in half. Most of the reporters were increasingly office-bound and barely used them, so Charley had reckoned it was a nifty way of cutting costs. Two days later, however, he'd had to face the humiliation of Gordon Osprey sending round a memo reversing his decision. He was the laughing stock of the newsroom.

His other big problem was Rebecca Wilson. Since sharing the bottles of bubbly, she'd taken to dropping into his office every so often to cry on his shoulder. Her shifts had now dwindled to about one a week, but she still seemed to spend all her time hanging around the *Clarion* on the off chance that John Fry might change his mind and bring her in more regularly. Charley kept resolving to bite the bullet and tell Rebecca to bugger off once and for all, but whenever the opportunity arose he simply didn't have the guts to do it. For all his bluster, he was terrified that she would seek out Kate and tell her the truth about New Year's Eve, tell her where he'd really been when she was in labour with Daisy. And that was something he simply couldn't risk happening.

*   *   *

Hugo stuffed the remains of a Brie and grape sandwich into his mouth, brushed the crumbs fastidiously from his fingers and opened up one of his growing number of Hollingberry Holdings files. He had to admit that he was enjoying himself hugely. The knowledge that his father-in-law trusted him sufficiently to handle a couple of potential acquisitions for the company had boosted his confidence sky-high.

Over the past few weeks Hugo had spent more time on Hollingberry Holdings than anything else in his portfolio. He'd swiftly ruled out the takeover of a large group of Midlands newspapers as being far too risky. After going through the numbers with a fine-tooth comb he'd pointed out to HH that the group had lost market share for five years in a row and advised him to avoid it like the plague. The other possibility, a medium-sized but thriving chain based on the west coast of Scotland, looked much more promising. He'd done the due diligence and concluded that not only did the group have most of the area sewn up, but by merging some of their titles together large-scale cost savings would be made instantly.

Hugo was well aware that with all the commuting back and forth to the group's head office in Campbeltown, he'd been neglecting Laura badly. They'd been married for more than a year now and it was only relatively recently that he had begun to realise what a fragile soul she was. He'd kept hoping and hoping that she would get pregnant, convinced that if she had a baby to care for she might get a grip and pull herself together. He'd been optimistic when he'd arrived home a month or so back to find her being violently sick, but it had turned out that she was just ill again. Their sex life seemed to have dwindled, too. Laura was so scrawny now that somehow he just didn't fancy her very much at the moment.

As he studied the Scottish group's latest results, there was a knock on his office door and Joanna King, his secretary, walked in carrying yet more files.

'Thanks Jo,' said Hugo without looking up from his papers. Joanna mimed a curtsy but Hugo didn't even notice.

It was a year since Joanna had started working for Hugo and she still couldn't fathom him out at all. At the beginning she'd found him so boorish and unappreciative that she'd predicted they'd come to blows within weeks and either he'd fire her or she'd walk out. Much to her astonishment, however, everything had settled down. She would never describe him as a charmer in a million years but at least he was appreciative. Sometimes he was so engrossed in his work that he barely spoke for days, but from time to time he put his head above the parapet and apologised for overloading her with work. She didn't particularly like him, though, and there was no doubt that he was deeply unpopular with his colleagues. She knew from the super-efficient office grapevine that some of them had nicknamed him Marie Antoinette because of his high-handedness.

Now, as she hurried back to the door, Hugo glanced up from the accounts he was reading and banged his fist on the table.

'Damn it,' he groaned. 'These don't make sense at all. I'm going to have to go up to bloody Scotland again.'

'When?' asked Joanna, trying not to sound too eager. Life was much easier when Hugo was out of town.

'This afternoon,' grunted Hugo. 'Can you get me

a flight to Glasgow and book a car? And ring Laura for me?'

Joanna dug her fingernails into the palms of her hands to stop herself commenting on the careless way in which Hugo treated his wife. Look at him now. He was so obsessed with his own pathetic wheeler-dealing that he couldn't even be bothered to ring her himself. On the few occasions that Joanna had encountered Laura, it was quite obvious that she was crying out for a good deal more warmth and affection than Hugo was either willing or able to provide. If Laura had been a dog, thought Joanna wryly, she would have been diagnosed as suffering from emotional neglect and carted off to Battersea Dogs' Home.

'Honestly, that man,' she hissed through her teeth as she sat down at her desk again.

'What's he done now?' asked Allison Taylor, the secretary who occupied the next desk and had no time whatsoever for Hugo. It had been she who had come to Laura's rescue after she'd fainted in Hugo's office. Allison had seen what a cold fish he was and even now she couldn't help marvelling at the fact that Laura had actually ended up marrying him. What had possessed her to contemplate such a mismatch was completely beyond her.

'Oh, he's just being a shit,' said Joanna, picking up the telephone to ring Laura. 'As per usual.'

When Joanna got through to Laura, however, she didn't think that Laura sounded particularly perturbed by the news. If anything she seemed curiously detached, as if she was on another planet.

'Are you all right?' asked Joanna. She wondered whether she should ask Hugo to have a word with his wife, then dismissed the thought. He'd find it hard to drag himself away from his precious papers if the office was on fire; he certainly wouldn't break off to chat to Laura now.

'What?' asked Laura absent-mindedly. 'Oh yes. Sorry, I'm fine. In fact I'm a bit busy. If you don't mind, I'd better get on.'

Joanna put the telephone down thoughtfully. There was definitely something wrong, she thought. Laura did not sound her usual self at all.

At home in Battersea – she kept begging Hugo to consider moving somewhere bigger but, penny-pincher that he was, he wouldn't hear of it – Laura stood and stared at the appalling mess on the kitchen table. Looking at it all now – the discarded chocolate wrappers, the family-sized tubs of ice cream (empty), the bag of oven-ready chips that she'd swallowed almost raw – she felt utterly disgusted with herself. Like a drunk who'd been making a concerted effort to dry out, Laura had convinced herself that she'd knocked this terrible habit on the head once and for all. And ever since her trip up north with Dodo, she'd definitely felt stronger. Even though their journey had been pretty much a waste of time, it had helped her enormously, made her realise that she was at least capable of *trying* to find her mother.

But now she'd gone and undone all those good intentions. If only Hugo had at least spoken to her before leaving for work at the crack of dawn. If only Kate hadn't rung and told her all about Daisy being able to sit up by herself now and how it was time she had a baby cousin. If only Dodo hadn't been out when she'd called round. Then Laura might have carried on walking past the tiny grocer's shop on the corner of her street and not gone inside and bought all this rubbish, the remains of which lay on the table now.

As Laura desultorily picked up the debris and chucked it into the bin, she started thinking about her mother again. Clare would be forty-seven this year. What was she like? Had her hair begun to turn grey? Was her face lined? Why had she never even tried to get in touch? Did she ever think about any of them?

Mulling over this last question in her mind, Laura smiled softly. Of course she thought about them. She would never have sent Dodo that postcard if she'd banished them from her mind completely.

Suddenly she remembered the quantity of food she'd rammed down her throat and rushed off to the bathroom to get rid of it.

Kate had plonked a very put-out Daisy into her babywalker and was trying to concentrate on applying her new Chantecaille eyeshadow to her eyelids. As if she knew that her mother was getting ready to leave her, Daisy kept banging the walker against Kate's shins in protest.

'My legs are going to be black and blue by the time you've finished, darling,' chuckled Kate to her daughter. At the sound of Kate's laughter, Daisy immediately beamed a toothless grin and gurgled merrily. She liked nothing better than being the centre of attention.

The sharp ring of the doorbell interrupted their laughter. Kate breathed a sigh of relief. Dodo was here at last, thank goodness. Her aunt had agreed to look after Daisy while Kate dashed off to a screening of a new Channel Four series about working mothers that Joe Harris had asked her to write about. It was the first time Kate had left her with anyone else and she was desperate for everything to go smoothly. She was still breastfeeding Daisy – her strong-willed baby daughter simply refused to take a bottle, batting the loathsome object away with her fists whenever Kate had the temerity to bring it anywhere near her – but she'd just fed her and prayed that Daisy would last out until she got back.

Still laughing at Daisy's antics, Kate pulled the door open, ready to give Dodo a huge thank-you hug. When she saw who was standing there, however, her laughter instantly died away. It was Rebecca Wilson. Rebecca Wilson looking svelte and stunning in a dark brown designer suit cinched at the waist with a wide suede belt, and with her hair held back in a loose chignon. Five minutes before, Kate had been feeling quite pleased with her own appearance – she'd even managed to squeeze into a pair of her old trousers (although they admittedly felt a little bit tight around the waist) – but now she felt like a boring frump.

For a few seconds they just stood and stared at each other. Rebecca was the first to break the silence.

'So are you going to ask me in or what?' she demanded.

Kate looked at her in amazement. The bloody cheek of the woman. How dare she come here? And what the hell did she want anyway?

'No, I'm not,' she said. 'You can say what you came to say and then leave.'

'Charming as ever I see,' murmured Rebecca under her breath. 'And by the way, you've got a bit of goo on your shoulder. Maybe it's just me but I just don't think it looks terribly professional. Do you?'

'Somehow it's very reassuring to see that you're

still the cow you always were,' said Kate calmly, willing herself not to lose her temper and slap the woman round the face. 'Now, perhaps you'll be so kind as to leave. I'm sure you must have quite a bit of job-hunting to do. Charley mentioned that you're on the point of being dumped because you're no bloody good at the job.'

At this last insult, Rebecca's eyes narrowed spitefully.

'Did he now?' she said in a soft voice. 'Well, that's not the impression he gave me, I can tell you.'

'What impression did he give you then?' Kate knew she shouldn't be getting into a slanging match with Rebecca but found that she was unable to stop herself. She'd managed to suppress her dislike for this woman for two years now and suddenly she couldn't contain herself any longer.

'Oh, he was very impressed with my . . . Now what should I call it? My technique,' said Rebecca. 'Very impressed indeed. And he thought I was bloody brilliant at the job, in fact.'

Kate gaped at Rebecca. What was the woman going on about? She wasn't talking about reporting any more, that was for sure.

'Look,' said Kate, scooping Daisy protectively out of her babywalker and into her arms. 'You've obviously come here to tell me something that I won't want to hear. So why don't you just spit it out and then get out of my life?'

Kate's coolness under fire momentarily took the wind out of Rebecca's sails. She'd been working up to this meeting for so long and now it wasn't turning out at all as she had planned. Desperate to get her own back, first on Charley for the indifferent way in

324

which he had treated her and then on Kate for having everything she herself wanted so badly, she'd finally decided to act. But she'd been fully expecting Kate to collapse in a heap of sobs and slam the door in her face. She'd hadn't anticipated this icy calm at all.

'I came to tell you that your husband's a complete and utter bastard,' Rebecca eventually burst out. 'If you've been wondering where he was the night your baby was born then I'm here to tell you. I saw in your column that she was born on New Year's Eve and that's when he was with me, screwing the living daylights out of me in my flat. And he never mentioned you once. Not once.'

Kate stared at Rebecca in horror, unable to take in what she had just said. But, much as she would have liked to dismiss her spiteful words out of hand as the malicious ranting of a jealous mind, she couldn't. She knew that it was all true. Everything was suddenly slotting into place. The way she hadn't been able to track Charley down anywhere when she'd gone into labour on New Year's Eve. The guilty look on his face when he'd rushed into the maternity ward the morning after. The fact that he'd looked so dishevelled and smelled so unfamiliar. Yes, in one sense Rebecca Wilson was absolutely bloody right about Charley. *He was a complete and utter bastard.*

It was at this precise moment that Dodo came clattering up the stairs and along the hall to the flat. Grateful for something to take her mind off the bombshell that Rebecca had just dropped on her doorstep, Kate looked at Dodo and did a double take. Her aunt's style was a million miles from her own but Kate freely admitted that Dodo always looked immaculate. She had her hair set every couple of days by her hairdresser off Sloane

Square, favoured neat wool suits from Jaeger and still wore the same style of court shoes from Russell and Bromley that she'd been wearing for the last twenty years. Today, however, her aunt was red-faced and distraught, and it was patently obvious from her puffy eyes and pale face that she had been crying.

'You can piss off now,' hissed Kate to Rebecca as she grabbed Dodo's hand and hurried her inside the flat.

'Darling,' said Kate to Dodo, who was now weeping quite openly. 'What on earth is the matter? What has happened? You *must* tell me.'

Kate plonked Daisy back into her babywalker and took Dodo in her arms. For the first time that she could remember, Dodo, the backbone of the entire family for so long, seemed desperately vulnerable. It was as if she had suddenly turned into a small child again and Kate had become the grown-up.

'It's your father,' moaned Dodo, sobbing into Kate's shoulder as if her heart was going to break. 'He's had a heart attack, and darling, he's dead.'

Chapter Thirty-One

The next few days passed in a complete blur for all of them. Later, when Kate looked back on the week between HH's death and the funeral, she couldn't remember how they got through it at all. In one way there seemed to be so much to do – arranging the death notices, planning the funeral, making sure that the company continued to run smoothly. In another way it was as if time had stood still. Kate had no recollection whatsoever of doing normal things, like getting dressed or feeding Daisy or cooking supper.

Kate had put the devastating revelation about Rebecca Wilson's affair with Charley to one side for now. If it hadn't been for the shock of her father dying, she would have let rip at Charley the instant he'd arrived home that night, asked him what the hell he thought he was playing at, demanded an explanation for all the lies and deceit. But, overshadowed by her father's death, even Charley's duplicity didn't seem particularly important any more. Kate was so consumed with sadness about HH that she'd temporarily filed the affair away in the back of her mind. All the same, she couldn't bring herself to show much warmth towards Charley. She darted out of the way whenever he came anywhere near her, desperate to avoid physical contact with him. After the dramatic upturn in their sex life in recent weeks, Charley couldn't help feeling puzzled by her behaviour. But, optimist that he was, he simply reassured himself that Kate was grieving for her father and vowed to make an extra special effort to be as compassionate and understanding as possible.

In truth, Charley was also questioning where exactly his father-in-law's death left him. He'd only been in his new job for a few months and now that HH was out of the picture he would have been a fool not to recognise that he was in an acutely vulnerable position. Gordon Osprey had shown his utter contempt for his abilities on a number of occasions and if, as was widely being assumed in the City, he was on the verge of being appointed chairman of Hollingberry Holdings, Charley would be out on his ear. Of that there was no doubt.

Charley did not realise it, but Hugo Bentley was beset with similar fears. He'd been stuck in Campbeltown when the news broke and the first that he'd heard of HH's death had been on the television news. For over an hour, he'd sat rigid in his hotel bedroom overlooking the storm-lashed Kilbrannan Sound, unable to take in the announcement. By the time that he'd finally pulled himself together sufficiently to ring Laura, it was midnight and there was no reply. Hugo gulped down a couple of aspirin and retired to bed to work out what to do about this irritating blip in his career plans.

Like Charley, Hugo had assumed that his career was made when HH asked him to get involved in the business. Hugo, who never underestimated his talents for a single second, was confident that he had made a cracking start to the Scottish acquisition but was all too aware that there was still a long way to go. He now reckoned that it would be a couple of months at least before Hollingberry Holdings was in a position to proceed, and by that time Gordon Osprey would probably have knocked the project on the head and booted him out altogether. If Gordon did that Hugo would be back shuffling papers at boring old Moneywise.

Hugo's work for HH had given him a definite taste for running his own show. He was undoubtedly talented and after all his years in merchant banking, running around at the beck and call of his clients and generally being treated like shit, it seemed only right that he should be in charge of something. He'd fully expected that as time went on and he showed his true worth HH would have given him the responsibility that he was due. But now, with HH's premature death at the age of fifty-seven, that was beginning to look increasingly unlikely. Hugo made a mental note to take Michael Portland, the head of the Moneywise venture-capital department, out to lunch as soon as he was back in London to talk over his future.

Dressed in black from head to toe and clutching Daisy tightly to her breast, Kate stood by the graveside and dropped a single red rose onto the oak coffin below. As the rose hit the wood a few scarlet petals flew off and scattered forlornly.

'Goodbye Daddy,' whispered Kate softly. A sob welled up inside her throat and for a moment she feared she was going to weep uncontrollably. Desperate not to do that – HH had always loathed public displays of emotion – she just about managed to restrain herself by turning abruptly and walking at a brisk pace into Dodo's arms. Dodo tightened her hold around Kate and murmured gently in her ear, urging her to be strong.

'For your own sake, as well as Daisy's,' whispered Dodo.

It was then that the tears came freely, coursing down Kate's cheeks like a torrent in full flow.

'I'm sorry, I'm sorry,' wept Kate into Dodo's comforting black woollen coat. 'I told myself I wasn't going to cry but I just don't seem to be able to help it.'

Dodo let go of Kate and took a step back to look at her younger niece. Kate, usually so colourfully dressed, was wearing a severe black trouser suit and had pulled her hair into a short ponytail. She seemed older, all of a sudden, as if her father's death had finally made her grow up.

'Of course you've got to cry,' whispered Dodo. 'It's important – and very therapeutic.'

'But Daddy couldn't stand people bursting into tears all over the place,' mumbled Kate. 'I never saw him cry, not once. Not even after Mummy went. So I feel as if I'm letting him down somehow.'

Dodo took a large embroidered handkerchief out of her pocket and gently wiped Kate's eyes for her.

'You know you've always got me, don't you?' she murmured. 'And Daisy too. Look, she knows that you're upset and she's smiling at you. Poor darling, she's trying to help.'

Kate tried to smile back at Daisy and Dodo but found that her mouth was too unyielding and dry and she just couldn't. All she could think of right now were the countless rows and disagreements she'd had with her father over the years. So many occasions flitted through her mind – the way she'd flounced off to Bowland in a fit of temper, his disappointment when she'd got pregnant and married so young, her cutting remarks after he'd got his knighthood. And why, why, why had she never told him she loved him? Because, despite all his bossiness and bluster, she really had. But now it was too late. He'd never know how she felt and it hurt.

Kate's sadness was exacerbated, too, by the knowledge that HH had taken the secret of Clare's departure to his grave. He'd never told her and Laura the truth about their mother and what had compelled her to leave them. Now it looked as though they'd never discover the truth. Not unless Clare, if she was even alive, learned of HH's death and belatedly came looking for them. That was the other thing, mused Kate. With a daughter of her own to care for, her mother's actions seemed increasingly incomprehensible. For God's sake, she found it hard enough to leave Daisy for a few hours; the thought of walking out on her for good and never seeing her again was impossible even to contemplate. What on earth had made Clare do such a terrible thing?

Dodo watched Kate anxiously. She couldn't bear to see her so distressed. Now that the initial shock of losing her younger brother so suddenly had begun to wear off, Dodo knew that she was going to have to be supremely strong over the coming months. It was her determination and common sense that had got Kate and Laura through Clare's disappearance eighteen years earlier, and she was adamant that she was going to get her beloved nieces through this tragedy too.

The person uppermost in Dodo's mind today, however, wasn't HH himself – she had to accept that he was gone now, she couldn't waste any more emotional energy on him – or even Kate. It was Laura. Given HH's high profile, the number of mourners who had turned out at the church was surprisingly low, but Dodo wasn't bothered by that. No. It was Laura's downright refusal to attend that was preying on her mind. She'd tried her utmost to coax her elder niece to come. She'd kept telling her that it was only right and proper that she should pay her respects and bid farewell to her father – and that she'd regret it for the rest of her life if she didn't – but Laura had just shaken her head obstinately and refused point-blank. Even Hugo hadn't been able to get through to her, though Dodo privately wondered how hard he'd really tried.

Now, standing in the sunlit graveyard, Dodo felt like weeping herself. She couldn't help thinking that she'd somehow let HH down in his hour of need. If only she had said the right things, then she could surely have persuaded Laura to be here today. She shot a cursory glance around her. Apart from Kate and Daisy, the only people she recognised were Charley and Hugo, the ubiquitous Gordon Osprey and a few vaguely familiar faces from Hollingberry Holdings. Considering Hubert's undoubted achievements over the years, it was all a bit pitiful.

Standing a few yards apart from his wife, Charley was surprised by how much the funeral service had affected him. He'd always thought of himself as being as tough as old boots. He'd covered scores of funerals in his time, after all – funerals of murder victims, funerals of people who'd died in terrible disasters. But somehow this was very different. This funeral inexplicably reminded him of the death of his own father. Charley's dad had cleared out of the family home soon after his son's tenth birthday, never to be heard of again until eight years later, when he'd been stabbed in a pub brawl and had bled to death on the pavement outside. Charley's mother, embittered by her years of suffering at her ex-husband's hands, had expressly forbidden Charley to attend the funeral. Not for the first time in his life, however, and certainly not for the last, he had completely ignored her wishes and gone.

Charley sighed heavily. His father's funeral, at a depressing church on the edge of a sprawling Blackburn housing estate, had been far removed from this one. A chill north wind had whistled through the two shattered windows above the pulpit, there had been no flowers to speak of and only a handful of mourners, a couple of them completely stoned out of their brains. Charley had never forgotten that day and the feeling of utter hopelessness that had descended on him. His dad had died in his early forties, totally alienated from his family, with a severe drink problem, no job to speak of and only a couple of quid in his pocket. What a bloody waste of a life.

Now he was about to see his father-in-law buried and he felt the same profound sense of regret. HH hadn't exactly covered himself with glory when it came to his family, either. He'd built his company into a massive empire and ensured that his daughters would never have any financial worries as long as they lived, but he'd been a loner too. His wife had walked out on him and in recent years his daughters hadn't had much time for him. Kate rarely mentioned him and Laura was obviously so screwed up that she couldn't even be bothered to turn out to his funeral.

Charley swallowed hard and picked up a handful of soil to scatter over HH's coffin. He had to make sure that he didn't make a hash of his own life. He just *had* to. With this in mind, he turned and walked back towards Kate and Daisy. It was important to remember that they were his future now.

Standing beneath a weeping willow in the corner of the graveyard, a young man of no more than seventeen or eighteen was watching the proceedings with interest. He'd arrived late for the service, tiptoeing in discreetly during the vicar's rambling tribute to HH, and he wasn't entirely sure who most of the mourners were. Apart, that is, from the young woman at the front with hair almost as blonde as his own. He took an old newspaper cutting out of his pocket and studied it carefully. Yes, it was definitely Kate, the bridesmaid in the picture. She looked pretty much the same, apart from the fact that now she was holding a young baby in her arms. He stared at the pair of them intently for a couple of minutes, making a mental note to remember every possible detail about both of them and the baby in particular.

As the principal group of mourners clustered around the grave began to murmur their final farewells, the boy suddenly panicked. Perhaps this wasn't really the most appropriate time to confront the past. Anxious to make his own exit as well as avoid anyone asking awkward questions, he turned and walked briskly towards the churchyard gate. It was imperative to escape before anyone had time to notice his presence. In his haste, however, he collided heavily with a slight blonde woman hurrying distractedly through the gate.

'Oh my God, I'm so sorry,' muttered the boy as she crashed onto the ground. He grabbed her by both hands, marvelling at how tiny they were for a grown woman, and pulled her to her feet. Apart from her cheeks, which were hot with embarrassment at having caused a scene, her face was dead white and she looked as if she had been weeping for days.

'I'm so sorry, I'm so sorry,' he kept repeating. 'Are you sure you're all right?'

Laura stared up at him in confusion. Compared with the pain of dragging herself here this morning, being knocked down by a speeding youth was absolutely nothing. Absolutely nothing at all.

'I'm fine,' she said, brushing imaginary particles of earth from her ankle-length black dress. 'Truly. I'm fine.'

At that moment their eyes locked and a shiver of recognition ran down Laura's spine. The boy was at least six foot tall, with white-blond hair and a kind, sensitive face, and there was something so familiar about him. It was almost like gazing into the depths of her own soul. Laura had barely had time to think about all this, however, before the boy glanced at the crowd of advancing mourners and ran for his life.

Puzzled by his obvious desperation to escape, Laura stared after him. Her eyes followed him intently until he became a tiny figure in the distance and finally disappeared around the street corner.

'I wish that you'd told me your name,' she murmured softly to herself.

Hugo wasn't entirely sure whether he felt relieved or irritated at Laura's belated arrival at her father's funeral. Relieved, certainly, because as HH's elder daughter, Laura was now the most senior member of her family and it was only right and proper that she should be there. But at the same time he couldn't help feeling a twinge of profound irritation as he recalled the appalling scene at home that morning when she had refused point-blank to attend.

'I can't go, I can't go,' she had cried hysterically. 'It's all too much. First I lose my mother and now this. It's too much to cope with. Too too much.'

Now Hugo felt slightly ashamed at the ferocity with which he had slapped her around the face and shouted at her that she *had* to come with him. He wasn't a violent man by nature but he had suddenly snapped, frustrated by both Laura's intransigence and the terrible thought that his short-lived career at Hollingberry Holdings was about to come crashing down around his ears. Laura had run weeping into the bathroom and locked the door behind her. Despite his fury with her, Hugo had drawn the line at breaking the door down and dragging her out, so after waiting for a few minutes he'd set off on his own.

Hugo's heart had lifted when he'd spotted her coming into the graveyard and he'd darted forward, eager to make amends for the way they had parted a few hours earlier. Perhaps he just wasn't cut out for marriage. No one had ever irritated him as much as Laura did, but then again he still felt oddly protective of her. She was such a mass of insecurities. Sometimes she drove him mad with her timidity and lack of confidence but at other times, like now, he just wanted to scoop her up into his arms and kiss all the hurt away.

As Hugo walked briskly towards Laura, full of good intentions, he couldn't believe his eyes when he saw her collide with a young man running in the opposite direction. He groaned. Trust Laura to show herself up, he thought crossly, all his earlier exasperation flooding back. She couldn't be relied on to do anything right.

First she had to be an hour late for the service and now she'd collapsed in a heap in the graveyard. He stood and watched as Dodo instantly sped forward to check that she was all right. Saint Dodo to the rescue, he thought sourly. Laura was seeing far too much of her at the moment. She kept coming home with all these ridiculous ideas about tracking down her mother when it would be far better if she could just forget about the past and concentrate on being married to him. He cleared his throat noisily behind Laura and the two women jumped apart as if they had been shot.

'Come on, Laura,' he instructed curtly, speaking to her as if she was a wilful child. 'It's about time you started thinking of someone apart from yourself for a change.'

Dodo watched with silent anger as Laura meekly took Hugo's arm and accompanied him to HH's grave to pay her respects.

Bloody, bloody man, she thought. When was Laura going to summon up the courage to stand up to him?

Chapter Thirty-Two

Gordon Osprey was having the time of his life. After all the years of having to put up with HH ordering him around and bellowing at him in disagreement over every last thing, Gordon had finally got what he wanted. He was in charge at last.

Within two days of the funeral the Hollingberry Holdings board had appointed him as acting chairman of the company. That was good enough for Gordon. For the first time in his very careful life, he had thrown caution to the wind and acted on impulse. He had immediately moved into HH's vast office and set about making it his own. He'd pulled the massive mahogany desk away from the window (he didn't want anything to distract him from work), placed his ten filing cabinets full of papers along the far wall and hung his own favourite watercolour of Big Ben next to HH's motley collection of oil paintings.

The Hollingberry Holdings board had decided to take its time nominating HH's successor. HH's will was to be read to all interested parties in a week's time and there would be a board meeting to appoint the new chairman a week after that. But it was pretty clear to all concerned that Gordon Osprey was the most likely person to be stepping into HH's shoes.

Everyone agreed that it made perfect sense. Gordon had been HH's number two for longer than anyone could remember, after all, and he knew the business like the back of his hand. Not only that, but it wasn't as if there were many other contenders waiting in the wings. All Gordon's fellow directors were either far too doddery and past it, or too young and inexperienced. No, Gordon knew in his bones that he was on the verge of being appointed as the new chairman of Hollingberry Holdings. It went without saying.

It was three days after HH's funeral that Gordon decided to take the bull by the horns and tackle a couple of issues that had been bugging him for months. In his head he knew that he had loads of more pressing things to attend to but his heart told him that they could wait. HH had made two decisions in the past couple of years that had enraged Gordon beyond belief and he was going to sort them out now. *Once and for all.*

Sitting in the back of HH's shiny black Jaguar (he had long coveted the chauffeur-driven limousine and had now appropriated it as his own), Gordon looked up from the new service contract that he was planning to discuss with the board in ten days' time. As he stared out of the window at the rows of terraced houses clinging to the side of the hill above Bowland he couldn't help shuddering. Bowland seemed like a completely different world from the one he inhabited.

It was rare that Gordon ventured out of London – the last time he'd come this far north had probably been the humiliating tour round the outer reaches of the Hollingberry Holdings empire that HH had inflicted on him a couple of years back. Gordon lived in a plush apartment overlooking Tower Bridge, worked in Docklands and hardly ever went further than Covent Garden for dinner. Now, looking at the redundant cotton mills that still towered over the grey Lancashire landscape, Gordon made himself a solemn promise. Once he had got this visit out of the way he intended to remain in London *all* the time. His minions could sort out the provinces.

Pam Newbold had plonked her bare feet up on the desk in front of her and was busy painting her toenails a particularly alarming shade of Tango orange. It was Thursday, the *Bugle*'s quietest day of the week, and she was taking it easy for a change. Pam had been in the office until ten the night before putting the *Bugle* to bed and as she contemplated the paper now, she felt a quiet sense of satisfaction creep over her.

After Kate had left the *Bugle* last year, the executives at Leadington Newspapers had studied the paper's declining sales figures and curtly told Pam that they couldn't possibly afford to replace her, lowly-paid trainee or not. She would just have to get the paper out somehow with her remaining staff of three – George Gibbs to sub it all, Danny Simpson, the photographer, who Pam suspected was getting increasingly itchy feet, and Pam herself to write every bloody word that went in. And somehow, against all the odds, they had managed to pull this feat off for the last twelve months. Some weeks were better than others, admittedly, but this week's paper – if she said it herself – was an out-and-out belter.

Pam put the brush back in the nail-varnish pot and picked up the paper for the umpteenth time.

'*Nicky's killer brother jailed for life*' said the splash

emblazoned across the top of the front page. Pam had also used a large picture of Nicky's family in happier times on the front and underneath in smaller type had written the strapline, *'Nicky's parents open their hearts to the* Bugle *in an exclusive interview'*.

It had taken more than a year for Dave Rawlinson to be tried for his sister's murder, but at Preston Crown Court the day before he'd finally been brought to justice and found guilty. He was now starting a life sentence for the brutal killing of fourteen-year-old Nicky. For a long time after Kate had left the *Bugle*, Bert and Vi Rawlinson had simply refused to talk to anyone else on the paper. But through sheer persistence and charm, Pam had eventually won them round and, like Kate before her, had become genuinely fond of the couple.

Pam was well aware that court cases were notoriously difficult for weekly newspapers. The Nicky Rawlinson murder was the biggest story to hit Bowland in twenty years, and Pam had feared that in the end sod's law would prevail and the trial would finish the day after the *Bugle* went to press. If that had happened she would have had to wait for a whole week to pass before publishing anything, by which time it would have been completely old hat.

But for once the *Bugle*'s luck had been in and the trial had finished late on Wednesday afternoon, perfect timing for the coming week's paper. Pam had already prepared a long background story on the case and got a (free) exclusive interview with Bert and Vi that all the nationals had been offering megabucks for. Last night she had just about had time to rush back to Bowland and write up the verdict, sentence and the judge's vitriolic condemnation of Dave Rawlinson and the state of British youth today before the paper went to press. The resulting story, lying on the desk in front of her now, was easily the best front page she had produced in her entire time as editor. And, to cap it all, she'd been inundated with calls from most of the nationals this morning, all clamouring to buy her interview with Nicky's parents.

Pam sighed happily. It had been a bloody hard year. Her relationship with her copper boyfriend had completely gone by the board because he'd got so pissed off with her always being at work and never having any time for him. She'd lost loads of weight too. Her once curvaceous figure was now down to a scrawny size ten, although – she quickly glanced down at her low-cut T-shirt for reassurance – the only comfort was that at least her boobs hadn't shrunk. She couldn't have borne that.

As Pam flicked the paper over onto page two, the newsroom door opened with a squeak and Gordon Osprey walked in.

Pam gaped at him in astonishment. Hurriedly taking her bare legs off the desk and shoving the nail varnish into a drawer, she couldn't help reflecting that he looked even more out of place in the scruffy *Bugle* newsroom than he had during his last visit. He was wearing a dark charcoal suit, a white shirt and a boring spotted tie, and she suddenly felt acutely aware that in her cheap T-shirt and short skirt she probably looked more like a holiday rep than a newspaper editor. One thing that didn't escape her notice, however, was the way his eyes lingered just a moment longer than was appropriate on her plunging neckline.

'Mr Osprey,' said Pam. She leapt to her feet and offered him her hand. 'How delightful to see you after all this time.'

'Quite,' said Gordon awkwardly. In his haste to come and shut this bloody white elephant down he'd completely forgotten about Pam Newbold and the extraordinary effect that she'd had on him during his last visit. Or was he just kidding himself? His eyes dropped to her bosom again, and then, in an attempt to pull himself together, he said sternly, 'And where, might I ask, are the rest of your staff?'

'Oh, I gave them the day off,' said Pam airily. 'All two of them. Any objection?'

Gordon glared at her. He'd always been screwed up about sex – apart from a high-class hooker that he very occasionally, maybe once a year or so, called upon, he hadn't slept with anyone since his wife walked out – but there was something about Pam that made him want to reach across and touch her. He felt so irritated by this thought that his voice sounded more brusque than he intended.

'I would have thought that a newspaper that was losing as much money as this one couldn't possibly afford to give two-thirds of its staff the day off in the middle of the week,' he said coldly. 'Have you taken leave of your senses? I must say that it merely serves to confirm that the action I am about to take is the right one.'

Pam stared at Gordon Osprey in amusement. He couldn't possibly have come all this way to fire her, because the *Bugle* was right down to the bare bone as it was. If the staff was reduced to two they quite simply couldn't get the paper out at all.

'And what is the action you are about to take?' she asked casually, bending down to put her sandals back on her feet.

Gordon stuttered for a moment as he got a glimpse of

343

Pam Newbold's glorious golden breasts. The thought of what it would be like to caress them occurred to him fleetingly, and he thrust his hands deep into his pockets to put it out of his mind.

'I'm sure that even the *Bugle* staff have read about Hubert Hollingberry's sudden death,' he began pompously.

Pam fixed him with a beady gaze. What was it about bloody Londoners that made them think they were so frigging superior to the rest of the country?

Gordon returned her stare, willing himself to keep his eyes on Pam Newbold's face and nothing else.

'For the past few months Hubert and I—' Gordon placed the utmost emphasis on Hubert – 'had been discussing the dire performance of the Leadington group and we were both increasingly of the opinion that we should close it down.'

Pam didn't say anything, so Gordon hurriedly continued. This was proving to be more difficult than he had envisaged.

'I have been given to understand by my contacts in the City that I am shortly to be appointed as chairman of Hollingberry Holdings, and I have therefore travelled north to put my dear friend Hubert's last wishes into practice.'

'And what if you're not?' asked Pam boldly.

'Not what?'

'Not appointed as chairman.'

Gordon regarded Pam with stupefaction. What was the woman thinking of? The closure of her paper had clearly come as such a shock that she'd lost her marbles. Of course he was going to be the next chairman of Hollingberry Holdings. He'd been talking to some tame fund managers over the last couple of days and they'd told him that it was virtually all signed and sealed. In the bag, as one of them had so succinctly put it.

'I'm sorry to be the bearer of bad news, obviously,' he said, 'but I'm certain that you will look back on it in later years and see that it was all for the best. I've got no doubts that you are young enough and bright enough to forge a new career elsewhere.'

'Have you actually looked at a single edition of the *Bugle* since I took over as editor?' asked Pam suddenly.

Gordon flushed awkwardly. He wasn't quite sure what to say.

'No, I thought not,' said Pam. 'Well, since you put me in charge, sales of the *Bugle* have gone up from twelve thousand a week to twelve thousand, seven hundred a week. Now, seven hundred copies of the *Bugle* might not mean much to you but shall I tell you what they mean to me and my staff of precisely two?'

She didn't pause long enough for him to answer.

'They mean a hell of a lot of blood, sweat and tears. That's what they mean. They mean all of us slogging our guts out for twelve hours a day, six days a week, to improve this paper without spending a penny more than Leadington has budgeted for. There should be at least six of us working on a paper this size, you know that as well as I do, and yet the three of us have been producing a bigger, better paper with half the manpower. And now you have the bloody nerve to come up here and tell me that after everything we've worked so hard for you're closing us down – without even looking at the paper. You make me bloody sick.'

If Gordon Osprey was slightly taken aback by Pam's outburst, he tried hard not to show it. He'd had to stand and listen to enough of HH's tirades over the years, after all. But even so, he couldn't help feeling a flash of sympathy for the woman standing in front of him. The *Bugle* didn't mean anything to him, she was right about that, but she had clearly put her heart and soul into it.

'Now, listen to me,' he said, his tone softer than before. 'If you want to get on in this group you'd be wise to try a different approach with me. I know that you are terribly disappointed – we all are – but we simply cannot carry on pouring money into a group of this size. Papers like the *Evening Clarion* are our core business and in the current economic climate we have to concentrate all our resources in them. And don't think that you're the only ones we're targeting. There are quite a few other people I shall be forced to lose over the coming months.'

Pam raised her eyebrows questioningly. It was hard to believe a bloody word he was saying.

'Now, do you remember what I was saying before about you having a bright future ahead of you?'

Pam nodded wearily.

'Well, look, I'm staying at the Royal Mile Hotel in Preston tonight. Why don't you come and join me for dinner and we'll discuss the possibilities open to you. I'm sure I can come up with a few proposals that might interest you.'

As Gordon's gaze suddenly dropped to Pam's cleavage once again, a germ of an idea planted itself inside her head. Judging by the lustful gleam in his eyes, she had a pretty good idea of what his 'interesting proposals' might entail.

'What do you think?' asked Gordon. 'Shall we say at about eight? I would make it earlier but I have a few things to sort out at Leadington's head office before that.'

I bet you have, reflected Pam, although she didn't voice her thoughts out aloud.

'I'd love to join you for dinner,' she said airily. 'I'll come straight to your room, shall I?'

Gordon Osprey's heart was beating wildly by the time he checked into his hotel that evening. He still wasn't entirely sure what he was expecting from Pam Newbold. He'd been utterly genuine when he'd told her she had a bright future ahead of her. She was clearly a talented editor who had tried desperately hard to turn the *Bugle* round. But if he was one hundred per cent honest with himself it wasn't her editorial talents alone that enthralled him. Gordon couldn't quite put his finger on the reason why, but he found himself oddly fascinated by this straight-talking, tarty-looking woman. She couldn't be more different from his ex-wife Josephine, with her neat suits and tidy perm, but maybe that was exactly why he had this perverse craving to strip Pam Newbold naked and bury his head in those breasts.

By eight pm Gordon had showered and changed into yet another charcoal suit and was sitting on his balcony sipping a gin and tonic. Preston wasn't quite the South of France, admittedly, but all the same life felt pretty good. He'd got his heart's desire of taking control of Hollingberry Holdings, he'd finally shut Leadington down and if he played his cards right he might be lying in Pam Newbold's arms in a couple of hours' time.

Three quarters of an hour later Gordon's buoyant

mood had all but evaporated. He'd chucked his large file on Charley Stone's recent performance down on the table in disgust and ordered a solitary smoked-salmon sandwich from room service. Pam Newbold had a bloody nerve, he thought furiously. How dare she stand him up? If anyone was going to be stood up, it should be her, the cheap-looking bitch, not him. And if she thought that he was going to give her a reference after this, she had another think coming.

Kate tucked Daisy's favourite pink blanket around her daughter and plonked her dummy into her mouth. Daisy's lips closed blissfully round the comforter and she began sucking. Kate smiled down at her little girl. She wished that something as simple as a plastic dummy would sort her own problems out.

Only a few days had passed since HH's funeral and Kate still felt profoundly depressed. It was a constant source of astonishment to her that all around her everyone else's lives seemed to be continuing perfectly normally while her own was falling apart.

Kate hadn't yet managed to broach the subject of Rebecca Wilson with Charley. During the week between her father's death and his funeral Charley's infidelity had been the last thing on her mind and though it pained her to admit as much, he *had* been a support on the day itself. Since the funeral, however, she'd barely seen her husband. Charley, fed up with being stuck in his office on his own every day, had taken to going out boozing most nights with Jake Horner and a bunch of other mates from the *Daily Recorder*.

Walking into the sitting room, Kate flicked Daisy's baby monitor on. Instantly the room was filled with the sound of Daisy's regular breathing. Kate grinned. Charley kept telling her that they didn't need the monitor any more and that Daisy's snuffling kept him awake at night, but Kate wouldn't hear of it. She'd hated it when they'd finally moved Daisy at six months old out of their own bedroom and into the tiny boxroom that Charley used as his dressing room. At least with the monitor she could still hear her.

'I've poured you a glass of wine, darling,' said Charley smoothly behind her.

Kate whirled round.

'God, you nearly made me jump out of my skin,' she said. 'How long have you been home?'

'About five minutes,' said Charley, handing her a glass of chilled white wine and kissing her sedately on the cheek. 'I thought it would be nice to spend the evening together.'

Kate took a sip of wine and slumped down on the sofa. She wondered why Charley was making such an effort.

'Has something happened?' she asked.

Charley looked puzzled.

'What do you mean? I've been at work as normal all day if that's what you're asking. Looking at the cost of a new computer system if you must know. The old one's getting hopelessly out of date.'

'Sounds exciting,' said Kate, clearly thinking the opposite. 'By the way, have you seen Rebecca Wilson lately?'

A guarded look appeared on Charley's face.

'No,' he said. 'Why should I? We're not exactly best mates, are we?'

Kate stared hard at him. She could see from his studied innocence that he was lying.

'That's not what I've heard,' she said lightly.

'What do you mean by that?' said Charley again. 'Honestly, Kate, I think HH's death has sent you round the twist. I virtually never see anyone, let alone Rebecca Wilson. I'm stuck in solitary confinement upstairs and she's hardly ever in, anyway. John Fry's dumped her from the rota for being next to fucking useless.'

Before Kate knew what she was doing she got up from the sofa, stalked across the room and chucked the remains of her white wine in Charley's face.

'Liar, liar,' she shrieked at him. 'You're a bloody liar. I could almost have forgiven you if you'd been straight with me but you're a compulsive liar, aren't you? You'd lie to your own grandmother, you bloody shit.'

Stunned by Kate's fury and with wine dripping down his face, Charley grabbed her by the hand and tried to take her in his arms. But Kate wasn't having any of it and wriggled to get free.

'I know all about your sordid little affair with that slut,' she shouted. 'I know all about where you were when I was in hospital giving birth to Daisy. There I was, in agony, hoping so desperately that you'd be rushing to be by my side. That you'd *want* to be by my side. When all the time you were screwing her . . .'

'It's not true,' said Charley quietly.

Incensed by his denial, Kate grabbed hold of a vase of white lilies from a side table and chucked it at him. Instantly Charley ducked and the vase smashed into a huge mirror on the far wall, scattering shards of glass all over the wooden floor.

'It bloody is true,' screamed Kate. 'She told me so herself and I believe her.'

At that moment, Daisy woke up, her roars of distress echoing through the baby monitor.

'And now look what you've bloody done,' yelled Kate, marching out of the room.

While she was attempting to pacify Daisy, the telephone rang. At first Charley ignored it, too shocked by Kate's tirade to think straight. After thirty seconds, however, it was still ringing and Charley angrily snatched it up.

'Can I speak to Kate, please?' demanded a female voice.

'Who is it?' bellowed Charley, not recognising the broad Lancashire accent at the other end of the line.

'Pam Newbold,' said Pam. 'And tell her it's urgent.'

Puzzled by Pam Newbold's pressing tone, Charley put the receiver down and went to fetch Kate. Pam couldn't help breathing a sigh of relief. She had to talk to Kate tonight. She just *had* to. Judging by Gordon Osprey's smug assumption that he was about to be appointed chairman of Hollingberry Holdings, there was no time to waste.

'What does she bloody want?' swore Kate under her breath. She was kneeling next to Daisy's cot by now, gently rubbing the baby's back in an attempt to get her back to sleep.

'I don't know, but she says it's urgent,' said Charley. 'Look, you take the call and I'll carry on rubbing Daisy's back. Then we'll sit down with a glass of wine and talk all this through without getting hysterical. Yes?'

'All right,' said Kate sullenly.

As she picked up the phone, Kate couldn't help wondering what Pam needed to talk to her about so desperately. She hadn't heard from her for months, not since Pam had sent a card and a pair of leopard-skin bootees to celebrate Daisy's arrival in the world.

'Hello,' said Kate tentatively. Surely Pam hadn't rung to offer her her old job back again?

'Kate, I've just had a visit from Gordon Osprey. Gruesome chap, isn't he? He says he's about to be appointed chairman of your father's company and the first thing he's done has been to close the *Bugle* down. After all that we've slogged our guts out for. And that's not the only thing he's up to. I think we need to talk. Can we meet? As soon as possible?'

Chapter Thirty-Three

Laura leaned over the side of the bed and threw up into the plastic washing-up bowl on the floor next to her. For a few seconds after she'd finished she felt better, her body purged of all the disgusting things she'd stuffed down her throat earlier on that morning; but once the elation had worn off, a black cloud of depression descended on her all over again.

It was an hour before she felt strong enough to lever herself out of bed and get dressed. She couldn't think what on earth Hugo would want her to wear for their lunch date. He'd left home at the crack of dawn and she'd forgotten to ask him last night. Not that there was much choice in the matter, come to think of it. Laura had been alternating between bingeing and vomiting and starving herself for a few weeks now, and a lot of the clothes she'd bought after their wedding were starting to hang off her tiny frame like rags on a scarecrow. Hugo hadn't commented on her appearance but he'd made it perfectly obvious that he didn't fancy her at all any more.

When Laura strolled into the Ritz soon after twelve thirty, Hugo and his companion were already seated at the table. The Ritz looked glorious, thought Laura appreciatively as she threaded her way in between the other tables and over to the window on the far side of the room. It always reminded her of something out of a fairy tale, with its huge glass chandeliers, painted cherubs and stunning gold, white and pink colour scheme. She wondered whether Hugo had chosen it for lunch as a romantic gesture, to remind her of their wedding night, then dismissed the thought out of hand. No. She knew him well enough now to understand that his mind didn't work like that at all. He would have booked the Ritz to impress his lunch guest. No other reason.

As Laura approached the table she put on her most radiant smile. Hugo had instructed her last night that his whole future depended on lunches like this and that she must make a concerted effort to charm all the people he introduced her to.

'Darling,' he said and his voice sounded warmer than it had for weeks. 'May I introduce you to David Lyons? David is the fund manager at Pennington's. They manage the pension funds of several very blue-chip companies. They also happen to own about ten per cent of your father's company. David, this is my wife Laura. Hubert's daughter.'

Laura glanced at Hugo quickly. He was definitely up to something, although she didn't have the first idea what it was. Ever since her father's funeral he'd been working all hours, leaving at dawn and not coming back until nine pm at the very earliest. Even when he was at home in the flat he closeted himself in the tiny study to make phone calls and pore over all the old Hollingberry Holdings accounts.

Laura had been dreading this lunch, but David Lyons turned out to be charming company. He was witty, urbane and despite a slight tendency to blow his own trumpet, made them both laugh with fond anecdotes about HH and extraordinary tales about the latest City scandals.

'So what do you think about Hugo's ambition to become the next chairman of Hollingberry Holdings?' asked David as he tucked into an exquisite-looking strawberry meringue.

Laura, who after her excesses of a few hours earlier had picked nervously at her sea bass and then refused any pudding, almost choked on her espresso.

'Er, I think it's an absolutely wonderful idea,' she said, trying to sound as loyal as she possibly could. 'I'm sure he would make a very worthy successor to Daddy.'

'Good,' said David Lyons heartily. 'That's what we think too. But I just wanted to be sure that you were right behind him, both as Hugo's wife and as a major shareholder in the company.'

Laura stirred her espresso thoughtfully. Up until David Lyons's comment, it genuinely hadn't occurred to her that of course HH would have left her and Kate a substantial number of shares in his will. She simply hadn't thought about it. She'd been so taken up with her own misery about her father, and her sadness that he'd died before revealing the truth about him and Clare, that the contents of his will had been the last thing on her mind.

'Of course Laura is right behind me,' said Hugo, patting Laura's hand proprietorially. 'You always are, aren't you darling?'

Laura stared at Hugo in confusion. These days it was becoming increasingly difficult to predict his moods. Every evening, when she heard the turn of his key in the lock, she'd remind herself to make an extra special effort to keep on the right side of him, tell herself that she must endeavour not to irritate him in any way. But no matter how hard she tried, he always found fault with something. The Chardonnay wasn't chilled enough. She hadn't made the bed as he liked it, with tight hospital corners and the sheets folded back exactly six inches. His favourite shirt hadn't been starched or his shoes collected from the menders. Every now and then, just as she was in the depths of despair, he would come home full of the joys of spring, bringing flowers and a bottle of champagne and throwing his arms around her shoulders.

'Of course I am, Hugo,' said Laura, making a mental note to ask Kate if she knew what the hell was going on at Hollingberry Holdings.

Sitting on the floor of her flat with Daisy wedged between her knees, Kate was trying her hardest to concentrate on what Pam Newbold was saying and finding it almost impossible. All through Pam's angry diatribe about Gordon Osprey and the man's crazy decision to close the *Bugle* down, her eyes had kept straying back to her friend's extraordinary new hairstyle.

When Kate worked for the *Bugle*, Pam had always worn her lustrous auburn hair down to her shoulders. But, a couple of days ago, after Gordon Osprey's bombshell, Pam had suddenly decided she was going to do something radical with it. Any other forty-two-year-old who felt as if they were in a rut would have been content with having a henna rinse and a couple of inches lopped off the bottom. But not Pam. Much to the consternation of the anxious hair stylist who'd done it, she'd insisted on having the whole lot shorn to within half an inch of her scalp and dyed bright peroxide blonde.

'You haven't been listening to a word that I've been saying, have you?' muttered Pam accusingly.

Kate, who had now lifted up her shirt to feed Daisy, couldn't help giggling at her friend's indignant face.

'I'm sorry, really I am,' she spluttered. 'I really like your hair. It's just, it's just that you don't look like yourself any more.'

'That's the whole point,' said Pam stiffly. 'I've been doing a lot of thinking over the past couple of days and I've come to the conclusion that it's high time I took control of things for a change. I'm sick of other people deciding what happens in my life. So from now on I'm going to do what I want, whether it's changing the colour of my hair or fighting tooth and nail to save the *Bugle*.'

Kate wriggled her little finger into Daisy's vice-like grip.

'Are you serious?' she asked.

'Deadly,' said Pam. 'I don't suppose there's much that I can do about Gordon Osprey becoming chairman of your dad's company but surely I can launch a management buy-out or something? What do you think? I can, can't I?'

Listening to Pam's angry words, Kate's mind had begun to spin into action. She'd *never* liked Gordon Osprey either, he was simply too slimy for words. But at this late stage in the day it was hard to see how she and Pam could foil his bid to take charge of Hollingberry Holdings.

'Leave it with me,' said Kate thoughtfully. 'My father's will is being read tomorrow and that might give us a few pointers. Can you wait that long?'

Pam nodded reluctantly. It was all very well ranting and raving about buying the *Bugle* herself but when it came to the crunch, she didn't have much of a clue as to how to go about it. If Kate could come up with a feasible plan, so much the better.

Kate, with Daisy still clutching her finger, accompanied Pam to the front door of the flat and kissed her exuberantly on both cheeks.

'Oh, and by the way, Pam,' she said.

'What?' asked Pam.

'I love the hair. Really I do. I admit it took me a while to get used to it but it makes you look ten years younger. Like a blonde Peter Pan.'

Perching on the edge of his antique desk, Oliver Brown cleared his throat authoritatively and surveyed the members of the Hollingberry family seated in front of him. He had been HH's solicitor for well over thirty years now but he'd never dreamed that the day would come when he'd be reading out the contents of his oldest friend's will. HH had always seemed so utterly invincible; Oliver had been convinced that he would be at the helm of Hollingberry Holdings long after he himself had snuffed it.

He was slightly appalled to see that HH's younger daughter Kate had brought her baby with her. Really, he thought crossly. His office was a place of work, not a crèche. Surely she could have left the baby with someone?

His irritation lifted slightly as he glanced across at Dodo Hollingberry, sitting in the middle of the clan. Oliver stared at HH's sister for a few seconds. It was hard to believe that it was a good thirty-five years since that magical summer when he'd fallen in love with her

– and thirty-four years since he'd taken leave of his senses and jilted her to marry his wife Irene. Oliver's face hardened at the thought of Irene. There was no doubt that he'd made the wrong choice there. What the hell had he been thinking of? While Dodo had more or less kept her looks and her figure and her acute sense of fun, Irene had turned into an overweight, nagging shrew who was far more interested in cream cakes and TV soaps than she was in him.

At that moment, Dodo looked up from the letter she'd been reading and Oliver flushed, embarrassed that she'd caught him gazing at her.

'Ahem,' he said again. 'Thank you all very much for coming here this morning to hear the last will and testament of Hubert Hollingberry.'

Oliver paused to check the date of the document he was reading, and then continued.

'Some of you may not be aware of this but this will is actually dated the 13th of January 1978. Hubert never saw fit to change it during the intervening years so it still stands.'

Kate and Dodo glanced at each other in surprise. January 1978. Two months after Clare left. Kate wondered whether there would be any mention of her mother in the will, then brushed the thought away. Of course not. It was ridiculous even to consider it. Her father had always avoided mentioning Clare while he was alive. He was hardly likely to broach the subject from beyond the grave.

In fact HH's will turned out to be surprisingly simple. Apart from a large bequest to 'my dear sister for her lifelong devotion and support' – Dodo wiped a tear from her eye as Oliver Brown read this part out – HH had split the rest of his assets between Laura and Kate.

The house in Chelsea and all its contents, his collection of paintings and his forty per cent shareholding in Hollingberry Holdings were divided fair and square between the pair of them.

At this point in the proceedings Oliver Brown peered at the sisters over the top of his half-moon spectacles.

'The only thing that your late father requested of both of you was that you should do all in your power to look after the best interests of the company. Hollingberry Holdings was his life's work and he was most insistent that its legacy should be continued long into the next century. Knowing the pair of you as I do, I have no doubts whatsoever that you will respect his wishes. And as your father's oldest friend, you may rest assured that I will do all in my power to help protect the interests of both you and the company.'

In the seat next to Laura, Hugo was doing a hasty series of sums on the back of his brand new Coutts chequebook. His smile of satisfaction widened as he totted up the number of institutions who had agreed to back his bid to become chairman of Hollingberry Holdings. Now that Laura officially owned a twenty per cent shareholding in the company he reckoned he was virtually home and dry. Getting Kate on his side would simply be the icing on the cake.

As Oliver Brown drew the meeting to a close, Hugo became charm itself. First he insisted on hailing a taxi for Dodo, carefully helping her into it and stuffing a crumpled ten-pound note into the driver's hand. As Dodo sank back into the squashy imitation-leather seat she shot him a suspicious look. Not only was Hugo notoriously tight-fisted but he couldn't usually be bothered to give her the time of day. He was clearly up to something.

Once Dodo's cab had roared off down High Holborn Hugo turned to Laura, Kate and Charley and suggested that he treat them to a glass of champagne at the American Bar to celebrate.

'Celebrate?' questioned Kate, raising her eyebrows in disapproval. 'Celebrate what? I hardly think that hearing the contents of Daddy's will constitutes something to celebrate. Do you, Laura?'

Torn between an inclination to agree with Kate and her loyalty towards Hugo, Laura looked questioningly at her husband. In the end, though, she didn't dare to contradict him.

'Oh come on, Kate,' said Laura, linking her arm through her sister's. 'Hugo's right. And anyway, we haven't seen each other properly for ages.'

And you know why that is, thought Kate sourly to herself. There was one reason and one reason alone why she and Laura had barely spent any time together since Daisy's birth. And that was Laura's determination to avoid all contact with her small niece. Not only that, but whenever Kate dared to start talking about babies and whether Laura had any problems that she hadn't told her about, her sister always changed the subject abruptly.

Charley consulted his Rolex. Much as he was tempted to adjourn to the Savoy's wonderfully civilised American Bar for the afternoon, he knew that it would be extremely unwise. For one thing, Kate was still barely speaking to him. And for another, Gordon Osprey had summoned him to his office for a meeting at noon, and standing him up would be the equivalent of some obscure backbencher blowing a raspberry at the Prime Minister.

'I'm sorry, sweethearts,' said Charley, kissing the top of Daisy's fluffy head, 'but you'll have to count me out on this one. Some of us have got work to do. Gordon Osprey has given me the three-line whip and if I don't show up on time he'll definitely sling me out on my ear.'

Hugo's eyes narrowed at Charley's mention of Gordon Osprey. He wasn't exactly his brother-in-law's number one fan either, but the thought of Gordon Osprey throwing his weight around before he'd even been appointed as chairman stuck in his gullet.

'Right,' said Hugo, taking charge. 'It's just Laura, Kate and me then.'

'Can you possibly hold Daisy while I get something out of the changing bag?' Kate asked Hugo, plonking her baby daughter into his arms before he even had time to reply. Somehow it was easier to ask him than Laura. She couldn't face seeing Laura's look of panic at the thought of coming into close contact with Daisy.

'What do you need?' asked Hugo, trying to hold Daisy at arm's length and as far away as possible from his suit.

Kate continued riffling through the heaps of nappies, wipes, bottles and other baby paraphernalia cluttering up the bag.

'I'm just looking for a cloth to wipe her mouth. She's had a feed and she often brings a little bit of it back up.'

Hugo sighed nervously. Kate was so much less inhibited than Laura. He had done his best to avert his eyes when Kate suddenly whipped out her breast in the middle of Oliver Brown's office.

'Ah, here it is,' said Kate triumphantly, waving a grubby-looking muslin cloth in front of him. 'I'll take her now—'

Suddenly Kate's words caught in her throat as Daisy deposited a small quantity of churned-up milk all over Hugo's immaculate shoulder.

'Oh dear,' she said, trying hard not to laugh at his outraged face. 'Come here. I'd better mop you up instead.'

It was at least a quarter of an hour before Hugo emerged from the gentlemen's cloakroom and joined them in the corner of the American Bar. Thanks to a kind cloakroom attendant who had taken pity on him, the milk stain was barely visible now, but Hugo was still clearly ruffled by the experience.

'This was the last thing I needed,' he said irritably after he'd ordered a mineral water for himself and glasses of white wine for Laura and Kate. His earlier offer of champagne seemed to have gone by the board, thought Kate ruefully.

'Anyway,' he added, clearing his throat in an irritating way. 'I've actually got something very serious to discuss with you both.'

'What's that?' said Kate, her curiosity getting the better of her. Her brother-in-law couldn't usually be bothered to discuss even the weather with her. He must want something.

'As we all expected, your father has left each of you twenty per cent of the Hollingberry Holdings shares,' began Hugo.

'Did we all expect it?' asked Kate. 'I must say it came as news to me.'

Hugo glared at her.

'May I continue?'

'Yes sir,' said Kate with mock obedience.

'Thank you. Now, I don't know if you are aware of this, but even though Gordon Osprey is foolishly assuming that he is going to be the next chairman he actually only has a three per cent shareholding.'

'Of course we know,' muttered Kate. 'We've been going into Daddy's office since we were in ankle socks.'

'Good,' said Hugo, slightly thrown off his guard. 'Now, where was I? Ah yes. I have been talking to a lot of my fund-manager contacts and it emerges that they aren't as impressed with Gordon as he has led us to believe. In fact, if the truth be known, they would rather appoint someone younger – and preferably someone with family connections too.'

'Like me,' said Kate.

Hugo stared at Kate in disbelief.

'You?' he said. 'You are joking, aren't you? You'd never get the support of the board. You know next to nothing about Hollingberry Holdings.'

'That's where you're wrong, Hugo. I know a lot more than you think. I worked there in practically all my university vacations.'

'Fine,' said Hugo. 'Now, where was I? Ah yes. The fund managers would like to see someone younger and less set in their ways in charge.'

Kate stared at her brother-in-law. It was gradually beginning to dawn on her what all this was about.

'Ahhhh,' she said slowly, 'and you reckon that *you* are the man for the job, do you?'

At this, Hugo had the grace to flush slightly.

'Look, Kate,' he said. 'I appreciate that we have had our differences in the past. But wouldn't you rather have me, your own brother-in-law, running the show and protecting Daisy's inheritance, than Gordon Osprey? That man is a one-man ego trip. He couldn't give a damn about the Hollingberry family. He just wants to get his hands on the business.'

Kate took a long sip of her white wine and considered the matter. In one sense, Hugo was right. If Gordon Osprey became the next chairman he wouldn't be interested in doing any of them any favours. She wasn't entirely sure that she trusted Hugo, either, but he was probably the lesser of two evils . . .

'Say I did give you my support,' she said thoughtfully.

'Yes,' said Hugo, his voice sounding just a touch too eager.

'Where would that leave Charley?'

Kate could hardly believe that she was saying this. After his bloody lies about Rebecca Wilson, Charley was far from being her favourite person right now. But then again, if Hugo was jostling for the position of chairman, it was imperative to make sure that both she and Charley had some say in the outcome.

'Er, I hadn't actually given that much thought,' faltered Hugo. 'Yet, I mean.'

Kate's brain was working overtime now. If she gave Hugo her backing, it was only reasonable that she should ask for a few things in return.

'Right,' she said. 'Look, Laura, I know that you are nervous of having anything to do with Daisy but could you just take her while Hugo and I work all of this out?'

Laura reluctantly held out her arms to Daisy. She noted how naturally both Hugo and Kate assumed that she didn't have any contribution to make to the discussion about the future of Hollingberry Holdings. It was almost as if she didn't exist.

'Now,' said Kate firmly. 'I might be prepared to

support you as the new chairman if you agree to a few conditions first. One: I want you to appoint Charley as the new editor-in-chief of the *Clarion*. I know that you don't rate his management abilities very highly, but he's a bloody good newspaper man. Two: I want your absolute word that you will not, *repeat not*, close the *Bowland Bugle* down. My father wouldn't have wanted that – and I don't either. I know that it isn't making any money yet, but from what I understand it's well on the way to becoming profitable. It would be no skin off your nose to keep it going, would it? And three, I want to be made a non-executive director. To look after my interests. And Laura's of course.'

As Kate finished what she was saying, Hugo couldn't help staring at her, half fascinated by the way she'd seized the initiative and turned it round to her own advantage, and half appalled.

'Right,' he said forcefully. 'It's a deal. Let's have a toast. To the future of Hollingberry Holdings.'

'To the future,' repeated Kate, clinking Hugo's glass playfully.

They were both so absorbed in their own personal victories that neither of them noticed that Laura hadn't joined in the toast. She sat staring into space, wishing that Daisy was her baby and not Kate's.

Chapter Thirty-Four

Considering that his appointment as company chairman was virtually in the bag, Gordon Osprey was surprised by how nervous he felt on the morning of the Hollingberry Holdings board meeting. He had changed his shirt twice already, rejecting a white Hilditch and Key one for a blue Turnbull and Asser, and after first choosing the gold cufflinks that his father had given him for his twenty-first birthday had then swapped them for more discreet silver ones.

Now Gordon was pacing up and down the length of the Hollingberry Holdings boardroom, muttering to himself. Everything was in place, he knew it was, but he still had a nagging fear at the back of his mind that he should have spent more time wooing the fund managers who ultimately held his fate in their hands. He had been so busy charging up north to shut the Leadington group down, and so obsessed with warning that awful layabout Charley Stone that his career was in grave jeopardy, that perhaps he'd neglected his contacts.

As eleven am drew closer, the boardroom began to fill up. In bustled Graham Travis, the self-important company secretary with whom Gordon had clashed on countless occasions in the past, followed by the five ageing non-executive directors who'd sat on the board for years. HH had always liked to keep board meetings formal and short, using them merely to rubber-stamp decisions that he had already taken in private.

At eleven precisely, Gordon rose to his feet and cleared his throat.

'Good morning, gentlemen,' he said. 'As you all know, Hubert Hollingberry, our esteemed and much-loved chairman, died suddenly and unexpectedly on the first of July. I wish to place on record the fact that we, the board of Hollingberry Holdings, the company to which he devoted his entire working life, deeply regret his passing. In his absence, I shall be chairing the meeting this morning but before we begin I think that in the circumstances it is only right and proper that we observe a minute's silence in memory of Hubert's name.'

As the remaining six members of the board duly stood up, Gordon couldn't help congratulating himself. His decision to hold a minute's silence had been a stunning master stroke. It showed that he was compassionate as well as tough, sensitive as well as authoritative.

After that, the agenda got off to its usual start. First Graham Travis, an absolute stickler for detail, ran through the minutes of the last board meeting and outlined several matters arising from the minutes. Next, Gordon got up again to read out the chairman's report, ranging from last month's sales figures (respectable) to whether the company was still on budget or not (thanks to Leadington's unimpressive performance, it wasn't quite).

Halfway through the meeting one of HH's team of secretaries wheeled in a trolley bearing a silver coffee pot, seven Wedgwood coffee cups and a plate of iced fancies (HH, who had a sweet tooth, had always insisted on this and the secretaries had decided to continue the tradition.) After the young woman had poured out the coffee and quietly withdrawn, Gordon took charge once more.

'Now, gentlemen, the next item on the agenda, as you know, is the appointment of the new chairman of Hollingberry Holdings.'

At this point, some of the non-executive directors shuffled uncomfortably in their seats. This was the moment that they had been dreading all morning. Gordon, however, was so fired up with what he was about to say that he didn't even notice their discomfiture.

'I should like to propose myself as the new chairman of the company. As you know, I have been Hubert's right-hand man for more years than I care to remember. I became finance director ten years ago and then in 1993 Hubert did me the honour of making me his deputy chairman. Not only have I worked flat out for many years to ensure that Hollingberry Holdings has become the highly profitable company that it is today, but I have also been responsible for a large part of our company strategy. As a result I am sure that you will all agree that I shall make a very good chairman. And I shall endeavour to serve the company to the best of my abilities. Just as I always have.'

If Gordon Osprey had been a more observant man, it would have struck him by now that the non-executive directors lined along either side of the table were taking great pains to avoid looking directly at him.

'Have any of you got any comments or questions?' asked Gordon, his tone jovial.

A deathly silence descended, and for the first time in the entire meeting Gordon felt a shiver of fear run down the back of his neck.

'Oh come on,' he entreated. 'Someone must have something to say. Let me go round the table. Henry, I'm sure that I can count on you being for the proposal.'

Gordon had started off with Henry Grace because he was supremely confident that he would give him his backing. Henry had been appointed to the board largely because he was an old friend of HH's, but he had always appeared to rate Gordon in the past and had given him his unequivocal support.

It was a few moments before Henry spoke. There was no easy way to say this, he thought, wishing that the ground would open up and swallow him whole.

'I have to say that I am against it,' he mumbled finally. 'I have been taking soundings from quite a few of my fund-manager acquaintances and they all seem to be of the opinion that at this stage Hollingberry Holdings would benefit from appointing a younger chairman, someone who is not quite so set in their views. Not only that, but I have taken the liberty of speaking to two of the main shareholders and they are both firmly of the opinion that fresh blood is needed. I'm sorry, Gordon, but I must say that I am inclined to agree with them.'

By this time, sweat was beginning to pour down the inside of Gordon's Turnbull and Asser shirt. Main shareholders, indeed. It was abundantly clear who Henry meant. He meant Kate and Laura, HH's daughters. And what did they know about business, for God's sake? They were just little girls. He wouldn't trust the pair of them to run a sweetshop.

Gordon put the same question to the rest of the board one by one, and almost to a man they shook their heads reluctantly and outlined their reasons for declining to appoint him as chairman. By the time Humphrey White, a retired merchant banker, had gently admonished Gordon for not taking the trouble to talk to them sooner, Gordon had heard quite enough.

'If that's all the bloody thanks I get for devoting my whole life to this shithole of a company, then I'm resigning right here and now,' he yelled, his face turning scarlet with rage. 'I've sacrificed everything for Hollingberry Holdings. Everything. For years and years I've had to sit and listen to that fucking bastard HH taking the most crazy decisions and then had to repair the damage on the quiet afterwards so as not to ruin his bloody pride. *His* bloody pride. I ask you. What about *my* bloody pride? And just when I think that I'm going to reap my rewards, take charge in name as well as deed, how do you repay me? How do you bloody repay me? You bloody throw all my bloody achievements back in my face, that's how you repay me.'

Gordon Osprey was shaking with fury by this time, but Graham Travis and the non-executive directors were so stunned by this unexpected turn of events that they sat mute. None of them dared to interrupt for fear of being turned on personally. Finally Gordon slammed all his board papers down on the table and stormed out, banging the door shut behind him.

Henry Grace was the first to break the silence.

'Well, I think that rather memorable performance shows that between us we have made exactly the right decision,' he said.

The others tittered nervously.

'Now,' continued Henry Grace smoothly. 'Shall we call Hugo Bentley in immediately? I understand that he's just down the corridor.'

Charley Stone leaned back in the editor's chair and beamed with contentment. He was completely in his element. His brief period in management seemed like a bad dream now that he was back in the newsroom, back where he belonged. He was well aware that loads of people had nearly fallen off their chairs when they'd heard the news of his sudden leapfrog up the executive ladder to the newly created position of editor-in-chief, but he didn't give a damn. The old editor, Drew Thompson, whom Charley had personally never had any time for, had promptly walked out claiming constructive dismissal (although not before collecting a hefty pay-off on the way). He certainly wasn't going to have a young upstart like Charley Stone lording it over him and telling him what to do. But taken all round, Charley's appointment had been pretty much a one-day wonder. Jonty Miller, the longest-serving reporter on the paper, had merely shrugged his shoulders and carried on with his work. After thirty years on the *Clarion*, nothing could surprise him any more. Jonty had seen a grand total of twelve editors come and go during his time and now he was busy taking bets on how long Charley would last in the hot seat. Knowing Charley's low boredom threshold as well as he did, he gave him eighteen months at the very most.

Charley laid out all four editions of yesterday's paper in front of him on the desk. He was due to get on his soapbox and address the troops in a few minutes' time, so he wanted to give them his thoughts on the paper and how he planned to go about improving it. He studied each edition's splash carefully in turn. Apart from the last edition, which had carried a cracking interview with the parents of a young girl who'd died at an illegal rave in Brixton a couple of days earlier, the paper looked turgid and dull. Charley knew that the news editor, John Fry, would lay the blame at the door of the 'silly season' – the tabloids' term for the uneventful months of July and August, when parliament is in recess, the football season is over and anybody who is anybody is away on holiday. But, in Charley's book, that was simply no excuse. Under his editorship, John Fry would just have to start sending his reporters out of the office in search of their own stories for a change, not leave them chained to their desks all day rewriting agency copy.

'This is a new start for all of us,' said Charley when he got up to speak to his two hundred-strong staff. 'I want to make the *Evening Clarion* an essential read for everyone who lives and works in London. We hit the streets the day before the dailies, so we have a fantastic opportunity to set the agenda. If we can go just that extra bit further I think we can produce the best paper in Britain. Reporters, that means you filing the instant you've got the story in your notebooks. Subs, that means creating tight, clean, *accurate* copy before your deadlines, not *after*. News and features desks, that means racking your brains to come up with the best ideas in Fleet Street. Our circulation has dipped below the five-hundred-thousand mark in recent months; let's set about getting it back above half a million again.'

Charley was elated when he left the newsroom. He knew that he'd only been appointed editor because he happened to be married to HH's daughter, but he was convinced that he had the flair to turn the *Clarion* into a great paper. He was brimming with ideas, too. He intended to give it a new masthead and a new layout. He'd bring in more news pages (that was the key demand emerging from every single readership survey he'd seen so far), more inspiring features, a cookery column and he was even going to start running short stories aimed at weary commuters heading home out of the capital.

Over the next few weeks Charley worked flat out to put his vision of the *Clarion* into action. In the two years that Drew Thompson, his predecessor, had been editor, Drew had always turned up at the office at eight forty-five, just in time for the daily news conference and only half an hour before the first edition went to press. But Charley, fired up by work for the first time in years, insisted on arriving at seven am on the dot, a cappuccino from the deli round the corner in one hand, a great sheaf of ideas in the other. He didn't skulk around in his office, either. His way of working was to prowl around the newsroom, peeping over reporters' shoulders to check that they were using the best line in their intros, suggesting headlines and straps to the subs and bellowing at the features people to come in earlier. His constant presence irritated the life out of the whole newsroom, Charley was well aware of that, but then again he had a sneaking suspicion that they respected him for being so 'hands on'.

Within two months of taking charge, Charley reckoned that he had really started to make a difference to the *Clarion*. The circulation figures had stopped falling – pretty good for the summer months – and the paper already looked cleaner and livelier.

No, the only part of Charley's life that wasn't so great was home. Kate still hadn't forgiven him for his moment of madness with Rebecca Wilson, and constantly reminded him that he owed his exalted new position to her and her alone. The only good bit of his family life was Daisy, but then again he was working such crazy hours at the *Clarion* that he barely got to see her during her waking hours. And that didn't do much to endear him to Kate, either.

Kate stared at her blank computer screen and wondered what the hell she was going to write about.

This was the second week that she had actually come into the *Clarion* office to do her column. She'd finally decided that balancing her laptop on her knee and bashing away at the keyboard with Daisy grabbing at her ankles wasn't the ideal way to churn out eight hundred words of golden prose. She reckoned that, at eight months, Daisy was old enough to be left at a day nursery for one day a week while she went to the office.

Daisy's first experience of nursery had been deeply traumatic for both of them. Daisy had yelled her head off when Kate left her and Kate had wept huge messy tears all the way to the *Clarion*. Her eyes had looked like a panda bear's by the time she got there, and she'd had to spend her first ten minutes scrubbing her face clean and then completely redoing her mascara.

But today hadn't got off to quite such a bad start. Daisy's key nursery nurse had immediately engaged her interest with a teddy bear that was almost as big as she was, and Kate had managed to creep out of the nursery without causing a scene. When she'd arrived at the office soon after ten, however, Charley had immediately dashed her sunny mood by suggesting that writing about babies was old hat now and that she should get her teeth into something more substantial for this week's column.

'But the whole point was to write about what it's like being a new mother,' protested Kate.

Charley perched himself on the edge of her desk and looked at her pityingly.

'Kate,' he said. 'You've got to get a grip. I know that Joe Harris has been encouraging you as much as possible but you've got to move on. You can't go on writing about soggy nappies and Babygros for the rest of your career. It's time you tackled much grittier issues.'

'Like what?' asked Kate, trying hard not to lose her temper. 'The decline of marriage? Husbands who screw around? Something along those lines?'

At least Charley had the grace to look a little embarrassed, thought Kate with satisfaction. And anyway, he had a blooming cheek to knock her column like this. She'd written stuff on loads of other subjects, from genetically modified foods to the dearth of nursery-school places in London. Not only that, but she knew from her bulging mailbag that her column was proving to be a huge hit with the readers. No, Charley definitely didn't have a leg to stand on. He simply hated having to feel grateful to her for his high-flying new job and was determined to put her in her place. She wasn't having it.

'Right, I'll leave you to it,' he said, a touch nervously. 'I think you get my gist though, don't you sweetheart?'

'And don't sweetheart me in the office – it's very unprofessional,' hissed Kate.

But it was too late. Charley had moved on to harangue some hapless young reporter who had missed a good line in a court case at the Old Bailey the day before. Talk about poacher turned gamekeeper, thought Kate. He'd only been in the job for a few weeks and he was rapidly turning into a tyrant.

Despite Kate's irritation with Charley, however, she couldn't help mulling over what he had just said. Perhaps he did have a point, she conceded grudgingly, but she definitely wasn't going to stop writing about the trials and tribulations of motherhood altogether. She picked up a pile of press releases that Joe Harris had left on her desk and began to leaf through them. What she needed now was a little bit of inspiration.

Chapter Thirty-Five

As Kate raced into the foyer at Channel Four she still wasn't utterly convinced that she was doing the right thing. She'd finished this week's column – a diatribe about husbands who stay at the office so late that they barely recognise their children – and had decided to make a start on the next by turning up to a preview of a new TV series about the growing problem of drugs in schools. She hadn't yet worked out whether she intended to follow Charley's advice about her column or – a tempting option – whether it would be more fun to wind him up by going on about babies as before. But she had nothing to lose by collecting some other material together.

Armed with a press pack emblazoned with the title of the series, *Drugs in the Playground*, and bulging with Just Say No leaflets, Kate followed the motley crew of other journalists into a large viewing room and found a seat right at the back. If the publicist showed more than one programme, she would have to make her excuses and dash for it. Otherwise she'd never get to the nursery in time to collect Daisy.

As the lights went down and the title music struck up, Kate closed her eyes for a second. This was absolute bliss, she thought, sitting in a darkened room on her own in the middle of the afternoon, with no puréed carrots to prepare and no telephones ringing.

It seemed like only five minutes later when Kate became aware of someone tapping her on the shoulder.

'What's the matter?' she murmured sleepily, not wanting to open her eyes and spoil the dream she was having. She was in the middle of mad, passionate sex with a man with fair hair – she wasn't quite sure who he was – on a deserted sandy beach. The feel of his lips on her skin was so delicious that she didn't want any of it to end.

'The programme's finished,' whispered a voice in her ear. 'It's chucking-out time. Come on. Time to go.'

'Go? Go where?' Kate's brain felt completely befuddled. She could still sense the sand between her toes and the sound of the waves lapping against the shore. Where the hell was she supposed to be going? And anyway, she couldn't possibly leave now.

'The programme's over,' the voice murmured again. 'There's another busload of journalists coming in to watch a series about life on Mars. I shouldn't think that's quite up your street, is it?'

Instantly Kate sat up straight and opened her eyes. Baffled by where she was, she blinked at the bright overhead lights and empty seats, then turned her head to find out whom the voice belonged to.

When she saw that it was Ben Maguire standing there, a wave of shock swept through her body.

'Oh my God, it's you,' she said, trying hard not to stumble over her words. 'After all this time. What on earth are you doing here?'

'I could ask you exactly the same thing,' muttered Ben. 'Did you pop in just to catch up on a bit of kip or something? And I don't suppose it's worth me asking you what you thought of the programme.'

Kate glanced down into her lap, slightly sheepish that she hadn't watched even a second of it. And what was even more embarrassing was the fact that Ben knew perfectly well that she hadn't.

'I'm sorry,' she said. 'Truly I am. But what's your involvement? I thought you were working for the *Daily Recorder* or something.'

'I was, but I gave it up a few months ago and started working for an independent TV company. I just wasn't cut out for all that rubbish about soaps and royals and the Spice Girls. I wanted to get my teeth into something a bit more . . .'

'Challenging?' suggested Kate, finishing his sentence off for him.

'Exactly,' smiled Ben.

'And have you?' asked Kate.

Ben's laugh was so infectious that Kate couldn't help joining in.

'You might be able to answer that question yourself if you hadn't slept your way through the entire programme,' he said.

'I'm sorry,' said Kate. 'I'm sure it's absolutely brilliant. Was it your idea to do it?'

'Yep. I still see a few old mates from my teaching days and they all keep telling me horror stories about kids of thirteen and fourteen doling out tabs of Ecstasy in the playground like sweeties. They said that someone should do a hard-hitting series to show what's really going on, so when I joined Inside TV I immediately suggested it.'

Kate stared intently at Ben. It was getting on for two years since she'd last seen him and she was amazed by how much he'd changed. He'd lost weight and his hair was much shorter, but that wasn't all. He wasn't as laid-back as he'd been in Lancashire; there was a harder edge to him, a wariness that hadn't been there before.

At that moment he caught her gaze and she flushed. This was totally ridiculous, thought Kate. Her relationship with Ben had been over a long time ago. She was married to someone else now and had an eight-month-old daughter; it was no use to either of them dwelling on what might have been. She was here to work and the more she thought about Ben's series, the more she was convinced that it could be the ideal subject to launch her gritty new column.

'Did you come across anyone who might make a good interview for the *Clarion*?' she asked abruptly. 'A schoolgirl who's seen the error of her ways maybe?'

'It's possible,' said Ben. 'But you'd have to give the series a good plug. Could I trust you to do that?'

Kate glanced at him sharply. His face looked as impassive as before but the meaning behind his words was perfectly clear. She couldn't quite get her head around it, though. *He* was the one who'd betrayed her in the past, *he* was the one who'd tipped the *Daily News* off about her father's identity when she'd asked him not tell a soul and yet *he* obviously bore some kind of grudge against *her*.

Suddenly Kate glanced at her watch and clapped her hand to her mouth.

'Oh my God, it's gone five thirty. I've got to collect my little girl from nursery. I'm sorry Ben, but I must dash. Could we have a drink sometime over the next few days to talk about all this? I'd love to interview someone you've featured in the series.'

It was as if the shutters had been slammed down on Ben's face.

'I don't think so,' he said coolly. 'I don't think that we've really got much to say to each other, do you? But I'll pass on your request to the press office. They'll come back to you if they can do anything for you.'

For the next couple of days Ben couldn't stop thinking about Kate. Try as he did, he couldn't get her out of his mind. It was almost two years since their break-up but he'd been a fool to think that he'd got over her. He'd thrown himself into his career, gone to bed with loads of different girls and almost managed to convince himself that he was deliriously happy. It was as if he'd covered all the heartache up with a big sticking plaster and carried on with his life. But now Kate had reappeared completely out of the blue and wrenched the plaster off to show what was really underneath – a raw, gaping wound that hurt like hell.

He was pretty sure that he had upset her after the preview. Perhaps it was his imagination, but when he'd turned all cool and told her that he had no intention of meeting up for a drink she'd looked as if she was on the verge of bursting into tears. Thinking about it now, Ben had the grace to feel a bit ashamed of himself. So Kate had walked out on him, that didn't mean he had to retaliate by behaving like a bastard himself. They were both grown-ups, after all; it must be perfectly possible for them to talk to each other in a civilised way. And refusing to have anything to do with Kate was a bit like cutting off his nose to spite his face. For a start, if she could write a piece on *Drugs in the Playground* for the *Clarion* it would boost the viewing figures no end.

Ben left several conciliatory messages for Kate at the *Clarion* but it was a couple of days before she got round to ringing him back. In the meantime she'd written another column – about the pressures of parenthood on marriage – and had had two more rows with Charley about cutting the fluffy stuff about babies and looking for new subject material. The second of these had ended up with him threatening to axe her column altogether and her yelling that if he did that she'd get him fired.

'I haven't heard anything from the press office,' Kate told Ben when he picked up his phone.

'No, you won't have. I've been handling it myself.'

'But I thought you didn't want to have anything to do with me. You said that—'

'I know,' said Ben, interrupting her in mid-flow. 'Look, Kate, I'm sorry. I was just pissed off at the way you behaved back in Lancashire and I suppose I wanted to get my own back. It was mean-spirited and immature. I'm sorry.'

'The way *I* behaved?' spluttered Kate. 'It was *you*. I completely trusted you – like no one before or since – and you went and . . .'

On the other end of the telephone Ben sighed heavily.

'Look, Kate,' he said again. 'There's been a lot of water under the bridge since then. You're married and have got a kid and I . . .' He stopped for a moment before continuing. What exactly did he have? '. . . I've moved on too. Let's just try and be adult about this, shall we? Now, if you want to do something on *Drugs in the Playground*, I've talked to one of the girls involved and both she and her parents would be willing to talk to you.'

'What's the story?' asked Kate, making a huge effort to sound professional.

'She's called Imogen and she nearly died after taking a tab of E she bought from a school pal. She's nearly fifteen and incredibly articulate for her age so she would make a great interview for the *Clarion*.'

'Does she mind her name being used?'

'We've just used her first name in the film so I think you should stick to that too,' said Ben. 'And don't identify the school. Or the town where she lives.'

'That sounds fine,' said Kate. 'We're always incredibly careful about interviewing minors these days.'

When Kate turned up at the shabby offices of Inside TV, just off Tottenham Court Road, the following Wednesday morning with a grumbling Gus Jones in tow, she prayed that Ben wouldn't be sitting in on the interview. They seemed to have come to some sort of a truce, thank goodness, but she certainly didn't want any disagreements to surface while she was chatting to Imogen. In fact, as it turned out, Ben wasn't even in the office – a taciturn secretary grudgingly told Kate that he'd gone out to do a recce for a new series he was working on for the BBC.

'Where can we do the interview?' asked Kate. She felt oddly disappointed not to see Ben.

'Dunno,' grunted the secretary. 'The only office not being used at the moment is Ben's so I s'ppose you'd better go in there.'

'Thanks,' said Kate, trying – with great difficulty – to summon up every ounce of charm she possessed. 'Could you possibly show Imogen and her parents in there when they arrive?'

As Kate pushed open Ben's office door she realised

that her heart was beating wildly. It felt strange walking into Ben's working environment, as if she was trespassing on private property. She couldn't help smiling at the tip that he'd left the place in, though. His flat in Lancashire had always been piled high with magazines and newspapers, clothes and old bits of motorbikes, and this was pretty much the same. The desk by the window was so cluttered with papers that you could barely see the surface at all. Kate sat down gingerly at the desk and cleared a few things to one side so that she could put her tape recorder, notebook and folder of newspaper cuttings down. When she glanced at Ben's computer screen, however, her heart began hammering so hard that she was sure even Gus Jones would be able to hear it.

'Hey, that's you, isn't it?' said Gus, staring at the passport-sized picture stuck to the side of the computer terminal.

'Don't be ridiculous – of course it isn't,' snapped Kate, wrenching the photograph down and stuffing it in her jacket pocket. 'She just looks a bit like me, that's all. My hair's much shorter than that.'

That at least was true, she thought with a frown, touching the back of her bob. And, in a way, the girl beaming sleepily in the picture was a different person altogether. This was a spirited girl of twenty-two in the throes of her first passionate love affair – Ben had taken the picture, if she remembered rightly, just after they'd made love. Not a weary twenty-four-year-old wife and mother of one, who never got enough sleep and whose husband irritated the hell out of her.

At that moment, the door opened and the secretary ushered Imogen and her parents in. Kate's jaw almost dropped to the floor at Imogen's appearance. She'd been expecting a spotty schoolgirl with pallid skin and fingernails bitten to the quick. The young girl standing in front of her looked as if she'd lived the purest life imaginable, never had anything whatsoever to do with drugs. Her skin glowed with health, her long auburn hair was glossy and lustrous, and, far from the shabby school uniform that Kate had been expecting, she was wearing a T-shirt and tight pedal pushers that showed off her slim figure to perfection.

'She's not supposed to look like that,' hissed Gus in Kate's ear. He was grateful at least that in order for Imogen not to be identified he'd been instructed to take a rear-view picture. 'She's so wholesome and fresh that she looks as if she's just stepped out of a toothpaste commercial.'

'Shut up and let me get on with the interview, will you?' whispered Kate, though, to be honest with herself, she was feeling a little bit anxious too. Imogen's story was supposed to be a salutary warning to other teenagers of the perils of taking drugs, for God's sake, not an advert for them.

But ten minutes into the interview, Kate started to relax. She really should have trusted Ben's news judgement in the first place. Imogen, she realised, might look amazingly healthy now, but she'd been one of the lucky ones. For two days after buying an Ecstasy tablet from a boy in her class and taking it in the school cloakroom her life had hung in the balance. It had been touch and go whether she would survive.

'I knew that there was something wrong the moment I got home from work that night,' said Imogen's mum, a quietly-spoken woman of about forty-five. 'The pupils of her eyes were huge, like golf balls, and she kept complaining that she couldn't feel her legs and arms. Then she began vomiting and collapsed into a coma. To this day I'm certain that if we hadn't got her to hospital so fast she would have died. We've got a picture of her taken in the hospital and when I look at it now I can't believe she came through.'

'Why have you decided to go public on this?' Kate asked Imogen, her voice gentle. 'It takes a lot of courage to talk about it.'

'I nearly died,' said the teenager, looking down into her lap. 'I know that if I'd had the slightest idea what taking just one Ecstasy tablet would do to me and my family I would never have swallowed it. So I want to do anything I can to warn other teenagers out there. And that includes doing the programme and sitting here with you now.'

Kate was chasing Daisy round the bedroom on her hands and knees the next morning when Charley rang from the office. Daisy had just begun to crawl and was enthralled by how clever she was.

'What do you want?' Kate asked, slightly out of breath. As a rule Charley never rang her during the day; he was claiming more and more that he was far too busy for domestic small talk.

'The first edition of the paper has just dropped and I had to ring you,' he said. 'I'm over the fucking moon with it, sweetheart. I just wanted to say that I'm glad to see that you do take my advice occasionally.'

Kate sat down abruptly. She couldn't remember the last time Charley had paid her a compliment. Not since her father's death, anyway.

'What are you talking about?' she said, though she knew perfectly well.

'Don't be ridiculous, sweetheart. Your column. Your

fucking amazing column. I didn't know you had it in you.'

'There's no need to swear at me, you know,' said Kate. She'd noticed that in the three months since Charley had become editor-in-chief the title had begun to go to his head. He now insisted on wearing nothing but Armani suits – 'we can afford it, can't we?' was his excuse – always went to Nicky Clarke's to have his hair cut and spent far more time at the Savoy than he did at home. He was also so used to swearing at people at work when they didn't do what he wanted that he'd begun to do it at home too.

'Do you want me to bike a copy of the first edition round to you?' asked Charley. 'We've even trailed it on the front, complete with your picture byline.'

For a split second, Kate was tempted. She had to admit that she was curious to see how the page looked and it would certainly save her getting Daisy dressed, bundling her into her pram and then lumbering down to Notting Hill Gate. But then again, she couldn't bear Charley to think that he was doing her a favour.

'It's all right,' she said curtly. 'I'll get one when I go out.'

'Fine, I was only trying to help,' said Charley and slammed the phone down.

It was another hour before Kate was finally ready to leave the flat. She cursed herself repeatedly for her pig-headedness. So Charley was being a pain at the moment – and a patronising one at that – but why had she insisted on making life even more difficult for herself by turning down his offer of biking the *Clarion* round?

She was in the middle of hunting for her front-door

keys, wishing that she could be better organised, when the telephone rang again.

'Hello,' she grunted, her bad temper all too evident.

'Kate?'

'Yes. Who is it?'

'It's Ben. Ben Maguire. I just wanted to congratulate you on the piece. You did a great job, you really did. It's so moving, so touching and yet it hammers home the dangers of taking drugs. Imogen and her mum and dad are really pleased with it too. They've just rung me.'

Overcome with confusion, Kate couldn't think what to say.

'But how did you get my number?' she asked eventually. 'We're ex-directory.'

Much to her surprise, Ben roared with laughter at this remark.

'You don't reckon much to my journalistic skills, do you?' he chuckled. 'Come on. You may be married to a newspaper editor but you're hardly MI5. It wasn't exactly taxing to get hold of it. I just rang one of my contacts and hey presto, I got it.'

It struck Kate forcibly all of a sudden that this was the first time that Ben had actually mentioned Charley. For a second or two she wondered what he thought of him, and then shuddered. It didn't bear thinking about. The pair of them were like chalk and cheese. Neither man would have any time for the other at all. Ben would reckon Charley was too flash and insubstantial, while Charley would dismiss Ben as 'a wishy-washy pinko'.

'I was thinking,' said Ben, the hesitation discernible in his voice.

'What?' said Kate.

'Do you remember suggesting that we meet up for a drink sometime?'

'Vaguely,' replied Kate. He'd been so vehement in his refusal that she wasn't going to make life easier for him now by biting his hand off with eagerness.

'Well, I was wondering whether you'd fancy meeting for lunch?'

'What? Today?'

'Yep. I know I haven't given you much notice but I just thought . . .'

'I've got Daisy with me today,' said Kate quickly.

'Who's Daisy?' asked Ben.

'My daughter,' said Kate. 'She's almost nine months old now.'

'Oh. Well, perhaps another time then.'

Kate paused for a moment. Then her words came out in a rush.

'It's such a fantastic day. I'd been thinking of taking Daisy for a picnic in Kensington Gardens. Nothing fancy or anything but why don't you come along too?'

'OK,' said Ben slowly. 'I will.'

'Great. Shall we meet by the Round Pond at, say, one pm? Oh, and Ben?'

'What?' said Ben.

'I'm afraid you'll have to be prepared to feed the ducks with us. It's Daisy's favourite thing.'

Chapter Thirty-Six

The Round Pond was virtually deserted when Kate arrived just before one. It was the end of September now, and the children who usually frequented the gardens on roller blades and racing bikes had been back at school for a couple of weeks. There was just one solitary nanny in a crisp blue uniform helping a laughing toddler to launch a miniature sailing boat, and a couple of elderly ladies walking their dogs. Despite the fact that it was early autumn the sky was azure blue and the trees, which hadn't yet begun to shed their leaves, gloriously green.

Kate reached inside the basket hanging from the pushchair handle and broke off a few hunks of the baguette she'd brought with her.

'Look,' she shouted to Daisy. 'Quack-quacks.'

Daisy, gurgling with delight from her seat, pointed excitedly at the birds. Apart from the fact that she hated going to bed, reflected Kate, who'd lost track of the number of times she'd had to climb into Daisy's cot herself to soothe her daughter to sleep, she really was the world's most perfect baby. Rosy-cheeked and pretty, with a mop of blonde curls, Daisy loved action, noise and colour. That made a walk around Kensington Gardens her absolute number one activity.

'Aren't you going to introduce us then?' said a man's voice from behind.

Kate swung round to see Ben standing there with a carrier bag in one hand and a huge bunch of bright blue delphiniums in the other. Caught by surprise, she felt her heart lurch like a teenager's. Dressed in an old pair of jeans and a soft suede jacket rather than the suit he'd been wearing at the preview, Ben somehow looked much more like the Ben she'd first met and fallen in love with.

'God, you nearly made me jump out of my skin,' said Kate, making a desperate attempt not to show the effect that he'd just had on her.

Ben stood there awkwardly. He wasn't sure whether to kiss her on the cheek or not, but in the end decided that it was perhaps better not to risk it. A kiss simply wasn't appropriate any more. Kate would probably go all frosty on him and that was the last thing he wanted.

For her part, Kate felt sad to see him being so cool towards her; but like Ben she didn't want to get too close for fear of rejection.

'Allow me to introduce you to Daisy Angelica Clare Stone,' she said, breaking the uncomfortable silence that had descended. Right on cue, Daisy turned her head and beamed a megawatt smile at Ben.

Clever girl, thought Kate. She watched as Ben, his confidence boosted no end by Daisy's favourable reaction to him, crouched down and solemnly took the little girl's hand.

'Hello Daisy,' he said softly. 'It's very nice to meet you. And may I say that I really like your red romper suit. I must get one myself some time.'

'You're good with babies,' said Kate. 'Lots of men

392

would run a mile if they were confronted with a nine-month-old. And especially a nine-month-old with a snotty nose and bread all over her face.'

'One of my sisters has got a kid of about the same age,' said Ben without looking up. 'She's called Grace and she's very nearly as gorgeous as you, Daisy. I've even been known to babysit for her on occasion.'

'That sounds useful,' grinned Kate. 'Babysitters are like gold dust around here. I'll bear you in mind if I ever get stuck.'

The sight of her with her small daughter had been far more unsettling than Ben had anticipated. Unbeknownst to Kate, he had stood and watched them together for a couple of minutes when he'd first arrived at the Round Pond. He'd noticed how she had handed Daisy a small piece of bread and then, with the utmost patience, had tried to show the little girl how to throw it to the ducks. But Daisy, much to Kate's indignation, had immediately stuffed it into her mouth and swallowed it.

Observing the two of them, Ben couldn't help wishing yet again that everything had turned out differently with Kate. He was haunted by the thought that if their relationship hadn't fallen apart so suddenly, Daisy could easily have been his daughter and not Charley Stone's. The three of them could have been the family of his own he'd always wanted.

Ben stood up quickly. It was ridiculous even to think about it. He'd drive himself mad if he carried on tormenting himself like this.

'Have you seen the *Clarion* yet?' he asked.

'I hadn't when you rang but I have now,' said Kate. 'Look in here.'

Ben glanced in her basket and chuckled out loud.

She hadn't just bought one copy of the *Clarion* but five or six.

'It's very uncool to do that, you know,' he said teasingly. 'But great minds think alike. I remember buying up every copy in the newsagent's when I got my first byline.'

'Very uncool,' agreed Kate. 'But it's the first decent piece I've written in ages and one copy didn't seem quite enough.'

Now that Daisy had devoured about a third of the baguette, Kate wheeled the pushchair around and they began walking east towards the Serpentine. When they found a shady expanse of grass beneath a tree Kate laid a huge tartan rug on the ground and took Daisy out of her pushchair. She handed Ben the remains of the bread, two different sorts of cheese and an ice-cold can of lager.

'I'm afraid I haven't brought anything very exciting,' she said apologetically. 'I have to cart so much stuff around for Daisy that I couldn't possibly manage a posh picnic hamper too.'

'It doesn't matter a bit,' smiled Ben, brandishing a bottle of champagne and two glasses. 'But I hope you won't say no to a glass of this. To celebrate your brilliant piece and . . .' He paused for a moment before continuing. 'Meeting up again.'

He deftly opened the champagne and before it had a chance to fizz out of the bottle poured them each a glass.

'To meeting up again,' said Kate, clinking her glass against his. She'd read somewhere that all the royals deemed clinking glasses terribly vulgar but what the hell, she *always* clinked. It was an absolutely integral part of the celebration of champagne.

Ben glanced at her, holding his gaze for a little longer than he'd intended, and repeated the words once more.

'To meeting up again,' he said simply.

The rest of the afternoon flew past without either of them being aware of it. In the twenty-one months that had elapsed since she'd last seen Ben, Kate had completely forgotten how effortless it was to talk to him. Whenever she and Charley spent any time together – which was rare these days – they either climbed straight into bed or began shrieking at each other. There was none of the easy companionship that she and Ben had always enjoyed. *And*, she reflected, despite everything it was exactly the same today. They'd discussed everything under the sun, from Ben's frustration with the tabloids and his move into television, to the death of Kate's father and her worries about Laura.

'Are you seeing anyone at the moment?' Kate asked casually, her courage fuelled by half a bottle of champagne.

'What? A woman, you mean?'

Kate burst into peals of laughter.

'Of course I mean a woman,' she giggled. 'I didn't mean a chimpanzee, did I?'

'Oh, I don't know,' said Ben. 'I know some very attractive chimpanzees.'

Kate threw Daisy's sunhat at him and dissolved into giggles.

'The answer to your question is no, by the way,' said Ben quietly.

'That's a shame,' said Kate, keeping her voice light. 'I would have thought that lots of girls would consider you quite a catch.'

'There was someone a while back,' said Ben. 'Someone really special.'

Kate almost caught her breath.

'What happened?'

'Oh, I don't know. It just didn't work out. No reason. You know how these things are.'

'What was she like?' asked Kate.

'The best,' murmured Ben. 'I'll never meet anyone like her again, that's for sure.'

His face looked so pensive now that Kate leaned forward and patted him on the knee in an effort to comfort him. She wasn't sure whether he was talking about her or not and she didn't quite dare ask.

'Surely you could try and make things up,' she said. 'Couldn't you?'

'Fraid not,' said Ben and his voice sounded oddly flat. 'She met someone else, you see. It's too late now. Far too late.'

Alexa Grainger walked purposefully up to the entrance of the red-brick mansion block and pressed the doorbell of number forty-four long and hard.

She'd been the world's worst friend to Laura over the last year or so and she knew it – but now she was going to start making amends.

Since Laura's wedding to the ghastly Hugo, Alexa had been working like a woman possessed to establish her name as an artist. And, just recently, friends in the art world had begun telling her that she could well be on the verge of success. Her style was still as bold and vibrant as ever, hot, zingy abstracts painted on huge canvases, but she'd exhibited at two prestigious shows recently and the critics had observed a new subtlety in her work.

'*Alexa Grainger is growing up at last,*' the *Clarion*'s newly appointed art critic had written. '*Her work still possesses the raw vitality and promise of her art-school days, but she is now starting to show signs of increasing maturity and thoughtfulness. If her work continues to develop like this she has the potential to become a great exponent of her art, not merely a competent one.*'

Alexa had been so overcome by these words that she carried the newspaper cutting with her at all times. Whenever she felt that her work wasn't progressing as smoothly as she would like it to, she would take it out and read it all over again. As a consequence the cutting was now so worn from being constantly folded and refolded that some of the words were barely legible.

'Who is it?' came Laura's voice through the intercom.

'Alexa,' shouted Alexa. 'I've come to take you out to lunch. To apologise for neglecting you so badly.'

Laura buzzed the front door open and Alexa clattered up the stone stairs to the first-floor flat.

When the two women confronted each other on the doorstep they were each stunned by the other's appearance. Laura hadn't set eyes on Alexa for so long that she'd forgotten how amazingly colourful she was. Today Alexa had swept her red curls into a topknot on her head and was wearing a turquoise silk shalwar kameez that clashed alarmingly with her hair. On her feet she wore flat open-toed sandals and she had painted her toenails navy blue. Laura couldn't help laughing at this. She hadn't even known that you could get navy blue nail varnish. She was more a pearly pink girl herself.

'What's so funny?' asked Alexa, pleased to see a smile on Laura's face.

'It's your nails,' chuckled Laura. 'I've never seen navy blue nails before.'

'Oh, that's nothing,' said Alexa. 'They were purple with yellow dots yesterday. Can I come in, by the way?'

Alexa noticed how Laura's eyes instantly clouded over, as if she had some deep dark secret to hide. The radiant Laura of her wedding day had all but disappeared. Her friend seemed shy and uncertain of herself, and her face looked shrunken and almost sallow. She couldn't possibly be happy, thought Alexa, not when she looked like this.

'The whole place is in complete chaos,' said Laura, a hint of desperation discernible in her voice.

Alexa stared hard at her.

'Do you remember who you're talking to?' she said with an engaging grin. 'Only the biggest slut in London. In fact the only reason I popped round to see you today was that I couldn't bear sitting in my hellhole of a flat for a minute longer. And my studio's almost as bad. So, Laura, you know that chaos is like water off a duck's back to me. Really. And anyway, nothing about you could possibly shock me.'

Looking at Alexa, Laura knew that she was right. Alexa had seen her through everything. Her terrible homesickness on being sent to boarding school, the row with HH over her dire GCSE results and, worst of all, the appalling excesses of bulimia she'd suffered with such monotonous regularity. Yes, Alexa was the only one who really knew how low she'd sunk over the years.

'OK,' said Laura, opening the door a little wider. 'But I'm afraid I'm going through a bit of a bad patch.'

That, thought Alexa, as she peeped surreptitiously

into the kitchen, must be the understatement of the year. Every single surface was covered with biscuit wrappers, pizza boxes, baked-bean tins with spoons sticking out of them and discarded ice-cream cartons. Laura always went for exactly the same things when her bulimia was bad. She always chose food that was quick and easy to shovel into her poor mouth; and food that was equally quick and easy to rid herself of afterwards.

'Come here,' said Alexa and Laura, craving the physical contact that she'd been lacking for so long, obediently stepped forward into her friend's arms.

Alexa had no idea how long she stood and hugged Laura for. Desperate to hide her shock at how weak Laura had become, she berated herself yet again for staying away for so long. Why the hell hadn't she come and checked up on Laura before this? Deep down, however, she knew the answer. She had somehow managed to convince herself that with Hugo to look after her Laura would be all right. But now Alexa had to confront the truth. Laura was quite patently not all right. She was very far from all right.

'Where's Hugo at the moment?' Alexa asked, standing back to take another good look at her.

Laura's face froze at the very mention of Hugo's name. Since his appointment as chairman of her father's company, Hugo had barely been at home at all. Not only had he taken it upon himself to visit every single newspaper in the far-flung Hollingberry empire, but he was still trying to finalise the acquisition of the Scottish newspaper group he was so keen on – a deal that seemed to entail spending a couple of days in Campbeltown every week. As a consequence, Laura could virtually count on the fingers of one hand the number of times they'd had a proper conversation recently, let alone anything else.

'At work, of course,' said Laura quickly. 'That's where he always is.' She tried to smile but couldn't quite pull it off.

'But he's home every night, isn't he?' asked Alexa.

'Not that much, no.'

'Why not?' asked Alexa. 'I know he's a Very Important Person these days but surely you get to see each other sometimes?'

Laura sighed. She'd forgotten how persistent Alexa was. When her friend got the bit between her teeth she always refused to let go. No matter how hard Laura tried to evade the question, Alexa would keep on asking it until she got an answer she was satisfied with. She should have been a lawyer, not an artist.

'We see each other sometimes, yes,' said Laura finally, 'but we never really talk. And anyway, Hugo can't think about anything apart from Hollingberry Holdings these days. It's ironic, really, isn't it? I spent my whole childhood competing with the family business for my father's attention. And now I'm going through exactly the same thing with Hugo.'

Alexa sat down on the shabby green sofa and patted the seat next to her. It was time to try a different tack with Laura, she thought, ideas spinning frantically in her head.

'Do you know what I think the problem is?' she said.

'What?' asked Laura, pulling absent-mindedly at a thread dangling from one of the cushions. She'd kept trying to persuade Hugo to let her get the sofa re-covered but he steadfastly refused.

'I don't want to sound harsh but you simply haven't got enough to do. It's ages since you jacked in your job at Moneywise, isn't it? So what do you do all day to keep yourself occupied?'

Laura shifted awkwardly in her seat.

'I've got absolutely loads to do,' she said. 'Shopping, cleaning, cooking. Oh, and I read masses of books. And sometimes I pop over to see Dodo – she's only round the corner – or Kate.'

'How's Kate's baby?' asked Alexa, her face lighting up. 'I love babies. If I could only meet someone willing to be a father I'd have one like a shot. Lenny would have been ideal but he spends virtually all his time in New York these days. The American designers just adore him, worse luck. Anyway, what about you? Have you and Hugo thought about having babies?'

Laura shook her head a little too vehemently. Fond as she was of Alexa, this was the one subject she didn't want to discuss. If she ever started talking to Alexa about the pain of being childless, she'd never be able to stop. She deeply regretted having mentioned it to Dodo. It was far better to keep the hurt locked safely away inside her, away from other people's prying eyes, no matter how well meaning they were.

'I sometimes wonder whether I should get another job,' she said, her voice tentative.

'That's a great idea,' said Alexa. 'Why don't you?'

'I'm not sure if Hugo would approve,' said Laura slowly. 'He made me give up the job at Moneywise and we've never discussed me working somewhere else.'

'Oh bugger Hugo,' shouted Alexa, slapping her hands down on her knees. 'Let him go and bloody jump in the river. *I* think a job is exactly what you need. You'll go bonkers if you carry on sitting in this flat by yourself much longer. And besides, I've got a proposition to put to you. Shall I tell you about it?'

Chapter Thirty-Seven

Hugo stood on the edge of the pavement and gazed up at the magnificent four-storey house in front of him. He remembered how stunned he'd been the first time he'd set eyes on it. It had been the day Laura fainted in his office and he'd accompanied her home in a taxi, fully expecting to drop her off at some grotty bedsit with countless pairs of tights drying on the fireguard and a bathroom shared by twenty other tenants. And instead he'd discovered that she lived here, in this imposing townhouse that must be worth millions.

All his life Hugo had dreamed of living in a house like this and now that his chairmanship of Hollingberry Holdings was progressing so well it looked as though he could be on the verge of fulfilling his heart-felt desire.

For all Hugo's self-importance, his background was not nearly as privileged as he liked to make out. He had been an introverted only child, a fact that probably accounted for his difficulties in forming relationships in later life. His father, a magistrates' clerk, and his mother, a librarian, had been in their late thirties by the time he was born and had stopped at absolutely nothing to give their son the chances they themselves had never had. Hugo had excelled at maths from a young age, and when he won a major scholarship to a minor public school his parents had crippled themselves financially to cobble together the remainder of the fees as well as to pay for his uniform and sports equipment.

His father had died of a heart attack during Hugo's first year at Oxford, and his mother had followed suit four years later, soon after her son had started his accountancy training. Even Hugo had been surprised by how remarkably little their deaths had affected him; he had always been a loner and life seemed to continue pretty much as it had before. Until he'd married Laura he'd never lived with anyone apart from his parents, and it had taken him a long time to get used to sharing his life. Now he was accustomed to it, he still wanted the relationship to be completely on his terms. Hugo liked having Laura to come home to and was actually quite fond of her in his own way – just so long as she didn't make any demands on him.

HH's house had been lying empty for more than six months. Dodo made it her business to pop in now and again to check that everything was all right, but apart from that it just sat there like a great white elephant, gathering dust. A couple of weeks after Christmas, however, Hugo visited the house and judged that the time was right to broach the subject of what should be done with it.

'I didn't want to upset you by mentioning it before,' he said to Laura when he got back home that evening. His voice was unusually gentle. 'But we can't just let your father's house sit there. I've been mulling the matter over and it seems to me that there are two realistic options. We can either sell it, which I'm sure you and Kate would never contemplate, or we can move into it ourselves.'

'What? All of us?'

Hugo tried hard not to lose his temper. Sometimes he wondered whether Laura was completely losing her marbles. Since she'd started spending all her time with Alexa Grainger again she'd become preoccupied, distant with him. Half the time she didn't even appear to be listening to anything he said. The pair of them were definitely up to something, he knew it, but he'd been so snowed under with work that he simply hadn't had the time to cross-question Laura and get to the bottom of all this.

'Of course I don't mean all of us,' he said irritably. 'I have quite enough to do with Charley Stone as it is without having to live under the same roof as him. No, I mean you and me. It seems such a shame to leave your father's house empty – and you're always going on about moving to something bigger.'

Laura twiddled a bit of blonde hair round her thumb. She'd lived in the Chelsea house virtually all her life and the idea of moving back in again now was oddly appealing. She hated seeing it neglected and unloved; it would be good to put a little bit of life back into the place again.

'I'll have to talk to Kate about it,' she said. 'It's her house too, you know.'

Hugo glanced up from his papers. A few months ago Laura would have immediately deferred to him and allowed him to get on with sorting all the arrangements out. But now she didn't seem quite so submissive as before – another development that he put down to Alexa's bad influence.

Kate, as it turned out, was perfectly happy to let

Laura and Hugo move into HH's house. She'd been slightly taken aback by the suggestion – she'd assumed that she and Laura would eventually get round to selling it and splitting the proceeds between them – but she certainly had no desire to live in it herself. She was quite happy in Notting Hill.

'How much rent are they going to pay you?' was Charley's immediate reaction when Kate told him the news.

Kate shrugged her shoulders.

'Oh, some nominal amount. We haven't really talked about anything like that yet.'

Charley looked aghast. Kate just didn't have a clue about anything, he thought savagely, least of all the dangers of letting her sister and brother-in-law move into a house that was half hers – and for free. She seemed to be living in her own little world these days, a world that included Daisy and virtually nobody else. He was amazed that she actually managed to produce her column on time each week. Mind you, her column was the one thing that Charley couldn't criticise her for. Since she'd transformed it from a soppy monologue about the joys of motherhood into a much tougher commentary about life in general it had become one of the most successful parts of the paper. The *Clarion* now sold more copies on Thursdays, the day Kate's column came out, than any other day.

After six months of being in charge of the *Clarion*, the novelty of editing had slowly started to lose its appeal – just as Jonty Miller had predicted. Charley had gone storming into his new job back in July, made loads of changes and completely revamped the paper. And what had been the result? He'd been rewarded for all his efforts by a slight rise in sales figures – but no more than that. Now he was increasingly coming to realise that the secret of being a great newspaper editor was slogging away week in, week out, year after year. No editor could double the *Clarion*'s sales figures overnight; he'd have to keep going for another twenty years to achieve that. But the prospect of still doing exactly the same job in his fifties was so depressing that he could hardly bear to contemplate it.

As Charley grew older – he was now thirty-two – it had gradually begun to dawn on him that his boredom threshold was spectacularly low. He was like a fox who, when he'd caught his prey, enjoyed playing with it for a bit and then cast it aside. Charley adored the thrill of the chase but once he'd got what he wanted he was always bored out of his brain within months. It seemed to apply to everything he touched. After the initial excitement of making it onto a London newspaper in the first place, he'd relaxed and taken things easy. After the struggle to make everyone at the *Clarion* sit up and take him seriously as an editor, he now wandered in late every morning, just like his predecessor had. And after stopping at nothing to charm Kate up in Lancashire, she now irritated the pants off him. Even Daisy, he was slightly ashamed to admit, didn't seem quite so entrancing as she had at first.

But, for all the frustrations at the *Clarion*, Charley couldn't deny that being editor had its plus points. The best part was all the film premières, book launches, parties and dinners he now got invited to. He occasionally took Kate along with him but just recently he had started going to many of them alone. A shiver of excitement ran through his bones as he thought back to the stunning young model he'd picked up at a wildly glamorous first night the week before. It was a bit like being single all over again – and he was loving every illicit minute of it.

A lump grew in Laura's throat as she stood in the middle of the attic bedroom that she and Kate had shared for so long. She hadn't been up here for years, but looking at the wooden floor, and the strawberry pink doll's house that Dodo had given them one Christmas, and the two small beds with matching floral counterpanes had suddenly brought all the memories flooding back. She remembered the countless nights when Kate had cried her heart out for Clare and how she'd always got out of bed to go and comfort her little sister. It was hard to believe now that it had been her consoling Kate and not the other way round.

The sound of a huge crash downstairs and a bellow of anger from Hugo suddenly interrupted Laura's reverie.

'And you can bloody well take more care,' he shouted. 'If you carry on like this you can tell your boss that I'll be knocking a hefty whack off his bill.'

Laura slumped onto the bed that had always been hers. Hugo was in such a filthy temper at the moment that she'd been trying desperately hard to keep out of the way all morning. Even though he was obviously stressed out of his mind with work he had insisted on taking the morning off to supervise the removal men. It had been totally pointless, thought Laura. She'd told him that she was perfectly capable of sorting everything out – she knew the house like the back of her hand after all – but he'd refused to listen. It wasn't even as if there was very much to move – just a few pictures and some scruffy bits of furniture from Hugo's flat. He'd decided to keep the flat as an investment property and had let it out at a vast rent. The new occupant, however, had turned her nose up at most of Hugo's stuff so it was all being moved to Chelsea instead. If Laura had had her way, she would have chucked the whole bloody lot out but Hugo wouldn't hear of it.

Laura glanced at her watch. It was one thirty now, so with any luck Hugo would be on his way back to the office soon and she could get on with unpacking boxes in peace. Even more appealing was the thought that she'd be out by the time Hugo returned from work this evening. She did a quick sum with her fingers. That meant she wouldn't have to talk to him properly for at least another *thirty* hours. Brilliant.

Over the last few weeks Laura had made a huge effort to pull herself together. She'd started eating more healthily, walked over the bridge to Battersea Park every day and had thrown herself into Alexa's project with an enthusiasm she hadn't known for years. Her new positive attitude was largely due to Alexa, of course. To Alexa and her bright idea that Laura should start working as her agent.

'This is my proposition,' Alexa had told her firmly, in a voice that Laura knew would brook no opposition. 'You need something to do, Laura, or you're going to go completely out of your mind. And I need an agent. Everyone says that I'm on the verge of making it if I can just get myself organised. The only trouble is that I'm so busy painting that I simply haven't got the time – or the inclination – to get organised. So I need someone to represent me. Someone who'll talk to the galleries on my behalf, organise viewings and exhibitions, talk to potential customers. What do you think?'

Laura had been so startled by Alexa's idea that for a few seconds she'd been completely lost for words.

'But I . . .' she mumbled finally '. . . I don't know if I can. You need someone who's far more pushy than me . . . someone who's far more knowledgeable about the art world.'

Alexa had waved her hands dismissively, cutting Laura off before she could run herself down any further.

'Listen to me, Laura,' she said bossily. 'And listen hard, because I'm only saying this for your own good. If you don't pull yourself together, get a grip on your diet problems and start standing up to that bully of a husband of yours, you're going to go under and never come up again. What you need is a project of your own to work on and make a success of. And that's what I'm offering you now. You've got a real understanding of art. You could have been a half-decent painter yourself if you'd only had the courage of your convictions. You need to know my work inside out, that's true, but I'll teach you. And as for the business side, you're your father's daughter, aren't you? You're steeped in bloody business. Not only that but you worked in the City for long enough. I bet you know a damn sight more about business than the average gallery owner. Come on. Admit it.'

Laura had been so astonished by Alexa's onslaught that she could scarcely think of any further objections to make. Somehow she'd found herself nodding and telling her friend that of course she'd act as her new agent.

And tonight she was going to be put to the test for the first time. A new gallery right in the heart of Soho was mounting an exhibition of three rising stars, artists who were tipped to be the Patrick Herons of the new millennium. Laura had read a piece about the exhibition in the *Clarion* a few weeks back and had cursed Alexa for not picking up on it earlier.

'Oh don't worry about it,' Alexa had told her airily. 'There'll be other exhibitions in the future. It's their loss, not ours.'

But Laura simply couldn't forget about it. In the end she had borrowed Alexa's portfolio and taken some new colour transparencies of her larger work, summoned up every ounce of courage she possessed and turned up at the Rye Gallery completely unannounced. Once there, she had proceeded to sell Alexa's work so convincingly to Dominic Janes, the gallery owner, that he'd agreed to include her in the exhibition too. Laura wasn't sure who had been more surprised by her triumph, her or Alexa.

'See?' Alexa had shrieked, throwing her arms around Laura. 'I told you that you could do it.'

Staring in through the gallery's enormous front window, Laura felt like a child watching a grown-ups' party from the top of the stairs and wishing that she could be part of it all. She was so nervous that she could hear her heart thumping. Tonight had to be a success. It just had to.

Laura pulled her long velvet coat around her narrow shoulders and pushed the door open. To her delight, Dominic Janes had hung Alexa's boldest work, a vast geometric abstract painted in glorious hues of vermilion and aquamarine, on the far wall so it was the first painting that guests saw as they came through the door. Laura sighed with pride. Until now, she had never seen Alexa's paintings displayed to their full effect. They were usually propped up against the wall of her chaotic studio or being carted around in her battered-looking portfolio. But seeing this painting hung on a plain white background and properly lit from below, it struck Laura forcibly how talented her friend actually was.

Within an hour, eight out of the ten paintings by Alexa had red 'sold' spots on them – a huge achievement for a private viewing. It was as if a massive weight had been taken off Laura's shoulders, and she began to relax and enjoy the party at last. She had finally found something that she was good at and she was going to make the most of it.

Laura took a sip of her champagne and gazed across the crowded room. Alexa, resplendent in a gold brocade coat that skimmed the floor, was standing next to one of her pictures and holding forth about her current work. It was strange, thought Laura, that even though she didn't really know anyone else in the room apart from Alexa and Dominic Janes it somehow didn't seem to matter. She felt at ease here. Perhaps it was because for the first time in years she was somewhere in her own right. Tonight she was herself. She wasn't HH's daughter or Hugo Bentley's wife. She was simply herself, Laura Bentley. And it felt good. In fact it felt better than good. It felt fantastic.

Suddenly her whole body stiffened as she caught sight of someone she most certainly did recognise. The man was standing sideways on to her but Laura knew without any shadow of a doubt that it was him. He was wearing a navy blue suit with his distinctive dark hair curling over the collar, just like it always did. What was disturbing Laura was the way his right hand kept nuzzling the shapely bottom of the young woman standing next to him. Laura couldn't see her face properly either but she didn't seem to be making any attempt to remove Charley Stone's wandering hand.

'Laura, you're an absolute genius. Promise me you'll never forget it.'

Laura dragged her eyes away from her brother-in-law's unsettling activities and whirled round to greet Alexa.

'Didn't I tell you that you'd be brilliant?' said Alexa, giving her a huge hug. 'We're really going places now, you and I.'

Laura couldn't help laughing at her friend's shining eyes and over-the-top manner. Everything was so black and white in Alexa's world. She never did anything in half measures.

'Are you enjoying the party?' asked Alexa suddenly. 'Oh, and by the way, you look gorgeous. You should show off that delectable figure of yours more often.'

Laura glanced down at her short red cocktail dress. A few months ago she would never have dared to wear something as revealing as this, but Alexa had bought it for her birthday and she hadn't wanted to offend her. Hugo would no doubt hit the roof when he saw it.

'Who's this delicious-looking hunk making his way over to you?' murmured Alexa. 'Oh bloody hell, he's got some stunning young blonde in tow. And she must be all of nineteen.'

Charley made straight for Laura, grabbing her by the hand and kissing her decorously on either cheek.

'What the hell are you doing here?' he said, just a touch too jovially.

'I could say the same to you,' murmured Laura,

surprised by his cheek. 'I had no idea that you were interested in art.'

'Oh, you know me. I'm interested in all sorts of things.'

At that moment the young blonde tucked her arm through Charley's proprietorially and asked if he was going to introduce them. The girl was gorgeous, thought Laura, there was no doubt about that. Tall and slim with white-blonde hair down to her waist, she was wearing a simple pale leather shift that barely covered her bottom and high strappy sandals.

'Laura, this is Ally Nicholson,' said Charley, trying to remove the girl's arm from his without drawing too much attention to it. 'She's the model who's going to be starring in the new TV ad for the *Clarion*.'

Laura raised her eyes slightly at this. As far as she knew, the *Clarion* had never done any TV advertising, either before or since Charley had taken over.

At least Charley had the grace to look uncomfortable, she thought, and waited for him to explain to Ally *who* exactly *she* was. When he made no attempt to do so, Laura seized the initiative herself.

'I'm Laura Bentley, Charley's sister-in-law,' she said placing as much emphasis as she could on the last three words. She was gratified to see Ally Nicholson choke on her champagne. '. . . And this is the artist Alexa Grainger, whom I represent. Everyone is predicting great things for her. Including your own paper, Charley, but you've probably had your hands too full to read it.'

A look of surprise crossed Charley's face as she said this. In all the time he'd known Laura she'd hardly had the balls to say boo to a goose. And here she was, holding forth about art. She looked different too. More

413

poised and sure of herself. He could quite fancy her himself, come to think of it.

'Now if you come with me, Charley, there's a particular picture of Alexa's that I want to show you.'

Stunned into submission by the way Laura was dictating the proceedings, Charley left Ally's side and obediently followed his sister-in-law across the room. She led him to the huge pink and blue abstract that dominated the gallery's far wall.

'It's Kate's birthday soon and I think she would adore this,' she said, keeping her voice light and sweet.

Charley cleared his throat nervously. He had the distinct impression that Laura was giving him little or no choice in the matter.

'It looks terribly expensive,' he mumbled. 'I'm not sure if I can afford it right now.'

Laura stared at him. If she hadn't been feeling so pole-axed by Charley's brazen performance with Ally Nicholson she might have been tempted to let him off the hook.

'It's only £5,000 so I think you can, don't you?' she murmured. Then her voice hardened. 'And once you've bought it, don't ever again let me catch you messing around with girls nearly young enough to be your daughter. And that reminds me. How is Daisy, by the way?'

Chapter Thirty-Eight

Kate was speechless when Charley presented her with the picture on the morning of her twenty-fifth birthday. She'd been lying in bed with Daisy bouncing up and down on her tummy, wondering if anyone would even remember what day it was. Charley was busy getting ready to go to the office and clearly didn't have a clue. There hadn't even been so much as a single card in the post.

'We'll just have to have our own private party, won't we?' said Kate, blowing a kiss to Daisy. 'What do you reckon?'

She was rewarded by a burst of babyish giggles from Daisy. At least it was a Monday, she thought, so she had the pleasure of spending the whole day with her daughter.

As Kate lay back on the pillow again, waiting for the door to slam behind Charley before she got up, she gradually became aware of the sound of rustling paper in the next room. Oh God, he *has* remembered, thought Kate, and he's desperately trying to cobble something together before leaving for the *Clarion*. It struck her suddenly that a year or so ago she might have been amused by his tendency to do everything like this at the last minute; now she simply felt irritated.

At that moment the door opened and Charley strolled in looking sheepish – and empty-handed.

'Happy birthday darling,' he said and gave her a decorous kiss on the cheek. Much to her exasperation, he ignored Daisy altogether.

'Oh, thanks,' said Kate in a cold voice and beamed pointedly at her daughter.

'Will you come next door? I've got something I want to show you.'

Kate wearily dragged herself out of bed and, heaving Daisy onto her hip, followed Charley into the sitting room. She noticed that he was wearing an ochre-coloured suit that she'd never seen before. She grimaced at him from behind. He seemed to be devoting far more time to preening himself and shopping for clothes these days than to actually editing the paper. She was sure that the eagle-eyed hacks at the *Clarion* must all be talking about his lack of appetite for work, too. No one had uttered a word to her but then they wouldn't let anything slip to the boss's wife, would they?

Kate stopped in her tracks as Charley led her over to a huge object swathed in brown wrapping paper and leaning against the sitting-room wall.

'Your birthday present,' he announced.

'What on earth is it?' asked Kate.

Charley gave a false-sounding laugh. 'If you open it, sweetheart, you'll find out, won't you?'

Kate put Daisy down and began pulling the brown paper off half-heartedly. This looked like great fun to Daisy so she immediately insisted on joining in. When the pair of them had finally ripped all the wrapping off to reveal the massive abstract underneath, Kate stared at Charley in astonishment. This was the last thing she'd expected.

'Wow, it's fantastic. I absolutely love it. Thank you so much. I thought you'd completely forgotten about my birthday this year.'

An embarrassed look crossed Charley's face but Kate chose to ignore it. Maybe he did love her after all. He'd just had a funny way of showing it over the last few months, what with his snappy behaviour at home and his new habit of rolling in at two in the morning, reeking of booze and something else she'd rather not think about.

'Of course I hadn't forgotten,' he said quickly. 'I'd never do a thing like that.'

Kate kept gazing, entranced, at the picture. She couldn't wait to see it hanging on the wall.

'The style looks oddly familiar,' she said. 'Who's it by?'

'Alexa Grainger,' replied Charley. He crossed his fingers that the name wouldn't mean anything to Kate. 'And it should be a fantastic investment, by the way. She's predicted to do great things.'

Kate took a few paces back from the painting and looked at it again.

'Oh I don't care about that,' she protested. 'But of course it's one of Alexa's. There are her initials at the bottom. I should have recognised it immediately.' She biffed her hand against the side of her head for being so stupid.

'Why?' said Charley. 'Do you know her work?'

'Alexa's one of Laura's oldest friends,' explained Kate. 'They were at school together and they've always stayed in touch. I don't know her nearly so well as Laura does, of course, but she's quite a character. You'd really like her. I'm over the moon to have one of her paintings. You couldn't have chosen anything more special in the whole world. Thank you, darling. You're a star.'

Much to Charley's surprise, Kate threw her arms around him and kissed him full on the mouth. He was suddenly intensely aware of the skimpy cotton nightshirt that she was wearing and the feel of her soft skin underneath.

'I don't suppose you feel like going back to . . .' he groaned, touching her breast through the thin fabric.

'Ssssh. We can't,' murmured Kate. 'We've got Daisy with us. Remember?'

After Charley had left for work, Kate felt more optimistic about her marriage than she had for ages. His behaviour this morning had shown that at least he must still care about her a bit. First the amazing present, and then his suggestion that they go straight back to bed together. A man who was totally indifferent to his wife wouldn't do either of those two things. Would he?

It was twelve fifteen and Kate had just about managed to get both herself and Daisy dressed when the doorbell rang. She abandoned the rickety tower of wooden bricks that she'd started building with Daisy and rushed to answer it. Perhaps it was Charley arriving to whisk them both off to a romantic birthday lunch.

'Don't look so stunned,' laughed Pam Newbold when she saw Kate's jaw drop.

'What on earth are you doing here?' shrieked Kate. 'You haven't been in touch for months. I thought I must have offended you in some way.'

Pam looked just as striking as always, although Kate was relieved to see that she'd got rid of the peroxide blonde and gone back to her familiar auburn colour. But she'd kept the weight off, slim and elegant in a well-cut navy trouser suit and high stilettos that looked hell to walk in.

'Don't be daft,' said Pam, her broad Lancashire accent as warm as ever. 'You couldn't do anything to offend me, love. You know that.'

Then the expression on her face changed and she added, 'But I'm afraid that's more than I can say for your bloody brother-in-law. He's been an absolute pain in the backside since he took over the group last year. He's made us slog our guts out for a pittance and penny-pinch to within an inch of our lives. But do you know what, love? He's gone too bloody far this time.'

Kate stared at Pam in bewilderment. Why was she going on about Hugo like this? What the hell had *he* done to get Pam in such a lather?

'You'd better come in,' she said.

Five minutes later, Kate, too, was gibbering with fury at what Pam had just told her.

'But he promised me,' she shouted. 'He made a solemn promise that if I supported his bid to become chairman of Hollingberry Holdings, then he would keep the *Bugle* open. I can't believe this, Pam, I really can't believe it. I can't believe he could close Leadington without a word to me or the rest of the board. He's a bloody double-crossing toerag. I should never have been so bloody trusting. I just let him get on with the business when I should have been checking up on what he was up to.'

Kate was so livid that she kept jabbing at the air with her finger as she spoke. Daisy, unaccustomed to seeing her mother in such a state, burst into tears and was completely inconsolable for five minutes.

419

'Ssssh, sssh, darling, I'm sorry,' murmured Kate, full of contrition for upsetting the little girl. 'Mummy didn't mean it. It's just that we've got to decide what we're going to do about your wicked Uncle Hugo. He sounds like the baddy in a pantomime, doesn't he?'

The first course of action, Kate decided, was to confront Laura. The two sisters hadn't seen each other for weeks but for some reason – Kate wasn't entirely sure why she felt so strongly – it was imperative to find out whether Laura had known about Hugo's plans. After all, Laura had been at the American Bar when Kate had told Hugo that she would only support his chairmanship on two conditions, the first that Charley be made editor-in-chief of the *Clarion*, the second that the *Bugle*'s future was guaranteed completely. So Laura had known beyond any doubt what Kate's provisos were. She'd been totally aware of how Kate would react if Hugo ever attempted to close the paper down.

Kate insisted that Pam must accompany her to Chelsea to see Laura.

'We've got to make her see that the *Bugle* isn't just some meaningless little rag hundreds of miles away,' she said as she busily stuffed Daisy's arms into her coat. 'I know I'm as sentimental about it as you are, but it gave me my first chance and I'm going to make bloody sure that Hugo doesn't shut it down. Not now and not ever.'

When the three of them arrived at HH's house – for some reason Kate still thought of it as her father's, rather than Laura and Hugo's – her sister was in the middle of hanging a selection of Alexa's pictures in the drawing room. After her triumph at the Rye Gallery, she had hit on the idea of mounting a permanent exhibition of Alexa's work in her own home. So instead of trailing round to galleries clutching transparencies in her hand, she could invite people here to view the pictures in their full glory. The only thing was that she hadn't quite summoned up the courage to break the news to Hugo yet.

Laura answered the door wearing an old pair of baggy dungarees that were far too big for her and holding a hammer and a load of picture hooks. Despite her eccentric apparel, it struck Kate that her sister seemed happier and more animated than she'd seen her look in years.

'Happy birthday,' beamed Laura, giving Kate a warm hug.

Kate hugged her back briefly and then marched inside with Pam.

'I'm sorry to interrupt you,' She said, 'but something urgent has come up that I've simply got to talk to you about.'

It didn't escape Kate's notice that a wary expression instantly appeared on Laura's face. She knew exactly what had crossed Laura's mind. It was the conclusion Laura always jumped to before anything else. She was hoping that Kate was here to bring her news about Clare.

'It's to do with Hugo,' Kate said quickly and she saw Laura's face fall. 'And Hollingberry Holdings.'

At the mention of the family business, Laura looked completely uninterested.

'It's lovely to see you, Kate,' she said in a cool voice. 'Really it is. But you know that I don't have anything whatsoever to do with the company. Hugo's the person you need to talk to.'

'I know,' said Kate grimly. 'And I sure as hell intend

421

to. But I need to talk to you first. This is Pam Newbold, by the way. She's an old friend of mine. I'll explain why she's here in a minute.'

Laura shrugged her shoulders and led Kate, Daisy and Pam along the black and white tiled hall and into the drawing room at the back of the house. It was a vast room with French windows opening on to the pretty town garden where Laura's wedding reception had been held two years before. It was late March now and the first of the cherry blossom was just coming into bloom on the trees outside. Kate let out a sigh of appreciation when she saw it; she'd forgotten how much the clouds of luscious pale pink blossom reminded her of her childhood. She and Laura had always adored it.

'This room looks absolutely fantastic,' exclaimed Kate, spinning round to take in the changes that Laura had made. 'It was always so dark and dingy when Daddy was alive. How clever of you to paint it all white. And are these Alexa's pictures?'

Laura had only managed to hang two pictures so far but another eight or nine were propped against the wall, waiting to be hung.

'Yes,' she said proudly, putting her hammer down on a side table. 'In fact I've just started working for her. I'm her new agent.'

All of a sudden, everything slotted into place. Kate had thought it strange that Charley should go and buy one of Alexa's pictures off his own bat. He'd obviously enlisted Laura's help.

'I simply love the picture Charley bought me for my birthday,' she said. 'Thank you so much for helping him choose it. I was thrilled with it. Alexa's work is just getting better and better, isn't it?'

Laura beamed with pleasure. But then, remembering the coercion she'd used to persuade Charley to buy the picture, she couldn't help frowning.

'Did he tell you what made him choose it?' she asked anxiously.

'No,' said Kate, slightly puzzled. 'Why? What happened?'

'Oh, it doesn't matter,' said Laura hurriedly. 'It's nothing. I'll tell you some other time.'

Kate and Pam sat side by side on HH's favourite leather chesterfield and Laura slumped onto a chair opposite them.

'So what have you got to talk to me about that's so important?' she asked.

'It's Hugo,' said Kate, leaning forward, unable to contain her anger. 'I'm sorry, Laura, I know he's your husband and you probably think he's Mr Wonderful but he's a lying, double-crossing toad. You deserve better, you really do.'

For a moment Laura looked startled but then she burst into fits of giggles.

'I'm sorry, Kate,' she said, finding it difficult to get her words out through her laughter. 'It's just that I've always known that you loathe Hugo with a vengeance. It was quite funny seeing you trying to keep it all bottled up for so long. But I knew it was bound to come out eventually. And now it has.'

Kate was speechless. Her sister had completely taken the wind out of her sails and for a moment she couldn't think what on earth to say.

'Oh and by the way,' said Laura, her face suddenly looking more composed. 'I know perfectly well what he's like. I don't think he's Mr Wonderful at all.

So whatever it is you've come to say, you'd better spit it out.'

Kate took a huge breath and launched into her account of Hugo's latest transgression.

'Do you remember that day when the three of us all had a drink together at the American Bar?' she asked Laura.

'What? After Daddy's will was read, you mean?' said Laura.

Kate nodded, her face incandescent with fury as she recalled the occasion.

'Yes. I told Hugo that I would support his bid to be made chairman on three conditions and three conditions alone. I wanted – God knows why, in retrospect – Charley to be made editor-in-chief of the *Clarion*, the *Bowland Bugle*'s future to be protected and me to have a seat on the board. He's never got round to putting me on the board, has he? And now look what's happened. Everything has fallen down about my ears. Charley has turned out to be far more interested in partying and buying up Armani than making a decent job of the *Clarion* and bloody Hugo has completely disregarded everything I ever said. Pam's the editor of the *Bugle* and he's just announced that he's going to shut it down. And all the other Leadington papers too. Without a word to any of us, either.'

'What's made him decide to do that?' asked Laura. 'Those papers are a tiny drop in the ocean alongside all the other titles.'

'I know,' said Kate. 'But they're still losing money. And that's the trouble with Hugo, you know. At least Daddy cared about his newspapers. Hugo doesn't give a damn about any of them. As far as he is concerned they're just commodities. They could be tins of baked

424

beans stacked on a supermarket shelf for all he cares. It never crosses his unimaginative little mind that people put their heart and soul into producing them and that they provide a real service to their communities. They're completely expendable to him.'

Laura sat in silence until Kate had finished ranting and raving about Hugo.

'You're right, Kate,' she said when she finally had the chance to get a word in edgeways. 'You're absolutely right. I didn't realise it when we got married but Hugo is a shit. A complete and utter shit. But then again maybe that's what the company needs. I promise you that I didn't have a clue what he was up to. He keeps everything bottled up. He never tells me anything. But then again, I do think that if you're running a business you can't let your emotions dictate what you do. You've got to take a long cool look at what's best for the company's future and I'm sure that's what Hugo is trying to do. And do you remember who put him in charge in the first place? It was us. You and me. We thought that he'd make a better job of it than Gordon Osprey. Yes? So even though we might not like his way of doing things there's nothing much we can do about it now, is there?'

Kate stared at Daisy, who was toddling around the room with two of HH's precious silver snuff boxes clutched in each chubby hand. Her daughter had been walking for a couple of months now but she was still a little unsteady on her feet and kept wobbling precariously, like a drunk on a pub crawl.

'We can't let ourselves be so defeatist,' she told her sister, the passion clear in her voice. 'For God's sake, Daddy worked his balls off to make Hollingberry

Holdings a success. And we own almost half the company between us. We can't just roll over and let Hugo destroy everything Daddy felt so strongly about. Do you remember what Oliver Brown told us about Daddy requesting that we do all in our power to look after the best interests of the company? Laura, we've got to do something. We've just got to.'

Laura stood up and picked up her hammer again.

'I'm sorry, Kate,' she said quietly. 'I can see why you and Pam are so upset about the *Bugle* but you're letting your hearts rule your heads. There's absolutely nothing we can do about it now. I know it's a pain but we've just got to let Hugo get on with his job.'

Laura rubbed her aching back. It was almost nine pm and she had just finished hanging the last of Alexa's pictures. If she said it herself, she'd done a fantastic job. She'd managed to transform HH's stuffy drawing room into a state-of-the-art gallery. Even Hugo would have to admit that the room looked sensational.

As she sank wearily into a squashy armchair she heard the front door slam. Her whole body stiffened. Hugo must be home but it was always impossible to predict whether he was in a good mood or a filthy one until she saw his face.

It was apparent as soon as Hugo's head appeared round the door wreathed in smiles, however, that he was feeling inordinately pleased with himself.

'Hello darling,' he said, bounding over to give her a kiss. He said nothing about Alexa's pictures. He either hadn't noticed them at all or considered them so unimportant compared to his own work that they were unworthy of comment.

'Have you had a good day?' asked Laura. On reflection she realised it was a pretty pointless question, because it was abundantly clear that he had.

'Very satisfying,' he said and, without enquiring whether she'd like one or not, poured them both a large gin and tonic. 'Very satisfying indeed.'

Any normal husband would have had the courtesy to ask her about her day, thought Laura. But then again, Hugo was very far from a normal husband.

'What happened?' she asked.

Hugo handed her her drink and sat down on the other side of the room.

'I've finally concluded our negotiations to move the head office from Docklands into the City,' he announced bluntly. 'There's a building just round the corner from the Mansion House that I've had my eye on for some time and we managed to sign the lease today. It's a great deal.'

Laura couldn't hide her shock.

'B . . . but you can't,' she stuttered. 'You can't possibly.'

Hugo stared at her in amazement. Who the hell did Laura think she was, telling him what he could and couldn't do? He was going to have to put a firm stop to her friendship with Alexa Grainger if she carried on like this.

'What on earth gives you the right to tell me what I can and can't do?' he said coldly. 'Of course I can. And I have.'

Laura tried again.

'But it was something that Daddy was so utterly opposed to. Gordon Osprey tried to persuade him loads of times to move the business to a more prestigious location but he wouldn't hear of it. As far as Daddy was concerned Hollingberry Holdings had been based in Docklands for years and that was where he wanted to keep it. And there's no point in paying extortionate City prices when the business functions perfectly well where it is. Is there?'

Hugo slammed his gin and tonic down on a small side table and stood up.

'Look Laura, this is none of your bloody business,' he said, his tone icy. 'You know nothing whatsoever about it so keep your nose out, will you? And who's hung all these appalling paintings on my wall?'

A shiver of panic ran down Laura's spine but she forced herself to continue.

'Oh but it is my business, Hugo,' she said, her words coming out in a nervous rush. 'I think you know that it's very much my business. Even you must be perfectly aware that you only managed to become chairman in the first place because you had the good fortune to be married to me. And if you won't listen to me about this then I'm sorry, but I'm going to have to do something about it.'

Chapter Thirty-Nine

Ben Maguire laid the sheaf of newspaper cuttings down on the desk and put his head in his hands. Of all the bloody assignments he had to be given, he groaned. Why on earth did it have to be this one? Anything would have been better. Even a month spent investigating the state of London's sewers.

It had been nine months since Ben began working for Inside TV and not a day had gone past without him thanking his lucky stars that he'd got out of tabloid newspapers when he had. On the *Daily Recorder* he'd usually had three hours at the most to get to grips with issues as complex as insider dealing or genetically modified foods and then to write the definitive story on them in eight paragraphs. His new job, however, was completely different, allowing him the time and space to research his subjects in depth.

But given the choice he would have avoided this latest assignment like the plague. He had almost jumped out of his skin when Mark Gudgeon, his genial boss – very different from the nervy news editors he'd worked for in the past – had asked him to take a look at what was going on at Hollingberry Holdings.

'Have you got any contacts in the company?' Mark had asked him at their first meeting.

For a moment Ben couldn't think what to say. God, if Kate knew that he was about to start delving into her father's company she'd hit the bloody roof. He hadn't seen her at all since their picnic in Kensington Gardens in the autumn, uncomfortably aware that he was still drawn to her and that it just wouldn't be wise.

'I, I vaguely know one of Hubert Hollingberry's daughters,' he'd said hesitantly.

Mark's eyes immediately lit up.

'Laura Bentley, you mean?' he'd said. 'That's great, Ben. I knew you were the right man for the job. We could find that very useful when it comes to getting a face-to-face interview with Hugo Bentley. He's the key to it all.'

'No,' said Ben, his voice flat. 'Not Laura. I know the younger one. Kate.'

His mind completely taken up with Hugo and Laura, Mark's eyes glazed over with disappointment.

'Oh well, never mind. You can't win 'em all. I'm sure she might come in handy later.'

'Why exactly do you want to do a whole programme on Hollingberry Holdings?' asked Ben. 'I mean, I know it's a very successful business in its field, but not exceptionally so. Why should we be looking at them rather than anyone else?'

Mark stared at him as if he was a total idiot.

'Don't you ever read the City pages?' he said witheringly. 'The word on the grapevine is that there's something fishy going on at Hollingberry Holdings. Something very fishy indeed. From what my contacts have told me, Hugo Bentley only managed to wangle the chairmanship in the first place because he happened to be married to Hubert Hollingberry's daughter. And just recently there have been signs

430

that all is not well. The share price has dropped significantly, Hugo Bentley's spent millions on some group up in Scotland that's turned out to be a complete waste of space and he's also begun shutting some of the smaller papers down. He's put his brother-in-law in charge of the *Clarion* and now that appears to be losing sales hand over fist too. And not only that, but at a time when he should be drawing his horns in he's just gone and paid mega money for plush new premises right in the heart of the City. According to my spies, he's getting far too big for his boots and there are rumblings of discontent among the smaller shareholders. Some of them aren't happy at all.'

Mark paused for a moment before continuing.

'So you can see, Ben, that it's definitely got all the hallmarks of a cracking documentary. I want you to put everything else on the back burner and get started on it straight away. Oh, and by the way, I thought that we'd call it *Family Business*. Good, eh?'

Ben had already spent two weeks researching the business, and from what he'd dug up so far, it was clear that Mark's instincts had been spot on. Something was definitely up at Hollingberry Holdings.

Now he was on the verge of doing something that he simply couldn't put off any longer. Kate was likely to fly off the handle completely but he had to come clean and tell her what he was up to. He knew that if he wasn't straight with her about this, she'd never forgive him. And, job or no job, that was something that he simply couldn't bear.

Kate thrust her hands deep into the pockets of her denim jacket and stared at the water. A lump had formed in her throat and she realised that she was on the point of bursting into tears. Her whole world was beginning to collapse around her and she felt powerless to stop it.

'No Daisy today?' said a voice behind her and she swung round to see Ben standing there.

Kate wiped her eyes quickly. She didn't want Ben to know the extent of her misery.

'No, she's at nursery today. Now that I've started doing a few interviews as well as my column she goes there two days a week.'

The two of them stood gazing at each other. Kate ached to touch him, just to check that he was real, but she couldn't bear the risk that he might turn away. He had made it quite clear on the phone, after all, that their meeting wouldn't take long. There was simply something that he had to tell her.

Her heart had begun thumping uncontrollably the moment she'd heard his voice on the telephone this morning. She'd been in the office, transcribing her interview with Ally Nicholson, Channel Four's glamorous new breakfast telly presenter, and trying desperately hard to avoid the other feature writers' sympathetic glances.

She still couldn't quite believe this latest humiliation that Charley had put her through. The features editor, Joe Harris, had told Charley of his intention to send Kate out to interview Ally and yet Charley hadn't lifted a finger to stop the two of them meeting. Charley really was a two-timing bastard, thought Kate. He must have known that there was a risk of Ally letting slip about their little fling but he obviously hadn't given a damn. The thought of his wife and his mistress having lunch together had probably appealed to his warped sense of humour or something.

Most humiliating of all as far as Kate was concerned was the fact that she'd actually liked Ally a lot. They'd done the interview over lunch at Joe Allen's and Ally had been completely frank about everything, from her teenage affair with soccer star Darren Gordon to her modelling career and her subsequent estrangement from her family. Kate had asked her persistently if she was seeing anyone right now – that was what the great British public would really be interested in – but Ally had kept flicking her long blonde hair back from her face and saying no, she only had time for her career these days.

But when the waiter brought them each an espresso and Kate finally switched off her tape recorder, Ally had leaned forward conspiratorially.

'Completely off the record,' she whispered, 'I *am* seeing someone. The only trouble is that he's married, with a kid.'

Kate was immediately sympathetic.

'Oh Ally, you're so young and you'll only get hurt, you know. I'm sure you can find someone much better. Who is he?'

Standing by the Round Pond now, Kate felt sick thinking about the terrible moment when Ally had opened her beautiful mouth and whispered: 'Your editor.' Kate had been so stunned that she'd barely been able to get any words out. Meanwhile Ally, who knew Kate only as Kate Grant – the name she still used for work – kept prattling on about how gorgeous Charley was and how caring and how brilliant in bed.

'I'm sorry,' Kate had mumbled. 'I've got to go. I'm not feeling very well. I think I'm going to throw up.'

'Are you sure you're all right?' asked Ben softly now.

He touched her fleetingly on the arm. 'You've gone awfully pale.'

'What?' said Kate. She blinked for a few seconds, then remembered where she was. 'Oh yes. I'm fine. Why did you want to see me?'

'Shall we walk?' asked Ben and Kate nodded in accord.

'I wanted to tell you this in person,' said Ben slowly. 'Because it might upset you.'

After the shock of finding out about Charley and Ally Nicholson this was too much for Kate. Her mind started to run riot. Had he met someone? Was he getting married? Oh God, she couldn't bear it if he was.

'Tell me,' she said.

Ben took a deep breath. He wasn't sure where to begin.

'You know that Inside TV, the company I work for now, makes news documentaries? Yep? Well, it's a bit embarrassing but my boss has asked me to start working on a programme about Hollingberry Holdings. I'm afraid I didn't have any choice in the matter.'

'Is that all?' said Kate. She lifted her head and beamed at him, amazed by how relieved she felt.

'Don't you mind?' said Ben. 'You see I'm afraid it's not going to be very flattering. Hugo Bentley's going to come out badly and I don't think it's going to reflect too well on your husband either.'

'Good,' said Kate, stopping in her tracks.

'What did you say?' asked Ben.

'I said "good". Hugo's a shit and Charley's a shit and any programme that shows the world that they are both shits is fine by me. Absolutely fine.'

Ben turned to look at her. He couldn't believe Kate was saying all this.

'But I thought that you were happy with Charley. That's the impression you gave me last year. And you've got Daisy now, too.'

Kate's face softened at the mention of her daughter.

'Yes, and she's the best thing in my whole life,' she said. 'But apart from the fact that Charley's her father, I wouldn't care if I never set eyes on him again. He's a lying, conniving, two-timing bastard.'

Ben grabbed her by the arm and pulled her round to face him.

'What do you mean, Kate? What's he done? Has he hurt you?'

'What bloody hasn't he done?' muttered Kate miserably. 'He had a fling with that bitch Rebecca Wilson while I was in hospital having Daisy – so he missed her birth completely. I pulled strings to get him the editorship of the *Clarion* and then he goes and screws that up because he can't be bothered to stick at it. And then yesterday I was in the middle of interviewing some new breakfast-telly bimbo, when, bold as brass, she announces she's having an affair with my bloody husband. So now do you see why I've had it with him?'

Ben's mind was reeling with shock at Charley Stone's behaviour. He couldn't believe that all this time he'd been assuming that Kate was blissfully happily married when in truth Charley had been treating her like dirt.

'So what are you going to do now?' he asked. 'Are you going to leave him?'

Kate looked down at her nails.

'It probably sounds mad but right now the state of my marriage isn't the only problem,' she murmured.

'So what is?' said Ben.

'How long have you got?' said Kate. 'Oh Ben, I've messed everything up so badly. The business is the problem. It turns out that all Hugo is bothered about is his own self-glorification. He's shut the Leadington papers down and fired all the staff when he swore he wouldn't. He's done some crazy deals that can't possibly work out and now he's spent millions on moving the head office into the City, when that's the last thing that Daddy would have wanted. Laura and I were supposed to watch over the interests of the company, that's what it said in Daddy's will, and instead the whole thing is falling apart.'

Ben thought for a moment, trying to take everything in.

'Couldn't you boot the pair of them out of the company altogether?' he said. 'You must be able to make a case for it.'

Kate's face looked stricken.

'How the hell do we go about doing that?' she cried. 'It's only nine months since we got rid of Gordon Osprey and gave Hugo and Charley our full backing. I can't believe how innocent Laura and I were. So bloody innocent.'

'Gordon Osprey,' said Ben thoughtfully. 'Wasn't he your father's right-hand man?'

'That's impressive,' said Kate, surprised that Ben should know his name. 'How do you know that? Have you started doing the research for your programme already?'

Ben flushed. He had in fact spent the last couple of weeks ringing around all his contacts in the City for titbits about Hollingberry Holdings.

'Yes, I have,' he admitted. 'But before I went any

436

further I wanted to tell you what I was doing. Do you remember when we broke up? When you just dropped me like a lead balloon?'

Kate closed her eyes for a second, remembering how devastated she'd been by Ben's betrayal. His actions seemed pretty tame now in contrast to Charley's duplicity.

'You hurt me a lot, you know,' she said softly. 'I really trusted you and then you went and tipped off the papers about who my father was. I'd asked you not to tell anyone and then it turned out that I couldn't trust you any more. It's all behind us now, I know that, but at the time I just couldn't cope with it. That's why I ended it. That's why I didn't want to see you any more.'

Hearing this, Ben felt as if he'd been smacked in the face by a cold, wet fish. It struck him forcibly that if only they'd sat down and talked about it back then, they might still be together now.

'It wasn't me, you know,' he said flatly. 'I don't know who it was but I swear to you that it wasn't me.'

Kate stared at him uncomprehendingly. She couldn't believe what Ben was saying.

'But you were the only person I'd told,' She protested. 'No one else had a clue who my father was.'

Ben couldn't help feeling exasperated by her naïvety.

'For God's sake, Kate, it could have been any one of a number of people. Someone on the *Bugle*, one of the trainees, anyone. You stood out like a sore thumb up there, with your posh southern accent and your outlandish clothes; *everyone* was wondering where the hell you came from.'

Slightly stung by his words, Kate thought back to

those first few months on the *Bugle*. Maybe Ben was right. Maybe they'd all been laughing at her behind her back. She remembered Thorndike's initial hostility to her and the way he'd questioned her name over and over again. He could easily have made a few enquiries and found out who she was. Oh what the hell did it matter now anyway? At least it hadn't been Ben. That was the important thing.

'I'm glad we've cleared our misunderstanding up,' said Kate. 'I should have known that you wouldn't do that to me.'

'Forget it,' said Ben briskly. 'You're right. It doesn't matter any more. What were we talking about before? Oh yes, Gordon Osprey. Now, from what I understand, you and Laura own forty per cent of the shares between you. Is that right?'

'Yes,' nodded Kate. 'But why do you want to . . . ?'

'Hang on. Let me think,' said Ben. 'Does anyone else close to you hold any shares? Your aunt, maybe?'

''Fraid not,' said Kate, shaking her head. 'As far as I know the bulk of the remaining shares are held by City institutions. Gordon's got two or three per cent, I think, but no one close to us.'

'Hmmm,' said Ben, thinking hard. 'It's worth taking a look at the shareholders' register though. Do you mind if I carry on researching this?'

'Who for?' asked Kate. 'For your programme or to help me?'

'That depends on you really,' said Ben enigmatically. 'Oh, and by the way, was it you who removed my favourite picture from my desk? Because if it was, I'd like it back. It's of someone pretty special and I've missed looking at it.'

* * *

Over the next couple of weeks, Ben worked all hours on the Hollingberry Holdings programme. It was remarkable, he reflected, quite how many people Hugo Bentley and Charley Stone had managed to cross in such a short time. He'd certainly encountered no shortage of people prepared to pour out their antipathy towards the two men and their ways of doing business. And on camera too. The only problem was going to be getting their vitriolic comments past the inside TV lawyer.

On the vexed question of what Kate and her sister could do to oust their husbands from the family business, however, Ben had drawn a complete blank. He'd talked to everyone he could think of and no one had come up with anything. His only real hope now was Gordon Osprey himself, who had finally agreed to speak to him – albeit off the record.

'Hubert's daughters should have stuck by me,' Gordon whinged to Ben when they met for afternoon tea at the Ritz. Unable to find anything other than a handful of non-executive directorships since his ignominious dismissal from Hollingberry Holdings, he made no attempt to hide his bitterness at the way he'd been treated.

'I think they realise that now,' said Ben diplomatically. 'But you can't blame them for what happened. They were young and inexperienced and they'd only just lost their father. Laura's husband was fighting his own rearguard action to take over and he convinced them that he'd be acting in their best interests. And anyway, it was the board that voted you out, not Kate and Laura.'

'Mmmm. I suppose you have a point,' said Gordon, taking a dainty sip of his Lapsang Souchong. 'They shouldn't have been such gullible little fools though. I know there's no room for sentimentality in business but I really would have made a very good chairman.'

'I'm sure you would,' said Ben soothingly. 'And you can see that the company still desperately needs your help now. I wondered if I could pick your brains as to what you know about the various shareholders?'

Flattered by Ben's sycophantic approach, Gordon nodded his assent. It was at times like this, when he was talking about Hollingberry Holdings, that it came home to him how very much he missed it. He'd spent his whole career there and nothing he'd done since had come anywhere near matching it.

'I've been through the list of shareholders with a fine-tooth comb,' said Ben, 'and there's one thing that doesn't quite add up. Kate and Laura own forty per cent, you own three per cent and the City institutions hold a total of forty-seven per cent. I've now discovered that a Guernsey-based outfit called the Fiddick Trust holds the remaining ten per cent. But that's all I know. I can't find out anything else about them. It's as if the trail has gone cold or something.'

Gordon took another sip of his tea and leaned back on his velvet-covered chair.

'It's Clare,' he said matter-of-factly.

'Who?' Ben couldn't believe he was hearing this.

'Clare. The girls' mother. Hubert gave her the shares when they were first married and they're held on her behalf through a nominee account. She's never done anything with them, of course, but as far as I know she's always hung onto them.'

Still pole-axed by Gordon's revelation, Ben struggled to get his words out.

'So, so where can I find her?' he stumbled finally.

'Oh, God knows,' said Gordon. 'You're on your own there, old boy. But there's one thing I can tell you. And that's that if you do find her the girls might have a way of getting rid of that waster of a chairman of theirs.'

Ben sat forward, eager to hear what Gordon had in mind.

'As long as a shareholder holds at least ten per cent of the shares,' he said, 'and of course Kate, Laura and Clare all do, then they can call an extraordinary general meeting.'

'And what would be the point of that?' asked Ben.

'If they can get together more than fifty per cent of the shareholders' votes then they can get rid of the board. It's a pretty radical thing to do, but looking at the mess Hugo's making of everything it's probably their only chance of saving the business.'

Chapter Forty

It was a bright clear morning in the middle of May and Kate and Laura were hurrying along the pavement towards the City conference hall where the Hollingberry Holdings extraordinary general meeting was about to take place.

Kate was visibly nervous, her back rigid and her teeth chattering uncontrollably, just as they had always done when she was little.

'Remember to keep your cool,' Laura instructed her sister. 'When it's your turn to speak, take a long deep breath and think about what you're going to say before you open your mouth. Think hard. Right?'

'Right,' said Kate. She couldn't help marvelling at Laura's calmness. It was strange how Laura had really shown her mettle over the last traumatic few weeks. Just as she'd held the pair of them together in the years after Clare's disappearance, so she was the one who was keeping them both going right now. It was hard to believe that it was Laura and not herself who'd nearly gone under in the intervening years.

'Oh, and Laura?' said Kate.

'What?' asked Laura.

On the spur of the moment Kate dropped the huge holdall of papers she was carrying and threw her arms around her older sister.

'Thanks,' she whispered into Laura's neck. 'Thanks for everything. I couldn't have got through any of this without you.'

As the sisters drew apart they were suddenly surrounded by a battery of photographers, their flash guns going like crazy.

'Bloody hell,' said Kate, her jaw dropping in astonishment. 'What the hell are you lot doing here?'

Call her naïve but it had never dawned on her for a second that the press might be interested in this meeting. Looking around, though, she realised that three TV crews were busy setting up their equipment and an army of noisy newspaper reporters was milling around the entrance to the conference hall. As a journalist, Kate couldn't blame them for being here. As far as the hacks were concerned this story had everything – money, sex, marital discord. Not only that, but this bitter family dispute could well be on the verge of turning into a boardroom coup. She spotted a few familiar faces in the crowd but managed to avoid catching anyone's eye. She kept reminding herself firmly that she was on the other side of the fence today.

Kate grabbed Laura's hand and barged through the throng.

'Come on,' she said. 'Let's get inside. And if anyone asks you anything at all, even what time it is, just say "no comment".'

The room where the meeting was to be held was vast. At the far end a long board table had been placed on a wooden dais and microphones had been installed along its length. As chairman, Hugo would be sitting in the middle, flanked either side, reflected Kate bitterly, by his team of toadying directors. Directly in front of the platform were rows and rows of red plastic conference seats, from where all the shareholders would watch the proceedings unfold. Side by side and with their heads held high, Kate and Laura walked straight to the front row and sat down without saying another word.

At eleven am precisely, the room fell silent and Hugo and the rest of the Hollingberry Holdings board marched down the room and mounted the stage. At the sight of her husband, it struck Laura how remarkably detached she felt from him. She had tried to bid farewell to him at home only three hours earlier but like a spoilt child he had refused even to speak to her. He'd simply shot her a look of pure hatred and stalked out of the front door without a word. Deep down, they'd both realised that, whatever happened at today's meeting, it sounded the death-knell of their marriage. Their relationship could never recover from this; nor did either of them want it to.

Hugo, looking the consummate professional in a sombre grey suit, white shirt and his club tie, was the first person to speak.

'I have been asked, against my better judgement, to convene this extraordinary general meeting,' he said.

He stopped for a moment and stared stony-faced at Laura.

'I must emphasize to all the shareholders present that in my opinion this is a mischievous and personal vendetta by my ailing wife and her misguided younger sister. Nevertheless, to clear this matter up once and for all I have agreed to convene this meeting.'

'You bloody hypocrite,' murmured Kate under her breath. 'You didn't have any choice in the matter. You *had* to convene it.'

Meanwhile Hugo, his voice icily calm, was continuing his opening speech.

'I hope that when this morning's meeting is over we can draw a line under this sorry affair and that I can get on with the important job of taking Hollingberry Holdings forward into the next century. Now, I think that without further ado we should get down to the business in hand. We have in front of us an ordinary resolution proposed by certain of our shareholders to remove myself as chairman . . .'

Hugo paused theatrically before delivering his next words.

'. . . And, preposterous as it may sound, the resolution also proposes that Kate Grant, as she calls herself, should be appointed as the new chairman and Laura Bentley as a director. I am sure that you will all agree with me that this is a totally ludicrous proposal. These are vindictive, spiteful women who, by virtue of their birth alone, fancifully believe that they are equipped to run their late father's company.

'I must admit that why what is essentially a family dispute should be allowed to wreck one of Britain's finest newspaper groups is completely beyond me and my fellow directors. I am sure that everyone present in this room today will see that to replace an experienced and able chairman such as myself with a young woman of twenty-five who couldn't even manage to complete her indentures on one of our smallest and least profitable newspapers is utterly farcical.

'I could go on but I believe that my record since I took over Hollingberry Holdings speaks for itself. If no one has anything to say on this ridiculous matter I should like to move swiftly to the vote. After that we can all get back to our work.'

For a moment Kate was so stunned by the vindictiveness of Hugo's attack that she sat paralysed in her seat. A sharp dig from Laura's elbow, however, was enough to make her jump to her feet.

'I most certainly have got something to say,' she shouted from the floor.

As Kate stood up, a small blonde figure in a businesslike navy blue trouser suit that made her look older than her years, a buzz of excitement rippled through the audience. The atmosphere was electric as everyone waited to see how Kate would respond to Hugo's onslaught.

Kate waited until all the noise had died down before continuing.

'My father gave his life to Hollingberry Holdings,' she said. 'I'm sure that everyone present appreciates that. He spent thirty years building this company into the highly successful business that we see before us today. But, throughout all that time, he never lost sight of the people who worked for the company; as far as he was concerned they were its most important asset.'

'Hear, hear,' said a northern voice from the back.

'In the short time that my brother-in-law, Hugo Bentley, has been chairman, however, he has shown utter contempt for all that my father stood for. Under my father's leadership our newspapers always maintained the highest moral standards. Never, in thirty years, did we have a single complaint against us upheld. But, under Hugo Bentley's command, all that has changed. The standards that my father applied so rigorously to everything he did have sunk into the gutter. Only last week the *Evening Clarion* was found to have paid a gangster's wife for her story, in complete defiance of the Press Complaints Commission's Code of Practice, while the week before that yet another of our papers was fined for contempt of court. I believe that I can safely say that my father would have been appalled by these events. As I am sure all of you present in this room today are.

'Since my brother-in-law has sunk to slinging outrageous insults at both myself and my sister, *his own wife*, I should now like to take the opportunity to tell my fellow shareholders a little bit more about *him*.'

Kate glanced down at Laura for support and Laura gave her hand a quick squeeze.

'Hugo Bentley has no interest in the newspapers that are the heart of our business,' she went on. 'Shortly before he was appointed chairman I asked him for his assurance that he would *never* close down Leadington newspapers, a group that I freely admit is particularly close to my heart. He gave me his solemn word. But several weeks ago, without any reference to either me or my sister, he proceeded to tell the Leadington editors that he was shutting them down with immediate effect – on cost grounds, or so he said. So, on the one hand he has closed a group of papers that mean a great deal to the local communities they serve. And yet on the other he has just spent an astonishing three million pounds on leasing new headquarters in the City – purely to satisfy his own ego. This last action, may I add, is something that my father was always completely opposed to. He felt that the company offices in the Docklands had always been perfectly adequate for our needs.

'Now, turning to my own husband, Charley Stone. I can honestly say that he has done almost as little for Hollingberry Holdings as Hugo Bentley. The *Clarion* has steadily lost sales over the last few months –

largely because of his laziness, uninterest and yes, it pains me to say it, his propensity to sleep around with every tart in London. I can assure you that in the event of my being appointed chairman he will be removed from his post.'

Almost everyone glanced across at Charley, who was sitting, an impenetrable look on his handsome face, just a few rows behind Kate and Laura.

Hugo rose to his feet again. He'd listened to quite enough of this and was anxious to get the meeting back under control.

'I think that we should at least behave like responsible adults and leave our personal grievances to one side,' he said, raising his voice by a couple of decibels to make himself heard over the mêlée. 'The tirade that we have just heard from Kate Grant proves my point exactly. She has shown conclusively that she is a misguided young woman who doesn't have a clue what she is talking about. I think that we must now move to a vote straight away before any further damage is done.'

The men in suits lined alongside Hugo immediately sat up to attention. Humphrey White, one of the most senior members of the board, gave Hugo a furtive thumbs-up sign behind his pile of papers.

'Those in favour of the resolution, please raise your hands,' roared Hugo.

A sea of hands, including those of Kate, Laura and Gordon Osprey, immediately shot up.

'And those against?' said Hugo.

Laura glanced frantically around the room. It looked too close to call. The two sides must be neck and neck.

Graham Travis, the company secretary, had got to

his feet and was making a huge show of counting the votes. As Hugo watched from the dais, a smirk of triumph was clearly discernible on his face. He and his non-executive directors were confident that all the company's institutional shareholders had sent their votes (mostly in his favour) by proxy rather than bothering to attend in person. Apart from Kate, Laura and that idiot Gordon Osprey, the other shareholders present at the meeting only had a handful of shares between them.

'It's in the bag, isn't it?' Hugo whispered to Graham Travis when he'd finished doing his calculations.

'Looks that way, yes,' said Graham. 'Are you going to announce it or shall I?'

'You can,' said Hugo. 'I want to enjoy watching the expression on my sister-in-law's face when she realises that she's lost.'

Graham Travis duly stood up again and cleared his throat self-importantly.

'Ladies and gentlemen, I can now announce the results of the shareholders' votes. Those in favour of the resolution – forty-three per cent.'

Kate and Laura glanced at each other in consternation. It didn't sound enough to oust Hugo.

'Those against – forty-seven per cent. I can therefore confirm that the resolution has not been pass—'

Suddenly Graham Travis stopped in mid-sentence as a woman sitting near the back got to her feet and waved the latest Hollingberry Holdings annual report in the air.

'Before you announce the results, I have something very important to say,' she said. 'Something that must be heard.'

Hugo groaned. This meeting was turning into a

Whitehall farce. God only knew who this was. A disgruntled *Bowland Bugle* reader who'd travelled south to protest against its closure, perhaps? No, on second thoughts, she didn't quite seem the type.

Before he had time to object, the woman walked coolly up to the platform and plucked the microphone that he'd been using from its stand.

Kate and Laura stared at her. She was tiny, with ash blonde hair streaked with grey and a tanned complexion. She looked slightly hippyish and unconventional, wearing a purple frock coat over narrow white trousers and a mass of gold bangles on her wrist that jangled as she spoke.

'Oh my God,' whispered Kate, unable to take her eyes off her. 'It's Mummy. I mean Clare.'

She quickly laid a restraining hand on Laura's shoulder, fearful that her sister might bolt straight up to the platform and throw herself at their mother.

'*Wait*,' she whispered to Laura. 'Just wait to hear what she's got to say. It's not over yet. We might still get Hugo and Charley out.'

The woman's eyes were roaming restlessly over the audience, as if she was looking for somebody. In the end, however, Graham Travis leaned over and told her that if she had something important to say she'd better get on with saying it before he wound up the meeting.

'Ladies and gentlemen,' she announced in a husky, upper-class voice. 'I apologise for arriving so late but I would like you to know that I am Clare Grant, Hubert Hollingberry's widow. I own ten per cent of the shares of this company and I am voting *for* the motion.'

Kate glanced at Hugo, fascinated to gauge his reaction to Clare's bombshell. He looked utterly defeated, she thought, his shoulders hunched and his face frozen in shock, and in a strange way she felt a twinge of compassion for him. He'd been so bloody sure that he'd win today and now he'd gone and lost everything – his job, his house and his wife – in one fell swoop. That was quite an achievement, by anyone's standards.

But Laura only had eyes for her mother. She'd dreamed of this moment for so long and at last it was here. Right now she didn't give a damn why Clare had walked out on her all those years ago. She was here now and as far as she was concerned nothing else mattered.

As Clare finished what she was saying and stepped back from the microphone, the whole room erupted into chaos. The news must have filtered through to the street because in an instant a crowd of photographers had barged into the conference hall and begun snapping crazily. First at Clare, who looked completely bewildered by what was going on, and then at Hugo, who was covering his face with his hands.

Gus Jones, the *Clarion* snapper who'd been sent down to cover the story, took out a large red and white spotted handkerchief and mopped his brow. This was a cracking story, there was no doubt about that, but talk about a conflict of loyalties. How on earth was the *Clarion* was going to treat it?

'This is better than *EastEnders*,' chuckled the *Recorder* photographer merrily. 'The only thing we need now is for Charley Stone to go and punch someone.'

In the midst of all this confusion, Graham Travis was still trying desperately to make himself heard above the hubbub.

'In the light of these, er, unexpected developments,' he bellowed, 'I should like to announce the results of the shareholders' vote again. Those in favour of the resolution – fifty-three per cent. Those against – forty-seven per cent. I hereby declare that the resolution has been passed.'

Kate's face went white and the tears began streaming down her face. It was all too much – first, the shock of Clare turning up out of the blue and now the realisation that she'd just become the new chairman of Hollingberry Holdings.

'Oh Laura,' she cried, collapsing into her sister's arms. 'We've done it. We've bloody done it.'

But Laura was miles away, still gazing transfixed at Clare.

'Come on,' she whispered to Kate. 'Let's go and introduce ourselves.'

'No, not yet,' murmured Kate. 'Not in front of all of Fleet Street's finest.'

'B . . . b . . . but we must,' stuttered Laura. 'We've been waiting all this time to find her. We've *got* to go and talk to her.'

Kate gripped Laura's hand firmly.

'Wait,' she said. 'If you go up to her now and throw yourself all over her, the press will have a field day and then we'll never get out of here. We want to sit down together in private somewhere and talk on our own, don't we?'

Laura nodded miserably.

'Right. So stay in your seat and let me think.'

Kate's mind raced as she tried to work out the best way of smuggling them all out of the building without being chased down the street by hordes of marauding photographers. She smiled to herself. At least being in the business herself gave her the added advantage of knowing how their minds worked.

She looked up suddenly and her heart started thudding. Ben Maguire was threading his way through the rows of empty seats towards her and Laura.

'Hello,' she said uncertainly. 'What on earth are you doing here?'

'I just wanted to come and congratulate you,' he smiled. 'I was sitting at the back of the room all the way through so I heard everything. Well done. I'm so happy that you got what you wanted. And have you talked to your mother yet? She's lovely, isn't she? You're very alike.'

Kate stared at him sharply. How the hell did he know that Clare was lovely? Unless, of course . . . Slowly the truth began to dawn on her.

'It was you, wasn't it?' she muttered. 'It was you who found her. After all this time of not having a clue how to go about looking for her, you did it. Oh Ben . . .'

A tear ran down her cheek and without thinking Ben leaned forward and brushed it away tenderly.

'Is it over with Charley now?' he asked softly.

'Yes,' she said. 'It's over.'

Chapter Forty-One

In the end it was Ben who managed to spirit the three of them away from the conference room without being trampled underfoot by the press. First he escorted Clare outside, hailed a taxi for her and hurriedly stuffed a key in her hand. Then five minutes later he came back to collect Kate and Laura and rushed them through the jostling snappers and out to another cab.

'Where on earth are we going?' asked Laura in panic as the cab sped over Blackfriars Bridge. 'All I want to do is to talk to Mummy. Or are we supposed to call her Clare now? Neither of them sounds quite right somehow, do they?'

Ben laid a comforting hand on hers.

'Don't worry. I know you want to see her. She's at my flat right now and that's exactly where I'm taking you.'

Kate stared out of the window. It crossed her mind that she didn't have a clue where Ben even lived. They'd already passed the monstrous pink shopping centre at Elephant and Castle and were heading south down the Walworth Road and on past Camberwell Green. Five minutes later, the taxi deposited them outside a tall, narrow Georgian house with a huge sycamore tree outside.

'Is this where you live?' asked Kate shyly.

'Yep,' grinned Ben. 'I've got a flat on the top floor. And hopefully Clare will have managed the stairs by now. It's quite a climb, I'm afraid.'

Ben led the way, galloping up the stairs two at a time, and Kate and Laura followed behind. Laura, sick with nerves, got slower and slower as they neared the top.

'I've changed my mind,' she whispered to Kate when there was only one more flight of stairs to climb. 'I don't think I want to do this any more.'

Kate grabbed hold of her hand and yanked her sister up.

'Never mind about whether you want to do it or not. You're meeting her now and that's all there is to it.'

Her resolve stiffened by Kate's firm words, Laura followed Ben and Kate through the front door and into a vast sitting room with windows overlooking the tree-lined street. It had a wooden floor and white walls but virtually no furniture at all. There was just one black sofa underneath the windows and Clare was sitting on it. She'd flung her shoes off and was hugging her knees to her chest like a small child.

'I've brought your daughters with me,' said Ben softly. 'But you certainly don't need me here kicking my heels so I'll get out of the way and leave you all to it.'

He tiptoed out of the room and shut the door behind him. Hearing the sound of his feet thundering down the stairs, Kate marvelled at how acutely aware he was. He knew how much talking the three of them needed to do and so he was letting them get on with it in private. But all the same she felt oddly downhearted. She couldn't bear it if he disappeared out of her life again.

The sound of Ben's footsteps had finally died away, but the two sisters were still gazing awkwardly at their mother. No one said anything at all for a few moments, none of them knowing quite how – or where – to begin.

It was Laura, however, who eventually broke the silence. During the half-hour taxi journey from the City she had promised herself faithfully that she would remain perfectly calm and composed when she faced her mother. She would be polite but cool, leave her to make all the running. But when it came to it, her earlier resolutions were completely forgotten.

'Why did you leave us?' she cried out pitifully. 'Why did you go?'

Clare flinched as if she had been shot. She hugged her knees even more tightly against her chest and buried her face from view.

Watching her mother sitting all alone, Kate couldn't help feeling sorry for her. It sounded crazy and she wasn't quite sure why she even thought it, but right at this second Clare somehow seemed more the victim than either her or Laura.

Twice Clare struggled to get her words out and failed, all too aware that nothing she could say would ever heal the hurt she'd inflicted on her daughters. The most she could really hope for now was their forgiveness. And perhaps, if she was lucky, their understanding.

After what seemed like an eternity Kate couldn't bear the silence any longer. On the spur of the moment she rushed forward and threw her arms around her mother's narrow shoulders. For what seemed like half a minute or more, Clare's whole body remained rigid and unyielding, but gradually she began to relax and soon she was hugging Kate back as if she'd never let her go.

When the two women finally drew apart, Clare looked up and met Laura's steady gaze from the far side of the room. She opened her arms wide and said, a little hesitantly, 'Laura?'

Laura stared back at her mother. After all the years of crying herself to sleep because she'd wanted her so badly, after all the years of praying that this moment would please one day come – now she couldn't even bring herself to cross the length of Ben Maguire's sitting room.

'How do you know that I'm Laura?' she said harshly. 'The Laura you knew was seven years old. She liked chocolate marshmallows and teddies and had nightmares about poisonous snakes. How do you know that I'm not Kate? Or someone else's daughter?'

'Of course I know that you're Laura,' murmured Clare softly. 'You're my daughter. My firstborn. I'd know you anywhere. I've kept my precious pictures of you and Kate by my side constantly for nineteen years. Every night I've kissed you both goodnight. Every night I've traced round your dear sweet faces with my finger. Every night I've hoped and prayed that you were all right and that Hubert was looking after you and loving and cherishing you. And every night I've asked myself why I did what I did.'

Laura angrily gulped back a tear. Kate was such a pushover, she thought. Such a traitor. How could she simply leap back into Clare's arms as if nothing had happened? She'd *left* them, for God's sake. Not just for a few days but for years and years and years. She'd walked out and left them when they were small and vulnerable and desperately needed her. How could she have done it? How could she?

'I'm sorry,' said Laura, sticking her bottom lip out like a sulky child. 'I've waited so long for you to come back. I've dreamed of how we would leap into each other's arms and kiss and make up and how everything would be all right again. But now you're here I can't do it. I can't just smile and pretend it never happened. I can't pretend that you've just popped out of our lives for nineteen years and now you're popping back. You've got to tell us why you did it. How could you do it? How could you leave a seven-year-old and a five-year-old without a word of explanation? How could you be there one minute and gone the next?'

Hearing Laura's sharp words and the bitterness in her voice, the tears began trickling down Clare's face. They rolled off her chin and splashed onto her white trousers.

'You say that you've dreamed about this moment,' sobbed Clare. 'Well so have I. Being without both of you was like being stabbed through the heart a million times every day. The hurt was there all the time. Not an hour went past without me thinking about you both and wondering how you were and what you were doing. And whether you still remembered me at all.'

'Of course we did,' murmured Kate, squeezing her mother's hand tightly. 'When we were little we used to cuddle up in bed together and talk about you all night.'

At this Clare began sobbing even harder, great cries of grief that sounded more like those of an injured animal than a human being.

But Laura refused to let herself be moved by Clare's

distress. She remained standing on the far side of the room, still waiting for an answer to her question.

After a few moments Clare took out a pristine white handkerchief and blew her nose loudly.

'You're right, of course, Laura,' she said eventually. 'You both deserve an explanation. I can see that it's impossible for you to ever forgive me for what I did, but if I try to tell you what happened will you at least make an effort to understand?'

Kate gave a quick nod of her head but Laura didn't respond at all. Clare swiftly began talking again.

'None of this was either of your faults. Whatever you may think of me you've got to remember that. You've got to. You've just got to. No, I'm the one to blame and it all goes back to the moment I met your father.'

Clare paused for a moment and wiped her eyes again before continuing.

'Dodo might have told you this already but my parents died in a car crash just after my eighteenth birthday. I was an only child and suddenly I found myself completely alone. Your father's family lived in the same street as us in Chelsea and they were very kind to me. They sort of took me under their wing. I'd just started studying at St Martin's and was pretty taken up with my student life but your father always went out of his way to look after me. He was ten years older than me but in lots of ways he seemed twice that. Compared to all the feckless young men I knew at college he was like a breath of fresh air. He was solid and strong and ultra-reliable – all the things I desperately needed at that time in my life.

'I'm not even sure how we came to get married but we did. When I was twenty. I was just a child really.

Far too young. Looking back now, I can see that it was a crazy thing to do but I was so alone. I needed someone and Hubert was just there. After we got married I carried on painting at home for a bit but your father found most of my pictures absolutely incomprehensible and so I suppose I began to lose heart.'

Clare broke off suddenly and glanced at her daughters. They were both completely silent, hanging on her every word.

'Then what?' Laura demanded impatiently.

'Then the best part of my life,' said Clare softly. 'First I had you, Laura, and two years later, Kate. I was so elated when you were both born. I'll never ever forget it. In a way you bound Hubert and me closer than we'd ever been before. I felt that we were a real family at last, the family I'd been yearning for since my own parents died.'

'The family you threw on the rubbish heap,' muttered Laura.

Clare rounded on her angrily.

'Never,' she cried out fiercely. 'Never. I made mistakes, yes. Mistakes that I've been paying for ever since. But I never planned to leave you.'

'Why did you then?' asked Laura, her voice so acerbic that even Kate shot her a beseeching look.

'By the time you were seven and five it was becoming apparent to both of us just how far apart we really were. Your father was absolutely obsessed with the family business. He couldn't think of anything else and because he was so much older he didn't see why he should be accountable to me in any way. All he really wanted me to do was to make his life comfortable and pleasant and to care for you two. When you both started school it slowly began to

460

dawn on me that there was nothing else in my life whatsoever. Between the hours of nine and three thirty I led a completely empty existence. It's hard to admit this but I was a pretty hopeless mother too. When you came home you both always seemed to prefer being with Dodo than me. She made fairy cakes with you and taught you to play draughts and when you were with her you always seemed to be laughing in a way you never laughed with me. I felt completely redundant. I was very young and I felt you didn't really need me at all.'

Laura was staring at her as if she was a complete imbecile.

'We were little,' she said and her voice sounded even more withering than before. 'Of course we needed you.'

'So what did you do?' asked Kate, placing a comforting hand on her mother's arm.

Clare ran her hands through her hair as she tried to describe what had happened.

'Much against your father's wishes, I started painting again. Just to occupy my time. And one afternoon, as I was going round the Summer Exhibition at the Royal Academy – on my own of course – I met Julian.'

'Who on earth's Julian?' said Laura.

'Julian Shaldon. The man I still live with,' murmured Clare. 'He was an art student too and we just got talking. We spent the whole of that summer visiting a different art gallery every single day. I was grateful to Hubert for what he'd done for me but he . . . he was more like a father figure to me than a lover. I never ever fell in love with him the way I fell in love with Julian. And by the end of the summer . . .'

Her voice trailed away for a moment before she found the courage to go on.

'. . . by the end of the summer I found out that I was pregnant.'

Laura cupped her hand over her mouth and gave a sob of distress.

'I'm sorry, I'm so sorry,' wept Clare, 'but you asked me for the truth and I've got to tell you everything now. I told Hubert everything too. And he . . . he just couldn't cope with it.'

She paused as she came to the most painful part of her story.

'Your father was such a good man in many ways. Oh, I know he had his faults, his obstinacy and his absorption in his work, but he wasn't a bad man. Not really. The trouble was that when I told him about Julian and the baby he simply couldn't cope. He couldn't accept it. I'm still not sure what I expected him to do but . . . oh, I don't know. I told him that I wanted to leave him and take you two with me to live with Julian. I begged him over and over again but he just went completely crazy. I'd never seen him so angry. He loved you both so much, you see. He just couldn't countenance life without you. I hate having to tell you this part but I'm afraid I've got to – to make you see exactly why I had to leave.'

'Go on,' said Kate evenly.

'Hubert wasn't a violent man at all. He'd never laid a finger on me before but this particular night he went mad. I was so scared that I'd lose the baby. He hit me and knocked me over and swore that if I didn't end everything with Julian and get rid of my baby he'd divorce me and make sure that he got custody of you two. He said that you loved him and Dodo much more than you'd ever loved me and that you'd be much better off with them. And he was such a powerful man, even then; I believed every word he said.'

Clare's voice was growing hoarse by now but she carried on regardless.

'Kate, you've got your own child now. You must understand how impossible it was for me to choose. I either sacrificed my unborn child and carried on living with Hubert as though nothing had happened, or I kept the baby and gave up my daughters. What could I do?'

'So it was us that lost out,' said Laura grimly. 'You chose the baby and left us behind. That does wonders for my self-esteem, I must say.'

Clare got up from the sofa and came and knelt down next to her.

'I thought that if I could just go off quietly and have the baby I could somehow persuade Hubert to change his mind later. But he was completely intransigent. Every time I rang he kept telling me that no court would ever take my claim seriously when I was so unstable and unreliable and I'd walked out on both of you in the first place. And he kept saying how settled you both were living with him and Dodo. He said that neither of you had ever even mentioned me once and that it would traumatise you both beyond belief if I tried to come back into your lives. And the same thing kept happening over and over again. Every time I tried to make contact Hubert bulldozed me into thinking that it would only do you both irreparable damage. He got child psychologists to make reports on you both – I don't know if you remember – and he said that they all advised that I should leave you alone. That I shouldn't risk churning your lives up again.'

'That was so wrong,' murmured Laura. 'And all the time I was quietly dying inside, longing for you to come back.'

'I'm so sorry,' sobbed Clare. 'I'm so sorry. If it's any comfort to you, I was so devastated by what I'd done that I started drinking to blot out the pain. Drinking so heavily that I had to go into a drying-out clinic for a while. But that just gave Hubert even more ammunition to keep me away from you. He wrote me a letter saying that I was an unfit mother.'

'You *should* be sorry,' snapped Laura. 'Even if I believe you, and I'm not sure whether I do or not, I don't see why you didn't come back when we were old enough to understand. And why didn't you come racing to be by our side when Daddy died? He couldn't have done anything then, could he?'

'I wish I had,' wept Clare. 'If you only knew the number of times I wanted to pick up the phone and try and speak to you both. I nearly did when I saw your wedding picture in the paper, Laura. *And* after Hubert died. When it comes down to it, I suppose all this is my punishment for being such a coward. So weak. But I was so scared that if I attempted to make contact you'd reject me out of hand. Pretty much like you're doing now, Laura.'

Kate stared at her mother, who was still kneeling next to Laura and wringing her hands.

'What happened to the baby?' she asked suddenly. 'Did you have it?'

Clare's eyes glazed over dreamily.

'Yes, I did. I had a little boy called Rupert. He was born in a hospital in Manchester and after that Julian and I bought a farm about fifty miles north of there. We've lived there ever since.'

464

She gave a hollow laugh and stared down at her hands. Kate noticed that they were weather-beaten and lined, the hands of a woman who lived an outdoor sort of life.

'A little boy. It sounds completely ridiculous now when he's a big strapping lad of eighteen. He looks like you both, though. He's got blond hair and fair skin like you but he's tall, over six foot.'

'Does he know about us?' said Kate. She wasn't sure why she wanted to know this but it seemed important somehow.

'Yes, he does,' said Clare. 'I told him a couple of years ago. He couldn't get his head round it at all – in fact he was almost as shocked as you are now – but he was intrigued to know that he had two older sisters out there somewhere.'

'I can't believe we've got a brother,' said Kate, her eyes shining. She turned to Clare again. 'Is he interested in meeting us?'

'Actually,' said Clare, 'in a way he already has. Well, he hasn't exactly *met* you. But he's seen you both. At Hubert's funeral. He's at medical school in London and when I told him that Hubert had died he decided that he was going to come and find you. He's a headstrong boy and he was determined to try and talk to you, tell you how much I loved you and longed to see you. But at the very last minute he bottled out. It obviously runs in the family, doesn't it?'

Laura stared at Clare thoughtfully. Suddenly that scene at HH's funeral, when she'd crashed into a beautiful young blond boy, was beginning to màke sense. She'd *known* there was something about him. Something that bound the two of them together. Call it intuition or something but she'd just known.

'I saw him,' she said slowly. 'He had a kind face and he seemed concerned about me. Then he ran off and just vanished into thin air. I wanted to reach out and grab him but I couldn't. He'd gone.'

Clare leaned across hesitantly and tried to take Laura's hand in her own. For a moment Laura let her touch her, but then she changed her mind and moved away again.

'That's strange,' said Clare quietly, 'because Rupert told me exactly the same thing. He wanted to speak to you properly but he simply couldn't summon up the courage. He told me that he couldn't think of the right words so he had panicked and run off.'

'I wish he hadn't,' said Laura.

Clare gazed at her elder daughter. Looking at her tense white face and delicate frame, she had the strongest sense that Laura had been damaged far more than Kate by what had happened in the past. It was going to take years before Laura forgave her for what she had done. Perhaps she never would.

'Do you think you might like to meet Rupert?' said Clare cautiously, directing the question to both of them.

'I'd love to,' said Kate immediately.

'And would you, Laura?' asked Clare.

'I don't know – it's too soon,' said Laura. 'I'll have to think about it.'

Clare sighed heavily. At least Laura hadn't actually said no. She supposed it was a start and for that she had to be grateful.

Kate was lying full-length on Ben's black sofa with her feet dangling off the end. If he didn't come back soon then she'd have to go. Dodo had been looking after Daisy all day and it simply wasn't fair to either of them to be away much longer.

Clare had been the first to leave the flat, drained by the day's events and the sudden longing to escape back home to the north-west. But before she left she'd extracted a promise from Kate and a maybe from Laura that they'd think about coming to stay with her the following weekend. Kate would bring Daisy with her and they'd get the chance to meet Julian and Rupert for the first time. It wasn't going to be easy, they were all acutely aware of that, but they had to try and put the past behind them.

Kate was on the point of giving up the wait when she heard the door of the flat gently click shut. She instantly jumped up from the sofa and tried hard to look natural.

'Where are Clare and Laura?' asked Ben, startled to find her all alone.

'They've gone,' said Kate. 'Clare had to catch her train back up north and Laura wanted time to think.'

'Was there a problem?' asked Ben. His face was full of concern. 'Didn't everything work out?'

Then Kate smiled, a grin that lit up her whole face. 'Everything worked out,' she said shyly. 'Thanks to you. Oh, I know we've got a hell of a lot more talking to do and Laura's not exactly falling over herself to try and make things easy for my mother, far from it, but I think that it might be all right. One day. In fact I'm taking Daisy up north to meet her new family next weekend. Laura might come too. I hope I can persuade her but I'm just not sure.'

Ben slumped down on the sofa, dizzy with relief and exhaustion.

'I'm so glad,' he said. 'I knew that I was taking a

huge risk trying to track Clare down like that. I wasn't convinced that I could do it at all in the time but it was obvious that she was the key to everything. If I could only find her I reckoned that you stood a reasonable chance of getting the business back. And finding out the truth about your mother too.'

Kate watched Ben closely as he spoke. All this really seemed to matter to him. She wasn't a hundred per cent sure but she had the distinct impression that this wasn't just another job to him. He really cared what happened.

'How did you find out about Clare still owning a ten per cent shareholding?' she asked all of a sudden. 'When I looked at the shareholders' register in Graham Travis's office, it was all City institutions and trusts. Clare wasn't listed at all. Not under her maiden name *or* her married name.'

'That's because her shares are held on her behalf by an outfit called the Fiddick Trust,' explained Ben. 'Mind you, I wouldn't have found that out either if it hadn't been for Gordon Osprey.'

'It's funny how Gordon has done a complete U-turn over the last few weeks,' said Kate thoughtfully. 'He was so anti me and Laura this time last year. But now we're beginning to see each other in a whole new light. In fact I'm seriously thinking of asking him to come back into the business.'

She thought about the family business for a few seconds – it wasn't exactly going to be a straight-forward task getting it back on the right track, but she had a hunch that she and Gordon might make a very effective team.

'Did Gordon help you to find my mother too?' she asked.

'I shouldn't really reveal my sources,' said Ben with a twinkle in his eye, 'but as it's you, yes, he did. It was very good of him. Actually he was so fired up about getting Hugo Bentley out of Hollingberry Holdings that he seemed to treat it as something of a personal crusade. He's a bit uptight about "correct procedure" and stuff like that but he agreed to speak to a few of his contacts and one of them eventually came back saying that he'd pass on a message to Clare. I wasn't at all sure that she would respond – not after all this time – but within a few days she was on the phone and we'd arranged to meet.'

'Where did you meet?' asked Kate, intrigued to think of Ben and Clare holding a secret assignation.

For a moment Ben looked self-conscious.

'Do you remember that little tea room on top of the moors above Bowland?' he said. 'Where we had tea that afternoon after putting flowers where Nicky Rawlinson died?'

'Yes,' said Kate. She still vividly remembered that afternoon together. She'd never felt so close to anyone, either before or since. They'd sat and talked and she'd told him things that she'd never told another living soul.

'Well, that was where Clare and I arranged to meet. In fact it turned out that she doesn't live very far away.'

Kate stared at him.

'That's amazing. Where does she live? I know it's somewhere within striking distance of Preston because she told us that she'd meet us off the train there at the weekend. But where exactly?'

'I went to her house the next day,' said Ben. 'Julian

and Rupert weren't there – I think Clare must have arranged for them to be away – but it's a farmhouse in the middle of nowhere, about twenty miles north of Bowland. It's stunning right now but God only knows what it must be like in winter. She told me that they get snowed in virtually every year.'

But Kate was only half-listening to this last bit. She was remembering that profound feeling of coming home that she'd experienced when she'd first arrived up in Bowland. She'd taken one look at the moors and sensed that for some inexplicable reason she somehow belonged there. And now it dawned on her why she'd felt so strongly. It was because all that time her own mother had been living just over the other side of the hill.

'Are you sure you're all right?' asked Ben. 'You've gone terribly pale.'

'What? Oh, I'm fine. It's just been quite a day, that's all.'

Ben laughed out loud at this.

'Kate, that must be the understatement of the year. You've taken over your father's business, you've been reunited with your long-lost mother and you've left your husband. I'd say that was pretty good going for anyone.'

Kate, gazing out of the window, didn't say anything.

'You have, haven't you?' demanded Ben more urgently.

'I have what?' asked Kate.

'You have left him.'

'Yes, yes, I have,' murmured Kate. 'I went into my marriage to Charley totally seriously and I really thought I could make it work. But I can see now that he

470

didn't feel the same way. Once the novelty had worn off, he'd had enough of me. *And* Daisy.'

'The novelty's never worn off for me,' muttered Ben under his breath.

'What are you mumbling about?' smiled Kate teasingly. 'People who work in TV are supposed to be highly articulate.'

'Not when they're on the point of declaring mad passionate love to the woman of their dreams, they're not,' grinned Ben, his eyes boring into hers. 'Then they're just as tongue-tied as the rest of the population.'

'And is that what you're about to do?'

'What?'

'Declare mad, passionate love to me?'

'Do you want me to?' said Ben, determined that she was going to give him a tiny bit of encouragement before he proceeded to make a complete and utter fool of himself.

'I *really* want you to,' said Kate. 'But it had better be quick because I just have to go and collect Daisy before she completely destroys Dodo's flat.'

'Bloody hell, I've never had a time limit imposed before,' laughed Ben.

'You make it sound as if you declare undying love every week.'

'Oh, at least,' said Ben. 'Right, here goes. I love you, Kate Grant. I've loved you since the day you failed your one hundred words per minute shorthand for the second time on the trot and I'll go on loving you for the rest of my life. Will that do?'

Kate gazed at Ben, unable to take her eyes off him. She still couldn't believe that after screwing things up so badly, after accusing him of betraying her trust and after going off to have a baby by another

471

man, he was really prepared to give her a second chance.

She threw her arms around his neck and kissed him long and hard.

'Yes, Ben,' she said. 'It'll do. It'll do brilliantly.'